USA TODAY BESTSELLING AUTHOR

Marie Ferrarella

NEW YORK TIMES BESTSELLING AUTHOR

Cindy Dees

COLTON BY MARRIAGE & DR. COLTON'S HIGH-STAKES FIANCÉE

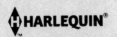

HARLEQUIN®

Special thanks and acknowledgment are given
to Marie Ferrarella and Cindy Dees
for their contributions to the Coltons of Montana miniseries.

ISBN-13: 978-0-373-60303-9

Colton by Marriage & Dr. Colton's High-Stakes Fiancée

Copyright © 2016 by Harlequin Books S.A.

The publisher acknowledges the copyright holders
of the individual works as follows:

Colton by Marriage
Copyright © 2010 by Harlequin Books S.A.

Dr. Colton's High-Stakes Fiancée
Copyright © 2010 by Harlequin Books S.A.

Recycling programs
for this product may
not exist in your area.

Printed in U.S.A.

www.Harlequin.com

Praise for *USA TODAY* bestselling author Marie Ferrarella

"Mixes unmatched humor, poignant situations and whimsical scenes."
—*RT Book Reviews* on *Dating for Two*

"Expert storytelling coupled with an engaging plot makes this an excellent read."
—*RT Book Reviews* on *Cavanaugh Undercover*

"Strong storytelling and sizzling chemistry between Ryan and Susie will keep readers turning the pages."
—*RT Book Reviews* on *Second Chance Colton*

"*Her Mistletoe Cowboy* is filled with moments of joy, caring, awakening and possibilities...a story that deeply touches the soul."
—*Fresh Fiction*

Praise for *New York Times* and *USA TODAY* bestselling author Cindy Dees

"A well-crafted plot with plenty of action, love and danger set within the intriguing city of New Orleans make this a must-read romance."
—*RT Book Reviews* on *Undercover with a SEAL*

"Dees blends action and intrigue in this character-driven romance with deft skill, keeping readers enthralled until the final secret is unveiled and the last chase winds down."
—*RT Book Reviews* on *Close Pursuit*

"A solid, suspenseful plot, tormented, vulnerable characters and beautiful, compelling writing will keep you turning the pages."
—*RT Book Reviews* on *Deadly Sight*

"[A] tightly plotted thriller with military authenticity."
—*Publishers Weekly* on *Close Pursuit*

USA TODAY bestselling and RITA® Award–winning author **Marie Ferrarella** has written more than two hundred and fifty books for Harlequin, some under the name Marie Nicole. Her romances are beloved by fans worldwide. Visit her website, marieferrarella.com.

Visit the Author Profile page
at Harlequin.com for more titles.

CONTENTS

COLTON BY MARRIAGE

Marie Ferrarella

To
Bonnie G. Smith.
Thank you for
having
such a wonderful daughter.

Prologue

"It's here, Sheriff." Unable to contain his excitement, Boyd Arnold all but hopped up and down as he pointed toward the murky body of water. "I saw it right here, in the creek, when Blackie ran into the water and I chased him out."

Blackie was what Boyd called his black Labrador retriever. Naming the dog Blackie had been the only unimaginative thing Boyd had ever done. Aside from that one example of dullness, the small-time rancher had an incredibly healthy imagination.

Some people claimed that it was a mite *too* healthy. At one time or another, Boyd had sworn he'd seen a ghost crossing his field, watched in awe as a UFO landed near Honey Creek, the body of water that the town had been named after, and now he was claiming to have seen a dead body in that very same creek.

As the town's recently elected sheriff, thirty-three-year-old Wes Colton would have liked just to have dismissed Boyd's newest tall tale as another figment of the man's overworked imagination. But, *because* he was the recently elected sheriff of Honey Creek, he couldn't. He was too new at the job to point to a gut feeling about things and so he was legally bound to check out each and every story involving wrongdoing no matter how improbable or wild it sounded.

Dead bodies were not the norm in Honey Creek. Most likely someone had dumped a mannequin in the creek in order to play a trick on the gullible Boyd. He hadn't put a name to the so-called body when he'd come running into the office earlier, tripping over his tongue as if it had grown to three times its size as he tried to say what it was he saw.

"Was it a woman, Boyd?" Wes asked now, trying to find the humor in the situation, although, he had to admit, between the heat and the humidity, his sense of humor was in extremely short supply today. Local opinion had it that a woman of the inflatable variety would be the only way Boyd would be able to find any female companionship at all.

Wes would have much rather been in his air-conditioned office, going over paperwork—something he usually disliked and a lot of which the last sheriff had left as payback for Wes winning the post away from him—than facing the prospect of walking through the water searching for a nonexistent body.

"I think it was a man. Tell the truth, Sheriff, I didn't stick around long enough to find out. Never can tell when you might come across one of them zombie types, or those body-snatchers, you know."

Wes looked at him. Boyd's eyes were all but bulging out. The man was actually serious. He shook his head. "Boyd, you want my advice? You've got to stop renting those old horror movies. You've got a vivid enough imagination as it is."

"This wasn't my imagination, Sheriff," Boyd insisted stubbornly with feeling. "This was a real live dead person."

Wes didn't bother pointing out the blatant contradiction in terms. Instead, he stood at the edge of the creek and looked around.

There was nothing but the sound of mosquitoes settling in for an afternoon feed.

A lot of mosquitoes, judging by the sound of it.

It was going to be a miserable summer, Wes thought. Just as he began to turn toward Boyd to tell the rancher that he must have been mistaken about the location of this "body," something caught Wes's eye.

Flies.

An inordinate number of flies.

Mosquitoes weren't making that noise, it was flies.

Flies tended to swarm around rotting meat and waste. Most likely it was the latter, but Wes had a strong feeling that he wasn't going to be free of Boyd until he at least checked out what the insects were swarming around.

"There, Sheriff, look there," Boyd cried excitedly, pointing to something that appeared to be three-quarters submerged in the creek.

Something that had attracted the huge number of flies.

There was no way around not getting his newly cleaned uniform dirty, Wes thought. Resigning himself to the unpleasant ordeal, Honey Creek's newly minted sheriff waded in.

Annoyance vanished as he drew closer to what the flies were laying claim to.

"Damn, but I think you're right, Boyd. That *does* look like a body," Wes declared. Forgetting about his uniform, he went in deeper. Whatever it was was only a few feet away.

"See, I told you!" Boyd crowed, happy to be vindicated. He was grinning from ear to ear like a little kid on Christmas morning. His expression was in sharp contrast to the sheriff's. The latter had become deadly serious.

It appeared to be a dead body all right. Did it belong to some vagrant who'd been passing through when he'd arbitrarily picked Honey Creek to die?

Or had someone dumped a body here from one of the neighboring towns? And if so, which one?

Bracing himself, Wes turned the body over so that he could view the face before he dragged the corpse out.

When he flipped the dead man over, his breath stopped in his lungs. The man had a single bullet in the middle of his forehead and he was missing half his face.

But the other half could still be made out.

At the same moment, unable to stay back, Boyd peered over his shoulder. The rancher's eyes grew huge and he cried out, "It's Mark Walsh!" No sooner was the name out of his mouth than questions and contradictions occurred to Boyd. "But he's dead." Confused, Boyd stared at Wes, waiting for him to say something that made sense out of this. "How can he look that fresh? He's been dead fifteen years!"

"Apparently Walsh wasn't as dead as we thought he was," Wes told him.

It was extremely difficult for Wes to maintain his decorum, not to mention an even voice, when all he could think of was that finally, after all these years, his brother was going to get out of jail.

Because Damien Colton had been convicted of a murder that had never happened.

Until now.

Chapter 1

Duke Colton didn't know what made him look in that direction, but once he did, he couldn't look away. Even though he wanted to.

Moreover, he wanted to keep walking. To pretend that he hadn't seen her, especially not like that.

Susan Kelley's head was still down, her short, dark-blond hair almost acting like a curtain, and she seemed oblivious to the world around her as she sat on the bench to the side of the hospital entrance, tears sliding down her flawless cheeks.

Duke reasoned that it would have been very easy either to turn on his heel and walk in another direction, or just to pick up speed, look straight ahead and get the hell out of there before the Kelley girl looked up.

Especially since she seemed so withdrawn and lost to the world.

He'd be doing her a favor, Duke told himself, if he just ignored this pretty heart-wrenching display of sadness. Nobody liked looking this vulnerable. God knew that he wouldn't.

Not that he would actually cry in public—or private for that matter. When he came right down to it, Duke was fairly certain that he *couldn't* cry, period. No matter what the situation was.

Hell, he'd pretty much been the last word in stoic. But then, he thought, he'd had to be, seeing as how things hadn't exactly gone all that well in his life—or his family's life—up to this point.

Every instinct he had told Duke he should be moving fast, getting out of Susan's range of vision. Now. Yet it was as if his feet had been dipped in some kind of super-strong glue.

He couldn't make them move.

He was lingering. Why, he couldn't even begin to speculate. It wasn't as though he was one of those people who was bolstered by other people's displays of unhappiness. He'd never believed in that old adage about misery loving company. When he came right down to it, he'd never had much use for misery, his own or anybody else's. For the most part, he liked keeping a low profile and staying out of the way.

And he sure as hell had no idea what to do when confronted with a woman's tears—other than running for the hills, face averted and feigning ignorance of the occurrence. He'd never lay claim to being one of those guys who knew what to say in a regular situation, much less one where he was front-row center to a woman's tear-stained face.

But this was Susan.

Susan Kelley. He'd watched Susan grow up from an awkward little girl to an outgoing, bright-eyed and bushy-tailed little charmer who somehow managed to be completely oblivious to the fact that she was as beautiful as all get out.

Susan was the one who cheered people up. She never cried. Not that he was much of an expert on what Susan did or didn't do. He just heard things. The way a man survived was to keep his eyes and his ears open, and his mouth shut.

Ever since his twin brother Damien was hauled off to jail because everyone in town believed he had killed Mark Walsh, Duke saw little to no reason to socialize with the people in Honey Creek. And Walsh was no angel. Most people had hated him. The truth of it was, if ever someone had deserved being killed, it was Walsh. Mark Walsh was nasty, bad-tempered and he cheated on his wife every opportunity he got. And Walsh and Damien had had words, hot words, over Walsh's daughter, Lucy.

Even so, Damien hadn't killed him.

Duke frowned as, for a moment, fifteen years melted away. He remembered watching the prison bars slam, separating him from Damien. He didn't know who had killed that evil-tempered waste of human flesh, but he would have bet his life that it wasn't Damien.

Now, like a magnet, his green eyes were riveted to Susan.

Damn it, what was she crying about?

He blew out an impatient breath. A woman who was that shaken up about something shouldn't be sitting by herself like that. Someone should be with her, saying something. He didn't know what, but *something*. Something comforting.

Duke looked around, hoping to ease his conscience—and not feel guilty about his desire to get away—by seeing someone approaching the sobbing little blonde.

There was no one.

She was sitting by herself, as alone as he'd ever seen anyone on this earth. As alone as *he* felt a great deal of the time.

Damn it, he didn't want to be in this position. Didn't want to have to go over.

What was the matter with him?

He didn't owe her anything. Why couldn't he just go? Go and put this scene of vulnerability behind him? He wasn't her keeper.

Or her friend.

Susan pressed her lips together to hold back another sob. She hadn't meant to break down like this. She'd managed to hold herself together all this time, through all the visits, all the dark days. Hold herself together even when she'd silently admitted, more than once, that one conclusion was inevitable. Miranda was going to die.

Die even though she was only twenty-five years old, just like her. Twenty-five, with all of life standing right before her to run through, the way a young child would run barefoot through a field of spring daisies, with enthusiasm and joy, tickled by the very act.

Instead, six months ago Miranda had heard those most dreadful of words, *You have cancer,* and they had turned out to be a death sentence rather than a battlefield she could somehow fight her way through.

Now that she'd started, Susan couldn't seem to stop crying. Sobs wracked her body.

She and Miranda were friends—best friends. It felt as if they'd been friends forever, but it only amounted to a tiny bit more than five years. Five years that had gone by in the blink of an eye.

God knows she'd tried very, very hard to be brave for Miranda. Though it got harder and harder, she'd put on a brave face every time she'd walked into Miranda's line of vision. A line of vision that grew progressively smaller and smaller in range until finally, it had been reduced to the confines of a hospital room.

The room where Miranda had died just a few minutes ago.

That was when the dam she'd been struggling to keep intact had burst.

Walking quickly, she'd made it out of Miranda's room and somehow, she'd even made it out of the hospital. But the trip from the outer doors to the parking lot where she'd left her car, that was something she just couldn't manage dry-eyed.

So instead of crossing the length of the parking lot, sobbing and drawing unwanted attention to herself, Susan had retreated to the bench off to the side of the entrance, an afterthought for people who just wanted to collect themselves before entering the tall building or rest before they attempted the drive home.

But she wasn't collecting herself, she was falling apart. Sobbing as if her heart was breaking.

Because it was.

It wasn't fair.

It wasn't fair to die so young, wasn't fair to have to endure the kind of pain Miranda had had just before she'd surrendered, giving up the valiant struggle once and for all.

Her chest hurt as the sobs continued to escape.

Susan knew that on some level, crying like this was selfish of her. After all, it wasn't as if she was alone. She had her family—large, sprawling, friendly and noisy, they were there for her. The youngest of six, she had four sisters and a brother, all of whom she loved dearly and got along with decently now that they were all grown.

The same could be said about her parents, although there were times when her mother's overly loud laments about dying before she ever saw one viable grandchild did get under her skin a little. Nonetheless, she was one of the lucky ones. She had people in her life, people to turn to.

So why did she feel so alone, so lonely? Was grief causing her to lose touch with reality? She *knew* that if she picked up the phone and called one of them, they'd be at her side as quickly as possible.

As would Linc.

She and Lincoln Hayes had grown up together. He'd been her friend for years. Longer than Miranda had actually been. But even so, having him here, having *any* of them here right now, at this moment, just wouldn't take away this awful feeling of overwhelming sorrow and loss.

She supposed she felt this way because she was not only mourning the loss of a dear, wonderful friend, mourning the loss of Miranda's life, she was also, at bottom, mourning the loss of her own childhood. Because Death had stolen away her own innocence. Death had ushered in an overwhelming darkness that had never been there before.

Nothing was every going to be the same again.

And Susan knew without being told that for a long time to come, she was going reach for the phone, beginning calls she wouldn't complete, driven by a desire to share things with someone she couldn't share anything with any longer.

God, she was going to miss Miranda. Miss sharing secrets and laughing and talking until the wee hours of the morning.

More tears came. She felt drained and still they came.

Susan lost track of time.

She had no idea how long she'd been sitting on that bench, sobbing like that. All she knew was that she felt almost completely dehydrated. Like a sponge that had been wrung out.

She should get up and go home before everyone began to wonder what had happened to her. She had a wedding to cater tomorrow. Or maybe it was a birthday party. She couldn't remember. But there was work to do, menus to arrange.

And God knew she didn't want to worry her parents. She'd told them that she was only leaving for an hour or so. Since she worked at the family restaurant and still lived at home, or at least, in the guesthouse on the estate, her parents kept closer track of her than they might have had she been out somewhere on her own.

Her fault.

Everything was her fault, Susan thought, upbraiding herself.

If she'd insisted that Miranda go see the doctor when her friend had started feeling sick and began complaining of bouts of nausea coupled with pain, maybe Miranda would still be alive today instead of...

Susan exhaled a shaky breath.

What was the point? Going over the terrain again wouldn't change anything. It wouldn't bring Miranda back. Miranda was gone and life had suddenly taken on a more temporary, fragile bearing. There was no more "forever" on the horizon. Infinity had become finite.

Susan glanced up abruptly, feeling as if she was being watched. When she raised her eyes, she was more than slightly prepared to see Linc looking back at her. It wouldn't be that unusual for him to come looking for her if he thought she wasn't where she was supposed to be. He'd appointed himself her keeper and while she really did value his friendship, there was a part of her that was beginning to feel smothered by his continuous closeness.

But when she looked up, it wasn't Linc's eyes looking back at her. Nor were they eyes belonging to some passing stranger whose attention had been momentarily captured by the sight of a woman sobbing her heart out.

The eyes she was looking up into were green.

Intensely green, even with all that distance between them. Green eyes she couldn't fathom, Susan thought. The expression on the man's face, however, was not a mystery. It was frowning. In disapproval for her semi-public display of grief?

Or was it just in judgment of her?

Duke was wearing something a little more intense than his usual frown. Try as she might, Susan couldn't recall the brooding rancher with the aura of raw sexuality about him ever really smiling. It was actually hard even to summon a memory of the man that contained a neutral expression on his face.

It seemed to her that Duke always appeared to be annoyed. More than annoyed, a good deal of the time he looked angry. Not that she could really blame him. He was angry at his twin for having done what he'd done and bringing dishonor to the family name.

Or, at least that was what she assumed his scowl and anger were all about.

Embarrassed at being observed, Susan quickly wiped away her tears with the back of her hand. She had no tissues or handkerchief with her, although she knew she should have had the presence of mind to bring one or the other with her, given the situation she knew she might be facing.

Maybe she hadn't because she'd secretly hoped that if she didn't bring either a handkerchief or tissues, there wouldn't be anything to cry about.

For a moment, she was almost positive that Duke was going to turn and walk away, his look of what was now beginning to resemble abject disgust remaining on his face.

But then, instead of walking away, he began walking toward her.

Her stomach fluttered ever so slightly. Susan straightened her shoulders and sat up a little more rigidly. For some unknown reason, she could feel her mouth going dry.

Probably because you're completely dehydrated. How much water do you think you've got left in you?

She would have risen to her feet and started to walk away if she could have, but her legs felt oddly weak and disjointed, as if they didn't quite belong to her.

Susan was actually afraid that if she tried to stand up, her knees would give way beneath her and she would collapse back onto the bench. Then Duke would *really* look contemptuously at her, and she didn't think she was up to that.

Not that it should matter to her *what* Duke Colton thought, or didn't think, of her, she silently told herself in the next breath. She just didn't want to look like a complete idiot, that was all. Her nose was probably already red and her eyes had to be exceedingly puffy by now.

Crossing to her, still not uttering a single word in acknowledgment of her present state or even so much as a greeting, Duke abruptly shoved his hand into his pocket, extracted something and held it out to her.

Susan blinked. Duke was holding out a surprisingly neatly folded white handkerchief.

When she made no move to take it from him, he all but growled, "Here, you seem to need this a lot more than I do."

Embarrassment colored her cheeks, making her complexion entirely pink at this point. "No, that's all right," she sniffed, again vainly trying to brush away what amounted to a sheet's worth of tears with the back of her hand.

"Take it." This time he did growl and it was an unmistakable command that left no room for refusal or even wavering debate.

Sniffing again, Susan took the handkerchief from him and murmured a barely audible, "Thank you."

He said nothing for a moment, only watched her as she slid the material along first one cheek and then the other, drying the tear stains from her skin.

When she stopped, he coaxed her on further, saying, "You can blow your nose with it. It won't rip. I've used it myself. Not this time," he corrected uncomfortably. "It's been washed since then."

A glimmer of a smile of amusement flittered across her lips. Susan couldn't begin to explain why, but she felt better. A lot better. As if the pain that had been growing inside of her had suddenly abated and begun shrinking back down to a manageable size.

She was about to say something to him about his kindness and about his riding to the rescue—something that seemed to suit his tall, dark, closed-mouth demeanor—when she heard someone calling out her name.

Linc. She'd know his voice anywhere. Even when it had an impatient edge to it.

The next moment, Linc was next to her, enveloping her in a hug. Without meaning to, she felt herself stiffening. She didn't want to be hugged. She didn't want to be pitied or treated like some fragile child who'd been bruised and needed protection.

If he noticed her reaction, Linc gave no indication that it registered. Instead, leaving the embrace, he slipped his arm around her shoulders, still offering protection.

"There you are, Susan. Everyone's worried about you," he said, as if he was part of her family. "I came to bring you home," he announced a bit louder than he needed to. And then his voice took on an affectionate, scolding tone. "I told you that you shouldn't have come here without me." Still holding her to him, he brushed aside a tear that she must have missed. "C'mon, honey, let's get you out of here."

A while back, she'd allowed their friendship to drift toward something more. But it had been a mistake. She didn't feel *that* way about Linc. She'd tried to let him down gently, to let him know politely that it was his friendship she valued, that there was never going to be anything else between them. But Linc seemed not to get the message. He seemed very comfortable with the notion of taking control of her life.

She found herself chafing against that notion and feeling restless.

He was being rude and completely ignoring Duke, she thought. Duke might not care, but *she* did.

Susan turned to say something to the rancher, to thank him for his handkerchief and his thoughtfulness, but when she looked where he'd just been, he was gone.

He'd left without saying another word to her.

The next moment, Linc was ushering her away, leading her toward the parking lot. She heard him talking to her, saying something about how relieved he was, or words to that effect.

But her mind was elsewhere.

Chapter 2

"You really shouldn't try to face these kinds of things alone, Susan," Linc quietly chided her as he guided Susan to his car. Once beside the shiny silver convertible, he stopped walking. "I'm here for you, you know that. And I'll *always* be here for you," he told her with firm enthusiasm.

"Yes, I know that." Fidgeting inside, Susan looked around the lot, trying to remember where she'd parked her own car. Linc meant well, but she really wanted to be by herself right now. "And I appreciate everything you're trying to do, Linc, but—"

Her voice trailed off for a moment. How did she tell him that he was crowding her without sounding as if she was being completely ungrateful? He was only trying to be kind, to second-guess her needs, she knew all that. But despite all that, despite his good intentions and her understanding, it still felt as if he was sucking up all the oxygen around her and she just couldn't put up with that right now.

Maybe later, when things settled down and fell into place she could appreciate Linc for what he was trying to do, but right now, she felt as if she desperately needed her space, needed to somehow make peace with this sorrow that kept insisting on finding her no matter which way she turned.

Linc opened the passenger door, but she continued to stand there, scanning the lot. He frowned. "What are you looking for?"

"My car." Even as she said it, Susan spotted her silver-blue four-door sedan. She breathed a sigh of relief.

He opened the passenger door wider, silently insisting that she get inside. "You're not up to driving, Susan. I'll take you home."

Her eyes met his. Susan did her best to keep her voice on an even keel, even though her temper felt suddenly very brittle.

"Don't tell me what I can or can't do, Linc. I can drive. I *want* to drive my car," she told him with emphasis.

He pantomimed pressing something down with both hands. Her temper? Was that what he was insinuating? She felt her temper flaring.

"Don't get hysterical, Susan," he warned.

The words, not to mention the action, were tantamount to waving a red flag in front of her. If the words were meant to subdue her, they achieved the exact opposite effect.

"I am *not* hysterical, Linc," she informed him firmly, "I just want to be alone for a while."

"You didn't look very alone a couple of minutes ago."

For a moment she thought he was going to pout, then abruptly his expression changed, as if he'd suddenly come up with an answer that satisfied him. "Was he bothering you?"

Susan stared at Linc, confused and wondering how he'd come to that kind of conclusion. Based on what? "Who?" she wanted to know.

"That Colton guy. You know who I mean. His brother killed Lucy Walsh's father," he said impatiently, trying to remember the man's name. "Duke," he finally recalled, then asked again as he peered at her face, "Was he bothering you?"

She felt as if Linc was suddenly interrogating her. Not only that, but she felt rather defensive for Duke, although she really hadn't a clue as to why. She'd had a crush on him when she was a teenager, but that was years in the past.

Still, he'd stopped and given her a handkerchief when he didn't have to.

"No, what makes you say that?"

Linc's shoulders rose and fell in a spasmodic shrug. "Well, you just said you wanted to be alone, and when I found you, he was in your face—"

Susan was quick to interrupt him. Linc had a tendency to get carried away. "He wasn't in my face, Linc. He hardly said a whole sentence."

Linc's expression told her that it hadn't looked that way from where he was standing. "Then he was just staring at you?"

Susan didn't like the tone that Linc was taking with her. He was invading her private space, going where he had no business venturing. He was her friend, not her father or her husband. And even then he wouldn't have the right to act this way.

"In part," she finally said. "Look, he saw I was crying and he gave me his handkerchief. No questions, nothing, just his handkerchief."

Linc snorted. "Lucky for you he didn't try strangling you with it."

It was a blatant reference to one of the theories surrounding Mark Walsh's death. The county coroner had said that it appeared Mark Walsh had been strangled, among other things, before his face was bashed in, the latter being the final blow that had ushered death in.

Susan just wanted to get away, to mourn her best friend's passing in peace, not be subjected to this cross-examination that Linc seemed determined to conduct. She lifted her chin stubbornly. "Duke's not Damien," she pointed out.

The look on Linc's face was contemptuous, both of her statement and of the man it concerned.

"I dunno about that. They say that twins have an unnatural connection. Maybe he's *just* like his brother." Linc drew himself up, squaring his shoulders before issuing a warning. "I don't want you talking to Duke Colton or having anything to do with him."

For a second, even with the emotional pain she was trying to deal with, Susan could feel her temper *really* flaring. Linc was making noises like a possessive *boyfriend*, and that was the last thing on earth she needed or wanted right now. "Linc, it's not your place to tell me what to do or not do."

Realizing the tactical error he'd just committed, Linc tried to backtrack as quickly as he could and still save face.

"Sure it is," he insisted. "I care about you, Susan. I

care about what happens to you. We don't know what these Coltons are really capable of," he warned. "And I'd never forgive myself if anything happened to you because I didn't say something."

Did Linc really think she was so clueless that she needed guidance? That she was so naive that she was incapable of taking charge of her own life? From out of nowhere a wave of resentment surged within her. She struggled to tamp it down.

She was just upset, Susan told herself. And Linc did mean well, even if he could come across as overbearing at times.

It took effort, but she managed to force a smile to her lips. "I'll be all right, Linc. Don't worry so much. And I'm still driving myself home," she added in case he thought he'd talked her out of that.

She could see that Linc didn't like her refusing his help, but he made no protest and merely nodded his head. She was about to breathe a sigh of relief when Linc unexpectedly added, "All right, I'll follow you."

Susan opened her mouth to tell him that he really didn't have to put himself out like that, but she had a feeling that she'd just be wasting her breath, and she was in no mood to argue.

Maybe she was being unfair. Another woman would have been thrilled to have someone voluntarily offer to all but wrap her in cotton and watch over her like this. There was a part of her that thought she'd be thrilled, as well. But now, coming face to face with it, she found it almost suffocating. All she wanted to do was run away.

Maybe she was overreacting, making too much of what was, at bottom, an act of kindness. But if she was overreacting, she did have a really good excuse. Someone she loved dearly had just died and blown a hole in her world, and it was going to take a while to come to terms with that.

Rather than prolong this no-win debate, Susan nodded. "All right, I'll see you at the house." With that, she turned and walked quickly over to where she'd parked her vehicle.

Duke watched the tall, slim, attractive young blonde make her way through the parking lot. More to the point, she was walking away from that annoying prissy little friend of hers.

Lincoln Hayes.

Now, there was a stalker in the making if he ever saw one, Duke judged. He wondered if Susan was aware of that, of what that Linc character was capable of.

Not his affair, Duke told himself in the next moment. The perky little girl with the swollen eyes was her own person. There was no reason for him to be hovering in the background like some wayward dark cloud on the horizon, watching over her. She might look like the naive girl next door, but he had a feeling that when push came to shove, Susan Kelley was a lot stronger, character-wise, than she appeared.

A fact, he had a feeling, that wouldn't exactly please Lincoln Hayes.

And even if she could be pushed around by the likes of Hayes, what was that to him? Why did he feel this need to make sure she was all right? The girl had his handkerchief and he wanted it back. Eventually. There was absolutely no other reason to pay attention to her, to her comings and goings and to whether that spineless jellyfish, Hayes, actually turned out to be a stalker.

Annoyed with himself, with the fact that he wasn't leaving, Duke watched as Susan crossed to the extreme right side of the lot and got into her car, a neat little sedan that would have been all but useless on his own ranch. It wouldn't have been able to haul much, other than Susan and some of her skinny friends.

Her sedan came to life. Another minute and she was driving off the lot.

Rubbing his hands on the back of his jeans, Duke got into the cab of his beat-up dark-blue pickup and drove away.

"Have you been crying?"

Bonnie Gene Kelley fired the question, fueled by concern, the moment her daughter walked into the rear of Kelley's Cookhouse, the restaurant that she and her husband Donald ran and had turned into a nation-wide chain.

Seeing for herself that the answer to her question was yes, Bonnie Gene quickly crossed to her youngest child and immediately immersed herself in Susan's life. "Did you and that boy get into an argument?" she wanted to know.

Ever eager for one of her children to finally make her a grandmother, the way all her friends' children had, Bonnie Gene fanned every fire that potentially had an iron in it. In Susan's case, that iron had a name: Lincoln Hayes.

Lincoln wouldn't have been her first choice, or even her second one. Bonnie Gene liked her men more manly, the way her Donald was—or had been before the good life had managed to fatten him up. But Linc was here and he was crazy about Susan. Her daughter could do a lot worse than marry the boy, she supposed.

But if he made Susan cry, then all bets were off. She absolutely wouldn't stand for someone who could wound her youngest born to the extent of making her cry. Sophisticated and worldly—as worldly as anyone could be, given that they were living in a place like Honey Creek, Montana—her maternal claws would immediately emerge, razor-sharp and ready, whenever one of her children was hurt, physically or emotionally.

"No, Mother," Susan replied evenly, wishing she'd waited before walking into work, "we didn't get into an argument."

Part of her just wanted to dash up to her room and shut the door, the other part wanted to be enfolded in her mother's arms and be told that everything was still all right. That the sun still rose in the east and set in the west and everything in between was just fine.

Except that it wasn't. And she needed to grow up and face that.

"Is Miranda worse?" her father asked sympathetically, coming out of the large storage room where they kept the supplies and foodstuffs that were being used that day. He pushed the unlit cigar in his mouth over to the side with his tongue in order to sound more intelligible.

Focusing on her husband for a moment, Bonnie Gene allowed an annoyed huff to escape her lips. She marched over to him, plucked the cigar out of his mouth and made a dramatic show of dropping it into the uncovered trash basket in the corner. It was an ongoing tug of war between them. Donald Kelley seemed to possess an endless supply of cigars and Bonnie Gene apparently possessed an endless supply of patience as she removed and threw away each one she saw him put into his mouth.

Susan had long since stopped thinking that her father actually intended to smoke any of these cigars. In her opinion, he just enjoyed baiting her mother.

But today Susan didn't care about the game or whether her father actually smoked the "wretched things" as her mother called them. All of that had been rendered meaningless, at least for now. Her friend was dead and she was never going to see Miranda again. Her heart hurt.

"Miranda's gone," Susan said in small, quiet voice, answering her father's question.

"Gone?" he echoed. "Gone where?" When his wife gave him a sharp look, a light seemed to go on in his head and Donald realized what Susan had just told him. "Oh. *Gone.*" A chagrined expression washed over his face as he came over to his youngest child. "Susan, sweetie, I'm so sorry," he told her. The squat, burly man embraced her, a feat that had been a great deal easier in the days before his gut had grown to the size that it had.

Coming between them, Bonnie gently removed Susan from Donald's grasp, turned the girl toward her and hugged her daughter closely.

For a moment, nothing was said. The other people in the kitchen, employees who had helped make the original restaurant the success that it was, went about their business, deliberately giving their employers and their daughter privacy until such time as they were invited to take part in whatever it was that was happening.

Still holding Susan to her chest and stroking her hair, the way she used to when she had been a little girl, Bonnie Gene said gently, "Susan, you knew this day was coming."

She had. Deep down, she had, but that didn't mean that she hadn't still hoped—fervently prayed—that it wouldn't. That a miracle would intervene.

"I know," Susan said, struggling again to regain control over her emotions, "it's just that it came too soon."

"It always comes too soon," Bonnie Gene told her daughter with the voice of experience. "No matter how long it takes to get here."

Bonnie Gene had no doubt that if Donald were to die before she did it wouldn't matter whether they'd been together for the past hundred years. It would still be too soon and she would still be bargaining with God to give her "just a little more time" with the man she loved.

"She's in a better place now, kiddo," Susan's father told her, giving her back a comforting, albeit awkward pat. "She's not hurting anymore."

Bonnie Gene looked at her husband, a flicker of impatience in her light-brown eyes. She tossed her head, sending her dark-brown hair over her shoulder. "Everyone always says that," she said dismissively.

"Don't make it any less true," Donald told her stubbornly, pausing to fish the cigar out of the trash. He brushed it off with his fingers, as if the cursory action would send any germs scattering.

Bonnie Gene's eyes narrowed as she looked at her husband over her daughter's shoulder. "You put that in your mouth, Donald Kelley," she hissed, "and you're a dead man."

Donald weighed his options. He knew his wife was passionate about him not smoking, and she seemed to be on a personal crusade these days against his beloved cigars. With a loud sigh, Donald allowed the cigar to fall from his fingers, landing back in the trash. There were plenty more cigars in the house—and a few of them stashed in various out-of-the-way places. Places that Bonnie Gene hadn't been able to find yet. He could wait.

The rear door opened and closed for a second time. All three Kelleys turned to see Linc walk in. He was accompanied by a blast of hot July air. It was like an oven outside. A hot, sticky, moist oven.

"I must have caught every red light from the hospital to the restaurant," Linc complained, addressing his words to the world at large.

Bonnie Gene felt her daughter stiffen the moment she heard Linc's voice. The reaction was not wasted on her. Her mother's instincts instantly kicked in.

Releasing Susan, she approached her daughter's self-appointed shadow. "Linc, I was wondering if you could do me a favor."

It was no secret that Linc was eager to score any brownie points with the senior Kelleys that he could. "Anything, Mrs. Kelley."

"The linen service forgot to send over five of our tablecloths. Be a dear and run over to Albert's Linens and get them." Taking the latest receipt and a note she'd hastily jotted down less than an hour ago, she handed both to Lincoln. "Nita at the service is already waiting for someone to come for them. Just show her these," she instructed.

Lincoln glanced at the receipt and the note, looking somewhat torn about the assignment he'd been given. It was obvious that he'd hoped that whatever it was that Susan's mother wanted done could be done on the premises and near Susan.

But then he nodded and promised, "I'll be right back." He looked at Susan, possibly hoping that she would offer to come with him, but she didn't. With a suppressed sigh and a forced smile, he turned on his heel and walked out of the kitchen through the same door he'd come in.

Susan looked at her mother. It completely amazed her how the woman who could drive her so absolutely crazy when the subject of marriage and babies came up could still somehow be so very intuitive.

She flashed her mother a relieved smile. "Thanks, Mom."

Bonnie Gene's eyes crinkled as she smiled with pleasure. "That's what I'm here for, honey. That's what I'm here for."

"Here for what?" Mystified, Donald looked first at his wife then at his daughter, trying to understand what had just happened. "And thanks for what?"

But rather than answer him, his wife and his daughter had gone off in completely opposite directions, leaving him to ponder his own questions as he scratched the thick, short white hair on his head. The action unintentionally drew his attention to the fact that his haircut, courtesy of his wife whom he insisted be the only one to cut his hair, was sadly lopsided. Again.

Though she'd been cutting his hair ever since they had gotten married all those years ago—originally out of necessity, now out of his need for a sense of tradition—Bonnie Gene had never managed to get the hang of cutting it evenly.

Donald didn't mind. He rather liked the way the uneven haircut made him look. He thought it made him appear rakish. Like the bad boy he'd never had time to be. And because he was who he was, the owner of a national chain of restaurants, no one ever attempted to tell him any differently.

Glancing over his shoulder in the direction that his wife had gone—to the front of the restaurant, undoubtedly to rub elbows with the customers—Donald quickly dipped into the trash basket and retrieved his cigar for a second time. This time, he didn't bother going through the motions of dusting it off. Instead, he just slipped it into his pants pocket.

With a satisfied smile, Donald assumed a deliberately innocent expression. Hands shoved into his pockets—his left protectively covering the cigar—he began to whistle as he walked toward the swinging double doors that led into the dining hall.

Life was good, he thought.

Chapter 3

The moment he'd realized that this time Boyd Arnold's discovery wasn't just a figment of his imagination, Wes had firmly sworn Boyd to secrecy. Knowing that Boyd had a tendency to run off at the mouth, words flowing as freely as the creek did in the winter after the first big snowstorm, he'd been forced to threaten the small-time rancher with jail time if he so much as breathed a word to *anyone*.

Boyd had appeared to be properly forewarned, his demeanor unusually solemn.

As for him, despite the fact that the words kept insisting on bubbling up in his throat and on his tongue, desperate for release, Wes hadn't even shared the news with his family. Not yet. He couldn't. He needed to be *absolutely* sure that the man with the partially destroyed face—he supposed the fish in the creek had to survive, too—actually *was* Mark Walsh.

There would be nothing more embarrassing, not to mention that it would also undermine the capabilities of the office of the sheriff, than to have to take back an announcement of this magnitude. After all, Mark Walsh had already been presumed murdered once and his supposed killer had been tried and sentenced. To say, "Oops, we were wrong once, but he's really dead now," wasn't something to be taken lightly.

His reasons for keeping this under wraps were all valid. But that didn't make keeping the secret to himself any easier for Wes. However, he had no choice. Until the county coroner completed his autopsy and managed to match Mark Walsh's dental records with the body that had been fished out of the creek, Wes fully intended to keep a tight lid on the news, no matter how difficult it got for him. Why dental records weren't used properly to identify the victim of the first crime was anybody's guess.

With any luck, he wouldn't have to hold his tongue for much longer. He desperately wanted to start the wheels turning for Damien's release. If the body in the morgue *was* Mark Walsh, then there was no way his older brother had killed the man over fifteen years ago. Not that he, or any of the family, including seven brothers and sisters, had ever believed that Damien was guilty. Some of the Colton men might have hot tempers, but none of them would ever commit murder. He'd stake not just his reputation but his life on that.

Damien was going to be a free man—once all that life-suffocating red tape was gotten through.

Damn, he thought, *finally.*

Deep down in his soul, he'd always known Damien

hadn't killed Mark. Been as sure of it as he was that the sun was going to rise in the east tomorrow morning.

He supposed that was one of the reasons he'd run for sheriff, to look into the case, to wade through the files that dealt with the murder and see if there was anything that could be used to reopen the case.

Now he didn't have to, he thought with a satisfied smile.

And he owed it all to Boyd, at least in a way. Granted, the body would have been there no matter what, but Boyd was the one who'd led him to it.

Who knew, if Boyd hadn't decided to sneak off and go duck-hunting—something that was *not* in season— maybe the fish would have eventually feasted on the rest of Walsh, doing away with the body and effectively annihilating any evidence that would have pointed toward Damien's innocence.

In that case, Damien would have stayed in prison, sinking deeper and deeper into that dark abyss where he'd taken up residence ever since the guilty verdict had been delivered fifteen years ago.

Wes made a mental note to call the county coroner's office later this afternoon to see how the autopsy was coming along—and give the man a nudge if he was dragging his heels. Max Crawford was the only coroner in these parts, but it wasn't as if the doctor was exactly drowning in bodies. Homicide was not a regular occurrence around here.

Smiling broadly, Wes poured himself his second cup of coffee of the morning. He was anxious to set his older brother's mind—if not his body—free. The sooner he told Damien about the discovery at Honey Creek, the sooner Damien would have hope and could begin walking the path that would lead him back home.

That had a nice ring to it, Wes thought, heading back to his desk. A really nice ring.

Miranda James had been an only child with no family. Her mother, Beth, had died two years ago, ironically from the same cancer that had claimed Miranda—and her father had taken off for parts unknown less than a week after Miranda was born, declaring he didn't have what it took to be a father. Because there was no one else to do it, Susan had taken upon herself all the funeral arrangements.

Bonnie Gene had offered to help, but one look at her daughter's determined face told the five foot-six, striking woman that this was something that Susan needed to do herself. Respectful of Susan's feelings, Bonnie Gene had backed away, saying only that if Susan needed her, she knew where to find her.

Susan was rather surprised at this turn of events, since her mother was such a take-charge person, but she was relieved that Bonnie Gene had backed off. It was almost cathartic to handle everything herself. Granted, it wasn't easy, juggling her full-time work schedule and the myriad of details that went into organizing the service and the actual burial at the cemetery, but she wasn't looking for easy. Susan was looking for right. She wanted to do right by her best friend.

Wanted, if Miranda *could* look down from heaven, to have her friend smile at the way the ceremony had come together to honor her all-too-brief life.

So, three days after she'd sunk down on the bench outside the hospital, crying and trying to come to grips with the devastating loss of her best friend, Susan was standing at Miranda's graveside, listening to the soft-voiced, balding minister saying words that echoed her own feelings: that the good were taken all too quickly from this life, leaving a huge hole that proved to be very difficult to fill.

Only half listening now, Susan ached all over, both inside and out. In the last three days, she'd hardly gotten more than a few hours sleep each night, but she had not only the satisfaction of having made all the funeral arrangements but also of not dropping the ball when it came to the catering end of the family business.

As far as the latter went, her mother had been a little more insistent that she either accept help or back off altogether, but Susan had remained firm. Eventually, it had been Bonnie Gene who had backed off. When she had, there'd been a proud look in her light-brown eyes.

Having her mother proud of her meant the world to Susan. Especially right now.

Susan looked around at the mourners who filled the cemetery. It was, she thought, a nice turnout. All of Miranda's friends were here, including mutual friends, like Mary Walsh. And, not only Susan's parents, Donald and Bonnie Gene, but her four sisters and her brother had come to both the church service and the graveside ceremony.

They'd all come to pay their respects and to mourn the loss of someone so young, so vital. If she were being honest with herself, Susan was just a little surprised that so many people had actually turned up. Surprised and very pleased.

See how many people liked you, Miranda? she asked

silently, looking down at the highly polished casket. *Bet you didn't know there were this many.*

Susan glanced around again as the winches and pulleys that had lowered the casket into the grave were released by the men from the funeral parlor. At the last moment, she didn't want to dwell on the sight of the casket being buried. She preferred thinking of Miranda lying quietly asleep in the casket the way she had viewed her friend the night before at the wake.

That way—

Susan's thoughts abruptly melted away as she watched the tall, lean rancher make his way toward her. Or maybe he was making his way toward the cemetery entrance in order to leave.

Unable to contain her curiosity, Susan moved directly into Duke's path just before he passed her parents and her.

"What are you doing here?" she asked.

It was a sunny day, and it was probably his imagination, but the sun seemed to be focusing on Susan's hair, making some of the strands appear almost golden. Duke cleared his throat, wishing he could clear his mind just as easily.

Duke minced no words. He'd never learned how. "Same as you. Paying my last respects to someone who apparently meant a great deal to you. I figure she had to be a really nice person for you to cry as much as you did when she died."

Susan took a deep, fortifying breath before answering him.

"She was," she replied. "A *very* nice person." She watched as the minister withdrew and the crowd began to thin out. The mourners had all been invited to her parents' house for a reception. "It just doesn't seem fair."

Duke thought of his twin brother, of Damien spending the best part of his life behind bars for a crime he *knew* beyond a shadow of a doubt his brother hadn't committed. They were connected, he and Damien. Connected in such a way that made him certain that if Damien had killed Walsh the way everyone said, he would have known. He would have *felt* it somehow.

But he hadn't.

And that meant that Damien hadn't killed anyone. Damien was innocent, and, after all this time, Duke still hadn't come up with a way to prove it. It ate at him.

"Nobody ever said life was fair," he told her in a stoic voice.

Susan didn't have the opportunity to comment on his response. Her mother had suddenly decided to swoop down on them. More specifically, on Duke.

"Duke Colton, what a lovely surprise," Bonnie Gene declared, slipping her arm through the rancher's. "So nice of you to come. Such a shame about poor Miranda." The next moment, she brightened and flashed her thousand-watt smile at him. "You are coming to the reception, aren't you?" she asked as if it was a given, not a question.

Duke had had no intentions of coming to the reception. He still wasn't sure what had prompted him to come to the funeral in the first place. Maybe it had been the expression he'd seen on Susan's face. Maybe, by being here, he'd thought to ease her burden just a little. He really didn't know.

He'd slipped into the last pew in the church, left before the mourners had begun to file out and had stood apart, watching the ceremony at the graveside. Had there been another way out of the cemetery, he would have used that and slipped out as quietly as he had come in.

Just his luck to have bumped into Susan and her family. Especially her mother, who had the gift of gab and seemed intent on sharing that gift with every living human being with ears who crossed her path.

He cleared his throat again, stalling and looking for the right words. "Well, I—"

He got no further than that.

Sensing a negative answer coming, Bonnie Gene headed it off at the pass as only she could: with verve and charm. And fast talk.

"But of course you're coming. My Donald oversaw most of the preparations." She glanced toward her husband, giving him an approving nod. "As a matter of fact, he insisted on it, didn't you, dear?" she asked, turning her smile on her husband as if that was the way to draw out a hint of confirmation from him.

"I—"

Donald Kelley only managed to get out one word less than Duke before Bonnie Gene hijacked the conversation again.

Because of the solemnity of the occasion, Bonnie Gene was wearing her shoulder-length dark-brown hair up. She still retained the deep, rich color without the aid of any enhancements that came out of a box and required rubber gloves and a timer, and she looked approximately fifteen years younger than the sixty-four years that her birth certificate testified she was—and she knew it. Retirement and quilting bees were not even remotely in her future.

Turning her face up to Duke's—separated by a distance of mere inches, she all but purred, "You see why you have to come, don't you, Duke?"

It was as clear as mud to him. "Well, ma'am—not really." Duke made the disclaimer quickly before the woman could shut him down again.

The smile on her lips was gently indulgent as she momentarily directed her attention to her husband. "Donald is his own number-one fan when it comes to his cooking. He's prepared enough food to feed three armies today," she confided, "and whatever the guests don't eat, he will." Detaching herself from Duke for a second, she patted her husband's protruding abdomen affectionately. "I don't want my man getting any bigger than he already is."

Dropping her hand before Donald had a chance to swat it away, she reattached herself to Duke. "So the more people who attend the reception, the better for my husband's health." Bonnie Gene paused, confident that she had won. It was only for form's sake—she knew men liked to feel in control—that she pressed. "You will come, won't you?"

It surprised her that the man seemed to stubbornly hold his ground. "I really—"

She sublimated a frown, keeping her beguiling smile in place. Bonnie Gene was determined that Duke wasn't going to turn her down. She was convinced she'd seen something in the rancher's eyes in that unguarded moment when she'd caught him looking at her daughter.

Moreover, she'd seen the way Susan came to attention the moment her daughter saw Duke approaching. If that wasn't attraction, then she surely didn't know the meaning of the word.

And if there was attraction between her daughter and this stoic hunk of a man, well, that certainly was good enough for her. This could be the breakthrough she'd been hoping for. Time had a way of flying by and Susan was already twenty-five.

Bonnie Gene was nothing if not an enthusiastic supporter of her children, especially if she saw a chance to dust off her matchmaking skills.

"Oh, I know what the problem is," she declared, as if she'd suddenly been the recipient of tongues of fire and all the world's knowledge had been laid at her feet. "You're not sure of the way to our place." She turned to look at her daughter as if she had just now thought of the idea. "Susan, ride back with Duke so you can give him proper directions."

Looking over her youngest daughter's head, she saw that Linc was heading in their direction and his eyes appeared to be focused on Duke.

Fairly certain that Susan wouldn't welcome the interaction with her overbearing friend right now, Bonnie Gene reacted accordingly. Slipping her arms from around Duke's, she all but thrust Susan into the space she'd vacated.

"Off with you now," Bonnie Gene instructed, putting a hand to both of their backs and pushing them toward the exit. "Don't worry, your father and I will be right behind you," she called out.

Without thinking, Susan went on holding Duke's arm until they left the cemetery.

He made no move to uncouple himself and when she voluntarily withdrew her hold on him, he found that he rather missed the physical connection.

"I'm sorry about that," Susan apologized, falling into step beside him.

He assumed she was apologizing for her mother since there was nothing else he could think of that required an apology.

"Nothing to be sorry for," he replied. "Your mother was just being helpful."

Susan laughed. She had no idea that the straightforward rancher could be so polite. She didn't think he had it in him.

Learn something every day.

"No, she was just being Bonnie Gene. If you're not careful, Mother can railroad you into doing all sorts of things and make you believe it was your idea to begin with." There was a fondness in her voice as she described her mother's flaw. "She thinks it's her duty to take charge of everything and everyone around her. If she'd lived a hundred and fifty years ago, she would have probably made a fantastic Civil War general."

Duke inclined his head as they continued walking. "Your mother's a fine woman."

"No argument there. But my point is," Susan emphasized, "you have to act fast to get away if you don't want to get shanghaied into doing whatever it is she has planned."

"Eating something your dad's made doesn't exactly sound like a hardship to me." Donald Kelley's reputation as a chef was known throughout the state, not just the town.

Susan didn't want Duke to be disappointed. "Actually, I made a lot of it."

His eyes met hers for a brief moment. She couldn't for the life of her fathom what he was thinking. The man had to be a stunning poker player. "Doesn't sound bad, either."

The simple compliment, delivered without any fanfare, had Susan warming inside and struggling to tamp down what she felt had to be a creeping blush on the outside. Pressing her lips together, she murmured, "Well, I hope you won't be disappointed."

"Don't plan on being," he told her. Duke nodded toward the vehicle he'd left parked at the end of the lot. "Hope you don't mind riding in a truck, seeing as how you're probably used to gallivanting around in those fancy cars."

When it came down to matching dollar for dollar, the Coltons were probably richer than the Kelleys, but despite his distant ties to the present sitting president, Joseph Colton, Darius Colton didn't believe in throwing money away for show. That included buying fancy cars for his sons.

Duke was referring to Linc's sports car, Susan thought. He had to be because her own car was a rather bland sedan with more than a few miles and years on it. But it was a reliable vehicle that got her where she had to go and that was all that ultimately mattered to her.

"I like trucks," she told him, looking at his. "They're dependable."

In response, Susan thought she saw a small smile flirt with Duke's mouth before disappearing again. And then he shrugged a bit self-consciously.

"If I'd known I'd be heading out to your place, I would've washed it first," he told her.

"Dirt's just a sign left behind by hard work," she said philosophically as she approached the passenger side of the vehicle.

Duke opened the door for her, then helped her up into the cab. She was acutely aware of his hands on her waist, giving her a small boost so that she could avoid any embarrassing mishap, given that she was wearing a black dress and high heels.

A tingle danced through her.

This wasn't the time or place to feel things like that, she chided herself. She'd just buried her best friend. This was a time for mourning, not for reacting to the touch of a man who most likely wasn't even aware that he *had* touched her.

Duke caught himself staring for a second. Staring at the neat little rear that Susan Kelley had. Funerals weren't the time and cemeteries weren't the place to entertain the kind of thoughts that were now going through his head.

But there they were anyway, taking up space, coloring the situation.

Maybe, despite the best of intentions, he shouldn't have shown up at the funeral, he silently told himself.

Too late now, Duke thought as he got into the driver's seat and started up the truck. With any luck, he wouldn't have to stay long at the reception.

Chapter 4

"Take the next turn to the—"

There was no GPS in Duke's truck because he hated the idea of being told where to turn and, essentially, how to drive by some disembodied female voice. He'd been driving around, relying on gut instincts and keen observation, for more years than were legally allowed.

For the last ten minutes he'd patiently listened to Susan issuing instructions and coming very close to mimicking a GPS.

Enough was enough. He could go the rest of the way to the Kelleys' house without having every bend in the road narrated.

"You can stop giving me directions," he told her as politely as he could manage. "I know how to get to your place."

She'd suspected as much, which was why she'd been

surprised when he'd allowed her to come along to guide him to the big house in the first place.

"If you didn't need directions, what am I doing in your truck?" she asked him.

He spared Susan a glance before looking back at the road. "Sitting."

Very funny. But at least this meant he had a sense of humor. Sort of. "Besides that."

Duke shrugged, keeping his eyes on the desolate road ahead of him. "Seemed easier than trying to argue with your mother."

She laughed. The man was obviously a fast learner as well. "You have a point."

Since she agreed with him, Duke saw no reason to comment any further. Several minutes evaporated with no exchange being made between them. The expanding silence embraced them like a tomb.

Finally, Susan couldn't take it any more. "Don't talk much, do you?"

He continued looking straight ahead. The road was desolate but there was no telling when a stray animal could come running out.

"Nope."

Obviously, he was feeling uncomfortable in her company. If her mother, ever the matchmaker, hadn't orchestrated this, he wouldn't even be here, feeling awkward like this, Susan thought. What had her mother been thinking?

"I'm sorry if you're uncomfortable," she apologized to him.

Duke spared her another glance. His brow furrowed, echoing his confusion. "What makes you think I'm uncomfortable?"

"Because you're not talking." It certainly didn't take a rocket scientist to come to that conclusion, she thought.

Duke made a short, dismissive noise. Discomfort had nothing to do with his silence. He just believed in an economy of words and in not talking unless he had something to say. "I don't do small talk."

She was of the opinion that *everyone* did small talk, but she wasn't about to get into a dispute over it. "Okay," she acknowledged. "Then say something earth-shattering."

For a moment, he said nothing at all. Then, because she was obviously not about to let the subject drop, he asked, "You always chatter like that?"

Blowing out a breath, she gave him an honest answer. "Only when I'm uncomfortable or nervous."

"Which is it?"

Again, she couldn't be anything but honest, even though she knew that if her mother was here right now, Bonnie Gene would be rolling her eyes at the lack of feminine wiles she was displaying. But playing games, especially coy ones, had never been her thing. "Both right now."

Despite the fact that he had asked, her answer surprised him. "I make you nervous?"

He did, but oddly enough, in a good way. Rather than say yes, she gave him half an answer. "Silence makes me nervous."

He nodded toward the dash. "You can turn on the radio."

She didn't feel like hearing music right now. Somehow, after the memorial service, it just didn't seem right. What she wanted was human contact, human interaction.

"I'd rather turn you on—" As her words echoed back at her, Susan's eyes widened with horror. "I mean, if you could be turned on." Mortified, she covered her now-flushed face with her hands. "Oh, God, that didn't come out right, either."

Despite himself, the corners of his mouth curved a little. Susan looked almost adorable, flustered like that.

"That's one of the reasons I don't do small talk." He eyed her for a second before looking back at the road. "I'd stop if I were you."

"Right."

Susan took a breath, trying to regroup and not say anything that would lead to her putting her foot in her mouth again. Even so, she had to say something because the silence really was making her feel restless inside. She reverted back to safe ground: the reason he'd been at the cemetery.

"It was very nice of you to come to the funeral," she said. "Did you know Miranda well?"

He took another turn, swinging to the right. The Kelley mansion wasn't far now. "Didn't know her at all," he told her.

The answer made no sense to her. "Then why did you come?"

"I know you," he replied, as if that somehow explained everything.

She was having a hard time understanding his reasons. "And because she was my best friend and meant so much to me, you came?" she asked uncertainly. That was the conclusion his last answer led her to, but it still didn't make any sense.

"Something like that."

But she and Duke didn't really know each other, she thought, confused. She knew *of* him, of course. Duke Colton was the twin brother of the town's only murderer. He was one of Darius Colton's boys. Each brother was handsomer than the next. And, of course, there'd been that crush she'd had on him. But she didn't really *know* him. And he didn't know her.

In a town as small as Honey Creek, Montana, spreading gossip was one of the main forms of entertainment and there were plenty of stories to spread about the Coltons, especially since, going back a number of generations, the current president of the United States and Darius Colton were both related to Teddy Colton who'd lived in the early 1900s. To his credit, the distant relationship wasn't something that the already affluent Darius capitalized on or used to up his stock. He was too busy being blustery and riding his sons to get them to give their personal best each and every day. He expected nothing less.

That kind of a demanding, thankless lifestyle might be the reason why Duke preferred keeping to himself, she reasoned.

She felt bad for him.

Following the long, winding driveway up to what could only be termed a mansion, Duke parked his pickup truck off to one side she supposed where it wouldn't be in anyone's way.

Still feeling a bit awkward, Susan announced, "We're here."

He gave her a look she couldn't begin to read. "That's why I stopped driving."

Susan waited for a smile to emerge, but his expression continued to be nondescript. She gave up trying to read his mind.

As she got out of the cab, Susan heard the sound of approaching cars directly behind them. The onslaught had begun.

"We might be first, but not by much," she observed. Within less than a minute, the driveway, large though it was, was overflowing with other vehicles, all jockeying for prime space.

The first to arrive after them were Bonnie Gene and her husband. Bonnie Gene was frowning as she looked around.

"Knew I should have hired a valet service," she reproached herself as she joined Susan and Duke. Donald came trudging up the walk several feet behind her. Since the driveway was at a slight incline, Donald was huffing and puffing from the minor exertion.

"Don't start carrying on, Bonnie Gene. People know how to park their own damn cars. No need to be throwing money away needlessly," he chided in between taking deep breaths.

Turning around to look at her husband, Bonnie Gene frowned. "Don't cuss, Donald," she chided him. "This is a funeral reception."

"I can cuss in my own house if I want to," he informed her, even though, since she'd chastised him, he knew he'd try extra hard to curb his tongue.

Bonnie Gene sighed and shook her head. "See what I have to put up with?" She addressed her question to Duke. Not waiting for a comment, she turned and raised her voice in order to be heard by the guests who had begun arriving. "C'mon everyone, let's go in, loosen our belts and our consciences just a little, and eat today as if it didn't count."

That definitely pleased Donald who laughed expansively. The deep, throaty sound could be heard above the din of voices coming from the crowd. "Now you're talking, Bonnie Gene."

His wife was quick to shoot him down. "That wasn't meant for you, Donald. That was for our guests." Keeping her "public smile" in place, Bonnie Gene uttered her threat through lips that were barely moving. "You eat any more than your allotted portion and there'll be hell to pay, Donald."

"I'm already paying it," Donald mumbled under his breath.

About to walk away, Bonnie Gene stopped abruptly and eyed her husband. "What was that?"

The look on Donald's round face was innocence personified. "Nothing, my love, not a thing."

Duke held his peace until the senior Kelleys had moved on. Once they had disappeared into the crowd filling the house, he lowered his head and asked Susan, "She always boss him around like that?"

"She does it because she loves him," Susan answered, feeling the need to be ever so slightly defensive of her mother's motives. "Mother's convinced that if she doesn't watch over him, Dad'll eat himself to death. It's because Mother wants him around for a good long time to come that she tends to police him like that."

Duke nodded, saying nothing. Knowing that if it were him being ridden like that, he wouldn't stand for it. But to each his own. He wasn't about to tell another man how to live his life.

They'd moved inside the house by now and Duke

looked around absently, noting faces. There were more people inside this room than he normally saw in a month.

He wondered how long he would have to stay before he could leave without being observed. As he was trying to come up with a time frame, his thoughts were abruptly interrupted by a flushed, flustered young woman who accidentally stumbled next to him. About to fall, she grabbed on to the first thing she could—and it was Duke.

Horrified that she'd almost pushed him over, Mary Walsh immediately apologized.

"Oh, I'm so sorry," she cried with feeling. "I didn't mean to bump into you like that." Her face was growing a deep shade of red. "New shoes," she explained, looking down at them accusingly. "I'm still a little wobbly in them."

He'd been ready to dismiss the whole thing at the word *Oh*. "No harm done," he assured her.

Drawn by the voice, Susan was quick to throw her arms around her flustered friend. "Mary, you made it after all! I wasn't sure if you were coming to the reception." She punctuated her declaration with a fierce hug.

"Yes, I made it. Just in time to step all over—" she paused for a moment, as if searching for a name, then brightened "—Duke Colton."

The next moment Mary made the connection. A sense of awkwardness descended because she wasn't altogether sure how to react. This was Duke Colton, the brother of the man who had been convicted of killing her father. Still, manners were manners and she thoroughly believed in them.

"I really am sorry. I didn't mean to bump into you

like that. New shoes," she explained to Susan in case Susan hadn't heard her a moment ago.

"She's wobbly," Duke added, looking ever so slightly amused.

"Who's wobbly?" Bonnie Gene asked, materializing amid them again with the ease of a puff of smoke. She looked from her daughter to her daughter's long-time friend, sweet little Mary Walsh.

The girl should have been married ages ago, Bonnie Gene thought. Maybe, if Mary was married, Susan wouldn't be such a stubborn holdout.

"I am, Mrs. Kelley," Mary explained. "These heels were an impulse purchase and they're too high for me. I really haven't had a chance to break them in yet," she added sheepishly.

"Well, break them in by the buffet table," Bonnie Gene urged. With a grand wave of her hand, she indicated the line that was already forming by the long table that ran along the length of the back wall. Leaning in closer to Mary, she added with enthusiasm, "Right next to that really good-looking young man in the tan jacket. See him?" she wanted to know.

"Mother," Susan cried, struggling to keep her voice low.

"Susan," Bonnie Gene responded in a sing-song voice.

She knew that none of her children appreciated her matchmaking efforts, but that was their problem, not hers. She intended to keep on trying to pair off the young people in her life wherever and whenever she had the opportunity—whether they liked it or not. People belonged in pairs, not drifting through life in single file.

Mary already knew what Susan's mother was like,

but Duke undoubtedly hadn't a clue. So Susan turned toward him and said in a soft voice, "I suggest we make our getaway the minute her back is turned. Otherwise, she'll probably have you married off by midnight."

"I don't think so," Duke answered with a finality that told Susan that not only was he not in the market for a wife, he'd deliberately head in the opposite direction should his path ever cross that of a potential mate.

Susan vaguely recalled that there had been some kind of scandal last year involving Duke and an older married woman. She thought she'd heard that the woman, Charlene McWilliams, had committed suicide shortly after Duke broke things off with her.

Something of that nature would definitely have a person backing away from any sort of a relationship, even the hint of a relationship, Susan thought sympathetically.

God knew she backed away from them and she had no scandal involving a man in her past. As a matter of fact, she had nothing in her past. But there was a reason for that. She just wasn't any good at relationships.

Her forte, Susan was convinced, lay elsewhere. She was very good at her job and at raising other people's spirits. For now, she told herself, that was enough. And later would eventually take care of itself.

"There's an open bar over there." Susan pointed it out. There were a number of people, mainly men, clustering around it. She wanted to give him the opportunity to join them if that would make him feel more comfortable. "If you'd rather drink than eat, I'll understand," she added, although she doubted that would make a difference to him one way or the other.

Duke wasn't even mildly tempted. He liked keeping

a clear head when he was on someone else's territory. Drinking was for winding down, for kicking back after a long, full day's work. He hadn't put in a full day yet.

"Nothing to understand," he replied. "I'd rather eat."

She couldn't exactly say why his answer had her feeling so happy, but it did.

"So would I," she agreed, flashing a wide smile at him. "Why don't I just go get us a couple of—"

She didn't get a chance to finish her sentence. Linc had swooped down on her like a hungry falcon zeroing in on his prey.

"There you are, Susan," he declared, looking relieved. "I've been looking all over for you. You shouldn't be alone at a time like this."

Oh, please, not now. Don't smother me now. She wanted to remain polite, but she wasn't sure just how long she could be that way. Linc was beginning to wear away the last of her nerves.

"I'm hardly alone, Linc," she informed him. "There're dozens and dozens of people here."

Her answer didn't deter Linc. "You know that old saying about being lonely in a crowd." He slipped his arm around her waist as comfortably as if he'd been doing it forever. At the same time, he looked smugly over at Duke. "I'll take it from here, Colton. Thanks for looking out for my girl."

She had to stop this before it went too far. Linc was being delusional. They'd dated a few times in the past, but it had gone nowhere. She thought they were both agreed on that point. Obviously not.

"I am *not* your girl, Linc," she insisted, lowering her voice so that she wouldn't embarrass him or wind up causing a scene.

She still had feelings for Linc, but they were all of the friendly variety. The romance that Linc apparently had so desperately hoped for had never materialized, although she really had tried to make herself love him the way he obviously wanted to be loved. It just wasn't meant to happen. Linc was handsome, funny and intelligent. But there was no spark, no chemistry between them. At least, she'd never been aware of any.

Apparently, Linc had been the recipient of other signals.

"You're just upset," Linc told her in the kind of soothing voice a parent used with a petulant child. "Once things get back to normal, you'll change your mind. You'll see," he promised.

"There's nothing to see," she informed him tersely, framing her answer more for Duke's benefit than for Linc's.

But she might as well not have bothered. Linc obviously wasn't listening and Duke, when she turned to look at him, wasn't there to hear.

What is he, part bat? she silently demanded. That was twice that he'd just seemed to disappear on her. Once outside the hospital and now here. Both times, it had been just after Linc had attached himself to her side as if they were tethered by some kind of invisible umbilical chord.

Stop making excuses for him. If Duke had wanted to hang around, he would have, Susan told herself.

Besides, she had more guests to see to than just Duke Colton.

The next moment, she was saying it out loud, at least in part.

"Excuse me, Linc, but I have guests to see to," she

told him, walking quickly away before he could make a comment or try to stop her obvious retreat with some inane remark.

When it came to being the perfect hostess, Susan had studied at the knee of a master—her mother. Bonnie Gene Kelley was the consummate hostess, never having been known to run out of anything, and always able to satisfy the needs and requirements of her guests, no matter what it was they wanted.

Like mother, like daughter, at least in this one respect.

Susan wove her way in and out of clusters of people exchanging memories of Miranda along with small talk. She made sure that everyone ate, that everyone drank and, just as importantly, that she didn't find herself alone with Linc again.

And all the while, she kept an eye out for Duke. She spotted him several times, always standing near someone, always seeming to be silent.

And watching her.

Their eyes met a number of times and, unlike with Linc, she felt a spark. There was definitely chemistry or *something* that seemed to come to life and shimmer between them every time she caught his eye or he caught hers.

She would have liked to put that chemistry to the test. Purely for academic purposes, of course, she added quickly.

But there was a room full of people in the way. Maybe that was the whole point, she thought suddenly. The room full of people made her feel safe. Not threatened by the tall, dark and brooding Duke.

Still…

Get a grip and focus, Susan, she upbraided herself. Her best friend was barely cold and she was exploring her options with Duke Colton. What was *wrong* with her?

She had no answer for that. Besides, right now, there was really nothing she could do about exploring any of these racing feelings any further.

And maybe that was a good thing. Everyone needed a little fantasy to spice up their lives and it only remained a fantasy if it wasn't tested and exposed to the light of day.

She was fairly certain that hers never would be. Not if Duke kept perform his disappearing act.

Chapter 5

"If I didn't know any better, I'd say you were trying to avoid me."

Startled, Susan swallowed a gasp as her heart launched into double time. She'd left the reception and come out here to the side veranda to be alone for a moment. She hadn't realized that Linc was anywhere in the immediate vicinity, much less that he'd follow her outside.

She took a deep breath to calm down. Linc was right. She *had* been avoiding him and she felt a little guilty about it. But at the same time, she felt resentful that he was making her feel that way.

Was it wrong not to want to feel hemmed in? And lately, that was the way Linc was making her feel—hemmed in. By avoiding him, she was trying to avoid having to say things she knew would hurt him.

She could see that he was hopeful that they could "give their relationship another chance." But kissing him was like kissing her brother and that was the way she felt about him, like a sister about a brother. She cared for him, but not in *that* way.

To try to turn that feeling into something more, something sexual between them seemed more than a little icky to her. But there was no graceful way to say that, no way to avoid hurting his feelings and his ego.

So she'd been trying to avoid Linc and avoid the awkwardness that was waiting out in the wings for both of them once she made her feelings—or lack thereof—plain to him.

Susan shrugged, hoping to table the discussion until she felt more up to having it out between them. "I'm not trying to avoid you, Linc, I've just been trying to be a good hostess."

He nodded his head, as if he was willing—for now—to tolerate the excuse she was giving him. "Well, now it's time for you to think about taking care of *you*," Linc said with emphasis.

If someone had asked her about it, Susan had nothing specific to point to as to why alarms were suddenly going off in her head, but they were. Loudly.

Survival instincts had her taking a step back, away from him. She wasn't sure where he was going with this, but it had her uneasy.

"What do you mean?" she asked him.

"I mean," Linc replied patiently, like someone trying to make a mental lightweight understand his point, "that you need someone to wait on you for a change."

As he spoke, he moved in closer and didn't appear to be too happy that she was taking a step back the moment he took a step forward. Pretending not to notice, he continued moving in toward her until the three-foot-high railing that ran along the veranda prevented her from moving back any further. He'd effectively managed to corner her.

"Someone who would put your needs ahead of their own," he continued. With a smile, he slowly threaded his fingers through her hair.

Susan pulled her head back with a quick, less-than-friendly toss. He was so close to her, if she took a deep breath, her chest would be in contact with his. She didn't want to push him back, but he wasn't leaving her much of a choice.

"Linc, don't."

His voice was low, almost hypnotic as he continued talking to her. "You're confused, Susan. Your emotions are all jumbled up. You need someone to take care of you and there's nothing I'd like more than to be that someone," he told her. He bent his head so that his mouth was closer to hers.

But when he brought it down to kiss her, Susan quickly turned her head. He wound up making contact with her hair. "Linc, no."

Despite her reaction, Linc gave no sign that he was about to back off this time, or let her step aside. Instead, he coaxed, "C'mon, Susan. You know I'm the one you should be with."

She moved her head in the opposite direction, awarding him another mouthful of hair. "Linc, no," she insisted more firmly. "I want you to stop."

Her words fell on deaf ears. "Might as well give in to the inevitable." This time, his voice was a little more forceful.

The next moment, Linc found himself stumbling backward. Someone had grabbed him by the shoulder and yanked him away as if he were nothing more than a big, clumsy rag doll.

"The lady said stop," Duke told him. His voice was deep, as if it was emerging from the bottom of a gigantic cavernous chasm. There was no missing the warning note in it.

Anger, hot and dangerous, flashed in Linc's eyes as he glared at the man who had interrupted his attempted play for Susan.

"This isn't any business of yours, Colton," he snapped at Duke.

Placing his range-toned muscular frame between Hayes and the target of Hayes' assault, Duke hooked his thumbs in his belt and directed a steely glare at the shorter man.

"Man forcing himself on a defenseless woman is everybody's business," Duke said in his steady, inflection-free voice.

Susan's chin shot up. She didn't care if this *was* Duke Colton, she was not about to be perceived as some weak-kneed damsel in distress.

"I am *not* defenseless," she protested with just enough indignation to make Duke believe that that little woman actually believed what she was saying.

She might be spunky, Duke thought, but there was no way that Susan Kelley could hold her own if Hayes decided to force himself on her. Or at least not without a weapon—or a well-aimed kick.

Still, he wasn't about to get drawn into a verbal sparring match with her over this. He'd had every intention of retrieving his truck and leaving, until he'd discovered the vehicle was barricaded in by two other cars that would have to be moved in order for him to get out. He'd been on his way to enlist Bonnie Gene's help in finding the owners of the other two vehicles when he'd seen Hayes crowding Susan.

So he shrugged now in response to Susan's protest. "Have it your way. You're not defenseless."

But Duke gave no indication that he was about to leave, at least, not until Hayes moved his butt and went back inside the house or into the hole he'd initially crawled out of.

Instead, Duke continued to stand there, his thumbs still hooked onto his belt, waiting patiently. The look in his eyes left absolutely no doubt what he was waiting for.

"I'll see you later, Susan," Linc finally bit off and then marched into the house, looking petulant and very annoyed.

Once Linc had retreated, closing the door behind him, Susan took a breath and let it out slowly. She turned toward Duke. "I suppose I should thank you."

A hint of a shrug rumbled across his broad shoulders. "You can do whatever you want to," he told her.

His seemingly indifferent words hung in the air between them as his eyes swept over her slowly. Thoroughly.

It was probably the heat and her own edgy emotional turmoil that caused her temporary foray into insanity. That was the only way she could describe it later.

Insanity.

Why else, she later wondered, would she have done what she did in response to Duke's words? Because she suddenly found herself wanting to do something that she would think in the next moment was outrageous. If she could think.

If nothing else, it was certainly out of character for her.

One minute, she was vacillating between being furious with the male species in general—both Linc and Duke acted as if they thought she was just some empty-headed nitwit who needed to be looked after.

The next minute, something inside her was viewing Duke as her knight in somewhat battered, tarnished armor. A tall, dark, brooding knight to whom she very much wanted to express her gratitude.

So she kissed him.

Without stopping to think, without really realizing what she was about to do, she did it.

On her toes, Susan grabbed on to his rock-hard biceps for leverage and support and then she pressed her lips against his.

It was a kiss steeped in gratitude. But that swiftly peeled away and before she knew it, Susan was caught up in what she'd initiated, no longer the instigator but the one who'd gotten swept up in the consequences.

That was *her* pulse that was racing, *her* breath that had vanished without backup. That was *her* head that was spinning and those were *her* knees that had suddenly gone missing in action.

Had she not had the presence of mind to anchor herself to his arms the way she had, Susan realized she might have further embarrassed herself by sinking to the ground, a mindless, palpitating mass of skin, bone and completely useless parts in between.

God, did he ever pack a wallop.

It wasn't often that Duke was caught by surprise. For the most part, he went through life with a grounded, somewhat jaded premonition of what was to come. Duke had been blessed with an innate intuition that allowed him to see what was coming at least a split second before it actually came.

It wasn't that he was a psychic; he was an observer, a student of life. And because he was a student who never forgot a single lesson he'd learned, very little out here in this small corner of the world managed to catch him by surprise.

But this had.

It had caught him so unprepared that he felt as if he'd just been slammed upside his head with a two-by-four. At least he felt that unsteady. Not only had Susan caught him completely off guard by kissing him, he was even more surprised by the magnitude of his reaction to that very kiss.

Because Charlene McWilliams' suicide over a year ago had left him reeling, he'd stepped back from having any sort of a relationship with the softer sex. Her suicide had affected him deeply, not because he'd loved her but because he felt badly that being involved with him had ultimately driven Charlene to take her own life.

Consequently, practicing mind over matter, Duke had systematically shut down those parts of himself that reacted to a woman on a purely physical level.

Or so he'd believed up until now.

Obviously he hadn't done quite as good a job shutting down as he'd thought, because this little slip of a girl—barely a card-carrying woman—had managed to arouse him to a length and breadth he hadn't been aroused to in a very long time.

Fully intending to separate his lips from hers, Duke took hold of Susan's waist. But somehow, instead of creating a wedge, he wound up pulling her to him, kissing her back.

Kissing her with feeling.

He had to create a chasm before his head spun completely out of control, Duke silently insisted, doing his best to rally.

With effort, his heart hammering like the refrain from "The Anvil Chorus," Duke forced himself to actually push Susan back—even though everything within him vehemently protested the action.

With space between them now, Duke looked at her, still stunned. And speechless.

His mind reeling and a complete blank, Duke turned on his heel and walked away from the veranda and Susan. Quickly.

The warm night breeze surrounding her like sticky gauze, Susan stood there, watching Duke grow smaller until he disappeared around the corner. Shaken, she couldn't move immediately. She wasn't completely sure if she'd just been caught up in some kind of groundbreaking hallucination or if what had just transpired— possibly the greatest kiss of all time—had been real.

What she did know was that she was having trouble breathing and that feelings both of bereavement and absolute, unmitigated joy were square-dancing inside her.

Confusing the hell out of her.

Taking as deep a breath as she could manage, Susan turned around and hurried back into the house. She needed to be able to pull herself together before she ran into her mother. One look from her mother in this present shaken-up condition and she'd be answering questions from now until Christmas.

Maybe longer.

* * *

"Where the hell have you been?" Darius Colton wanted to know.

Home to replenish his supply of water before heading back out to the range and his men again, Darius had seen his son's dusty pickup truck on the horizon, on its way to Duke's house. Like several of his other offspring, Duke lived in a house located on the Colton Ranch.

Duke had been conspicuously absent, both this morning and now part of the afternoon. He'd been absent without clearing it with him and Darius didn't like it.

Darius Colton didn't consider himself an unreasonable man, but he needed to know where everyone was and what they were doing at any given hour of the day. It was his right as patriarch of the family.

To him it was the only way to run a ranch and it was the way he'd managed to build his ranch up to what it now was.

Getting on the back of the horse he'd tethered to the rear of his truck, Darius rode up to meet Duke. Within range of the pickup, Darius pinned his son with the sharply voiced question.

When he received no answer, he barked out the question again. "I said, where the hell have you been, boy?"

Stopping the truck, Duke met his father's heated glare without flinching. He'd learned a long time ago that any display of fear would have his father pouncing like a hungry jackal on unsuspecting prey. His father had absolutely no respect for anyone who didn't stand up to him.

The confusing flip side of that was that the person who opposed him incurred his wrath. There was very little winning when it came to his father. For the most part, to get on his father's good side, a person had to display unconditional obedience and constant productivity. Anything less was not tolerated for long—if at all.

"I went to a funeral," Duke told his father, his voice even.

The answer did not please Darius. He wasn't aware of anyone of any import dying. "Well, it's going to be your own funeral you'll be attending if I catch you going anywhere again during working hours without asking me first."

"I didn't tell you because you were busy."

Duke deliberately used the word *tell* rather than *ask*, knowing that his father would pick up on the difference, but it was a matter of pride. He wanted his father to know that he wasn't just a lackey, he was a Colton and that meant he expected to be treated with respect, same as his father, even if the person on the other end of the discussion *was* his father.

His horse beside the driver's side of the truck's cab, Darius looked closely at his son. His eyes narrowed as he stared at Duke's face.

"This a frisky corpse you went to pay your respects to?" he finally asked.

There was no humor in his voice. Before Duke could ask him what he was talking about, Darius leaned in and rubbed his rough thumb over the corner of his son's lower lip.

And then he held it up for Duke's perusal.

There was a streak of pink on his father's thumb. Pink lipstick.

The same shade of lipstick he recalled Susan wearing.

"That didn't come from the corpse" was all that

Duke said. And then he preemptively ran his own thumb over his lips to wipe away any further telltale signs that Susan might have left behind.

"Well, that's a relief," Darius said sarcastically. "Wouldn't want the neighbors talking." He drew himself up in the saddle. "You're way behind in your chores, boy," he informed Duke coldly. "Nobody's going to carry your weight for you."

Darius had long made it clear that he expected his offspring to work the ranch every day, putting in the long hours that were necessary. No exceptions.

"Don't expect anyone to," Duke replied. "I just came home to change," he added in case his father found fault with his coming back to his own house rather than heading directly to the range.

"Well, then, be quick about it," Darius barked. He was about to ride his horse back to his own truck parked before the big house, but he stopped for a second. Curiosity had temporarily gotten the better of him. "Whose funeral was it?"

"Miranda James," Duke answered.

Bushy eyebrows met together over a surprisingly small, well-shaped nose. Darius scowled. "Name doesn't mean anything to me."

His father's response didn't surprise him. Darius Colton didn't concern himself with anyone or anything that wasn't directly related to the range or the business of running that ranch.

"Didn't think it would," Duke said more to himself than his father.

Darius snorted, muttered something under his breath about ungrateful whelps being a waste of his time and effort, and then he rode away, leaving a cloud of dust behind in his wake.

Duke shook his head and went into the house to change. Despite the hour, he had a full day's work to catch up on. His father expected—and accepted—nothing less and he didn't want to give the man another reason to go off on him. He wasn't sure how long his own temper would last under fire.

Chapter 6

Admittedly, though it had been close to a year since he was elected sheriff, Wes was still rather new on the job. However, some things just seemed like common sense. According to the unofficial rules of procedure in cases where there was a dead body involved, the next of kin was the first to be notified.

Usually.

But in this particular troubling case, the next of kin had already *been* notified. Fifteen years ago. After getting confirmation from the county medical examiner that the body in the morgue really was Mark Walsh, Wes figured that he could put off notifying Jolene Walsh about her husband's murder for an hour or so, seeing as how this was the second time she would be receiving the news.

Since this turn of events was really disturbing—who

would have thought he'd get a genuine, honest-to-God mystery so soon after being elected?—Wes wanted to turn to a sympathetic ear to run the main highlights past. Again, he didn't go the normal route. Since this case did involve his older brother, by rights the family patriarch should be the one he would go to with this.

Should be, but he didn't.

He and Darius had a prickly relationship—the same kind of relationship, when he came right down to it, that his father had with each of his children. Darius Colton, for reasons of his own that no one else was privy to, was *not* the easiest man to talk to or get along with. He never had been.

But someone in his family should be told and since this was Wes's first time notifying anyone about the death of a loved one—or, in Mark Walsh's case, a barely tolerated one—he wanted to practice it before upending Jolene Walsh's world a second time with what amounted to the same news.

So he rode out to his family's ranch and headed toward the section he knew that Duke was assigned to tending.

Wait 'til Duke hears this, Wes thought. If this didn't shake his older brother up, nothing would.

Blessed with excellent vision, Duke saw Wes approaching across the range a good distance away. Just the barest hint of curiosity reared its head as he watched his brother's Jeep grow larger.

Today was his day to mend fences—literally—and he could do with a break, Duke thought. Putting down his hammer and the new wire he was stringing across the posts, Duke left his cracked leather gloves on as he wiped the sweat from his brow with the back of his wrist.

Once he did, that brow was practically the only part of him that wasn't glistening with sweat. His shirt had long since been stripped off and was now tied haphazardly around his waist.

"Slow day in town?" he called out just before Wes pulled up beside him. "If you're tired of playing sheriff and want to do some real work, I've got another hammer around here somewhere." He glanced around to see if he'd taken the second tool out of his battered truck or left it in the flatbed.

Though no one would ever call him laid-back, Duke was considerably more at ease around his siblings, and even his nephew, his sister Maisie's son, than he was around most people. And that included his father, who he viewed as a less-than-benevolent tyrant.

When Wes made no response in return, Duke narrowed his eyes and looked at his brother more closely.

Now that he thought about it, he'd seen Wes look a lot less serious in his time.

"Who died?" he said only half in jest.

Pulling up the hand brake, Wes turned off the ignition and got out. He pulled his hat down a little lower. Out here, on the open range, the sun seemed to beat down almost mercilessly. He'd forgotten how grueling it could be out in the open like this.

"Mark Walsh," Wes answered his brother.

Duke frowned. What kind of game was this? "We already know that, Wes. Damien's in state prison doing time for it."

Wes looked up the two inches that separated him from his brother. "Damien didn't do it."

"Also not a newsflash," Duke countered. He picked up his hammer again. If Wes was out here to play games, he might as well get back to work. "Although the old man hardly lifted a finger to advance that theory." It wasn't easy, keeping a note of bitterness out of his voice. He'd always felt his father could have gotten Damien a better lawyer, brought someone in from the outside to defend his twin instead of keeping out of it the way he had. "But the rest of us know that Damien didn't do it." Bright-green eyes met blue. "Right?"

"Absolutely right," Wes said with feeling. He took a breath, then launched into his narrative. "Boyd Arnold found a body the other day in the creek."

Duke waved his hand in dismissal. He paid little attention to what went on around Honey Creek these days—even less if it involved people like Boyd Arnold.

"Did it have one head or two?" he asked sarcastically. "That lamebrain's always claiming to find these weird things—"

Wes stopped him from going on. "What he found was Mark Walsh's body."

That managed to bring Duke up short. He stared at Wes, trying to make sense out of what his brother had just told him. "Somebody dug Walsh up and then tossed him in the creek?" Nobody had ever really liked the man, but that seemed a little excessive.

Wes shook his head. "No. Whoever's in Mark Walsh's grave isn't Walsh."

Duke went from surprised to completely stunned. He waited for a punch line. There wasn't any. "You're serious."

"Like the plague," Wes responded. "County coroner just confirmed it from Walsh's dental records. Nobody else knows yet," he cautioned, then added, "except for the coroner and Boyd, of course. Boyd's sworn to secrecy," he explained when he saw the skeptical look that came into Duke's eyes.

"That'll last ten minutes," Duke estimated with a snort. And then he realized something. "You haven't told Jolene yet?" he asked, surprised.

Wes shook his head. "Not yet. I planned to do that next. I wanted to tell you first."

Duke didn't follow his brother's reasoning. They got along all right, but he wasn't any closer to Wes than he was to some of the others. "Why me first?" Duke wanted to know.

Wes gave him an honest answer. "Because telling you is almost like telling Damien." The two weren't identical, but it was close enough. Wes sighed deeply. The guilt he bore for not being able to find something to free his brother earlier weighed heavily on his soul. "I'm going up to the county courthouse after I tell Jolene, get the wheels in motion for Damien's release."

"Why don't you go there first?" Duke suggested. He saw he'd caught Wes's attention. "Seeing how 'fast' those wheels turn, you need to get the process started as soon as possible." He gave Wes an excuse he could use to assuage his conscience. "You won't be telling Jolene anything she hasn't heard before. The only thing that's different is the timeline. She's still going to be a widow when you finish talking to her. There's no hurry to deliver the news."

Wes gave the matter a cursory thought, then nodded, won over. Duke's plan made sense. "I guess you're right."

"'Course I'm right." A small, thin smile curved Duke's

lips. "I'm your big brother." And then he rolled the news over in his head as the impact of what this all meant hit. "Hell, Mark Walsh...dead again after all this time." He shook his head. "Don't that beat all? You got any idea who did it?"

Wes didn't have a clue. What he did know was the identity of the one person who didn't do it. "Not Damien."

The thin smile was replaced with a small grin on Duke's lips. "Yeah, not Damien." And that, he thought, a wave of what he assumed had to be elation washing over him, said quite a lot.

Wes checked his watch. "See you," he said, beginning to get back into his vehicle. And then, shading his eyes a little more, he stopped to squint in the direction he'd come from. "Looks like you've got company coming, Duke. This place isn't as desolate as I remember," he commented with a short laugh, getting behind the wheel of his Jeep.

Still stunned by the news Wes had delivered, even though he didn't show it, Duke looked down the road in the direction Wes had pointed.

His green eyes narrowed in slight confusion as he made out the figure behind the wheel of the silver-blue sedan.

Hell, if this kept up, they were going to need a traffic light all the way out here, Duke thought darkly, watching Susan Kelley's little vehicle approach.

Woman didn't have enough common sense to use a truck or Jeep, he thought in disdain. Cars like hers weren't meant for this kind of road, didn't she know that?

His brother passed Susan's car, pausing a second to

exchange words Duke wasn't able to make out at this distance.

He thought he saw Susan blush, but that could have just been a trick of the sunlight. The next minute, she was driving again, getting closer. This was blowing his schedule to hell.

He ran his hand through his hair, trying not to look like a wild man.

Duke wasn't wearing a shirt. She hadn't thought she'd find him like this.

Susan could feel her stomach tightening into a knot. At the same time her palms were growing damper than the weather would have warranted.

God, but he was magnificent.

For the length of a minute, Susan's mind went completely blank as her eyes swept over every inch of the glistening, rock-hard body of the man standing beside the partially completed wire fence. His worn jeans were molded to his hips, dipping down below his navel—she found her breath growing progressively shorter.

Focus, Susan, focus. The man's got other parts you could be looking at. His face, damn it, Susan, look at his face!

But that didn't exactly help, either, because Duke Colton was as handsome as Lucifer had been reported to be—and most likely, she judged, his soul was probably in the same condition.

No, that wasn't fair, she upbraided herself. The man had come to her aid at the funeral reception. If he hadn't been there, who knew how ugly a scene might have evolved when she tried to push Linc away? She'd loudly proclaimed that she could take care of herself, but Linc outweighed her by a good fifty pounds. He could have overpowered her if he'd really wanted to.

And Duke hadn't been the one to kiss her after Linc had slunk away. She was the one who had made that fateful first move.

Duke waited until Susan was almost right there in front of him before he left the fence and walked over to her vehicle in easy, measured steps.

"Lost?" he asked her, allowing a hint of amusement to show through.

Preoccupied with thoughts that had caught her completely by surprise and made her even warmer than the weather had already rendered her, she hadn't heard him. "What?"

"Lost?" Duke repeated, then put the word into a complete sentence since her confused expression didn't abate. "Are you lost? I've never seen you this far out of town."

There was a reason for that. She'd never been this far out of town before. There hadn't been any need to venture out this way—until now.

Forcing herself to pull her thoughts together, she shook her head. "Oh. No, I'm not lost. I'm looking for you."

Suspicion was never that far away. His eyes held hers. "Why?"

She felt as if he was delving into her mind. "To apologize and to give you this."

This was a gourmet picnic basket. The general concept was something she'd been working on for a while now, attempting to sell her father on the idea of putting out a mail-order catalogue featuring some of their signature meals.

Donald Kelley was still stubbornly holding out. He thought that shipping food through the mail was ridiculous, but her mother saw merit in the idea, so currently, the "official" word was that Kelley's Cookhouse was in "negotiations" over the proposed project. The final verdict, Bonnie Gene insisted in that take charge-way of hers, was not in yet.

Duke eyed the picnic basket for a long moment before finally taking it from her. "What, exactly, are you apologizing for?" he wanted to know.

It wasn't often that she found herself apologizing for anything. The main reason for that was that she never did anything that was out of the ordinary—or exciting. Until now.

"The other afternoon," she told him, lowering her eyes and suddenly becoming fascinated with the dried grass that was beneath her boots.

"The whole afternoon, or something in particular?" Duke asked, his expression giving nothing away as he looked at her.

He was going to make this difficult for her, she thought. She should have known he would. Duke Colton had never been an easygoing man.

"For you feeling as if you had to come to my rescue," she murmured, tripping over her own tongue again. He seemed to have that effect on her, she thought. But she was determined to see this through. "For me putting you on the spot by kissing you."

Pretending to be inspecting the picnic basket, Duke drew back the crisp white-and-red checkered cloth and looked inside. The aroma of spicy barbecued short ribs instantly tantalized his taste buds. It mingled with the scent of fresh apple cinnamon pie and biscuits that were still warm. She must have brought them straight from the oven.

He glanced down at her. "Still haven't heard anything to apologize for," he told her. "I enjoyed taking that little weasel down a couple of pegs. As for you kissing me," his eyes slowly slid over her, "you *definitely* don't have anything to apologize for in that area."

Trying not to grow flustered beneath his scrutiny, Susan tried again. "I didn't mean to make you uncomfortable...."

Duke cut into her sentence. "You didn't," he told her simply.

Susan cleared her throat. This wasn't going as smoothly as she'd hoped. How was it that he made her feel more tongue-tied every time she tried to talk to him?

"Well, anyway, I just wanted to say thank you for being so nice."

That made him laugh. It was a sound she didn't recall ever hearing coming from him. She caught herself smiling in return.

"Nobody's ever accused me of being that," Duke responded, more than slightly amused by the label, "but have it your way if it makes you happy."

Susan brushed her hands against the seat of her stone-washed jeans. She couldn't seem to shake the nervous, unsettled feeling that insisted on running rampant through her. The fact that he was still bare-chested, still wearing jeans that dipped precariously low on his hips, didn't help matters any. If anything, they caused her breath to back up in her lungs and practically solidify.

Try as she might, she couldn't seem to ignore his sun-toned muscles or his washboard abs. Her mouth felt as if it was filled with cotton as she tried to speak again. "They told me at the house that I'd find you out here. I asked," she tacked on and then felt like an idiot for stating the obvious.

Duke nodded at the information. "They'd be the ones to know."

She licked her overly dry lips and tried again. She definitely didn't want him thinking of her as a village idiot. She normally sounded a lot brighter than this. "What are you doing out here, working out in the sun like this?"

He was smiling now, enjoying this exchange. Ordinarily, he had no patience with flustered people, but there was something almost…cute about Susan hemming and hawing and searching for words. "Haven't found a way to turn down the sun while I do my work."

She didn't understand why he had to be out here in this heat, doing things that could just as easily be handled by a ranch hand. "Don't you have people to do this?"

One side of his mouth curved more than the other, giving the resulting smile a sarcastic edge. "My father thinks his sons should learn how to put in a full day's work each day, every day. Besides," he added, "it saves him money if we do the work."

She thought that was awful. "But your father's the richest man in the county." She realized that sounded materialistic, not to mention incredibly callous. "I mean—"

Duke took no offense at her words. He was well aware that his father had amassed a fortune. The fact didn't mean anything to him one way or another. It certainly didn't make him feel as if he was entitled to a special lifestyle or to be regarded as being privileged. He believed in earning his way—and maybe he had his father to thank for that—if he were given to thanking his father.

He saw the blush creeping up her neck. "You do get flustered a lot, don't you?"

She looked embarrassed by the fact. "I'm not a people-person like my mom."

He didn't think she should run herself down like that. The way she was was just fine. "No offense to your mom, but she does come on strong at times. You, on the other hand," he continued in his off-hand manner, "come on just right."

Susan felt her pulse beginning to race.

More.

If she was being honest with herself, her pulse had started racing the instant she saw Duke's naked chest. All sorts of thoughts kept insisting on forming, thoughts she was struggling very hard not to explore.

Right now, she was just barely winning the battle. Emphasis on the word *barely*.

She licked her lips again, fearing that they might stick together in mid sentence if she didn't. "I—um—I've got to be going."

By now he'd reached into the basket and plucked out a short rib. He glanced into the interior. He could probably transfer the rest of the food into the cab of his truck, out of the sun, not that in this heat it would buy him much time.

"Want the basket back?" he offered.

"No!" she heard herself saying a bit too forcefully. *Calm down, Susan.* "I mean, that's yours. A token of my appreciation."

She'd said that already, hadn't she? Or had she? She couldn't remember. It was as if he'd just played jump rope with her brain and absolutely everything was tied up in a huge, tangled knot.

Duke nodded. "It's good," he told her, holding the short rib aloft. "But I considered any debt already paid by your first token of appreciation."

Confused, she was about to ask what token he was talking about when it hit her. He was referring to when she'd kissed him.

Pleased, embarrassed and breathless, she could only smile in response. Widely.

The next moment, she was back in the car and driving away. Quickly. She thought it was definitely safer that way. Otherwise, she ran the risk of ruining the moment by tripping over her own tongue. Again.

Chapter 7

Going to the county seat to officially file Mark Walsh's autopsy report with the court had taken longer than Wes had expected. He didn't mind. There was a certain rush that came from knowing that he could finally—finally—get Damien free, and he savored it.

He'd known all along in his gut that Damien hadn't killed that worthless SOB.

Granted, he could have saved himself a lot of time if he had called the information in over the phone or started the ball rolling via the computer, but Wes had always favored the personal touch. In this highly technical electronic age, he felt that human contact was greatly underestimated. It was easy enough to ignore an email or a phone message, but not so easy to ignore a man standing outside your office door, his hat in his hand. The gun strapped to his thigh didn't exactly hurt, either.

But doing it in person had caused him to be rather late getting back to Honey Creek. He'd been gone the better part of the day and a growling stomach was now plaintively asking him to stop in town for dinner before ultimately heading toward the ranch and the small house where he lived.

The old sheriff, he knew, would have put notifying Jolene Walsh off until some time tomorrow, tending to his own needs first. After all, as Duke had said, it wasn't like telling Jolene that her husband was dead was actually going to be much of a surprise to the woman. And there certainly wasn't anything to mourn over. Everyone in town felt that Mark Walsh had been a nasty-tempered womanizer who'd had an ugly penchant for young girls. Moreover, Walsh made no secret of the fact that he'd treated Jolene more like an indentured servant than a wife throughout their marriage.

There hadn't been a single redeeming quality about the man. He hadn't even been smart, just lucky. Lucky that he had picked the right man to run his company.

His CFO, Craig Warner, was and always had been the real brains behind Walsh Enterprises. It was Warner, not Walsh, who had turned the relatively small brewery located right outside of town into a nationally known brand to be reckoned with.

But somewhere along the line, Walsh must have stumbled across a cache of brains no one else knew he had acquired. How else had he managed to fake his own death and pull it off all these years, hiding somewhere in the vicinity? Someone had finally done away with the man, but it had taken them fifteen years to do it.

But why, Wes couldn't help wondering, had the original murder been faked to begin with? What was Walsh trying to accomplish?

And what was *he* missing?

Tired, resigned to his duty, Wes brought his vehicle to a stop before the Walsh farmhouse. Jolene had gone on living there after her husband had been murdered. The first time, Wes added silently.

It was late and he was hungry, but it just wouldn't seem right to him if he put this off until morning. She had a right to know about this latest, bizarre twist and the sooner Jolene Walsh was informed of this actual murder of her husband, the sooner she could begin to get over it. Or so he hoped.

There were several lights on in the large, rambling house. Walsh wouldn't have recognized the place if he'd had occasion to stumble into it, Wes mused. Five years after the man's supposed death, Jolene had had some major renovations done to the house, utilizing some of the profits that the business was bringing in.

Jolene had become a different woman since Walsh had vanished from her life, Wes thought. More cheerful and vibrant. She smiled a lot these days and there was a light in her eyes that hadn't been there when Walsh was around. It was good to see her that way.

This was going to knock her and Craig for a loop, Wes thought, wishing he didn't have to be the one to break this to the woman. But he couldn't very well postpone it or shirk his duty.

Standing on the front porch, Wes rang the doorbell. Then rang it again when no one answered.

He was about to try one more time before calling it a night when the door suddenly opened. Mark Walsh's widow—rightfully called that now, he couldn't help thinking—was standing in the doorway, her slender body wrapped in a cream-colored robe that went all the way down to her ankles. Her long hair was free of its confining pins and flowed over her shoulders and down her back like a red sea.

Warm amber eyes looked at him in confusion a beat before fear entered them. She was a mother and thought like one.

"Is it one of the children?" she asked. She had four, the youngest of whom, Jared, was twenty-five and hardly a child, but to Jolene, they would always be her children no matter how many decades they had tucked under their belts. And she would always worry about them.

"No, ma'am," Wes said respectfully, removing his hat. Uncomfortable, he ran the rim through his hands. "I'm afraid I've got some really strange news."

She hesitated for a moment, as if debating the invitation she was about to extend to him, then moved aside from the doorway. "Would you like to come in, Sheriff?"

He didn't plan on staying long. He had no desire to see how this news was going to affect her once the shock of it faded. "Maybe it'd be better if I didn't." He took a short breath. "Mrs. Walsh, your husband's body turned up in the creek the other day."

She stared at him as if the words he was saying were not computing.

"Turned up?" she echoed. "Turned up from where?" Horror entered her expressive eyes. "You don't mean to tell me that someone dug up his body and—"

"No, ma'am, I don't mean to say that. According to the county coroner, Mark Walsh has only been dead for five days."

Stunned, Jolene's mouth dropped open. "But we buried Mark almost sixteen years ago. He was definitely dead." It had been a closed-casket service. Whoever had killed her husband had done it in a rage, beating him to death and rendering him almost unrecognizable, except for his clothes and the watch on his wrist. The watch that she had given him on their last anniversary. "How is this possible?"

He tried to give her a reassuring smile. "Well, we buried *somebody* sixteen years ago, but it wasn't your husband." Wes made a mental note to have that body exhumed and an identification made—if possible—to see who had been buried there. "I'm really sorry to be the one to have to tell you this," he apologized.

Jolene looked as if the air had been completely siphoned out of her lungs and she couldn't draw enough in to replace it. For a second, he was afraid she was going to pass out. Jolene clung to the doorjamb.

"You're just doing your job," she murmured, her thoughts apparently scattering like buckshot fired at random into the air. "Do you want me to come down to make a positive I.D.?" she asked in a small voice. It was obvious that she really had no desire to take on the ordeal, but would if she had to.

"No, ma'am, there's no need." He was glad he could at least spare her that. "The coroner's already made a positive identification, using your husband's dental records. I just wanted you to hear it from me before word starts spreading in town." She looked at him blankly, as if she couldn't begin to understand what he was telling her. "Boyd Arnold was the one who found the body in the creek," he explained. "And it's only a matter of time before he lets it slip to someone. Boyd's not exactly a man who can keep a secret."

Jolene nodded, seeming not altogether sure what she was nodding about. "Do you have any idea who did it?"

"That's what I aim to find out, ma'am," Wes told her politely.

Horror returned to her expressive eyes as her thought processes finally widened just a little. "Oh, my God, Sheriff, your brother, he's been in prison all this time for killing Mark. We have to—"

He anticipated her next words and appreciated the fact that Jolene could think of Damien's situation when she was still basically in shock over what he'd just told her.

"I've already started the process of getting him released from prison," Wes assured the woman. "Again, I am sorry to have to put you through this."

"It's not your fault, Sheriff." Pale, shaken, Jolene began to close the door, retreating into her home. She felt as if she was in the middle of a bad dream. One that would continue when she woke up. "Thank you for coming to let me know," she murmured.

Shutting the door, she leaned against it, feeling incredibly confused. Incredibly drained.

Jolene shut her eyes as she tried to pull herself together. When she opened them again, she wasn't alone. Craig Warner, the man who had singlehandedly helmed the brewery into becoming a household name and the sole reason she'd become the happy woman she was, was standing beside her.

"That was the sheriff. He came to tell me that Mark wasn't dead before. But he is now." Did that sound as crazy as she thought it did?

Craig nodded. "I heard," he said quietly.

Jolene blew out a breath as she dragged her hand through her long, straight hair. At fifty, she didn't have a single gray hair to her name. Astonishing, considering the trying life she'd led until Mark had been killed—or reportedly killed, she amended silently.

Her eyes met Craig's, searching for strength. "What do I do now?"

Shirtless and wearing only jeans that he'd hastily thrown on when he'd heard the doorbell, Craig padded over to her. Linking his strong, tanned fingers through hers, he gave her hand a light tug toward the staircase.

"Come back to bed," he told her.

She couldn't pull her thoughts together. Was she to have a second funeral? Did she just have the body quietly buried? There were so many questions and she just couldn't focus.

"But, Mark—" she began in protest.

"Is dead and not going anywhere," Craig told her. "He'll still be there in the morning. And he'll still be dead. You've had a shock and you need time to process it, Jo." He kissed her lightly on the temple, then looked down at her face. "Let me help you do that."

Jolene blew out another shaky breath, then smiled a small, hesitant smile reminiscent of the way she'd once been. Craig was right. He was always right.

Without another word, she let him lead her up the stairs back to her bedroom and the bed that had become the center of her happiness.

"You think he'll stay dead this time?" Bonnie Gene asked her husband the next afternoon. The story was all over town about Mark Walsh's second, and consequently, actual murder.

Donald Kelley was in his favorite place, the state-of-the-art kitchen that he had installed at great cost in his restaurant. Feeling creative, he was experimenting with a new barbecue sauce, trying to find something that was at once familiar yet tantalizingly different to tease the palates of his patrons. Bonnie Gene had come along with him, whether to act as his inspiration or to make sure that he didn't sample too much of his own cooking wasn't clear. But he had his suspicions.

"Who?" Donald asked, distracted. Right now, the hickory flavoring was a little too overpowering, blocking the other ingredients he wanted to come through. The pot he was standing over, stirring, was as huge as his ambitions.

"Mark Walsh," she said with an air of exasperation. Didn't Donald pay attention to anything except what went into his mouth? "That man must really have enemies, to be killed twice."

"He wasn't killed the first time," Donald pointed out, proving that he *was* paying attention. "He had to fake that."

Bonnie Gene was never without an opinion. "Most likely he faked it because he knew that someone was out to get him. And apparently they finally did. Mark Walsh is really dead this time," she told her husband with finality. "Boyd Arnold's running around town volunteering details and basking in his fifteen minutes of fame for having found the body in the creek." She shivered at the mere thought of seeing the ghoulish sight of Mark Walsh's half-decomposed body submerged in the water.

"Found whose body?" Susan asked, walking into the

kitchen, order forms for future parties tucked against her chest.

She set the forms down in her section of the room. It was an oversize kitchen, even by restaurant standards, which was just the way her father liked it. The size was not without its merit for her as well. It allowed her to run the catering end of the business without getting in her father's way—or anyone else's for that matter.

Bonnie Gene swung around in her daughter's direction, delighted by Susan's obvious ignorance of the latest turn of events. There weren't all that many people left to surprise with this little tidbit.

Crossing to her, Bonnie Gene placed her arm around her daughter's slender shoulders, paused dramatically and then said, "Mark Walsh."

Susan looked at her mother, confused. "What about Mark Walsh?"

"Boyd Arnold just found his body. Well, not just," Bonnie Gene corrected herself before her husband could. "Boyd found it several days ago."

That cleared up nothing. Susan stared at her mother, trying to make sense of what she was being told. She knew that in New Orleans, whenever the floods covered the various cemeteries in that city, the waters disinterred the bodies that had been laid to rest there, but there'd been no such extreme weather aberrations here.

What was her mother talking about? "But Mr. Walsh's been dead for the last fifteen years," she protested. "His body's buried in the cemetery."

There was nothing that Bonnie Gene liked more than being right. She smiled beatifically now at her daughter. "Obviously not."

Susan jumped from fact to conclusion. "Then Damien Colton is innocent."

Donald sneaked a sample of his new sauce, then covertly slipped the ladle back into the pot and continued stirring. "It would appear so," he agreed.

Susan couldn't help thinking of all the years that Damien had lost, cooling his heels in prison for a crime he hadn't committed. The years in which a man shaped his future, made his reputation, if not his fortune. All lost because a jury had wrongly convicted him.

She looked from her mother to her father. "My God, what kind of a grudge do you think Damien's going to have against the people who put him away for something he didn't do?"

The thought had crossed Bonnie Gene's mind as well. "There's something I could live without finding out," she responded.

Susan's mind went from Damien to Duke, his twin. They said that most twins had an uncanny bond, that they felt each other's pain. That was probably why he'd been so solemn all these years, she thought. How would Duke take the news of his brother's innocence?

Or did he already know?

If he did, Duke had to be filled with mixed feelings. She knew that he'd never believed that Damien had been the one to kill Mark Walsh and he'd turned out to be right. He had to feel good about that, she reasoned.

But now Mr. Walsh really *was* dead. Who *had* killed the man after all this time? And had someone tried to frame Duke's twin brother for that first murder?

Or maybe whoever had made it look like Mr. Walsh was killed that first time had tried to frame Duke and Damien had mistakenly been accused of the crime.

But wait a minute.

Her thoughts came to an abrupt halt. Mark Walsh *hadn't* been dead at the time and he never came forward. That meant what, that Mark Walsh had been behind all this? That he had been the one who had deliberately tried to frame Damien? Or Duke?

Why?

She had to see Duke, Susan thought suddenly. This was a huge deal. The man was going to need someone to talk to, to be his friend. He'd been there for her, albeit almost silently, but he'd made his presence known. Returning the favor was the least she could do for the man.

She made up her mind. "Mother, I don't have an event to cater today."

Bonnie Gene looked at her, trying to discern where Susan was going with this. "And your point is?" she prodded, waiting.

Susan saw that one of the kitchen staff had cocked her head in her direction, listening. She moved closer to her mother, lowering her voice. "I think I'll see if Duke Colton needs a friendly ear to talk to."

Bonnie Gene nodded. "Or any other body part that might come into play," she commented with an encouraging smile.

No, no more matchmaking, Mother. Please. "Mother, I just want to be the man's friend if he needs one," Susan protested.

"Nobody can ever have too many friends," Bonnie Gene agreed, doing her best to keep a straight face. She failed rather badly.

Susan rolled her eyes. "Mother, you're incorrigible."

"What did I say?" Bonnie Gene asked, looking at her with the most innocent expression she could muster.

Susan turned to her other parent. "Dad, back me up here."

Her father spared her a quick glance before turning his attention back to the industrial-size pot he was standing over. He chuckled under his breath, most likely happy that someone else was drawing Bonnie Gene's fire for a change.

"This is your mother you're dealing with. You're on your own, kiddo," he told her.

Bonnie Gene raised her hands, as if she was the one surrendering. "I have no idea what you two are inferring," she declared. "But I have guests to mingle with," she told them. And with that, she crossed to the swinging doors that led out into the Cookhouse's dining room. But just as she was about to walk out, she stopped and stepped back into the kitchen.

When she turned to look at Susan, there was a very pleased smile on her lips. "Looks like you won't have to drive out of town to play Good Samaritan, honey."

As was the case half the time, Susan had no idea what her mother was talking about. "What do you mean?" she asked, crossing to her.

Bonnie Gene held one of the swinging doors partially open so that Susan could get a good look into the dining area.

"Well, unless my eyes are playing tricks on me, Duke Colton just took a seat at one of the tables in the main dining room." She let the door slip back into place. "Why don't you go see what he wants?"

That was being a bit too pushy, Susan thought, suddenly feeling nervous. "I can't just go out and play waitress."

"You can if I tell you to," Bonnie Gene countered,

then turned toward the lone waitress in the kitchen. The girl was about to go on duty. "Allison here is feeling sick, aren't you, Allison?"

Confusion washed over the woman's broad face. "I'm fine, Mrs. Kelley," Allison protested with feeling.

Bonnie Gene was not about to be deterred. "See how sick she is? She's delirious." Placing both hands to Susan's back, Bonnie Gene gave her a little push out through the swinging doors. "Go, take his order. And follow it to the letter," she added, raising her voice slightly as the doors swung closed again.

"You're shameless, Bonnie Gene," Donald commented with a chuckle, never looking away from the sauce, which now was making small, bubbling noises and projecting tiny arcs of hot red liquid in the air.

"As long as I get to be a grandmother, I don't care what you call me," she told him.

With that, she went to the swinging doors to open them a crack and observe Susan and Duke—and she hoped that she would have something to observe.

Chapter 8

Duke looked up just as Susan reached the two-person booth where he had parked his lean, long frame.

"Duke, I just heard."

She was breathless, although she wasn't certain exactly why. It wasn't as if she'd rushed over to his table and she hadn't been doing anything previous to this that would have stolen the air out of her lungs, but she was definitely breathless.

Subtly, Susan drew in a deep breath to sustain herself and sound more normal.

Duke continued to look at her, arching a brow, as if he was waiting for her to finish her sentence.

So she added, "About Wes finding Mark Walsh's body. I don't know whether to congratulate you or to offer my condolences."

"Why would you feel you had to do either?" Duke

asked her in that slow, rich voice of his that seemed to get under her skin so quickly.

She shifted uncomfortably. Why did he need her to explain? "Well, because this means that Damien didn't do it."

"I already knew that," he told her, his voice deadly calm.

She had no idea how to respond to that, especially since Duke was definitely in the minority when it came to that opinion. Most of the town had thought that Damien was guilty and were quick to point out that there'd been no love lost between Damien and Mark Walsh. Matters had grown worse when Walsh had discovered that Damien was in love with his daughter, Lucy.

Never in danger of being elected Father of the Year, Walsh still wanted to control the lives of all of his offspring. None of his plans included having his oldest daughter marry a Colton and he made that perfectly clear to Damien. He was the one who had broken things up between Lucy and Damien. When Walsh was discovered beaten to death in the apartment he kept expressly for romantic trysts in Bozeman shortly afterward, everyone assumed that Damien had killed Walsh.

"Why condolences?" Duke finally asked when Susan said nothing further but still remained standing there.

She took his question as an invitation to join him. Sliding into the other seat, she faced him and knotted her fingers together before responding. "Because your brother had to spend so much time in prison for a crime he hadn't committed."

Duke lifted one shoulder in a careless shrug. "Yeah, well, that's life."

Susan stared at him, stunned. How could he sit there so calmly? Did the man have ice water in his veins? Or didn't he care? She felt excited about this turn of events and she wasn't even remotely related to Damien. As a matter of fact, she hardly remembered him. She'd been barely ten years old when Damien Colton had been sent off to prison.

"Don't you have any feelings about this?" she questioned.

"Whether I have feelings or don't have feelings about a particular subject is not up for public debate or display," he informed her in the same stony voice.

Well, that certainly put her in her place, Susan thought, stung.

Angry tears rose to her eyes and she silently upbraided herself for it. Tears, to Duke, she was certain, were undoubtedly a sign of weakness. But ever since she was a little girl, tears had always popped up when she was angry, undercutting anything she might have to say in rebuttal.

The tears always spoke louder than her words.

So rather than say anything, Susan abruptly rose and walked away.

Duke opened his mouth to call out after her. He'd caught sight of the tears and felt badly about making her cry, although for the life of him he saw no reason for that kind of a reaction on her part. But then he'd long since decided that not only were women different than men, they were completely unfathomable, their brains operating in what struck him as having to be some kind of an alternate universe.

Still, he did want to apologize if he'd somehow hurt her feelings. That hadn't been his intent. However, Bertha Aldean was sitting with her husband at the table over in the corner. A natural-born gossip, the woman was staring at him with wide, curious eyes. She was obviously hungry for something further to gossip about.

There was no way he was going to give the woman or the town more to talk about.

So he went back to scanning the menu and waited for a waitress to come and take his order. Susan Kelley was just going to have to work out what was going on in her head by herself.

"He's been alive all this time?" Damien's hand tightened on the black telephone receiver he was required to use in order to hear what his brother, Duke, was saying to him.

They were seated at a long, scarred table, soundproof glass running the length of it, separating them the way it did all the prisoners from their visitors. He was surprised at the middle-of-the-week visit from Duke. Weekdays were for doing chores on the ranch according to his father's rigid work ethic.

And he was utterly stunned by the news that Duke had brought. With a minimum of words, his twin had told him about the body that Wes had discovered.

Damien had received the news with fury.

"Yeah," Duke replied to his twin's rhetorical question. "Until the other day. Now, according to Wes, Walsh is as dead as a doornail."

Duke saw the anger in his brother's eyes and hoped that no one else noticed. He didn't want Damien doing anything to jeopardize his release.

Damien fairly choked on his anger. "That bastard

could have come forward any time in the last fifteen years and gotten me released."

"Not likely, since he hated your guts," Duke reminded him in a calm, collected voice. "And more than that," Duke pointed out, "he was afraid."

Dark-brown eyebrows narrowed over darkening green eyes. "Afraid of what? Me?"

"You, maybe," Duke acknowledged. His twin was a formidable man, especially now. He'd used all his free time to work out and build up his already considerable physique. There's always the possibility that Mark framed Damien himself, but that seems like an awful lot of trouble to go to. The victim was wearing Mark's clothing and watch. "More likely, he was afraid of whoever killed that guy they found in his apartment fifteen years ago and mistook for him. He probably figured that the killer thought the same thing, that he'd killed him—Walsh," Duke clarified. "As long as people thought he was dead, Walsh thought he was safe. If that meant that you had to stay in prison, well, Walsh probably saw that as being a bonus."

"Bonus?" Damien echoed incredulously. "What do you mean bonus?"

Duke would have thought that was self-evident. "If you were in prison, you weren't making babies with his daughter."

Damien snorted. "Small chance of that. Lucy hates my guts." She'd made that perfectly clear the last time he'd seen her. But before then…before then it had been another matter. He'd thought they really had something special, something that was meant to last.

"Because she thinks you killed her father," Duke

emphasized. "That's the reason she hates you. Since you didn't, there's nothing for her to hate any more."

"It's too late," Damien said quietly. *Too late.* Too much time had been lost.

Damien scrubbed his hand over his face. Joy filtered in to mix with the rage. Impotent rage because there wasn't anyone to direct that rage toward, now that Walsh was dead. Holding the jury—and his father who should have stood up for him—accountable for his being here all these years seemed pointless.

Nonetheless, he had a feeling it was going to take him a long time to work out all these anger issues he had going on inside of him.

"How much longer do I have to stay here?" he wanted to know. "And why isn't Wes here, telling me all this himself?"

"Cut the guy a little slack, Damien," Duke said. "He's been seeing everyone he can, trying to cut through the red tape and get you released. He's always been on your side, right from the start." Duke could see how restless Damien was, so he added, "There are forms to file and procedures to follow. Nothing is ever simple."

"Throwing me into jail was," Damien said bitterly.

Damien told him what they could do with the procedures and the forms. Duke laughed shortly under his breath, then advised, "You better can that kind of talk for a while, Damien. Don't give anyone an excuse to drag their feet about letting you out of here."

The veins in Damien's neck stood out as he gripped the phone more tightly. "They *owe* me."

"No argument," Duke answered, his voice low, soothing. "But you can't start to collect if you do something to get your tail thrown back into prison. You're

a free man in name only right now. Hold your peace
until the rest of it catches up." His eyes held Damien's,
clearly issuing a warning. "Hear me?"

Damien blew out a long, frustrated breath. "I hear
you." And then the barest hint of a smile crept across
his lips as the reality of it all began to sink in. "I'm really getting out?"

"You're really getting out," Duke assured him, feeling a great deal of relief himself.

"How about that," Damien said more to himself than
his brother. And then he looked at his twin. "What's
the old man say?"

Darius Colton's expression hadn't changed an iota
when Wes had told him about the new development. Instead, he'd merely nodded and then said that he could
use the extra set of hands.

Damien stared at his twin. He would have thought,
after all this time, that their father would have registered
some kind of positive emotion. "That's it?" he pressed.

For Damien's sake, Duke wished that there had been
more. But he wasn't going to lie about it. It would only
come back to bite him in the end. "That's it. He never
was much of a talker," Duke reminded him.

His father hadn't come to see Damien once in all the
years that he'd been confined. "Not much of a father,
either," Damien bit off.

Duke shrugged. It was what it was. There wasn't
anything he could do or say to change things. "Yeah,
but we already knew that."

Oh, God, not again.

The thought echoed in Susan's brain the moment she
saw the dead roses on the mat outside the private en-

trance to her catering business. She'd gotten the wilted flowers before but hadn't thought anything of it. She'd thought it was someone's idea of a bad joke.

Preoccupied with the challenging feat of keeping an ice sculpture frozen and firm in the middle of a July heat wave long enough to look good at a reception, she hadn't seen the bouquet on the ground until she'd stepped on the roses and heard them crunching under her shoes.

Startled, she'd backed up and saw what was left of them. And the envelope lying next to them. It was the type of envelope that was used for greeting cards. But if this was like the two other times, there was no greeting card inside. Instead, there was probably a note. A note written in childish block letters that made no sense to her.

Taking a deep breath, Susan stooped down and picked up the bouquet and the envelope. Steeling herself, she opened the envelope.

Sure enough, there was a folded piece of paper tucked inside it. Taking it out, she unfolded the paper. Uneven block letters spelled out another threat, similar to the one that she'd received yesterday.

DEAD FLOWERS FOR A DEAD WOMAN.

The warning might have been downright scary if it didn't make her so mad. She held the note up to the light. And what do you know, the Coltons' watermark.

It wasn't Linc. As aggressive as he'd become lately, he was too smitten to pull something like this. It wasn't his style. She knew exactly who was behind this. It was just the kind of thing he'd do.

Duke.

But why?

Just what was he trying to pull? Was this his ob-
scure way of saying that he thought she was childish, as
childish as the block letters in the message? Or was he
trying to get her to back off? But back off from what?
From expressing a few feelings about the current state
of affairs regarding his brother? She was only trying
to be neighborly.

Just what the hell did Duke Colton think he was
doing?

The more Susan thought about it, the angrier she
became.

While she willingly acknowledged that she might
not be the bravest soul God had ever created, she was
definitely *not* about to be intimidated by rotting flowers and stupid, enigmatic notes that sounded more de-
ranged than anything else.

It was damn well time to put a stop to this before
she found herself knee-deep in dead roses and dried-
up thorns.

Still clutching the flowers, she marched to the kitch-
en's threshold.

Since this was between meals and there was no one
else around, she told her father. "I'm going out, Dad."

Donald Kelley had his back to her. He was still experimenting with the new sauce he was determined to
create. Currently, he was on his sixth theme and vari-
ation of the new recipe, and he barely acknowledged
that he'd heard her.

"That's nice. Have fun," Donald muttered. Reaching for the long yellow tablet he'd been making all his

notations on, he crossed out an ingredient near the bottom of the list.

Susan doubted that her father had actually heard what she'd said.

But her father wasn't a problem right now. Duke was. Duke Colton was insulting her with these childish notes and bouquets of dead roses. It had to be him. Who else could it be? She had every intention of putting a stop to this behavior—and give him a piece of her mind while she was at it.

The sooner the better, she thought, storming out to her car.

A head full of steam and indignation propelling her, Susan was torn as where to go first in order to locate Duke. As luck would have it, she actually found him in the first place she looked.

Wanting to cover all bases, at the last minute, rather than going to the main house on the ranch, she'd decided to stop at his house first since it was actually closer. She'd stopped her car right in front of the front door, got out and rang his doorbell. She gave him to the count of ten.

He opened the door when she got to six.

Duke's face registered a trace of surprise when he saw her. His sister, Maisie, had said that she might be stopping by and that was who he had expected to see on his doorstep, not a five-foot-ten caterer whose brown eyes were all but shooting lightning at him.

Before he could ask Susan what had brought her out to the Colton ranch for a second time in such a short period of time, she yelled "Here!" and threw what looked like a bouquet of flowers way past their prime at his feet.

Dried petals rained right and left, marking the passage before the bouquet landed.

Duke glanced down at the all but denuded bouquet and then back up at her.

"I don't remember asking for dead flowers," he said in a voice as dry as the flowers.

"Don't try to be funny!" Susan retorted angrily, her arms crossed before her.

"All right, how about confused?" he suggested. What the hell was going on? Susan was acting as crazy, as unstable as his older sister Maisie was. He toed the bouquet. More petals came loose. "Why'd you just throw those things at me?"

Duke was behaving as if he'd actually never seen the bouquet before. Maybe the man should become an actor, she thought sarcastically. "Because you left them on my doorstep."

Her answer only confused things more, not less. "I don't believe in wasting money," he told her. "But if I did decide to give you flowers, trust me, I could afford ones that weren't so damn shriveled up."

She drew herself up indignantly. He was lying to her face, wasn't her?

Or was he?

She began to vacillate ever so slightly. Her eyes on his, she asked, "You're telling me you didn't leave those flowers on my doorstep?"

"I'm telling you I didn't leave those flowers on your doorstep," he echoed.

He saw no reason to plead his case any further. If Susan had half a brain—and he was fairly confident that the youngest of the Kelleys was a very intelligent young woman—she would realize that there was no reason for him to do something so bizarre.

A little of Susan's fire abated. "What about the note?"

"What note?" he challenged.

Digging the last missive she'd received out of her purse, she held it up in front of his face. "This note."

Taking the note out of her hand, Duke held it at the proper distance so that he was able to read it. When he did, he frowned and folded it up, then handed it back to her.

"I didn't write this," he informed her flatly.

She was beginning to believe him, but she couldn't just capitulate and back away. He might be a very good liar. She knew she wasn't experienced enough when it came to men to tell the difference.

"If you didn't write this, then who did?" she challenged.

Outwardly, her bravado remained intact, but inwardly, she knew she was beginning to lose ground. Embarrassment was starting to take hold.

He paused for exactly one second, thinking. "My first guess would be Linc."

"Linc?" she echoed incredulously. "Why would he keep sending me dead flowers?" she asked, not wanting to go there. She and Linc had been friends forever. If he actually was the one sending her these horrid bouquets, that meant that he wasn't the kind of person she thought he was. And that meant that she was completely incapable of judging *anyone's* character.

"Why would I?" Duke countered, then suddenly realized what she'd just said. "This isn't the first time you've gotten dead flowers?"

She shook her head, her straight blond hair swinging back and forth, mimicking the motion. "No. I got a bouquet of rotting roses yesterday, and one the day before that. They each had notes like this one."

Once was a stupid prank. Twice was something more. Three times meant that there was a dangerous person on the other end of those notes. She could very well need protection. "Have you gone to Wes about this?" Duke wanted to know.

She was beginning to get nervous. If Duke wasn't sending the flowers as some kind of nasty prank, then who was? She refused to think it was Linc. She'd just seen him yesterday and aside from seeming a little morose, he was the same old Linc. He *couldn't* be the one sending these notes.

"No, I haven't," she said quietly.

"Maybe you should."

She looked uneasy, he thought. He hadn't meant to scare her, but on the other hand, Susan should be aware that this might be more than just some really stupid joke. If it did turn out to be that spineless Linc character, he was going to beat the tar out of him.

The chores and his father's obsession with having all his offspring working from sunup to sundown could wait. He felt responsible for the sliver of fear he saw entering her eyes.

After reaching into the house for his hat, he closed the door. "C'mon, I'll go with you."

It was an offer she couldn't refuse.

Chapter 9

Wes had sat quietly, unconsciously rocking ever so slightly in his chair as he listened to what the young woman his brother had brought in to see him had to say.

He could feel the hairs at the back of his head rising. Wes didn't like what he was hearing.

"And this isn't the first time you've found a note like this on your doorstep?" he asked her, indicating the envelope in the center of his desk. Taking a handkerchief, he turned the envelope over, not that he expected to notice anything now that neither he nor the other two people in the room hadn't up until now.

Susan set her mouth grimly before she shook her head. "No."

"She already told you that," Duke reminded his brother impatiently. He'd taken a seat beside Susan in front of Wes's desk, but it was obvious that he would have felt more comfortable standing, as if he had better control over a situation if he was on his feet.

"Just double-checking the facts, Duke," Wes replied mildly. He wondered if there was ever going to be a point where Duke wouldn't think of him as his little brother but as a sheriff first. Probably not. Wes directed his next question to Donald and Bonnie Gene Kelly's youngest offspring. "Do you still have the other notes somewhere?"

Susan knotted her hands in her lap and shook her head. "No. I threw them away along with the flowers." She realized now that she should have hung on to them, just in case. But it had never occurred to her that the person sending this was dangerous. "I thought it was only a stupid prank."

Wes's face remained expressionless but he nodded, taking the information in. "So what changed your mind?"

"I didn't change it," Susan contradicted. "I just got fed up and mad."

Wes continued making notes in the small spiral pad he always kept on his person, replacing it only when he filled one. He wrote in pen so that the notes wouldn't fade away before he needed them.

Eventually, the pad would find its way into a file. A real file rather than a virtual one. Computers were for law-enforcement agents who had to contend with crime in the big cities and had a lot of information to deal with. In comparison to those places, Honey Creek seemed like a hick town.

A hick town with a murderer and a possible stalker, Wes reminded himself. He finished writing down what Susan was saying and couldn't help wondering what else would crawl out from under the rocks while he was sheriff.

"Any particular reason you thought Duke was the one sending you the notes and flowers?" he wanted to know, sparing his brother a quick, sidelong glance.

Susan drew herself up, like a schoolgirl in a classroom when things like posture and radiating a positive attitude mattered. "Not now, no."

"But before?" he coaxed sympathetically.

Slim shoulders rose and fell beneath the bright pink-and-white-striped tank top. She actually did look more like a girl in high school than the successful head of the catering division of Kelley's Cookhouse.

"I thought it was Duke's way of saying I was acting like a kid," she murmured. Looking back, she realized that her reasoning didn't make any real sense. But admittedly, she wasn't thinking as clearly as she normally did, what with dealing with Miranda's death and viewing life through new, sobered eyes.

"Now that you don't think that it's Duke anymore, do you have any new thoughts about who might be sending you these threats and dried flowers?" Wes asked gently, as if he was trying to coax words out of a witness who had just been intimidated.

Susan began to shake her head because she really couldn't think of anyone this nasty, but Duke interrupted anything she might have to say. "You should check out that Lincoln character," he suggested. There was no uncertainty in his voice.

There was only one person with that first name around the area, but Wes asked anyway, wanting to make sure. "You mean Lincoln Hayes?" When his brother nodded his response, Wes continued questioning him. "What makes you think that Lincoln Hayes is behind this?"

"It's not Linc," Susan interjected before Duke could respond.

Duke ignored her. The woman was too soft. She probably wouldn't want to think the worst of Satan. Seeing the skeptical look on Wes's face, he gave his brother what he felt was proof. "I caught him trying to force himself on her," he nodded toward Susan, "after the funeral."

Susan waved her hand at the statement, dismissing it. "Linc has this notion that we should give dating another chance. I told him it wasn't going to work. He thought it would." Duke snorted his contempt for the man. She slid forward on her chair and tapped the envelope that she'd brought in to the sheriff. "That's not Linc's handwriting."

"He write you notes in block letters often?" Duke asked her sarcastically.

Why was it that this rancher with the hard body could get to her faster than any other human being on the face of the earth? She'd never met anyone else who could scramble her emotions so quickly, making her run hot then cold within the space of a few moments.

"No, but—"

His point made, Duke looked at his brother. "I'd check it out if I were you," he repeated firmly to Wes. "See if there're any fingerprints on the envelope or the note that belong to Hayes."

Wes raised his eyes to Duke's, his patience stretched to what he figured was his limit. "I know what to do, Duke."

"Just makin' suggestions," Duke replied.

That was, Wes knew, as close to an apology as he

would ever hear from Duke. Rather than comment, he merely nodded, then turned to Susan again.

"Anything else you can think of?" he asked her. "Something Linc or someone else might have said that would make you think that they were the one sending you these threats?"

Coming up empty, Susan shook her head. "Nothing comes to mind."

"That's all right," he told her sympathetically. "Give it some time. And if something *does* come to you, give me a call," Wes instructed. He debated his next words, then said them—just in case. "It's probably harmless—a prank like you said—but for a while," he told her, offering her an encouraging smile, "I wouldn't go anywhere alone if I were you."

Instead of the expected fearfulness, Duke was surprised to see anger entering Susan Kelley's expressive eyes. She tossed her head, once again sending her short, straight blond hair swinging back and forth about her chin.

"Honey Creek is my home, Sheriff. I'm not about to let anyone make me afraid to walk around my home," she declared fiercely.

"I'm not asking you to be afraid, Ms. Kelley, I'm asking you to be sensible. Cautious," he tagged on when she continued looking at him as if she found his choice of words offensive. "There's a lot to be said for 'better safe than sorry,'" Wes told her.

"She'll be sensible," Duke chimed in, solemnly making the promise for her.

Wes nodded. "I'll hang on to this for now," he said, indicating the envelope on his desk.

"Keep it," she replied, her voice rather cool and formal. "I was just going to throw it away anyway."

"I'll get back to you on this," Wes said, then added, "we'll find out who's behind this, Susan."

"Yeah, we will," Duke added his voice to the promise as he strode out of the one-story building that had been the sheriff's office for the last fifty-some years. It was hard to say exactly to whom he was addressing his words, his brother, Susan or some invisible force he meant to vanquish.

Right now, Susan was fit to be tied and would have wanted nothing more than just to walk away from Duke Colton, but she couldn't. She'd left her car parked in front of Duke's house and he was her ride back. She had no choice but to hurry after him.

Oh, she knew she could ask someone at the Cookhouse to drive her to the Colton Ranch so she could get her car, but she really didn't want word getting back to her mother or her father about this. Neither of them knew about the notes and the flowers and she wanted to keep it that way. She didn't want them worrying.

She also didn't want her mother finding out that she'd gone to see Duke for *any* reason. The way her mind worked, her mother would be sending out invitations to her wedding by nightfall if she suspected that there was something going on between them.

Right now, Susan thought as she wordlessly plunked herself down in the passenger seat of Duke's truck, the only thing going on between them was anger. At least there was anger on her part.

She stole a look at Duke's chiseled profile as he turned the ignition on and his truck's engine coughed to life. On Duke's part, she was willing to bet, there was nothing but complete ignorance of the offense he'd just committed.

Typical male, she thought. Her anger continued to

smolder and grow, like a prairie fire feeding on shoots of grass and tearing a path through the land.

Pressing her lips together, she stared straight ahead at the road and said nothing.

She'd been quiet the entire trip back to his ranch. Not that he actually minded the quiet, Duke thought, but it seemed somehow unnatural for her. The girl was nothing if not a chatterbox.

Which meant, if he remembered his basic Women 101, that there was probably something wrong. Or at least *she* thought that there was.

Nothing occurred to him.

Duke debated not staying quiet about her silence. The purpose of this trip back was to reunite her with her car. Once that happened, then she'd be on her way. And out of his hair, so to speak.

And it wasn't as if he was given to an all-consuming curiosity. Pretty much most of the time, he couldn't care less if he knew something or not. Rabid curiosity was not one of his shortcomings.

So exactly what was it about this slip of a girl that made things so different? That made *him* behave so differently?

The question ate at him.

Duke saw his house in the distance. They'd been on Colton land for a while now, all traveled in annoying silence.

A couple of more minutes and he'd be home-free, he told himself. He'd pull up his truck beside her prissy little sedan, let her get out and then she'd be gone. And he could get back to his work and anything else he felt like getting back to.

The problem was he didn't feel like getting back to work. He felt like—

Startled, Duke abruptly clamped down his thoughts. There was absolutely no point in letting his imagination go there. He had no business thinking about that. It wasn't going to happen. Moreover, he definitely didn't want it to.

Liar.

Five minutes, just five more minutes and he'd be at the house and she'd be unbuckling. And then—

Oh, hell.

Duke turned toward her. Her face was forward and her features were almost rigid. He stifled an inward sigh. So much for letting sleeping dogs lie.

"Something wrong?" he asked her in a voice that was fairly growling.

She made no answer, which told him that he'd guessed right. Something *was* wrong. He found no triumph in being right, only annoying confusion because he hadn't a clue what was sticking in her craw.

"All right, *what's* wrong?" he demanded, sparing her a second look.

He heard her sigh.

That makes two of us, honey.

Still facing forward, Susan pressed her lips together. It had been eating away at her all the way back to his ranch.

The reason she hadn't said anything was because she knew damn well that it wouldn't do any good. It would be like banging her head against a wall. Men like Duke Colton didn't learn from their mistakes. And the reason they didn't learn from their mistakes was because they didn't believe they *made* mistakes.

He'd probably say something like, she was being too sensitive, or imagining things.

Or—

But if she didn't say anything, she silently countered, she was going to explode. The man *needed* a dressing down.

She shifted in her seat and looked at him. "I don't need you to make promises for me."

Duke silently cursed himself for saying anything. He was better off with her not talking. But now that she had, he had to respond. It was going to be like picking his way across quicksand, he just knew it. "What are you talking about?"

She might have known that he wasn't aware of his transgression. Nobody probably ever challenged him. At least no woman. "You told the sheriff that I'd 'be sensible.'"

He spared her a glance. Funny how her face seemed to glow when she got excited about something. "Well, won't you be?"

Didn't he understand anything? "Whether I will or won't be isn't the point—"

Damn but women should come with some kind of a beginner's manual. Something like *A Guide to Women for the Non-Insane*.

"So what the hell is the point?"

She did have to spell this out for him, didn't she? Susan could feel her temper fraying and growing shorter and shorter.

"The point is you have no right to think you can speak for me. You don't know the first thing about me."

"I've known you all your life," he snapped indignantly.

He actually believed that, didn't he? she thought incredulously.

"No, you've been *here* all my life. In Honey Creek," she pointed out. "But you don't know anything about me, Duke."

This time the sidelong glance was more of a glare. "I know you like picking fights."

"I'm not picking a fight," she cried, exasperated. "I'm making a point." *You big, dumb jerk. Don't you even know the difference?*

Duke snorted. "Seems like the same thing from where I'm standing."

God, but there were times when she hated being right. He *was* being obtuse. "Because you're not paying attention."

"When you say something worth listening to, then, I'll pay attention," Duke told her in his cold, offhand manner.

She suddenly shut her eyes. "What color are my eyes?" she asked him.

Approaching his house, Duke looked at her. Now what was she doing? "What the hell does that have to do with anything?"

Susan kept her eyes shut. She intended to show Duke how wrong he was in terms that even a thick-headed idiot like him could understand.

"If you 'know' me like you claim, you've got to at least know what color my eyes are. You were just looking at me a second ago. Okay, come on, tell me. What color are they?"

He was really beginning to regret this good deed he'd undertaken. "This is stupid," he told her between gritted teeth.

Susan was not about to back off. "What color?" she

demanded again, then laughed. She'd proven her point. "You don't know, do you?"

She heard him huff and half expected a cuss word to follow.

Duke surprised her.

"They're brown," he finally told her. "Chocolate brown. Warm and soft when you look at a man. Warm," he repeated, "like the inside of a pan-baked brownie fresh out of the oven on Christmas morning."

Stunned, Susan slowly opened her eyes to make sure she was still sitting next to Duke Colton and that someone else hadn't slipped into the driver's side in his place.

"Lucky guess." The two words dribbled out of her mouth in slow motion. There was absolutely no conviction to them.

"Like hell it was," he retorted.

Finally home, Duke pulled up the hand brake, put the manual transmission into Park and turned off the ignition. His engine sighed audibly before shutting down. Getting out of the cab, he rounded the hood and came over to the passenger side.

He opened the door for her. Then he took her hand and, rather roughly, "helped" her out of the truck.

To be honest with himself, he wasn't exactly sure who he was angry at. Her for stirring up feelings he wanted no part of, or himself for *having* these feelings in the first place and for not being able to rein them in the way he'd trained himself to.

After that numbing fiasco with Charlene—first the affair and then her suicide—he'd sworn to himself that he wasn't going to get caught up in any kind of a relationship again. Women just weren't worth it. A few minutes of pleasure in the middle of weeks of turmoil and grief was what it usually amounted to. Hell, it just wasn't worth it.

And then she came around, this naive little girl-next-door with the heart-shaped face. Looking at her, he would never have thought that she could get under his skin, but she had.

He still didn't understand how or why. He was ten years older than she was. Ten damn years. She was only seven years old when he'd had his first woman. Seven years old. Just a baby, nothing more.

What was he doing, having feelings for someone who was so young? Yet, there it was. He had feelings for this slip of a thing. Feelings he couldn't seem to cap or harness.

Feelings that threatened to tear him apart if he gave in to them even a little.

Yeah, like he had a choice, Duke silently mocked himself.

He bracketed her arms with his strong, calloused hands. But it was his eyes that pinned her in place, his eyes that held her prisoner.

"I know everything there is to know about you," he told her angrily, biting off each word. "I don't want to, but I do."

Pulling her into his arms, he didn't give her a chance to say anything in reply, whether to challenge him or perhaps, just possibly, to admit to having feelings for him herself, the latter being a long shot in his estimation.

Susan didn't have time to say or do anything except brace herself because, in the next second, Duke's mouth came down on hers and the world, as she knew it, exploded.

It most definitely stopped turning on its axis.

Chapter 10

Duke only meant to kiss her. It was a way of venting his feelings for a moment. Maybe he even meant to scare her away by showing her the intensity of what he was feeling.

If that was his intent, it backfired. Because he wasn't scaring her away. If anything, kissing her like this had the exact opposite effect.

And worse than that, he somehow managed to lose himself completely within his own attempt at a defensive maneuver.

She tasted sweet, like the first ripe strawberries of the summer. More than that, she caused the spark within him to burst into flame, consuming him. Making his head swirl and causing his thought processes to all but disintegrate.

What was going on certainly wasn't logical.

He sure as hell hadn't meant to push this up to the next level.

But he had, and he could feel Susan's willingness to have this happen. Could feel the way she was yielding to him, silently telling him it was all right to press on. Given that, it was impossible for him to stop. Hell, it was hard for him to maintain control, not just to take her out here, with the warm sun as a witness and the hot July breeze caressing her bare skin.

The only thing that *did* stop him was that someone might ride by at the worst time and the last thing he wanted was to embarrass her. Nor did he want to share with that passerby what he felt certain in his heart was a magnificent body.

So, as he continued pressing his lips urgently against hers, drawing his very reason for existing out of the simple act, Duke scooped her up in his arms and took the three steps up to the porch.

He didn't keep the front door locked. It wasn't so much that he trusted people as that he knew he had nothing worth stealing. Someone would have to be a fool to risk coming onto the Colton Ranch solely for the purpose of breaking into his house. There was nothing to be gained by that.

Elbowing open the door, he carried Susan inside, then closed the door with his back. Only then did he allow her feet to touch the floor.

His pulse was racing and he could have sworn that there were all sorts of fireworks, crafted by anticipation, going off inside him. Who would have ever thought—?

Duke drew his head back.

He'd stopped kissing her. Was it over? Had she done something to make him back away? To suddenly change his mind?

Because she'd thought...

Determined not to come so far only to have it abruptly end, Susan rose on her toes, framed the handsome, chiseled face between her long, slender hands and kissed him.

For a moment, she felt a surge of triumph. He was kissing her back. But then that triumph faded because he drew his head back again. This time he took her hands between his, holding them still.

His eyes delved into hers. Susan struggled to catch her breath.

"You sure?" Duke asked, looking straight into her soul.

Susan didn't want to talk, didn't want to stop. She had never felt like this before and she just wanted that feeling to continue. Wanted it to flower and grow until it reached its natural conclusion. Until he made love with her.

So instead of answering him, she started to kiss Duke again. But for the second time, he took her hands in his. His eyes were deadly serious as they pinned her in place and he repeated his question.

"Are you sure?"

"Yes," she breathed, her pulse doing jumping jacks. "I'm sure."

Well, he wished he was. But he wasn't. Wasn't sure at all that this was the right thing to do. All he knew was that he really *wanted* to be with her, wanted to make love with this fresh-faced young woman and experience that incredible feeling that ultimately defied all description.

He hadn't been with a woman since he had broken things off with Charlene and she had killed herself.

Hadn't thought it worth the trouble to get to that point with a woman. Duke didn't believe in paying for sex, and getting sex any other way required putting in time. Setting down groundwork.

He wasn't interested in doing that. Wasn't interested in getting tangled up with another woman.

He really had no idea how this had managed to happen so quickly. And with a woman—a girl—he'd never even thought of in this particular light.

But he was attracted to her, there was no denying that. And he wanted her. There was no denying that, either.

She made his blood rush the way he couldn't remember it rushing in a very long time.

Susan struggled to keep from losing consciousness. She'd never, *ever* felt like this before. Never experienced passion to this level before. Never experienced the desire to go the distance and find out just what there was about this ultimate bond between a man and a woman that was so seductively compelling. An eager curiosity propelled her on.

Her relationship with Linc that brief time when they'd attempted to be more than just friends was the only other time she'd even contemplated being intimate with a man—and the moment that Linc began kissing her, she'd stopped contemplating and wound up pushing him away. There'd been no bright, swirling lights, no surges of heat coupled with all but unmanageable desire. There had only been the deep, bone-jarring sense of disappointment.

That wasn't what was going on here.

This was a whole brand-new brave world she was entering.

The excitement she felt at every turn was almost un-manageable. It fueled her eagerness. They moved from the front hall into the living room area.

When she felt Duke's strong, sure hands on her, touching her, being familiar, caressing her with a gentleness she hadn't thought he was capable of, it almost completely undid her.

She wanted to know what those hands felt like on her bare skin.

Her own hands were shaking as she began unbuttoning his shirt. She knew what she would find underneath the material and the excitement of that knowledge was making her fumble.

Damn it, he's going to figure out you're a novice before he gets to the last part. She upbraided herself, telling herself to slow down, to be calm.

She couldn't calm down.

One of the buttons got stuck and she tugged at it to no avail, feeling inept.

"Having trouble?"

Was he laughing at her? No, Duke wasn't laughing at her she realized, raising her eyes to his face. He was smiling.

Really smiling.

She couldn't remember if she'd *ever* seen Duke without at least a partial scowl on his face.

Having no experience at lying, she went with the truth. "I'm not used to doing this," she murmured, feeling somewhat embarrassed at her ineptitude.

The smile on the rugged face deepened. "Good," she thought she heard him say.

The next moment, he helped her take off his shirt,

then proceeded to do the same with hers, employing a great deal more ease than she had used.

There was no time for hesitation, no time for thought. No time to contemplate whether she was going to regret this later. The only thing Susan knew was that she didn't regret it now, and now was all that mattered.

When the rest of their clothes were shed, Duke inclined his head toward her again. Her heart was pounding as she felt his lips skim the side of her neck, then her throat. By then, she could hardly breathe. There were all sorts of wondrous, delicious things going on within her, and Susan gave up the effort of trying to catch her breath.

All she could do was fervently hope that she wasn't going to pass out.

Hungry for the taste of him, hungry to explore everything there was about this wondrous, exciting familiarity that was unfolding before her, Susan ran her hands along the hard contours of Duke's body, thrilling to his muscularity.

Thrilling even more to the evidence of his wanting her.

She knew that someone else would have pointed out that he was just having a physical reaction, that it meant nothing.

But it meant something to her.

Because this was Duke Colton and he wanted her. Wanted her as much as she wanted him. She felt a throbbing sensation within her inner core she'd never experienced before.

As he continued kissing Susan, acquainting himself with every inch of her, Duke found himself both wanting to go slow, to savor every second of this—and to go quickly so that he could experience the ultimate pleasure that tempted him so relentlessly.

Somehow, he managed to continue going slow.

To his surprise, he enjoyed watching her react to him, enjoyed the decidedly innocent way surprise registered on her freshly scrubbed face when he teased a climax from her using his fingertips and then his lips. Enjoyed, too, the urgency with which Susan twisted and bucked against him, seeking to absorb the sensation he'd created for her as she also gasped for air.

The expression of wonder on her face made him think that she hadn't ever—

Duke abruptly stopped what he was doing and looked at her.

Susan felt the change in him immediately. A shadow of fear fell over her and something inside her literally froze.

Her eyes flew open. "What? Why did you stop?" she cried, then immediately questioned, "Did I do something wrong?"

Troubled, Duke sat up and dragged a hand through his hair. It didn't seem possible in this day and age, and yet…

"Susan, are you a virgin?" he asked her quietly.

Susan pressed her lips together. "No," she cried with feeling.

Too much feeling, Duke thought, looking at her face. "Susan," he asked in the same tone he'd just used to inquire after her virginity, "are you lying?"

She closed her eyes for a moment and sighed. She really wasn't any good at this, she thought. Lying came so naturally to other people, why did it have to stick in her throat?

"Yes."

She couldn't read his expression. Was he angry at her? Disgusted?

"Why?" he asked.

For a moment she stared down at the cracked leather sofa they'd tumbled onto. When she raised her eyes again, there was a look of defiance in them. She had as much right to this, to making a choice, as anyone.

"Because I want it to be you," she told him. "I want you to be the first."

He needed to understand her reasoning. He wanted her to make him understand. "Why?"

Why did they have to discuss this now? Why couldn't it just happen? She was fairly certain that other women didn't have to explain themselves before they made love for the first time.

"Because I never felt this way before," she told him truthfully. "Never wanted to make love with anyone before. I promise I won't hold you to anything, won't expect anything. Not even for you to do it again," she added, her voice soft. She touched his arm, silently supplicating. "Just don't turn away from me now. Please."

He looked at her. Never in a million years would he have thought that he'd be trying to talk a woman out of making love with him. But he couldn't just take her innocence from her without trying to make her understand what she was doing.

"Susan, you don't know what you're asking. I'm not any good for you," he insisted.

Susan raised her eyes to his. "That's not for you to decide," she told him simply. "That's my decision— and I've made it."

He should have been able to get up and walk away,

Duke thought. The act of lovemaking—of having sex—had never been so all consuming to him that he couldn't think straight, couldn't easily separate himself from his actions. Couldn't just cut it off with no lingering repercussions.

But this time it was different.

This time, there was something about it, about Susan, about the sweetness that she was offering up to him, that robbed him of his free will, of his ability to stop, get up and walk away. He *always* could before.

He couldn't now.

He lightly cupped her cheek with his hand, the tender expression all but foreign to him. "You're going to be sorry," he predicted.

Susan's voice was firm, confident, as she replied, "No, I'm not."

He had nothing left in his arsenal to use in order to push her away. He didn't want to push her away. Every fiber of his being suddenly wanted her, wanted the life-sustaining energy he saw contained within her. Wanted, he knew, to completely wrap himself up in her and lose himself, lose the huge weight he felt pressing down on him.

Making love with Susan made him feel lighter than air and he didn't want to surrender that. Not yet. Not until he had a chance to follow that feeling to its ultimate conclusion.

Taking her into his arms again, Duke lay back down with her. He kissed Susan over and over again until he felt as if he were having an out-of-body experience.

And when he finally couldn't hold back any longer and he entered her, the small gasp of surprise that escaped her lips almost had him pulling back. The last thing he wanted was to cause her pain.

But she wouldn't let him stop. And for a single moment, she was the strong one, not Duke. She took the choice out of his hands.

They became one, rushing to the final, all-fulfilling moment, one of body, one of soul. And when it happened, when the final burst overtook him, Duke realized that he had never felt this complete before.

He had no idea what that meant. But now wasn't the time to explore it.

He held her to him, waiting for his heart to stop pounding so hard.

Maisie Colton didn't realize she was crying until she blinked and a tear slid down her face.

She'd seen them.

Had seen them kissing.

Had seen that two-bit floozy, Susan Kelley, sinking her claws into her little brother. Into Duke. Casting a spell over him.

Five years older and six inches shorter than Duke, Maisie bore a striking resemblance to her brother, except for her dramatic aqua eyes, and she felt closer to Duke than she did to anyone.

She wasn't going to stand for it. Wasn't going to allow that Kelley slut to make off with the only person on the ranch who was her ally. Duke didn't look down his nose at her, didn't judge her the way her father and the others did. Duke understood what it felt like to be a loner. Moreover, he'd never questioned her about her son, Jeremy, never even asked her who the boy's father was. Unlike their own father, Darius, who even now never missed an opportunity to badger her about her "shameless" betrayal of the family honor.

Like her father knew anything about honor, she thought contemptuously.

It was Duke who knew about honor. Like a strong, silent knight in shining armor, Duke had always been there for her. She could actually *talk* to him, tell him how she felt about things and he'd listen to her. Listen without judging.

She'd come to rely on him a great deal.

But if Duke got mixed up with that little whore, then everything would change. She'd lose him, lose the only friend she had around here.

She'd be all alone.

Suddenly feeling cold, Maisie ran her hands up and down her arms.

It wasn't going to happen, she promised herself. Duke wasn't going to take up with that little twerp. Not if she had anything to say about it.

Not even if she had to do something drastic to Susan Kelley to make her back off.

Permanently.

They'd gone inside.

Holding her breath, Maisie made her way slowly toward the house. She had to see what they were up to, had to see if it was as bad as she thought.

Maisie hated the Kelleys, hated the idea of any of her family getting mixed up with them. She couldn't stand the idea of Susan Kelley even *talking* to her brother. If the little bitch was doing anything else, that would be so much worse.

Maisie looked around. The terrain was as flat as the pancakes she'd made for Jeremy for breakfast this morning. If anyone was coming, she'd see them. But there was no one around. No one to see what she was about to do and chastise her for it.

She had a right to protect herself, Maisie silently argued. A right to protect what was hers.

Tiptoeing over to the window beside the front door, Maisie moved in what amounted to slow motion the last foot. And then she peered into the window by degrees to ensure that they didn't see her.

Maybe there was nothing going on.

Maybe he didn't like the way she kissed.

Maisie looked in, hoping.

Praying.

Her heart froze within her chest.

Pressing her lips together to stifle a gasp, she pulled back against the wall, her heart hammering in her shallow chest.

Damn it, it was worse than she thought.

That whore was naked. Stark-naked. So was Duke. How *could* he? He was letting that little whore throw herself at him. Tempt him. Didn't he know that the little bitch was no good for him? Why wasn't he throwing her out? Telling her to leave?

She squeezed her eyes shut as more tears filled them. A sob clawed its way up her throat but she deliberately kept her mouth shut. She couldn't take a chance on them hearing her.

God but she wished she'd thought to bring her gun with her. Just to fire over that bitch's head. Just to scare her a little.

Or maybe a lot.

Susan Kelley had no right to take Duke away from

her. No damn right! If her brother abandoned her, if he chose that whore over her, who was she going to talk to?

She had to find a way to scare this little two-bit whore off. And if she couldn't scare Susan off, then she was just going to have to kill her. There'd be no other choice.

The thought made Maisie smile.

Chapter 11

Dragging air into his lungs, Duke sat up on the sofa, watching Susan. Trying to reconcile what he knew about her with what he'd just discovered about her. That she seemed to have the capacity to do the impossible. She had rocked his world.

"You can stay, you know. If you want to," Duke was quick to qualify. That way, the ball was in her court and not his. He wasn't asking her to stay, he was telling her she could if she wanted to. That put the emphasis on her desire, not his.

He was having trouble wrestling with these new-found sensations and emotions and didn't want to make things worse by exposing them to public scrutiny.

Susan was gathering up her clothes from the floor as quickly as she could. Now that the passion and the ensuing euphoria had both faded away, she felt awkward. Naked was not exactly her normal state of being. Naked made her uncomfortable.

Very uncomfortable.

Not to mention she had this strange feeling she couldn't seem to shake that they had been observed. She could have sworn that when she'd thrown back her head at one point, she'd seen something move by the window. And if there was someone outside, wouldn't they have knocked by now?

A tree branch, it was probably just a tree branch, swaying in the hot breeze, she silently insisted to herself. She was just being jumpy.

Be that as it may, Susan knew she'd feel better once she had her clothes back on. And as for Duke, well, he didn't sound as if he cared one way or another if she stayed or if she left.

So she was determined to leave while there was still a shred of dignity available to her—or for her to pretend that it was available.

"I've got to get back to the restaurant," Susan murmured in response to Duke's cavalier invitation of sorts.

"You do what you have to do," he told her matter-of-factly.

Totally unselfconscious about being stark-naked he fetched his jeans and slid them on.

Even battling embarrassment, Susan had trouble drawing her eyes away from Duke from the moment that he got up.

She couldn't help thinking that Duke Colton was one hell of a specimen of manhood.

Wearing only his jeans, barely zipped and still unsnapped, consequently dipping precariously low on hips that put the word *sculptured* to shame, Duke turned to her. Very slowly, as if he was drawing out scattered leaves, he ran his fingers through her hair.

His eyes held hers.

She hadn't a clue as to what he was thinking or feeling.

"Sure you have to go?" he asked her.

A very firm yes! hovered on her lips, but somehow couldn't manage to emerge. The lone word was seared into place by the heat of the lightning bolts that insisted on going off inside her all over again. She could hardly even breathe.

One by one, Duke removed the clothes she was clutching against her, never looking at either them or at the bit of her that was uncovered once the clothing was cast aside. Instead, his eyes remained on hers, doing a fantastic job of unraveling her.

She finally found her tongue. It was thick and clumsy—and definitely not cooperating. "I…really… have to…go."

"If you say so," Duke murmured. Tilting her head up toward his, he brought his mouth down to hers again.

And succeeded in keeping her there for yet another go-round, another hour filled with salvos of ecstasy and brand-new peaks that begged to be explored and then went off like rocket flares.

"You know he's only toying with you."

Two days later, lost in her own world, her mind only partially on working out the menu for the next dinner she and her staff were scheduled to cater, Susan looked up, startled by the intrusion of the harsh voice.

She was in her office and although she distinctly remembered leaving her door open, it was closed now.

And there was a woman in the office with her. Glaring at her.

It took Susan a moment to realize who the woman was. Maisie Colton, the oldest of eight full- and half-sibling Colton offspring. The woman looked a little wild-eyed. And not a hundred-percent mentally stable.

Susan knew all about the whispers, the rumors. Maisie Colton had borne a love child, fathered by a man she refused to name. Speculation, even now, fourteen years later, ran high and rampant as to who that man might be. But Maisie's lips were sealed.

Guarding her secret so zealously despite her father's unrelenting attempts to uncover the man's identity might be the reason that Maisie seemed to be so off-kilter these days. To everyone who dealt with her, she seemed to be two cards shy of a full deck, if not more. That was the way Susan had heard her father describe Maisie. There'd been pity in his voice when he'd said it.

There were times, like now, when Maisie appeared to be going off the deep end.

"I'm afraid I don't know what you're talking about, Maisie," Susan answered, her tone politely dismissing the woman.

But Maisie wasn't about to be brushed aside that easily. She drew herself up, looming over Susan, "Sure you do," she insisted, then fairly shouted at her. "I'm talking about my brother."

Susan raised her chin. She was *not* about to let herself be chastised.

"You have lots of brothers." Whereas she had only one and she really wished Jake was here right now to rid her of this menace.

The next moment, Susan silently upbraided herself.

She was twenty-five years old, running a successful business and had, due to that romantic interlude with Duke, crossed over into the world of womanhood. It was time she stopped looking to others to champion her and took up weapons to fight her own battles.

"Duke, I'm talking about Duke!" Maisie shouted at her impatiently. "He's just toying with you. You don't mean anything to him, so why don't you save yourself a lot of grief and just stop hanging around him?" Maisie fairly spat out.

For a moment, Susan stared at the older woman. Was she guessing, or had Duke actually told her about their afternoon? Had he thought so little of her that he'd broadcast what they had done together for anyone to hear? How many other people knew?

And then, for no apparent reason, it came to her out of the blue. She had her answer. She hadn't imagined that there was someone watching them that day at Duke's house, there *had* been someone watching. Maisie.

She thought she was going to be sick.

But in the next moment, the feeling passed. Instead, Susan became angry. Very, very angry. "You watched us, didn't you?" she demanded, her eyes narrowing into blazing slits.

Taken by surprise by the accusation, Maisie had no ready answer at her disposal.

She stumbled over her own tongue, then tossed her long brown hair over her painfully thin shoulder. "What if I did?" she retorted haughtily.

Susan would have preferred to be friends with the older woman. She liked to think of herself as friendly and outgoing. The kind of woman another woman would have welcomed as a friend.

But by attacking her, Maisie left her no choice. This was *not* her fault.

"There are names for people like you," she informed Duke's unstable sister, making no secret of the disgust she was experiencing.

Nothing Susan could have actually said could have been worse than the names that were running now through Maisie's head. Names her father had flung at her more than once. Wanting to strike out, she doubled up her fists. But rather than hit Susan, Maisie uttered an angry cry and swiped her hand along Susan's desk, sending a vase of daisies crashing to the floor. The vase broke, leaving the flowers homeless.

"You'll be sorry," Maisie predicted furiously, yanking open the office door. "Wait and see, you'll be sorry."

And with that, Duke's sister slammed the door and stormed out.

Susan closed her eyes for a moment, gathering herself together. Part of her wanted to run after Maisie, to pin the thin, fragile woman down and send for the sheriff to file a complaint.

Not a wise move, she pointed out to herself. After all, the sheriff was one of Maisie's brothers.

The other part just felt sorry for Maisie. She knew that the woman had had a hard time of it, being harassed not only by the holier-than-thou people in town, but by her own father. Darius Colton allowed his daughter to live on the Colton ranch—along with her son he had never accepted into the family—but he made her pay for the so-called kindness. Made her pay for any tiny crumb he sent Maisie's way.

It made her eternally grateful for her own set of parents—even if her mother did tend to drive her insane with broad hints about not getting any younger and needing to get started on creating a family *now*, if not yesterday.

Well, if nothing else, the Coltons were certainly not a dull lot, Susan thought. Carefully getting down on her knees, she gingerly began to gather up the shards of glass that had once been a cut-glass vase.

That was the way Duke found her, on her knees, piling up pieces of glass onto a tissue that was spread out on the floor beside her desk. Opening the door in response to her wary "Come in," he took one look at the mess and crouched down to help her.

"What happened?" It was actually meant as a rhetorical question. The answer he received didn't fall into that category.

She took a breath before giving Duke an answer. "Your big sister had a 'run in' with my vase." She grimaced. "The vase lost."

Duke sat back on his heels, looking at her. "My sister?" he repeated, confused. "Maisie?"

"You have any other sisters I don't know about?" Susan asked drolly.

There was his half-sister Joan, a product of one of his father's affairs, but that's clearly not who Susan meant. Duke frowned. Deeply. This wasn't making any sense. Why would Maisie cause a scene like this? He hadn't even thought that his sister *knew* Susan. "No, but—what was she doing here?"

Susan sighed, reliving the event in her mind. She couldn't quite separate herself from it. It had really bothered her.

"Telling me that you were just toying with me and that I should walk away if I knew what was good for me." She stopped picking up pieces of glass and looked at Duke. He wasn't reacting. "Is she right? Did you send her to warn me off?"

She couldn't fathom his expression as he looked at her. "Is that what you think?"

Susan looked up toward the ceiling, thinking. And not getting anywhere. "I don't know what to think— except that Maisie could be dangerous if she got angry enough."

If he were being honest, Duke would have to admit that there was part of him that agreed with Susan. There were times when he worried that Maisie might do something that couldn't be swept under the rug or just shrugged off. Something that would go badly and backfire on her.

But family loyalty made him feel compelled to dismiss Susan's concerns, so out loud he said, "Maisie's harmless. She's just a little off at times, that's all. But she's been through a lot and the old man hasn't exactly made life easy for her. He rides everyone, especially Maisie and she's a little fragile."

There was merit to his argument, Susan thought. But he was missing a very significant point. He might even be blind to it, she judged. "I think Maisie's afraid I might try to take you away from her."

"That's ridiculous," he scoffed. The shattered vase forgotten, Duke rose to his feet, not a little indignant over what he assumed that Susan was implying. "Why would Maisie think that? She's my sister, not some woman I've been seeing."

Susan quickly stood up and placed her hand on his

chest, in part to calm him, in part to keep him from leaving before she explained herself. She hadn't meant to insult him.

"I'm not saying that's how you see her, but I think in Maisie's world, things are a little…confused. She probably looks to you as someone she can trust, someone she can share her thoughts with."

The man might be stoic, but there was a gentleness in his manner when he mentioned his sister's plight with their father. Her guess was that Duke didn't want to see Maisie hurt. She liked him for that, even if Maisie had overtly threatened her.

His eyes were angry as he promised, "I'll have a talk with her."

"Don't yell at her, Duke," Susan cautioned, in case what she'd just told him caused his temper to flare. "I think your sister is really scared." She paused for a moment, debating, then decided that Duke had a right to know what she suspected had happened. "I also think she saw us."

Duke's gaze grew very dark as he stared at her. "Saw us?" he echoed.

Now what was Susan talking about? Women were way too complicated, never coming right out and saying what was on their minds. They had to hint, to skirt around the words until a guy's head got painfully dizzy.

"Yes, *saw us,*" Susan emphasized meaningfully, her eyes on his.

Because his mind didn't work that way, for a moment he didn't know what Susan meant by that cryptic phrase. And then it hit him.

"Oh."

Anger over having his privacy invaded battled with

the general compassion he normally felt for his sister. He'd always cut her a lot of slack, especially after Damien had been sent to prison.

"Hell," he sighed, shaking his head, "now I really *am* going to have a talk with her." One hand on the doorknob, he was about to leave when Susan called his name.

"Duke?"

He stopped abruptly, his mind already back at the main house. "What?"

"What are you doing here?" Susan wanted to know. When he looked at her blankly, she became a little more specific. "You don't usually come into town," she pointed out. Was this a casual visit, or was there something more behind it? She knew which way she would have wanted it. She tried not to sound too eager as she asked, "Why did you come by my office?"

"I was in town on an errand." It seemed rather foolish now to say that he'd just wanted to see her. To see if he'd just imagined the whole thing back at the ranch the other day or if the sight of her actually could make his stomach feel as if it was at the center of a Boy Scout knot-tying jamboree. "Thought I'd stop by," he mumbled.

Damn, but this wasn't him, Duke thought in disgust at his own behavior. He was never tongue-tied. He was quiet by choice, not out of necessity to keep from sounding like some kind of babbling idiot. And yet, this bit of a thing had him tripping over his own tongue, badly messing with his thought processes.

What *was* it about her that made him act like a village idiot?

Pushing all thoughts of Maisie aside, Susan smiled at him as she drew closer.

"I'm glad you did," she told him. "Are you hungry?" she asked him, suddenly thinking of it. Glancing over her shoulder at the small refrigerator where she kept all sorts of samples for her catering business, Susan made him an offer. "If you are, I could just whip up something for you to nibble on, take the edge off."

What he found himself wanting to nibble on required no special preparation by Susan. All she had to do was stand there.

Where the hell had that come from?

The next moment, stifling an annoyed sigh, Duke mentally shook his head. It was official. He had become certifiably crazy. And all it had taken was two consecutive rolls in the proverbial hay with the Kelley girl.

Maybe this dropping by wasn't such a good idea. He didn't like discovering that he had these needs knocking around inside him. At least, not to this extent. He'd known he was attracted to her, but he'd figured he could keep it under control.

Time to go. "No thanks," he muttered, begging off. "I'm good."

Yes, you are, Susan thought, then realized that she could probably go straight to hell for what she was thinking right now.

Clearing her throat, she nodded in response to what he'd just said to her. "Well, thanks for stopping by. It was nice seeing you again."

"Yeah, well…" For the second time, he began leaving the office, his hand on the doorknob, ready to pull it shut behind him and make good his escape. He was almost home free when the words seemed to escape of their own volition. "You free tonight?"

Her mother had taught her that it was never a good thing to appear to be too available because that made it seem as if no one else wanted her. But no one else did, other than Linc and there was no way she wanted even to entertain that thought. Besides, her mother was a big one for playing games. Playing games had never held any appeal to her. And to that end, she just wasn't any good at it. Lies had a way of tripping her up.

"I'm free," she told him. "Why?" She crossed her fingers behind her back, hoping that the reason he was asking was because he wanted to see her.

Duke knew he was voluntarily putting a noose around his neck, but he assured himself that he could remove it at any time and would, once he grew tired of Susan. But for now, he was very far from being tired of her. "I was thinking maybe I could come by, pick you up and we could go out to eat."

He liked the way a smile came to her eyes when he asked her out. It was almost as if he could feel the warmth. "Sounds good to me."

He did his best to appear as if he was indifferent to the actual outcome. It was rather adolescent of him, but this was a brand-new place he found himself traveling through. "So if I come by, you'll be there?"

"That better be 'when,' not 'if,'" she informed him, doing her best to sound serious and not letting him hear the way her heart was pounding, "and yes I'll be there when you come by. Oh, by the way, I'm staying in the guest house behind the main house."

Duke nodded. He understood how that was. There were amenities that were hard to give up, but they weren't worth trading hard-won independence for, either. A compromise was the best way to go. "All the comforts of home without having them underfoot."

She didn't really consider her parents being "underfoot" but it was too early in this budding whatever-it-was to admit that to him outright. He might look down at her for that.

"Something like that," she answered vaguely.

He nodded, not pressing the issue. "Seven o'clock sound all right to you?"

"Seven o'clock sounds fine." Hesitating, Susan knew she'd have no peace about the evening ahead unless she asked. "Maisie won't be coming with you, will she?"

"Don't worry," he assured her. "She'll be staying home tonight. Even if I have to tie her to a chair," he promised.

"You don't have to go to those drastic measures," she told him. But secretly, the thought of knowing that Maisie would be unable to suddenly pop up and ruin their evening was rather appealing, not to mention comforting. "Just make sure she doesn't know where you're going—and with whom."

He looked at her closely. "She really did spook you, didn't she?"

Susan was going to say no, because that sounded braver, but it was also a lie. So she shrugged, trying her best to look casual. "Let's just say I'm not used to being threatened."

"Don't worry, you won't have to get used to it. It won't happen again," he promised.

There was definitely something of the knight in shining armor about the dusty cattle rancher, Susan thought with a smile, watching him leave.

Chapter 12

"Is it true?"

Wes hadn't heard the door to the sheriff's office open, had been too preoccupied working at his desk to even hear anyone come in.

Only in office for a little more than a year and it was already looking as if every unaccounted-for piece of paper in the county had somehow found its way to his desk, presumably to die. A man had to have access to a thirty-hour day—without any sleep—in order to do this job properly and still take care of all this annoying paperwork, he thought darkly.

Right about now, Wes was convinced that he would welcome any distraction to take him away from these damn reports he needed to file. But when he looked up to see his sister standing before his desk, looking every bit like a commercial seeking pledges of money for food for a starving third-world country, he wasn't quite so sure about welcoming *any* distraction.

Maisie, at forty, was his older sister—as well as his only sister—but there were a lot of times when he felt as if he were the older one, not Maisie. These days there was something of the waif about her. Seeing her like that usually brought out his protective instincts.

But dealing with Maisie took a great deal of patience, which in turn meant a great deal of time, and time was something he was rather short on right now. As sheriff of Honey Creek he had a murder with a twist on his hands and the sooner he got to the bottom of it, the sooner life in this small town would go back to normal. Back to people engaging in harmless gossip instead of looking at one another with suspicion and uneasiness. Too many people were heading to the hardware store to buy deadbolts for their doors, something that had been, heretofore, unheard of in Honey Creek.

Maisie's thin but still beautiful face was now a mask of consternation. Wes couldn't even begin to guess why.

His first thought was that whatever had brought her here to him might have something to do with her son, his nephew Jeremy. Or maybe with their father.

And just possibly, both.

His guess turned out to be wrong.

"Is what true?" he finally asked her when she didn't elaborate.

Maisie drew in a shaky breath, as if that would somehow help her push out the next words she needed to say. "Is it true that Mark Walsh came back from the dead?"

That pulled him up short. Where the hell had that come from? There just seemed to be no end to the annoyances this dead man could stir up. "Who told you that?"

Her thin shoulders scratched the air in a hapless shrug. "I heard talk. They said that you found Mark Walsh in the creek." Maisie paused, clearly waiting for him to confirm or deny the statement.

Wes folded his hands on top of the opened report on his desk and looked into his older sister's eyes. "I did."

Maisie stifled a strange, hapless little noise. "Then he did come back from the dead."

She began to tremble visibly, her busy fingers going to her lips as if they could help her find the right words to say next. But only small frightened sounds escaped.

Getting up, Wes abandoned the tiresome work that was spread over the surface of his desk. He considered his sister's peace of mind—or what he was about to coax forward—to be far more important than filing something on time.

Rounding his desk, Wes came over to where Maisie was standing and put his arm around her shoulders in an effort to comfort her. Maisie responded to kind voices and a soft touch.

"No, Maisie, Mark Walsh didn't come back from the dead," he told her in a firm, gentle voice.

But it didn't help. She pulled away from him, her aquamarine eyes wide and frightened. "But we buried him. There was a casket and a body and they were buried," she insisted, her voice bordering on hysteria. "Fifteen years ago, they were buried. I *saw* it."

"It was someone else—" Wes began, still patient. His voice was low, soothing. Damn, he wished Duke was here. Duke always seemed to be able to manage her better than the rest of them could.

"Who?" Maisie wanted to know, almost begging to be convinced she was wrong. If she was wrong, if Mark hadn't come back from the dead to haunt her, then the nightmares she was afraid of wouldn't start again, the way they had when Mark was first buried.

"I don't know," Wes told her wearily, "but it wasn't Walsh." He tried talking to her the way he would to anyone else. To a stable person. "I'm having the first body exhumed to try to see if we can determine who it was." No one else had been reported missing at the time, so for now, he still held to his drifter-in-the-wrong-place-at-the-wrong-time theory.

It was obvious that Maisie was desperately trying to come to terms with what had happened. "But that body you found in the creek, that was Mark?"

"Yes, Maisie, that was Mark Walsh."

Just when he thought he'd made her understand, she suddenly challenged him. "How do you know that was Mark Walsh?"

He supposed it was a fair enough question. He did his best to hang on to his patience. "The county medical examiner matched up Walsh's dental records with the man we fished out of the creek."

Maisie blew out another shaky breath, her eyes never leaving her brother. "And he's really dead?"

Wes tried to give her an encouraging smile. "He's really dead."

She still looked fearful, still unable to believe what he was telling her.

"You're sure?" Clutching at his shirt with her damp fingers, she implored him to convince her. "You're really sure it's him? And that he's dead?"

Very gently, he separated her fingers from his shirt.

"Maisie, what's this all about?" An uneasy feeling undulated through him. Could his sister have had something to so with Walsh's death? She did seem unhinged at times and there was no way to gauge what was going on in her head.

She didn't answer his question, she just repeated her own. "Are you sure, Wes?" she pressed, enunciating each word.

"I'm sure. There's no mistake this time. It *is* Mark Walsh and he's dead." Still holding her hands in his, Wes looked into her eyes, trying to make sense out of what was going on. "Maisie, why are you so agitated about this?"

"I don't want the nightmares to start again," she said, more to herself or to someone who wasn't in the room than in response to his question. For a moment, Maisie looked as if she was going to cry, but then she raised her head defiantly, as if issuing a challenge to that same nonexistent person. "Not again."

Wes did what he could to reassure her. He really didn't have time for this. "They won't," he promised her. "Everything's going to be fine, Maisie. Just fine. Look, why don't I take you home? You're too upset right now to be alone."

"All right," she agreed docilely, the agitation leaving her as quickly, as suddenly, as it had come. Subdued, she followed him outside to the street like some obedient pet.

About to open the passenger side of his police vehicle for her, Wes happened to look across the street, to the side entrance of Kelley's Cookhouse. He saw Duke walking out of the restaurant and heading toward his truck.

Wes saw his way out.

"C'mon, Maisie," he urged, "I think I just found you a ride home."

His sister looked at him blankly as he took hold of her arm and propelled her down the street. "I thought you said you were taking me home."

"I was, but then I'd have to come back." But Duke didn't, he thought. Duke was going home.

His brother had already started up his truck. Waving, Wes hurriedly put himself directly in Duke's path. The latter was forced to pick up his hand brake again and turn his engine off.

Now what? Duke wondered.

He stuck his head out through the driver's-side window, looking at Wes. "From what I recollect, they issued you a bulletproof vest when you took this job, not a car-proof vest. You got a death wish, Sheriff?"

Wes came around to Duke's side of the cab. "I need you to get Maisie home."

Duke scowled as he looked at his sister. "Maisie." There was no inflection whatsoever in his voice, no way of telling what he was thinking.

"Yeah, Maisie." And then, because he *was* the sheriff, he had to ask. "Something wrong?"

Maybe Duke knew the reason why Maisie seemed to be on the verge of hysteria this afternoon. Was it really only about the discovery of Mark Walsh's body—something that was upsetting a lot of people—or was there something else going on? And why was Duke looking at their sister that way? Was he missing something?

Duke suppressed an annoyed sigh. He was not about to tell Wes that their sister had threatened Susan. Even if he wasn't the sheriff, Wes would want to know why

Maisie was behaving that way. What was going on—or not going on—between him and Susan was nobody's business but his—and maybe Susan's, he added silently. There was no way he was going to talk about it with anyone.

"No, nothing's wrong," Duke said. His eyes shifted toward his sister who was hanging back. "Get in, Maisie," he told her.

Maisie looked a little hesitant; her initial smile when she'd seen Duke had all but vanished. But when Wes opened the passenger-side door for her, she got into the truck's cab docilely.

Securing the door, Wes crossed back around to Duke's side. Once next to his brother, he lowered his voice and said, "Something about my finding Walsh's body in the creek has her spooked." He paused for a second, debating whether to add the last part. But he decided it couldn't hurt. "Go easy on her."

"I have for the last fifteen years," Duke told his brother.

And maybe that was the problem, Duke thought. Maybe he'd gone too easy on Maisie and that had eventually allowed her to slip into a place where he couldn't readily reach her. Maybe if he'd made her behave a little more responsibly, he'd have done them both a favor.

They were going to have a little talk, he and Maisie, and get things straightened out, Duke promised himself. Once and for all.

Duke started up his truck again and pulled away without saying another word to Wes.

"You don't have to worry about Maisie anymore," Duke told Susan that evening when she opened the door to admit him to her home. A man who believed in getting down to business, he'd skipped a mundane greeting in favor of setting her mind at ease as he walked into the Kelley guest house.

Susan did her best to look composed and nonchalant—not like someone who'd spent the last forty-five minutes two steps away from the front door waiting for Duke to finally arrive.

Duke wasn't late, she was just very early. "Oh?" That came out sounding a little too high, she upbraided herself as she closed the door behind him. He could probably tell she was nervous.

Duke looked around the living room. The house was neat, tidy, with sleek, simple lines. With just enough frills to make him think of her. But then he'd noticed that, lately, a lot of things made him think of her.

"Yeah," he responded. "I had a talk with Maisie." He'd used the time it took him to get his sister back to the main house to his advantage. And Maisie had listened solemnly—and crossed her heart. "She promised not to bother you anymore."

What a woman said was one thing, what she did was another, Susan thought. But she didn't want to spoil the evening by getting into any kind of a discussion about his sister's possible future behavior. So she offered him a bright smile and pretended that she thought everything was going to be just peachy from then on.

"That's good." She knew she should just drop it here, but there was a part of her that was a fighter. That didn't just lie down and wait for the steam roller to come by and finish the job. So she said, "Does that mean she'll stop leaving dead flowers and nasty notes too?"

He looked at her sharply. "You got more?"

She pressed her lips together and nodded. "I got more."

Damn it, who the hell was stalking her? He didn't like thinking that she could be in danger. This was Honey Creek. Things like this didn't happen here—until they did, he thought darkly. Like with Walsh.

"Well, they're not from Maisie," he told her, measuring his words slowly. "I took her home from town and left her sleeping in her room. Jeremy's looking after her," he added.

Though no one would have guessed it, he couldn't help feeling sorry for his nephew. The poor kid had been dealt one hell of a hand. No father, a mother who was only half there mentally and a grandfather whose dislike for the boy was all but tangible whenever the two were in the same room together.

He and his brothers did what they could to make Jeremy feel that he was part of the family, but it wasn't easy when Darius was just as determined to make Jeremy feel like an outsider subsisting solely on the old man's charity.

"Anyone else in my family you think is sending them?" he asked her archly.

She bristled slightly. "I didn't mean to sound as if I was focusing on your family," she apologized. "But this has me a little shaken up. There's no reason for *anyone* to be sending me dead roses and threatening notes, but they still keep on coming."

He heard the distress in her voice, even though she struggled to hide just how nervous this was making her. Nobody was going to hurt her if he had anything to say about it.

"For my money I still think it's that Hayes character," he told her, then repeated his offer. "You want me to talk to him?"

She shook her head. "It's not Linc. He wouldn't do something like this." She was certain of it. They were friends, good friends. He wouldn't resort to this kind of mental torture.

Duke didn't quite see it that way. "'Fraid you've got a lot more faith in Hayes than I do. Let me take the latest note and the last batch of flowers with me when I leave. I'll bring them over to Wes tomorrow, see if he's gotten anywhere with his investigation."

Susan wondered if he realized the significance of his offer. In case the small detail eluded him, she pointed it out. "That means you'll have to admit to seeing me. Are you ready to do that?"

Duke knew a challenge when he saw one. And Susan, whether she knew it or not, was definitely challenging him. Calling him out.

"Woman, I've been on my own for a lot of years," he told her. "I don't have to ask anyone's permission to do anything I want to do." He left the rest unsaid and let her fill in the blanks.

"What about your father?" she asked. "Don't you have to run things by him?"

She'd heard that the patriarch of the Colton clan could make life a living hell for anyone who crossed him. He was a strict man who demanded allegiance and obedience from the people he dealt with, especially from his own family.

"Only when it comes to things that concern the ranch," he allowed. And there was a reason for that. "The ranch is his. My life is mine. Any other questions or things you'd like to clear up?"

She had to admit she felt a little more at ease. Susan smiled at him. "Can't think of a thing."

"All right, then let's go," he prodded. It was getting late and he'd promised her dinner in town. When she made no move to follow him out the door, Duke raised one eyebrow. "Change your mind?"

"Only about where we're eating," she replied. He raised his eyebrow even higher. "I thought maybe we could eat in. I threw some things together," she explained, then stopped, wondering if maybe she was taking too much for granted or sending out the wrong signals again. This creating a relationship was hard work. Worth it, but hard work.

Duke asked, "Edible things?"

He was teasing her. Susan didn't bother attempting to hide her smile. She considered herself a very good cook, having inherited her father's natural instincts for creating epicurean miracles.

"Very."

That was good enough for him. Duke took his hat off and let it fall onto the cushion of the wide, padded leather sofa to his right.

"Talked me into it," he told her.

His eyes caught hers. He felt something stirring inside him. Anticipation. It surprised him and he savored it for a moment. In so many ways, Charlene had been superior to Susan. Experienced, clever and worldly, she'd been a woman in every sense of the word. And yet, there was something about Susan, something that pulled him to her, that had him looking forward to being with her, more than he'd *ever* looked forward to being with Charlene. Who would have thought—?

"This way," he continued pointedly, "we won't have to go so far or wait so long for dessert."

Dessert. Was that what he was calling it? Or was she reading too much into his words? Too much because she desperately wanted him to mean that he wanted her. Wanted to believe that he had planned the evening around dinner and lovemaking.

Because she'd thought of nothing else since he'd asked her about her plans when he came to her office earlier today.

"Come this way," she invited. Turning on her heel, she led him into her small dining room.

Duke entertained himself by watching the way Susan's trim hips moved as she walked ahead of him. It reminded him of a prize show pony he'd once owned, a gift from his grandfather when he'd been a young boy. The pony had had the same classy lines, the same proud gait as Susan did now. It had been a thing of beauty to watch when it ran, he recalled.

Just like Susan was a thing of beauty to behold when she was in his arms. Making love with him.

Wow.

He hadn't realized he was even capable of having thoughts like that. Susan was definitely bringing out the best in him, he mused. Making him want to be a better man. For her.

He found himself hoping she hadn't made very much for dinner because whatever was on the table wasn't going to whet his appetite one-tenth as much as the taste of her mouth would.

And that was what he craved right now. Her. But she'd gone to all this trouble, it wasn't right to ask her to skip it because he was having trouble holding back his more basic appetites.

"Sit down," she told him. "This won't take long, I promise."

"Need any help?" he offered, raising his voice so that it would carry into the kitchen.

Her back to him, Susan's mouth curved in pure pleasure. She would never have believed that Duke Colton would actually offer to help out in the kitchen. As a matter of fact, she would have been fairly certain that Duke didn't even know what to do in a kitchen. You just never knew, did you?

"No, everything's fine," she answered, tossing the words over her shoulder. "All you have to do is sit there and enjoy yourself."

Susan's casual instruction brought an actual grin to Duke's lips before he could think to stop it.

He fully intended to, he thought. He fully intended to.

Chapter 13

Susan sighed.

She finally put down her pen and gave up her flimsy pretense that she hadn't noticed the looks Bonnie Gene had been giving her each time the woman walked by the open office door. Which was frequently this morning. Susan had lost count at eleven.

"All right, Mother, what is it?"

Bonnie Gene had already gone by and had to backtrack her steps in order to present herself in the doorway.

"What's what, dear?" her mother asked innocently.

The stage had lost one hell of a performer when her mother had decided not to pursue an acting career, Susan thought.

"You know perfectly well 'what's what,'" Susan insisted. "You must have walked by my office about a dozen times this morning. And each time, you looked in with that self-satisfied smile of yours." When her mother raised a quizzical eyebrow, Susan continued to elaborate. "You know, the one you always wear whenever you place first in the annual pie-baking contest."

"I *always* place first in the pie-baking contest," Bonnie Gene informed her regally. "Unless the judges were being bribed that year or had their taste buds surgically removed."

Susan stopped her mother before she could get carried away. "Don't change the subject."

Another innocent look graced Bonnie Gene's face as she placed a hand delicately against her still very firm bosom. "I thought that was the subject."

Okay, Susan thought, *we could go around like this indefinitely.* She worded her question more precisely. "Mother, why do you keep looking in at me?"

Bonnie Gene crossed the threshold, her smile rivaling the summer sun outside. "Because you're my lovely daughter—"

"Mother!" Susan cried far more sharply than she would have ordinarily, impatience shimmering around the single name. "Come clean. What's going on?"

Bonnie Gene adopted a more serious demeanor. "I should be asking you that."

"You could," Susan allowed, feeling her patience being stripped away. "*If* you explained what you meant by your question."

"Don't play innocent with me, my darling." Bonnie Gene looked at her daughter pointedly, having lingered on the word *innocent* a beat longer than the rest of her sentence. "The time for that is past, thank goodness. All right, all right," she declared, giving up the last shred of pretense as Susan began to get up from her chair. "I can't stand not knowing any longer."

"Not knowing *what?*" Susan cried, completely frustrated. What was it that her mother was carrying on about? It couldn't possibly be about her and—

"How things are going with you and Duke Colton."

Oh, God, it was *about her and Duke.*

In response, Susan turned a lighter shade of pale and sank back down in her chair. She'd been afraid of this.

"What are you talking about?" she finally asked in a small, still, disembodied voice that didn't seem to belong to her.

With a superior air, one hand fisted at her hip, Bonnie Gene tossed her head, sending her hair flying jauntily over her shoulder. "Oh, come now, Susan, you didn't *really* think that you could keep this to yourself, did you?"

In retrospect, Susan supposed that had been pretty stupid of her. Her mother had eyes like a hawk and the sensory perception of a bat; all in all, a pretty frightening combination. Especially since it meant that *nothing* ever seemed to escape her attention.

"I had hopes," Susan murmured, almost to herself. She raised her eyes and blew out a breath, bracing herself for the answer to the question she was about to ask. "Who else knows?"

Bonnie Gene laughed. She staked out a place for herself on the corner of Susan's desk and leaned over to be closer to her youngest.

"An easier question to answer, my love, is who else *doesn't* know. I must say though, I've had my work cut out for me."

"Your work?" Susan echoed, really lost this time. What was her mother talking about now?

"Yes." Bonnie Gene looked at Susan as if completely surprised that she didn't understand. "Defending your choice. Defending *Duke*," she finally stressed.

"There is no 'choice,' Mother," Susan informed Bonnie Gene, knowing that she really didn't have a leg to stand on. She *had* chosen Duke. The problem was, as of yet, she had no idea how the man really felt about her. There were no terms of endearment coming from him, no little gifts now that she had ruled out that those awful flowers had been from him.

For all she knew, Duke was just seeing her because he had no one better within easy access at the moment. She knew that making herself available to him if she believed that made her seem like a pathetic woman, but she couldn't help it. She was so very attracted to Duke, she would accept him on almost any terms as long as it meant that the evening would end with them sharing passion. When she was away from him, she was counting off minutes in her head until they were together again.

But that was by no means something she wanted her mother—or anyone else for that matter—to know. At least, not until she knew how Duke felt about her.

And for that matter, maybe it was better that she didn't know how he felt. She was more than a little aware that the truth could be very painful.

"And exactly what do you mean *defending Duke?*" Susan suddenly asked, replaying her mother's words in her head.

Bonnie Gene rolled her eyes dramatically. "Well, I can't begin to tell you how many people have come up to me, wanting to know what a nice girl like you is doing with a man the likes of Duke Colton. If I hear one more 'concerned' citizen tell me about Charlene's suicide after Duke broke it off with her, I'll scream—if I don't throw up first."

Susan squared her shoulders, indignation shining in her eyes. She resented the gossipmongers having a field day with Duke's past behavior, and they were all missing a very salient point.

"Duke broke it off with Charlene when he found out she was married. He told me that he would have never been involved with her in the first place if he'd known that she wasn't single." In her eyes, he had done the right thing, the honorable thing. Why couldn't anyone else see that?

"Simmer down, Susan, I believe you." Bonnie Gene smiled into her daughter's face, lightly touching the hair that framed it. "As much as I want to see you married, I wouldn't let you throw your life away on someone I didn't think was good enough for you. What kind of a mother would that make me, if all I wanted was just to get you married off?" She looked at her daughter pointedly.

She was right, Susan thought. There were times that she forgot that, at bottom, her mother loved and cared about all of them. Worried about all of them. She'd lost sight of that amid all the less than veiled hints that came trippingly off Bonnie Gene's tongue about time running out.

"Sorry," Susan said quietly.

Bonnie Gene beamed, looking more like her older sister than her mother. "Apology accepted. Now," she drew in closer, her eyes lively and hopeful, "how *is* it going between the two of you?"

Her mother deserved the truth, Susan thought. "I don't know," Susan confessed. "It's a little early to tell. We've only been seeing each other for two weeks," Susan pointed out, using the innocent phrase *seeing each other* as a euphemism for what was really going on: that they had been making pulse-racing, exquisite love for those two weeks.

In truth, she felt as if she was living in a dream. But dreams, Susan knew, had a terrible habit of ending, forcing the dreamer to wake up. She dreaded the thought of that coming to pass and could only hope that it wouldn't happen too soon. She'd never felt like this before, as if she could just fly at will and touch the sky, gathering stars.

"Time isn't a factor. I knew the first time your father kissed me," Bonnie Gene told her with pride. She saw the skeptical expression that descended over the girl's face. "Oh, I know what you're thinking—your father is this overly round man with an unruly gray mane and a gravelly voice, but he didn't always look like that."

Bonnie Gene closed her eyes for a moment, remembering. The sigh that escaped was pregnant with memories.

"When I first met your father, he was beautiful. And what that man could do—" Bonnie Gene stopped abruptly, realizing who she was talking to. Clearing her throat, she waved her hand dismissively. "Well, never mind. The point is, it doesn't take months to know if you want to spend the rest of your life with someone or not. It just takes a magic moment."

That rang true. For her. For Duke, not so much.

"Well, as far as I know, Duke hasn't had a magic moment," Susan told her.

Bonnie Gene heard what wasn't being said. "But you have." It wasn't a question.

Susan didn't want to go on record with that. "Mother, if I don't get back to putting together a spectacular menu, Shirley and Bill Nelson are going to let her sister take over cooking for the party," she protested. "And I don't want that to happen."

Bonnie Gene leaned even further over the desk and lightly kissed the top of her daughter's head. "Go, work. Make your father proud. I have what I wanted to know," she assured Susan.

"Mother." There was a note of pleading in Susan's voice.

Bonnie Gene smiled. "My lips are sealed."

Susan sincerely doubted that.

"Only if you get run over by a sewing machine between here and the kitchen," Susan murmured. No one would have ever recruited Bonnie Gene to be a spy whose ability to keep secrets meant the difference between life and death in the free world.

Bonnie Gene stuck her head in one last time. "I heard that."

"Good, you were supposed to."

Susan attempted to get back to work. She really did need to finish this menu today. *Something exciting that isn't expensive*—those had been Shirley Nelson's instructions. So far, she really hadn't come up with anything outstanding.

Her ability to concentrate was derailed the next moment as she heard her mother all but purr the words, "Oh, how nice to see you again," to someone outside her door, then adding, "Yes, you're in luck. She's in her office."

The next second, Susan heard a quick rap on her doorjamb. She didn't have to ask who it was because he was there, filling up her doorway and her heart at the same time.

And looking far more appealingly rugged and handsome than any man had a legal right to be.

"Hi," Duke said, his deep voice rumbling at her, creating tidal waves inside her stomach and an instant yearning within the rest of her.

"Hi," Susan echoed back.

"I just ran into your mother," Duke told her needlessly.

He was at a loss as to how to initiate a conversation with Susan, even at this point. Coming to see a woman was new for him. Usually, the women would come seeking him out, their agendas clearly mapped out in their eyes. Conversation had very little to do with it. This was virgin territory he was treading—appropriately enough, he added to himself as an afterthought.

The thought hit him again that he had been Susan's first. He couldn't really say that had ever mattered to him before, but this time around was different. He realized that he liked being her first.

Her only, at least for now.

Even though it brought with it a rather heavy sense of responsibility he'd never felt before. A heavy sense of responsibility not because of anything that Susan had said or demanded, but just because he felt it.

"Yes, I heard," Susan answered.

The first few moments were still awkward between them every time they met and she couldn't even explain why. It wasn't as if they hadn't seen each other for a while. Duke had come over just last night. As he had every other night since the first time they had made love. The time they spent pretending that they intended to go somewhere or do something had been growing progressively shorter. They were in each other's arms, enjoying one another, enjoying lovemaking, faster with each day that passed by.

What pleased her almost as much was that he did talk to her once the lovemaking was over. Talked to her about little things, like what he'd done at the ranch that day, or his plans for a herd of his own. It meant the world to her.

Please don't let it end yet. Not yet, she prayed, watching him walk into the room.

Out loud, she asked, "Um, can I get you anything?"

The hint of a wicked little smile touched the corners of his mouth, sending yet another ripple through her stomach.

"Not here," he told her.

To anyone else, it might have sounded like an enigmatic response, but she knew exactly what he was saying to her. And it thrilled her. She had absolutely no idea where any of this was headed, or even if it was headed anywhere, but she knew she was determined to enjoy every moment of this relationship for as long as it lasted.

Susan was well aware that in comparison to the other women Duke had been with, she could be seen as naive and completely unworldly. Consequently, she wasn't about to fool herself into thinking that she and Duke actually had some kind of a future together. Not in this world any way, she thought. He wasn't the marrying kind. Everyone knew that.

She blushed a little at his response and heard Duke laugh as he crooked his finger beneath her chin and raised her head until her eyes met his.

Damn, but there was something about her, something that just kept on pulling him in, he thought, watching the pink hue on her cheeks begin to fade again. Each time he made love with her, he expected that was finally going to be that. That he'd reached the end of the line.

But he hadn't.

He hadn't had his fill of her, wasn't growing tired of her. He wasn't even aching for his freedom the way he normally did whenever something took up his time to this extent.

Maybe it was a bug going round, he reasoned, searching for something to blame, to explain away his odd behavior satisfactorily.

"I just came by to let you know that I'm going to be late coming by your place tonight," he told her. "I'm in town to pick up some extra supplies and what I'm doing's going to take more time than I thought."

Susan nodded, thrilling to his slightest touch. And to the promise of the evening that was yet to come. She didn't care how late he came, as long as he came.

"I'll keep a candle burning in the window for you," she promised.

Why did the silly little things she said make him want to smile? And why did she seem to fill up so much of his thoughts, even when he should be thinking of something else?

If he didn't watch out, he was going to get sloppy and careless. And then he'd have his father on his back, watching him like a hawk. That was all he needed. He could guarantee that a blow-up would follow.

"You do that," he told Susan.

Still holding his finger beneath her chin, he bent his head and brushed his lips quickly over hers.

Her eyes fluttered shut as she absorbed the fleeting contact and reveled in it. She could feel her pulse accelerating.

When she opened her eyes, she found him looking at her. More than anything, she wished she could read his thoughts.

"Um, listen, since you're here, can I get you something to eat?" she wanted to know. "It's almost lunch time and I'm assuming that your father lets you have time off for good behavior."

The smallest whisper of a smile played along Duke's lips. She ached to kiss him again, but managed to restrain herself.

"Who says I have good behavior?" he asked. His voice sounded almost playful—for Duke. It sent more ripples through her, reinforcing the huge tidal wave that had washed over her when he'd kissed her.

"No, really," she tried to sound more serious. "Aren't you hungry?" She nodded in the general direction of the kitchen. "I could just whip up something quick for you—"

Yes, he was hungry he thought, but the consumption of food had nothing to do with it. He wanted her. A lot. Another first, he realized.

"If I stay to eat," he told her, his eyes holding hers, "I might not leave anytime soon."

They weren't talking about food. Even she knew that. And the idea that she could actually entice someone like Duke Colton thrilled her beyond measure.

"Wouldn't want to do that."

Her words were agreeing with him, her tone was not. Her tone told him that she wanted nothing more than to have him stay and do all those wondrous things to her that he had introduced her to. Just the thought of it stirred his appetite.

He looked at her for a long moment, debating. The door had a lock on it.

"Oh, I don't know about that," he answered speculatively, allowing his voice to trail off.

But the thought of being interrupted by one of the staff, or either of her parents, tipped the scales toward behaving more sensibly. He told himself that passing up a chance to make love with her now meant that there was more to look forward to tonight.

Suppressing a sigh, Duke gathered himself together and crossed to the doorway. He nodded his head. "See you tonight."

"Tonight," she echoed to his retreating back.

Tonight.

The single world throbbed with promise. If she weren't afraid of her mother passing by again and looking in, she would have hugged herself.

Chapter 14

The extra feed he'd come for all loaded up in his truck, Duke got behind the wheel, put his key into the ignition and turned it on.

Then he turned it off again.

He'd never been a man given to impulsive moves. He thought things through before he did them. But he was here, so he took advantage of time and opportunity. Taking the note that Susan had given him, he got out of the truck's cab, secured the door and went to the short, squat building across the street.

Wes's car was parked outside. That meant that Wes was most likely inside or close by. Duke walked into the sheriff's office without bothering to knock. He was a man with a timetable.

"I know you're busy with looking into Mark Walsh's latest murder, but I really need you to look into this for me," he declared, holding the crudely handwritten note out in front of him. "Susan got another one. Along with more dead flowers."

About to leave to grab some lunch, Wes took a step backward in order to allow his older brother to come in. Taking the note that Duke held out to him, he glanced at it quickly. Same block letters, an equally childish threat on the sheet.

"You mean you want me to look into this in my spare time between midnight and 12:04 a.m.?" he asked wryly. He wasn't a man who complained, but venting a little steam wasn't entirely out of order. He'd been hunting for Walsh's killer even before the autopsy had confirmed his identity—and getting nowhere. "I had no idea there were so many people who hated Mark Walsh." Wes walked back to his desk and sat down, placing the note on top of the pile of papers that were there. "Right now, the only ones who I know aren't suspects are Damien and me."

Hooking his thumbs onto his belt, Duke continued to stand, his countenance all but shouting that he was a man with things to do, places to go. "That bad?"

"Pretty much. Hell, the spooked way Maisie's been acting lately, if I didn't know any better, I'd say that she did the guy in herself." Wes rocked back in his chair, glancing again at the note that Duke had brought in. He'd hoped that the previous notes and flowers had been a prank that had played itself out. Obviously not, he thought. "I'm starting to think that maybe getting elected sheriff was not the wisest career move I could have made."

Duke had never seen the appeal of the position, but

he'd backed Wes's choice nonetheless. "Still better than ranching with the old man."

"You do have a point." Straightening up, Wes frowned as he perused the note more closely. "Now, remind me again what is it I'm looking for?" he asked, *other than a little sleep,* he added silently.

"Find out who sent the notes and the flowers," Duke replied simply.

Wes raised a quizzical eyebrow. "This is important to you, isn't it?"

Duke was about to say no, that it was all one and the same to him, but it was upsetting Susan, but that would have been a lie and Wes had a knack of seeing through lies.

Maybe he shouldn't have come here, pushing the issue, Duke thought. He didn't want Wes picking through his business. But then, this wasn't about him, it was about Susan, about her safety. He was beginning to get worried that maybe whoever was sending these notes and the dead flowers wasn't exactly up for the most sane person of the year award. If that person turned out to be dangerous as well…

He shrugged. "She's afraid. I don't like seeing women threatened."

Wes looked at him knowingly. "You seeing Susan Kelley?" It wasn't really so much a question as it was a statement seeking verification.

Duke managed to tamp down his startled surprise. "What makes you say that?" he asked in a toneless voice.

"Because I'm a brilliant detective, because I've got fantastic gut instincts—" and then he gave Duke the real reason "—and because Maisie complained to me that you're going to ruin the family line by getting the Kelley girl pregnant."

Damn it, he thought Maisie and he had settled this. Apparently he needed to have another talk with her, Duke thought, annoyed. Out loud, he confirmed Wes's guess. "Yeah, maybe I'm seeing her."

"Either you are, or you're not," Wes pointed out, looking at him, waiting for an answer.

"Okay, I am. For now," he qualified, leaving himself a way out. "Now, are you going to look into this for her sometime before the turn of the next century?" he asked irritably. "Someone's been leaving these on her doorstep the last couple of weeks, along with bunches of dead flowers," he reiterated, in case Wes had forgotten.

"And you really don't have any idea who's been doing this?"

Duke looked down at his brother pointedly. "I wouldn't be talking to you if I did."

"Good point, although I'd rather not have one of my brothers turn vigilante on me. Especially not now when we're finally getting Damien out." He figured there was nothing wrong with issuing a veiled warning to his brother. If it didn't come out in so many words, there was more of a chance of Duke complying with it.

A cynical smile touched the corners of Duke's mouth. "When she first started getting them, Susan really thought that I was the one sending them."

Wes surprised him by nodding. "I can see why she might." Duke looked at him sharply. "You're so damn closed-mouthed, nobody ever knows what's going on in that head of yours. You're like this big, black cloud on the horizon. Nobody can make an intelligent guess if it's going to rain or just pass through. And you're always frowning. Hell, when I was a kid, I thought that scowl of yours was set in stone."

Duke blew out an impatient sigh. "I don't have time for memory lane, Wes. Just take a few hours away from the Walsh thing and look into this for me, okay?" He couldn't remember when he'd asked Wes for something, so he took it for granted that Wes's response would be in the affirmative.

He wasn't prepared for the slightly amused grin that curved his brother's mouth.

"What?" Duke demanded.

"You and Susan Kelley, huh?"

Duke's eyes narrowed to small, dark slits. "That is none of your business."

Wes would have been lying if he hadn't admitted that contradicting Duke stirred up more than a small amount of satisfaction. "Well, actually, with my being sheriff, it kinda is if for some reason the two of you being together made someone write these." He nodded at the note on his desk for emphasis. "And if we're talking personal—"

"We're not," Duke quickly bit off.

Wes ignored Duke's disclaimer and continued with his thought. "I think it's great that you've finally moved on and put that whole Charlene McWilliams thing behind you. Susan looks like a really great girl—and she's just what you need."

Duke was not about to admit anything, even if, somewhere in his soul, he secretly agreed with his brother's pronouncement. That was his business, not anyone else's. Just like he felt something lighting up inside of him every time he saw Susan was his business.

"I wasn't aware that I needed anything," Duke said, his voice a monotone.

"That just means that you need it more than the rest of us," Wes told him with a knowing smile. "Not a single one of the Almighty's creatures does better without love than with it."

Annoyed, Duke asked him with more than a small touch of sarcasm, "You thinking of becoming a philosopher now, too?"

Wes took no offense. He hadn't expected Duke to suddenly profess how he felt about the girl. Duke had trouble coming to grips with feelings, they all knew that.

"No, just happy someday, if the right woman crosses my path," Wes qualified.

Duke sighed and shook his head. He was not about to get into a discussion over this. "Just get back to me on that," he instructed, nodding at the note.

Wes rose and walked with his brother to the door. "Don't let that bit about being 'a servant of the people' fool you, big brother. Just so we're clear, I find this guy, *I'll* handle it, not you." There was no negotiation on this point.

Though he wouldn't say it in so many words, Duke gave his younger brother his due. "Whatever," he muttered as he walked out.

"Nice talking to you too, big brother," Wes said to Duke's back.

The phone in Susan's office rang as she got up to walk out for the evening. She looked longingly toward the doorway.

It wasn't like her to ignore a call. Susan was one of

those people who felt a compulsion to answer every phone that rang, whenever it rang. But she knew that if she picked up this time, she'd wind up leaving the office and town later than she wanted to.

She didn't want to have to amend her schedule. What she wanted to do was hurry home and get ready for her evening with Duke. Granted there was nothing special planned—just being together was special enough as far as she was concerned—but she wanted to take her time getting ready tonight. That meant actually indulging in a bubble bath for a decadent twenty minutes—fifteen minutes longer than she usually spent in the shower.

And there was this new scent she wanted to try out, something that she had ordered via the Internet and that smelled like sin in a bottle. She was anxious to wear something as different as possible from her usual cologne whose light scent brought fresh roses to mind. After being on the receiving end of all those dead roses, roses were the last thing she wanted wafting around her as she moved about.

Susan had almost made it out of the office when she finally stopped. Guilt got the better of her.

Turning around, she hurried back to her desk and picked up the receiver just as her answering machine clicked on.

"This is Susan," she told the caller, raising her voice above the recorded greeting. "Wait until the tape in the answering machine stops before talking."

But her instructions came too late. Whoever was on the other end of the line had hung up.

Well, she'd tried, she thought, replacing the receiver into its cradle. At least this way, she told herself silently, she didn't have to feel guilty.

Guilt was the last emotion she wanted lingering around when Duke was with her.

Glancing one last time at the package she was bringing home with her—she'd made beef tenderloin with a green chili and garlic sauce as well as a double serving of grilled vegetables for dinner tonight—she smiled and hurried out.

The dinner's warm, welcoming aroma followed her to her car and then filled up the space around her as she closed the door. Susan started up her car.

Ultimately, this aroma would probably tempt Duke more than the expensive perfume she just bought would, she thought.

But she hoped not.

Reaching home, she parked her car, grabbed her package and raced inside. It struck her, as she closed the door behind her, that she'd left it unlocked again. She was forever forgetting to lock the door when she left in the morning. But this was Honey Creek, she reasoned. Other than Mark Walsh's death—and those stupid notes along with the dead flowers—nothing ever happened here. It was a nice, safe little town.

Hurrying, she took the warming tray out of the cabinet and got it ready to be pressed into service once she finished her bubble bath. She put the package on the counter beside the tray and raced off to the bathroom.

Too excited to come close to relaxing, Susan shaved six minutes off her bubble bath and utilized that extra time fixing her hair and makeup.

She'd decided to show Duke that she wasn't just another fresh-scrubbed face. That she could be pretty—

maybe even more than a tad pretty—if she set her mind to it, given the right "tools."

So she carefully applied the mini battalion of shadows, mascara and highlighters she'd amassed and redid her hair three times before she was ultimately satisfied with the woman she saw looking back at her from the mirror.

Throwing on a light-blue, ankle-length robe to protect the shimmery royal-blue dress that only went half way down her shapely thighs, Susan hurried back to the kitchen. She wanted to do a few last-minute things to the dinner so she could put the meal out of her mind until it was time to serve it.

Just as she entered the kitchen, Susan could have sworn she saw something hurry past the large window located over the double sink.

Probably just some stray animal, lost, she decided, and looking to find its way back.

Aren't we all? she mused, grinning.

It wasn't unheard of to catch a glimpse of a stray deer every so often, although now that she thought about it, there'd been fewer sightings in the last couple of years.

That was the price of progress, a trade-off. Two-legged creatures instead of four-legged ones.

Plugging in the warming tray, she froze, listening. She was certain she'd heard a noise coming from the front of the house.

It *wasn't* her imagination. She *had* heard something.

Her parents—even her mother—didn't just come over without either calling first or at the very least, ringing the doorbell to give her half a second's warning before they walked in.

And she *knew* that Duke wouldn't play games like

this, making noise to scare her. The man didn't play games at all.

Grabbing a twelve-inch carving knife out of the wooden block that held the set of pearl-handled knives that her mother had given her for her catering business, Susan tightly wrapped her fingers around it.

"Is anyone there?" she called out.

Susan thought of the gun her father had tried to convince her into taking when she had moved in here. She wished now that she hadn't been so stubborn about it. A gun would have made her feel more in control of the situation.

It was probably nothing, she told herself as she inched toward the front of the house. Just the wind causing one of the larger tree branches to bang against the living-room bay window.

It was the last thing to cross her mind before the searing pain exploded at the back of her skull.

The next moment, everything went black.

Susan dreamt she was drowning. She struggled to reach the surface and gulp in air. It took her a beat to realize that she wasn't in the creek, desperately trying to swim for the bank while Mark Walsh tried to pull her back under. She was in her house.

And then she gasped, trying to breathe. Someone had just thrown water in her face. A lot of water, all at once.

Coughing and gasping, it took her another couple of beats before she became completely aware of her surroundings.

She *was* still in her house, in the kitchen. But instead of standing by the counter, she was sitting on a chair. Not just sitting but sealed onto it. Duct tape all but co-

cooned her waist and thighs, holding her fast against the wood. Her hands were bound behind her. She couldn't move no matter how hard she pulled against the silvery tape.

Afraid, wild-eyed, Susan looked around, trying to understand what was going on. Her head felt as if it was splitting in half, the pain radiating from the back of her skull to the front.

She couldn't see anyone but she *knew* that there was someone in the house with her. Someone who had hit her from behind and then bound her up like an Egyptian mummy. But who could have done this?

Maisie?

Linc?

And if not either of them, then who? And why?

Her thoughts collided as she struggled to control the hysteria that threatened to overwhelm her.

"Who's there?" she cried. "Why are you doing this? Show yourself," she demanded, doing her best to sound angry and not as afraid as she really was. "Show yourself so we can talk. You don't want to do this."

She heard someone moving behind her and tried to turn her head as far as she could in that direction. But she needn't have bothered. The person who had put her in this position moved into her line of vision.

"Oh, but I do," the thin-framed, weatherbeaten, nondescript man told her. "You can't even *begin* to understand how much I want to do this."

Susan stared at the man. He was maybe as tall as she was, maybe shorter. She didn't know him. His face meant nothing to her and no name came to mind. No frame of reference suggested itself.

Why did he hate her?

"Why?" she managed to ask hoarsely, fear all but closing up her throat. "Why do you want to tie me up like this?"

"I don't want to tie you up," he informed her condescendingly. "That's just a means to an end." He brought his face in close to hers. The man reeked of whiskey. Had he worked himself up, seeking courage in a bottle before going on this rampage? "I want to hurt you," he said, enunciating each word. "I want to make you slowly bleed out your life, just like she did."

This was a mistake. It had to be a mistake. She needed to get this man to talk, to make him see that what he was doing was crazy.

If nothing else, she needed to stall him. To stall him until Duke came to save her from this maniac.

"Like who did?" she asked urgently. "Who are you talking about?"

His face contorted, as if someone had just hit him in the gut and the pain was almost too much to bear. "My wife. My wife killed herself because that worthless scum you're playing whore for walked out on her." Again he stuck his face into hers. "Do you know how that feels?" he demanded. "Do you have *any* idea how it feels to know that your wife would rather kill herself than come back to you?"

He straightened up, reliving the memory in his mind. Staring off into space, he sucked in a long, ragged breath.

"I thought my gut had been ripped out when I had to go and identify her body. They found her in her car, her wrists slashed." There were angry tears shimmering in his eyes. The next second, the tears were replaced with rage. "Well, that's what I want Duke Colton to feel. I want him to feel like he's been gutted when he looks at what I've left behind for him."

Picking up the knife that she had dropped when he'd knocked her unconscious, Hank McWilliams held it for a moment, as if contemplating the would-be weapon's weight and feel.

A strange look came into his eyes as he looked back at her. "Had a notion to become a doctor once. Studied on my own. Didn't matter, though. Never got to be a doctor because there weren't enough money." The smile that slipped across his lips made her blood run cold. "But I know where every vital organ is. And I know how and where to cut a man so that he stays alive for a very long, long time." His smugness increased. "Same goes for a woman," he concluded, delivering the first cut so quickly, she didn't even see it coming.

Susan heard the shrill, bloody scream and realized belatedly that it was coming from her.

The next second she felt the sting of his hand as he slapped her across the face.

"Damn it, whore," he exclaimed, then seemed to regain control over himself. "My fault," he mumbled under his breath. "Forgot that you'd scream."

Leaving the knife on the floor for a second, Mc-Williams ripped off an oversize piece of duct tape and clamped it hard over her mouth. He smoothed it down over and over again to make sure it stayed in place.

"That should keep you quiet," he announced, deftly slicing her two more times in her chest and abdomen. As the blood began to flow, he laughed gleefully, his eyes bright and dancing. "This might go quicker than I thought," he told her, his tone as unhurried as if he was timing something in the oven instead of watching her life drain from her.

Susan struggled to stay conscious, trying to focus on what time it was. How long had she been out? Where was Duke?

And then she remembered. He'd said he was going to be late tonight.

Fear wrapped itself around her, making it all but impossible to breathe as the blade of the maniac's knife sliced through her flesh as quickly and easily as if she was only a stick of butter.

The duct tape stifled the scream that tore from her throat, diffusing it. Susan still screamed for all she was worth, her head spinning wildly from the effort and from the pain.

She was barely hanging on to consciousness by her fingertips.

He slashed into her flesh again, twisting the knife this time.

Chapter 15

Duke had worked at a quick, steady pace all afternoon, taking no breaks, creating shortcuts when he could. Though he told himself he was only being practical and that working this quickly would get him out of the sun faster—a sun that was beating down on him without mercy—he knew that he was just feeding himself a line of bull. That wasn't the real reason he was working this hard and he knew it.

The real reason had soft brown eyes that could melt a man's soul and even softer lips. Lips that made him forget about everything else. Lips that, for the first time in his life, actually made him glad to be alive instead of just feeling as if he was marking time until something of some sort of import happened.

For him, it already had.

He'd met someone he'd known, more or less, for most

of his life. Certainly for all of hers. Someone who, the more he saw her, the more he *wanted* to see her.

Damn, he didn't even know where all these complicated thoughts were suddenly coming from. What was going on with him anyway, Duke scolded himself as he drove up to Susan's house.

Stopping the truck, he took one last look at himself in the rearview mirror, angling it so that he could see if his hair still looked combed or if the hot breeze had ruffled it too much.

He'd taken a quick shower and changed before coming here but still looked sweaty. It had never bothered him before, but now it mattered that he looked his best.

Though he'd never told her, he liked the way Susan ran her fingers through his hair, liked the way she looked up at him, half innocent, half vixen. And when he came right down to it, he didn't know which half he liked better. Was a time he would have known, would have picked vixen hands down.

Now, though...

Tabling his thoughts, he got out of the truck. Duke walked up to Susan's front door and raised his hand to knock.

The sound of a man's voice, coming from within the house, stopped him. There wasn't another car parked in the driveway to give a clue as to who it may be.

That wasn't her father, he thought. The timbre of the voice was all wrong. Donald Kelley had a raspy, coated voice, the kind that came from decades of sipping whiskey on hot, summer nights. This voice belonged to someone else.

To another man.

Duke glanced at his watch. He was early, at least earlier than he'd told her he'd be. Was she "entertaining" someone else while she waited for him?

Well, why the hell not? It wasn't as if any pledges had been made between them. Hell, there wasn't even any wordless understanding. They were both free to do whatever they wanted with whomever they wanted.

Even so, the thought of Susan being with another man angered him more than he thought it would. More than he'd ever felt before.

He glared at the door. He could hear the man talking again.

The hell with her.

He didn't need this, didn't need the aggravation or the humiliation. Turning on his heel, he started to walk away. He was better off giving the whole breed a wide berth, just as he had before he'd gotten roped in by doe eyes and a shy smile.

Shy his as—

Duke's head whipped around toward the door.

Was that a scream? It sounded awfully muffled if it was. But what he had absolutely no doubt about was the streak of fear he'd heard echoing within the suppressed scream.

Making up his mind to go in, he tried the doorknob and found that it wouldn't give. She'd finally learned to lock her door, he thought.

There it was again. A muffled scream, he'd bet his life on it.

Duke's anger gave way to an acute uneasiness, which in turn gave way to fear, even though he couldn't logically have explained why.

Susan was in trouble. His gut told him so.

Instead of calling out to her, Duke braced his right

shoulder, tightened his muscles the way he did whenever he lifted one of the heavier bales of hay on his own and slammed his shoulder hard against the door.

It gave only a little.

With a loud grunt that was 50 percent rage and 50 percent fear, Duke slammed his aching shoulder into the door again. As he braced himself for another go-round, he caught a glimpse of Bonnie Gene and Donald coming out of their house and heading in his direction. There was a puzzled look on Bonnie Gene's face.

Had they heard the strange scream, too? Or were they coming because they'd heard him trying to break down Susan's door?

He had no time to explain what he was doing or why he was doing it. For the same mysterious reason that was making him try to break down her door, his sense of urgency had just multiplied tenfold.

The third meeting of shoulder to door had the door splintering as it separated itself from the doorjamb. What was left of the door instantly slammed into the opposite wall as Duke ran in, bellowing Susan's name at the top of his lungs.

In response he heard that same muffled, strange scream, even more urgent this time than before.

It took him more than half a minute to realize what was going on, the lag due to the fact that it all looked so surreal, literally as if it had been lifted from some bad slasher movie.

Susan had silver tape wrapped around over half her body, sealing her to one of her kitchen chairs. There was blood on her, blood on the floor and a deranged-looking man wielding a knife which he nervously shifted back and forth, holding it to Susan's throat, then aiming it toward Duke to keep him at bay. The man continued to move the knife back and forth in jerky motions, as if he couldn't decide which he wanted to do more—kill Susan or kill Duke.

Duke wasn't about to give the man a chance to make up his mind.

With a guttural yell that was pure animal, Duke sailed through the air and threw himself against Susan's attacker, knocking the man to the floor. The assailant continued to clutch his knife. Duke saw the blood on it.

Susan's blood.

Sick to his stomach, he almost threw up.

And then a surge of adrenaline shot through him. Duke grabbed the man's wrist, forcing him to hold the knife aloft where, he hoped, the sharp blade couldn't do any harm.

Restraining Susan's attacker wasn't easy. The man turned out to be stronger than he looked, or maybe it was desperation that managed somehow to increase his physical strength. Duke didn't know, didn't have the time to try to analyze it and didn't care. All he knew was that he had to save Susan at any cost, even if it meant that he would wind up forfeiting his own life in exchange.

It was at that moment, with adrenaline racing wildly through his veins as he faced down a madman with a knife, that Duke realized that without Susan, he didn't have a life, or at least, not one that he believed was worth living.

It was a hell of an awakening.

"Who the hell are you?" Duke bellowed as he continued to grapple with the man.

"I'm Hank McWilliams, the husband of the woman you killed," he replied angrily, stunning Duke.

McWilliams wrenched his hand free and slashed wildly at Duke's shoulder. He hit his target, piercing Duke's flesh and drawing blood. He also succeeded in enraging Duke further.

The fight for possession of the weapon was intense, but ultimately short if measured in minutes rather than damage. Disarming McWilliams amounted to Duke having to twist his arm back so hard that he wound up snapping one of the man's bones.

Sounding like a gutted animal, McWilliams's shrill scream filled the air.

Duke was aware of the sound of running feet somewhere behind him and cries of dismayed horror. Prepared for anything, he looked up to see Donald and Bonnie Gene charging into the house.

"I need rope to tie this bastard up," he yelled at Bonnie Gene, sucking in air. "Donald, call the sheriff. Tell my brother I caught the guy stalking Susan."

Grabbing a length of cord from one of the upper kitchen cabinets, Bonnie Gene ran back into the living room.

"Someone was stalking Susan?" she cried, alarmed.

Panting, Duke had already allowed Donald to take over holding McWilliams down. Donald had done it wordlessly by planting his considerable bulk on the man, who was lying facedown on the floor. Taking the rope from his wife, he tied McWilliams up as neatly as he'd tied any horizontally sliced tenderloin that had come across his work table.

Not waiting for an answer to her question, Bonnie

Gene hurried over to her daughter, who was struggling to remain conscious.

Duke had already begun removing the duct tape from around her. Susan was trying not to whimper but every movement he made, however slight, brought salvos of pain with it.

"I'm sorry," Duke kept saying over and over again as he peeled away the duct tape. "I'm trying to be quick about it."

"It's okay," Susan breathed, struggling to pull air into her oxygen-depleted lungs.

"Oh, my poor baby," Bonnie Gene cried, feeling horribly helpless. A sense of torment echoed through her as she took in her daughter's wounds.

Standing back as Duke worked to remove the rest of the duct tape, Bonnie Gene quickly assessed the number of wounds that Susan had sustained. A cry of anguish ripped from her lips when she reached her total.

Bonnie Gene swung around and kicked McWilliams in the ribs six times, once for each stab wound that her daughter had suffered. As she kicked, Bonnie Gene heaped a number of curses on the man her husband had no idea she knew. Donald looked at her with renewed admiration.

"You're going to be okay, Susan, you're going to be okay. I don't think the bastard hit anything vital," Duke told Susan as he looked over her wounds.

He felt his gut twisting as he assessed each and every one. As gently as he could, he picked Susan up in his arms and turned toward the door. He almost walked into Bonnie Gene, who was hovering next to him, trying hard not to look as frightened as she probably felt.

"I'm going to take Susan to the hospital," he told her mother.

Bonnie Gene bobbed her head up and down quickly, glad for the moment that someone had taken over.

"We'll use my car," she told him, digging into her pocket for her keys. "It's faster than your truck," she added when he looked at her quizzically.

"I'll get...blood...all over...it," Susan protested haltingly. The fifty-thousand-dollar car was her mother's pride and joy, her baby now that her children were all grown.

"Like I care," Bonnie Gene managed to get out, unshed tears all but strangling her. Getting out in front, she quickly led the way out of the house.

"Don't let him out of your sight until my brother gets here," Duke cautioned Donald just before he left the house with Susan.

"I'm not even going to let him out from under my butt," Donald assured him, raising his voice. "Just get my daughter to the hospital."

But he was talking to an empty doorway.

Looking back later, Duke had no idea how he survived the next few hours.

The moment Bonnie Gene drove them into the hospital's parking lot, he all but leaped out of the vehicle, holding an unconscious Susan in his arms, pressed against his chest. Silently willing her to be all right.

Terrified that she wasn't going to be.

A general surgeon was on call. One look at Susan and Dr. Masters had the nurses whisking her into the operating room to treat the multiple stab wounds on her torso. The surgeon tossed a couple of words in their general direction as he hurried off to get ready himself.

That left Duke and Bonnie Gene waiting in the hall as the minutes, which had flowed away so quickly earlier, now dragged themselves by in slow motion, one chained to another.

There was nothing to do but wait and wait. And then wait some more.

Duke wore a rut in the flat, neutral carpeting in the hallway directly outside the O.R. His brain swerved from one bad scenario to another, leaving him more and more agitated, pessimistic and progressively more devastated with every moment that went by.

Sometime during this suspended sentence in limbo, Donald arrived to ask after his youngest daughter and to tell them what had happened at the guest house after his wife and Duke had left. The sheriff had arrived soon after they drove off for the hospital, and Donald had quickly filled Wes in on what he knew, which wasn't much. After turning McWilliams over to the sheriff, Donald had sped to the hospital.

"She's a strong girl," Donald assured Duke, taking pity on the young man. "She takes after my side of the family."

Bonnie Gene looked up, leaving the dark corridors of her fears. Though she was trying to keep a positive outlook, it was still difficult not to give in to the fears that haunted every mother.

"Susan gets her strength from my side of the family," Bonnie Gene contradicted.

"Right now, she needs all the strength she can beg, borrow or steal from both sides," Duke told the pair impatiently. The last thing he was in the mood for was to listen to any kind of bickering.

Bonnie Gene rose, taking a deep, fortifying breath and doing her best to look cheerful, even as she struggled with the question of how this could have happened to her baby. And right under her nose, too.

She put her hand on Duke's shoulder, giving it a quick squeeze. "She'll pull through, Duke. Susan might not look it, but she's a fighter." Her eyes met Donald's for affirmation. "She always has been."

Duke made no response. He really didn't feel like talking. So, instead, he took a deep breath and just nodded, silently praying that Bonnie Gene was right.

With effort, he maintained rigid control over his mind, refusing to allow himself to think about what might have happened if he hadn't come when he had.

If he'd worked more slowly and arrived an hour later.

There was a definite pain radiating out from his heart. A pain, he was certain, he would have for the rest of his life if Susan didn't pull through.

"She didn't look very strong when they took her into the O.R." Until he heard his own voice, he wasn't even aware of saying the words out loud.

Bonnie Gene pressed her lips together, pushing back an unexpected sob.

"That's my Susan, soft on the outside, tough on the inside. You're not giving her enough credit," she told Duke. "But you'll learn."

The woman said that as if she believed that he and her daughter would be together for a long time, Duke noted. Bonnie Gene had more confidence in the future than he did, he thought sadly.

The next moment, the O.R. doors swung open, startling all three of them. It was hard to say who pounced on the surgeon first, Bonnie Gene, Donald or Duke.

But Duke was the first who made a verbal demand. "Well?"

Untying the top strings of his mask and letting it dangle about his neck, Dr. Masters offered the trio a triumphant, if somewhat weary smile.

"It went well. She's a tough one, luckily," he declared.

"I told you," Bonnie Gene said to Duke. She almost hit his shoulder exuberantly, stopping herself just in time, remembering that McWilliams had sliced him there and he'd had to have it treated and bandaged.

Duke wasn't listening to Bonnie Gene. His attention was completely focused on the surgeon. "Will she be all right?"

Masters looked a bit mystified as he continued filling them in. "Yes. Miraculously enough, none of her vital organs were hit. Don't know how that happened, but she is an extremely lucky young woman." He looked at the trio, glad to be the bearer of good news. "You can see her in a little while. She's resting comfortably right now, still asleep," he added. "A nurse will be out to get you once she's awake."

Duke didn't want to wait until Susan was awake. He just wanted to sit and look at her, to reassure himself that she was breathing. And that she would go on breathing. He slipped away from Susan's parents and went in search of her.

He slipped into Susan's room very quietly, easing the door closed behind him.

She did look as if she was sleeping, he thought. He fought the urge to reach out and touch her, to push a strand of hair away from her face and just let his fingertips trail along her cheek.

She was alive. Susan was alive. She'd come close to death today, but she was still here. Still alive. Still his.

He let out a long, deep breath that had all but clogged his lungs. He never wanted to have to go through anything like that again.

Seizing one of the two chairs in the room, he brought it over to her bed, sat down and proceeded to wait for Susan to wake up.

He didn't care how long it took, he just wanted to be there when she opened her eyes.

Chapter 16

Consciousness came slowly, by long, painfully disjointed degrees. Throughout the overly prolonged process, Susan felt strangely lightheaded, almost disembodied, as if she was floating through space without having her body weighing her down.

Was this what death felt like?

Was she dead?

She didn't think so, but the last thing she remembered was Duke carrying her to the car—her mother's car—and she was bleeding. Bleeding a lot and feeling weaker and weaker.

After that, everything was a blank.

Was heaven blank?

Struggling, Susan tried to push her eyelids up so that she could look around and find out where she was. But she felt as if her eyelids had been glued down. Not only that, but someone had put anvils on each of them for good measure. Otherwise, why couldn't she raise them at will?

She was determined to open her eyes.

Something told her that if she didn't open them, she was going to fade away until there was nothing left of her but dust. Dust that would be blown off to another universe.

She liked *this* universe.

This universe had her parents in it. And her siblings.

And Duke.

Duke.

Duke had saved her. Did that mean that he loved her? Whether he loved her or not, she didn't want to leave Duke, not ever.

With a noise that was half a grunt, half a whimper, she concentrated exclusively on pushing her eyelids up until she finally did it.

She could see.

And what she saw was Duke.

Duke was standing over her, looking worn and worried. More worried than she remembered ever seeing him. His left arm was in a sling, but he was holding her hand with his right hand.

He didn't believe in public displays of affection, she thought. But he was holding her hand. In a public place.

Was she dead?

"Duke?" she said hoarsely.

He'd never cried. Not once, in all his thirty-five years. Not when Damien was convicted of murder and they had taken him out of the courtroom in chains. Not even when that horse had thrown him when he was ten and had come damn near close to stomping him to death, only his father had jumped into the corral and dragged him to safety at the last minute, cursing his "brainless hide" all the way.

He hadn't cried then.

But he felt like crying now. Crying tears of relief to release the huge amount of tension that he felt throbbing all through him.

She was alive.

"Right here," he told Susan, his reply barely audible. Any louder and she'd be able to hear the tears in his throat.

"I know... I can...see...you," she answered, each word requiring a huge effort just to emerge. Her hand tightened urgently on his. "Charlene's...husband...tried to...kill...me."

"He won't hurt you any more," Duke swore. *Not even if I have to kill him with my bare hands,* he promised silently.

"He...didn't want to...hurt...me, he...wanted to... hurt...you," she told Duke, then rested for a second, the effort to talk temporarily draining her.

"Hurt me?" Duke echoed incredulously. Was she still a little muddled, reacting to the anesthetic? She'd been the one to receive all the blows, he thought angrily. Again he promised himself that if by some miracle, Hank McWilliams was ever released from prison, he was going to kill the man. Slowly and painfully, to make him pay for what he'd done to Susan. And even then it wouldn't be enough.

"Yes... By hurting...someone you...loved," she told him. A weak smile creased her lips. "I...guess...he... wasn't...very...smart."

Duke realized what she was saying. That McWilliams had made a mistake. But the man hadn't. McWilliams had guessed correctly. "No, I guess he's smarter than he looks," he told her pointedly.

Susan's eyes widened. The words were still measured, but were now less labored coming out. "That... would mean...that...you—"

"Love you," he finished the sentence for her. And then he smiled. "Yes, it would. And yes, I do."

This had been the hardest thing he had ever had to say. But today had taught him that not saying this would have taken an even heavier toll on him. Because he would have carried the weight of this lost opportunity around with him for the rest of his life.

Susan passed her hand over her forehead. She was back to wondering if she had indeed died. At the very least, "I...must be...hallucinating."

He smiled. "No, you're not. I'll say it again. I love you."

It was a tad easier the second time, he thought. But not by much. If he was going to say it the way he felt it, it was going to take practice. Lots and lots of practice.

"Maybe I'm...not...hallucinating," she allowed slowly. "Maybe this...is a dream...and if it is... I just won't...let...myself...wake up." Because hearing Duke say he loved her made her supremely happy and ready to take on the whole world—in small increments. "So, if that's...the case...if I'm...asleep...then I don't...have to worry...about sounding...like an idiot...when I...tell you...that I...love you."

"You wouldn't sound like an idiot. You *don't* sound like an idiot," he assured her softly.

So this was how it felt.

Love.

Exciting and peaceful at the same time. Duke grinned to himself. Who knew?

"Ask her to marry you already." Bonnie Gene's disembodied voice ordered impatiently from the hallway. She'd gone to fetch them both coffee and arrived back in time for this exchange. She'd been waiting outside the door for the last ten minutes. "I can't stand outside this door much longer."

Duke laughed, shaking his head. These Kelleys were a hell of a lively bunch. They were going to take some getting used to. In a way, he had to admit he was looking forward to it.

"So don't stand outside the door any longer. Come on in, Bonnie Gene," he urged.

The next moment, Susan's mother, carrying two containers of coffee, one in each hand, eased the door open with her back and came into the room.

"The heat of the coffee was starting to come through the containers," she informed them with a sniff, putting both coffees down on the small table. "I felt like I was standing outside in the hall forever, waiting for you to get around to the important part."

"And what makes you think I was going to get around to the 'important part'?" he asked, wondering if he should be annoyed at the invasion of his privacy, or amused that the woman just assumed that everything was her business. He went with the latter.

Bonnie Gene waved her hand, dismissing his attempt to be vague.

"Oh, please." She rolled her eyes. "You risked getting yourself killed to save my daughter, then, your shoulder bleeding like a stuck pig, you picked her up in your arms and looked like you were ready to carry her all the way to the next town on foot. Besides—" Bonnie looked up into his face and patted his cheek "—one look into your eyes and anyone would know how you feel."

"I didn't," Susan protested, weakly coming to her hero's aid.

"That's because you're still a little out of your head, my darling. You're excused." Taking her container back into her hands, Bonnie Gene removed the lid, then looked up at Duke pointedly. "All right, so when's the wedding?"

"Mother!"

Susan had used up the last of her available breath to shout the name as if it were a recrimination. It was one thing to kid around. It was completely another to put Duke on the spot like this.

In addition to beginning to really hurt like hell, Susan was now also mortified. Didn't her mother take any pity on her?

"As soon as she's well enough to pick out a wedding dress," Duke replied quietly, answering Bonnie Gene's question.

"Mother, please, you can't just—" And then Susan's brain kicked in, echoing the words that Duke had just uttered. Stunned, Susan attempted to collect herself. She had to ask. "Duke, did you just say something about a wedding dress?"

"He did," Bonnie Gene gleefully answered the question before Duke could.

"Whose?" Susan all but whispered. They'd established that she wasn't dead. But maybe she had a concussion.

"Yours," Duke told her, beating Bonnie Gene to the punch this go-round. And then he looked at the older woman who seemed so bent on being involved in all the facets of their lives. "You *are* going to stay home when we go on our honeymoon, aren't you?"

Delighted, Bonnie Gene smiled from ear to ear. "I don't think you two need any help there."

Duke breathed a genuine sigh of relief. For a second, he'd had his doubts. "Good."

"Hey, wait a minute," Susan did her best to call out, feeling completely out of it and ignored. "Haven't you forgotten something?"

With effort, she pushed the button that raised the back of the bed, allowing her to assume the semblance of a sitting position.

Duke thought for a moment, stumped. And then it came to him. "Oh, right." Duke reached for her with his free arm, lowering his head to hers in order to kiss her.

Susan put her hand up in front of her mouth, blocking access. "No, wait. I mean you didn't ask me."

He pulled his head back, looking at her. "Ask you what?"

Either the man had an incredibly short attention span, or she was just not making herself clear. "To marry you."

"Oh."

He had taken her compliance for granted. It hadn't occurred to him, after what they had just both been through, that she would turn him down. But maybe he was wrong. Maybe she didn't feel about him the way he did about her. Maybe this life-and-death experience had had a different effect on Susan, making her want to run into life full-bore and sample as much of it as she possibly could.

Because Bonnie Gene was looking at him expectantly, he went through the motions. Part of him was dreading the negative answer he might receive at the end. "Susan Kelley, will you marry me?"

"That's better." Pleased, Susan nodded her head in approval. "And yes, I'll marry you," she said with a deceptively casual tone, followed up with a weak grin. The grin grew in strength and size as she added, "Now you can kiss me."

"You going to give me orders all the time?" he asked, amused.

"No, I think you'll get the hang of all this soon enough." She glanced at Bonnie Gene. It was time for her mother to retreat. Far away. "Mother?"

"You want me to kiss him for you?" Bonnie Gene offered whimsically.

"Mother," Susan repeated more firmly this time, using all but the last of her strength.

With a laugh, Bonnie Gene raised her hands in total surrender. "I'm going, I'm going." But she stopped for a moment, growing a little serious. "Treat my daughter well, Duke Colton, or I will hunt you down and make you sorry you were ever born."

To his credit, he managed to keep a straight face. "Yes, ma'am."

Susan pointed toward the door. "Leave, Mother."

"Don't have to tell me twice," Bonnie Gene assured her, backing out of the room.

As the door closed behind her, a broadly grinning Bonnie Gene began to hum to herself.

One down, five to go.

* * * * *

New York Times and *USA TODAY* bestselling author **Cindy Dees** started flying airplanes while sitting in her dad's lap at the age of three and got a pilot's license before she got a driver's license. At age fifteen, she dropped out of high school and left the horse farm in Michigan where she grew up to attend the University of Michigan. After earning a degree in Russian and East European studies, she joined the US Air Force and became the youngest female pilot in its history. She flew supersonic jets, VIP airlift and the C-5 Galaxy, the world's largest airplane. During her military career, she traveled to forty countries on five continents, was detained by the KGB and East German secret police, got shot at, flew in the first Gulf War and amassed a lifetime's worth of war stories.

Her hobbies include medieval reenacting, professional Middle Eastern dancing and Japanese gardening.

This RITA® Award–winning author's first book was published in 2002, and since then she has published more than twenty-five bestselling and award-winning novels. She loves to hear from readers and can be contacted at www.cindydees.com.

Books by Cindy Dees

Harlequin Romantic Suspense

Soldier's Last Stand
The Spy's Secret Family
A Billionaire's Redemption
High-Stakes Bachelor
Code: Warrior SEALs
Undercover with a SEAL
Her Secret Spy

HQN Books

Close Pursuit
Hot Intent

Visit the Author Profile page
at Harlequin.com for more titles.

DR. COLTON'S
HIGH-STAKES FIANCÉE

Cindy Dees

This book is for all the generous and compassionate
people who volunteer in animal shelters, rescue
programs and animal protection programs
everywhere. I am brought to tears
often by your kindness and caring.
All of our lives—both human and nonhuman—
are made better by your loving work.

Chapter 1

Rachel Grant sighed down at her chipped and dirt-encrusted fingernails. What she wouldn't give to be at Eve Kelly's Salon Alegra right now, getting a manicure and not staring at a shelf of toilet parts in a hardware store. But such were the joys of home ownership on a shoestring budget.

Whoever said that men didn't gossip as much as women was dead wrong. But they would be right about one thing: Man-gossip left a lot to be desired in comparison to girl-gossip. Floyd Mason, owner of the hardware store, was gossiping with someone whose voice she didn't recognize the next row over in Paint, and, of course, she was shamelessly eavesdropping. Floyd drawled, "Seems like there's Colton boys all over town all of a sudden."

The customer replied, "I hear Damien Colton's back.

The missus sent me over here to get a dead bolt for the back door because of 'im."

Bless Floyd, for he replied, "Why's that? Damien didn't murder Mark Walsh the first time around or else the bastard wouldn't have turned up dead for real a few months ago."

"Yeah, but fifteen years in a penitentiary...that's gotta change a man. Make him hard. Mean. Maybe even dangerous."

She might have her own bone to pick with the Colton family, but she bristled at the suggestion that Damien had become a criminal. She'd never for a minute thought he was capable of murder, not fifteen years ago, and not now. She had half a mind to march around the corner and tell the guy so.

Thankfully, Floyd drawled, "Ahh, I dunno 'bout Damien bein' dangerous. Those Colton kids might'a been wild, but they was never bad. At least not that kind of bad."

"I hope you're right," the customer drawled. "Ever since Damien got outta jail, it's been like old-home week over at the Colton place. Wouldn't be surprised if they's all back in town by now to welcome home the prodigal son."

Rachel's heart skipped a beat in anticipation and then just as quickly thudded in dismay. Please God, let it not be *all* of the Coltons back home. She really, truly, never needed to see Finn Colton again as long as she lived. He'd been the best-looking boy in the high school. Maybe the entire town. Smartest, too. Was so effort-lessly perfect that she'd fallen in love with him before she'd barely known what had happened to her. Oh, and then he'd broken her heart for fun.

The bell over the hardware store's front door dinged, jolting her from a raft of old memories. Very old. Ancient history. Water *way* under the bridge—

"Speak of the devil!" Floyd exclaimed. "Long time, no see, boy! You're looking great. All growed up...got the look of your daddy about you."

Rachel glanced toward the front of the store. It took no more than a millisecond for certain knowledge to hit her that a Colton had just walked through that door. The brothers were all tall, broad-shouldered, hard men who dominated any room they entered. And one of them was here now. A wave of loss slammed into her. Its backwash was tempered by bits of humiliation, fear, and a few specks of nascent anger swirling around like flotsam. But mostly, it just hurt.

Rachel ducked, wishing fervently that the shelves were at least two feet taller than their five-foot-tall stacks. Which Colton was it? Several of them had left town after high school and gone on to bigger and better things than Honey Creek had to offer.

It didn't matter which Colton it was. She didn't want to see any of them. And she especially didn't want to see Finn. Her knees were actually shaking at the prospect. Lordy, she had to get out of here *now*. Preferably unseen. She randomly grabbed the nearest rubber toilet gasket and took off crawling on her hands and knees for the front of the store and the cash register. *Pleeease let me make it out of here. Let me be invisible. Let me make it to the front door—*

"Ouch!" She bumped into something hard, nose-first, and pulled up short. That was a knee. Male, covered in denim. And it smarted. She grabbed the bridge of her nose, which was stinging bad enough to make her eyes water.

"Lose something?" a smooth voice asked from overhead.

Oh. My. God. She knew that voice. Oh, how she ever knew that voice. It was dark and smooth and deep and she hadn't heard it in fifteen years. It had gained a more mature resonance, but beyond that, the voice hadn't changed one iota.

"I asked you a question, miss. Did you lose something?" the voice repeated impatiently.

Her mind? Her dignity? Definitely her pride.

She forced her gaze up along the muscular thighs, past the bulge that was going to make her blush fiercely if she dwelled on it, past the lean, hard waist beneath a black T-shirt, up a chest broad enough to give a girl heart palpitations, and on to a square, strong jaw sporting a sexy hint of stubble. But there was no way her gaze was going one millimeter higher than that. She was *not* looking Finn Colton in the eye. Not after he'd caught her fleeing the hardware store on her hands and knees.

"Uh, found it," she mumbled, brandishing the hapless gasket lamely.

"Rachel?" the voice asked in surprise.

Her gaze snapped up to his in reflex, damn it. She started to look away but was captured by the expression in his green-on-brown gaze. What was he so surprised at? That she was crawling around on the floor of the hardware store? Or maybe that she still lived in this two-bit town? Or that she looked like hell in ratty jeans and a worse T-shirt and had on no makeup and her hair half coming out of a sloppy ponytail? Or maybe he was just stunned that she'd dared to breathe

the same air as he, even after all these years. She hadn't
been good enough for him then; she surely wasn't good
enough for him now.

Her gaze narrowed. She had to admit Finn looked
good. More than good. Great. Successful. Self-assured.
The boy had become a man.

For just one heartbeat, they looked at each other. Really *looked* at each other. She thought she spotted something in his gaze. Longing, maybe. Or perhaps regret.
But as quickly as it flashed into his eyes that unnam-
able expression blinked out, replaced by hard disdain.

Ahh. That was more like it. The Finn Colton she
knew and loathed. "Finn," she said coldly. "You're
standing in my way. I was just leaving."

With a sardonic flourish of his hand, he stepped aside
and waved her past. *Jerk.* Watching him warily out of
the corner of her eye, she took a step. She noted that
his jaw muscles were rippling and abruptly recalled
it as a signal that he was angry about something. All
the Coltons had tempers. They just hung on to them
with varying degrees of success. Finn was one of the
calmer ones. Usually. He looked about ready to blow
right now, though.

Hugging the opposite side of the aisle, she gave him
as wide a berth as possible as she eased past. She made
it to the cash register and looked up only to realize that
just about everyone in the store was staring at her and
Finn. Yup, men were as bad as women when it came
to gossip.

She had to get out of there. Give them as little fodder
for the rumor mill as possible. She was finally starting
to get her life together, she had a new job, and she didn't
need some new scandal to blow everything out of the

water when she was just getting back on her feet. She fumbled in her purse for her wallet and frantically dug out a ten-dollar bill. The clerk took about a week and a half to ring up her purchase and commence looking for a small plastic bag to put her pitiful gasket in.

She snatched it up off the counter, mumbling, "I don't need a bag," and rushed toward the exit. But, of course, she couldn't get out of there without one last bit of humiliation.

"Miss! Miss! You forgot your change!"

Her face had to be actually on fire by now. She was positive she felt flames rising off her cheeks. She turned around in chagrin and took the change the kid held out to her.

"Don't you want your receipt? You'll need it if you have to return that—"

She couldn't take any more. She fled.

She didn't stop until she was safely locked inside her car, where she could have a nervous breakdown in peace. She rested her forehead against the top of the steering wheel and let the humiliation wash over her. Of all the ways to meet Finn Colton again. She'd pictured it a thousand times in her head, and not once had it ever included being caught crawling out of the hardware store in a failed effort to dodge him.

Knuckles rapped on her window and she jumped violently. She looked up and, of course, it was *him*. Reluctantly, she cracked the window open an inch.

"If you're going to faint, you should lie down. Elevate your feet. But don't operate a motor vehicle until any light-headedness has passed."

He might be a doctor, but that didn't mean he needed to lecture her on driving safety. Sheesh. He didn't even bother to ask if she was feeling all right! She snapped, "Why, I'm feeling fine, thank you. It was so kind of you to ask. I think I'll be going now. And a lovely day to you, too."

She rolled up her window and turned her keys in the ignition. Thankfully, her car didn't choose this moment to act up and coughed to life. She stomped on the gas pedal and her car leaped backward. Finn was forced to jump back, too, or else risk getting his toes run over. It might have been petty, but satisfaction coursed through her.

She pulled out of the parking lot with a squeal of tires that had heads turning up and down Main Street. How she got home, she had no real recollection. But a few minutes later, she became aware that she was sitting in her driveway with her head resting on the steering wheel again.

Finn Colton. Why, oh why, did he have to come back to Honey Creek after all these years? Why couldn't he just stay in Bozeman with his perfect job and a perfect wife, two point two perfect kids, and a perfect life? Heck, knowing him, he had a perfect dog and drove a perfect car, too.

All the joy had been sucked right out of this day. And she'd been so excited to cash her first paycheck and have a few dollars in her pocket to start doing some desperately needed repairs around the house. Cursing Colton men under her breath, she dragged herself into the house and got to work fixing the toilet.

The gossip network took under thirty minutes to do its work. She'd just determined that, although she'd miraculously managed to get the right-size gasket, her toilet was officially dead. She was going to have to replace all the tubes and chains and floaty things that made up its innards.

Her phone rang and she grabbed the handset irritably. "Hello."

"Hi, Raych. It's me."

Carly Grant, her sometimes best friend, sometimes pain in the ass, second cousin. They'd been born exactly one week apart, and they'd had each other's backs for their entire lives. Carly had stuck by her when no one else had after Finn dumped her, and for that, Rachel would put up with a lot of grief from her scatterbrained cousin. Rachel's irritation evaporated. "Hey. What are you doing?"

"I'm wondering why my home girl didn't call me to tell me she ran into the love of her life down at the hardware store. Why did I have to hear it from Debbie Russo?"

"How in the heck did she hear about it?" Rachel demanded.

"Floyd Mason told his wife, and she had a hair appointment at Eve's salon at the same time Debbie was having a mani-pedi."

Rachel sighed. Telephone, telegraph, tell a woman. Sometimes she purely hated living in a small town. Actually, most of the time. Ever since she'd been a kid she'd dreamed of moving to a big city. Away from nosy neighbors and wide open spaces…and cows. Far, far away from cows.

She'd have left years ago if it wasn't for her folks. Well, her mom, now that her dad had passed away. A sharp stab of loss went through her. It had been less than a year since Dad's last, and fatal, heart attack. Sometimes his death seemed as if it had happened a lifetime ago, muted and distant. And sometimes it seemed like only a few days ago complete with piercing grief that stole her breath away. Today was one of the just-like-yesterday days, apparently.

"So. Spill!" Carly urged.

"Finn Colton is *not* the love of my life!"

"Ha. So you admit that you did see him!"

"Fine. Yes. I saw him. I was crawling on my hands and knees, my rear end sticking up in the air, trying to make a break for it, and he walked right up to me."

Carly started to laugh. "You're kidding."

"I wish I were," Rachel retorted wryly. "I can report with absolute certainty that his cowboy boots are genuine rattlesnake skin and not fake."

"Oh, my God, that's hilarious."

Rachel scowled. She was *so* demoting Carly from BFF status. "I'm glad I amuse you."

"What did he say?" Carly asked avidly.

"Not much. He said my name, and I said his. Then I got the heck out of Dodge as fast as I could." She added as a sop to Carly's love of good gossip, "He did knock on the window of my car to tell me that I looked like crap—and that if I was going to faint, I shouldn't drive."

"What a jerk!" Carly exclaimed loyally.

Okay, she'd just regained her status as best friend forever.

"You'll have to fill me in on the details while we drive up to Bozeman."

Rachel groaned. She'd forgotten her promise to go with Carly to shop for a dress for the big celebration of the high school's hundredth anniversary, which was scheduled for next weekend in conjunction with the school's homecoming celebration.

"You forgot, didn't you?" Carly accused.

"No, no, I'll see you at three. But right now I have to go back to the hardware store and get more parts for my toilet."

"Hoping to see your favorite Colton brother again?"

"When they're having snowball fights in hell," she retorted. She slammed the phone down on Carly's laughter and snatched up her car keys in high irritation.

Finn threw his car keys down in high irritation. He remembered now why he hated Honey Creek so damned much.

His older brother, Damien, finished off his sandwich and commented, "Funny how you can want worse than anything in the world to get back home. And then you get here, and in under a week, you'd do anything to get away."

Finn rolled his eyes. Nothing like being compared to a recent ex-con and the analogy working. Especially since he'd been working like crazy for the last fifteen years to recover the family reputation from Damien's murder conviction. He dropped a brown paper bag from the hardware store onto the kitchen table. "Here are your fence fasteners. Need some help installing 'em?"

Damien shrugged. "Sure. If you don't mind getting those lily-white doctor hands dirty."

Finn scowled. "I grew up working a ranch. I didn't go completely soft in medical school."

"We'll see."

An hour later, Finn was forced to admit that compared to his massively muscled brother, he qualified as a bonified sissy. But the sweat felt good. They were restringing the barbed wire along the south pasture fence.

His hands were probably going to be blistered and torn tonight, but he wasn't about to complain after the lily-white doctor-hand crack.

Seeing Rachel Grant again had rattled him bad. He needed to get out and do something physical. Something strenuous that would distract him from memories of her. He'd loved her once upon a time. Been dead sure she was the one for him. And then she'd up and—

"Hey! Watch it!" Damien exclaimed.

Finn pulled up short, swearing. He'd almost whacked off his brother's hand with the sledgehammer.

"How 'bout I take that?" Damien suggested warily. "In fact, why don't we take a break and go get a bite to eat? Maisie made chili this morning."

As a bribe, it was good one. His oldest sibling might be nosy and overbearing, but the woman made a pot of chili that could put hair on a guy's chest. He stomped into the mud room of the main house a few minutes later. The warmth inside felt good after the hint of winter in the air outside.

"Hey, boys," Maisie called. "Pull up a chair."

Damien led the way into the enormous gourmet kitchen. "Watch out for him—" he hooked a thumb in Finn's direction "—Honey Creek's already getting on his nerves."

Maisie commented slyly, "The way I hear it, it's someone in Honey Creek who's getting on his nerves."

Finn's head jerked up. How did she do that? That woman knew more gossip faster than anyone he'd ever met. And she wasn't afraid to use it to get exactly what she wanted. Or to manipulate and hurt the people around her. She saw herself as the real matriarch of the clan in lieu of their reclusive and withdrawn mother and, as such, responsible for shaping and controlling the lives of everyone named Colton in Honey Creek. Maisie had been one of the reasons he'd bailed out of town as soon as he could after high school.

He moved over to the stove and served up two bowls of steaming chili. He plunked one down on the table in front of Damien and sat down beside his brother to dig into the other bowl.

He heard arguing somewhere nearby and looked up. Damien's twin brother, Duke, and their father, Darius, were going at it about something to do with the sale of this year's beef steers. Those two seemed to be arguing a lot since he'd gotten back two days before. Not that he had any intention of getting involved, but Duke seemed to have the right of it most of the time. But then, Darius always had been a dyed-in-the-wool bastard. A hard man taming a hard land.

Maisie sat down across from him. "So tell me. How'd your meeting with that Jezebel go?"

No need to ask who she was talking about. Maisie always had called Rachel "that Jezebel." He also knew Maisie would badger him until he told her exactly what she wanted to know.

He answered irritably, "We didn't have a meeting. I bumped into her in the hardware store." Amusement flashed through his gut at the recollection of her crawling for the door as fast as she could go. Her pert little derriere had been wiggling tantalizingly, and her wheat-blond hair had been falling down all around her face. Which was maybe just as well; it had partially hidden the sexy blush staining her cheeks.

"Come on. You know I'll find out everything anyway," Maisie said.

He sighed. Like it or not, she was right. "That's all there was to it. I saw Rachel, she saw me, she walked out. I bought Damien's fasteners and came home."

"You men. No sense of a good story. I swear, we'll never get on *The Dr. Sophie Show* unless I do all the work." She scowled and pressed, "What was she wearing? How did she look at you? Did she throw herself at you? Did she look like she's still scheming to land herself a Colton?"

Actually, Rachel had looked pissed. Although he didn't see why she had any right to be angry. She was the one who'd betrayed him and wrecked what they had between them. He supposed he did have Maisie to thank for finding out the truth about her before he'd gone and done anything dumb like propose to Rachel. How could she have—

He broke off the bitter train of thought. Her betrayal had happened a lifetime ago, when they were both kids. It was time to let it go. Beyond time. He was so over her. And as long as he was home in Honey Creek, he damned well planned to stay over her.

Chapter 2

Rachel's heart wasn't in shopping today. Not only was she still badly shaken after having seen Finn, but watching Carly spend money when she didn't have a dime to spare kind of sucked. Edna down at the Goodwill store had spotted a perfect dress for her a few weeks back and had offered to alter it to fit her slender frame, and for that Rachel was grateful. But she didn't dare dream of a day when she could waltz into a fancy department store like her cousin and buy a nice dress for a party. Not until her mother passed away and the nursing home bills quit coming. And as hard as it was to cover those bills, she dreaded them stopping even worse. Her mother was all she had left.

She felt guilty for secretly counting the days until her mother finally slipped away. But her mom was the only thing holding her in Honey Creek. Ever since they'd found out the summer after Rachel's sophomore year in high school that her mom had early-onset Alzheimer's disease, she'd been trapped here. Her dad had already had his first heart attack by then, and there was no question of Rachel going away to college. He needed her to stay home to help out with her mom.

Not that she was complaining. Well, not too much, at any rate. She loved her folks. They'd been a close-knit trio, and she'd been willing to set aside her big dreams of seeing the world for her parents. And after Finn had left, taking their dreams of escaping Honey Creek together with him, it had been easier to reconcile herself to sticking around.

But sometimes she imagined what it would have been like to travel. To see Paris and Rome and the Great Pyramids of Egypt. Heck, at this point, she'd be thrilled to see Denver or Las Vegas.

If only she knew why he'd dumped her like he had, so publicly and cruelly. The worst of it was that everyone else in town followed his lead and blamed her for whatever had broken them up. Nobody seemed to know exactly why Finn did such an abrupt one-eighty about her, but she was a girl from the poor side of town, and he was Honey Creek royalty. Clearly the whole thing must have somehow been her fault.

It was no consolation knowing that it wouldn't be much longer before she was free to leave. Her mother's health was fragile, and truth be told, her mother was so far gone into Alzheimer's she usually had no idea who Rachel was. She could probably leave town and go start a new life somewhere else and her mother wouldn't know the difference. But *she'd* know. And unlike Finn

Colton, she wasn't the kind of person who turned her back on the people she loved.

"Oh!" Carly exclaimed. "There it is!"

Rachel looked up, startled. Her cousin was making a beeline for the far display case. Must've spotted the perfect dress. Carly might be a ditz, but the girl had impeccable taste in clothes. Rachel tagged along behind, wondering if it were the little black number or the dramatic red dress that had caught Carly's eye.

Another woman was closing in from their right, and Rachel watched in amusement as both Carly and the other woman reached for the black dress at the same time.

"You take it."

"No, you take it."

Rachel finally caught up and suggested diplomatically, "Why don't you both try it on, and whoever it looks best on can have it?"

Laughing, the other two women dragged her into the dressing room to act as judge. Like she'd know fashion if it reached out and bit her. Her whole adult life had been a financial scramble, first to work herself through college online and have enough left over to give her folks a little money, then to help her folks fix up the house and now to pay for her mom's medical bills. What clothes she didn't make for herself she picked up at the Goodwill store, mostly. Of course, because she was a volunteer, she got dibs on the best stuff before it went out on the sales floor. Still. Just call her Secondhand Rose.

Carly disappeared into the dressing room first. The other woman turned out to be the chatty type and struck up a conversation. "Do you live here in Bozeman?"

"No. We live in Honey Creek. It's about twenty miles south of here as the crow flies."

"Oh!" the woman exclaimed. "I've heard of it! One of the doctors at the hospital is from there. I'm a nurse down at Bozemen Regional."

Rachel's stomach dropped to her feet. She had an idea she knew exactly which doctor her impromptu companion was talking about. Desperate to distract her, Rachel asked, "So, what's the special occasion you're shopping for?"

"A first date. With this cute radiologist. He just divorced his wife and is *very* lonely, if you catch my drift."

Rachel smiled. "Sounds like fun."

"So. Do you know Dr. Colton? I mean, to hear him talk about it, Honey Creek's about the size of a postage stamp. He says everyone knows everyone else."

Rachel nodded ruefully. "He's right. And yes, I went to school with Finn."

"Oh, do tell! He's so private. None of the nurses know much about him. Gimme the dirt."

Rachel winced. Nothing like being the dirt in someone's past. "There's not much to tell." She paused, and then she couldn't resist adding, "So, what's he up to these days? Is he married? Kids?"

"Lord, no. If he wasn't so...well, manly...we'd all think he was gay. He never dates. Says he has no time for it. But we nurses think someone broke his heart."

Great. She was dirt *and* a heartbreaker. But something fluttered deep inside her. He'd never gotten seriously involved with anyone else? Funny, that. She commented lightly, "Huh. I'd have thought the girls would've been hanging all over him. He was considered to be a good catch in Honey Creek."

The nurse laughed gaily. "Oh, he's got women hanging all over him, and he's a good catch in Bozeman, too. Thing is, he just doesn't seem interested. That is, assuming he doesn't have some secret relationship that none of us know about. But, it's pretty hard to hide your personal life in a hospital. We spend so much time working together, especially down in the E.R., you pretty much know everything about everybody."

So. No perfect wife and no two point two perfect kids yet, eh? What was the guy waiting for? He'd talked about wanting a family of his own when they'd been dating. Of course, in his defense, she'd heard that medical school was grueling. Maybe he just hadn't had time yet to get on with starting a family. Well, she wished him luck. With someone emphatically not her. She'd had enough of Colton-style rejection.

"What do you think?" Carly asked. She came out of the changing room and twirled in the clingy black dress.

The nurse laughed. "It's not even a contest. That dress was made for you. I'm not even trying it on. I'll go find another one."

Carly hugged the woman. "C'mon. I'll help you. I have a great eye for fashion. I saw a red satin number that would be a knockout with your hair color..."

Rachel sat in the deserted dressing room. A few plastic hangers and straight pins littered the corners. Why was she so depressed to hear about Finn's single state? Maybe because it highlighted her own lack of a love life. At least he was still a good catch. Truth be told, she'd never been a good catch, and everyone had thought their dating in high school was an anomaly to begin with.

His older sister, Maisie, had called her a phase. Said that Rachel was Finn's rebellion against what all his family and friends knew to be the right kind of girl for him. Yup—dirt, a heartbreaker and the anti-girlfriend. That was her.

"Raych? You gonna sit there all day?"

She looked up, startled. "Oh. Uhh, no. I'm coming."

"So when do I get to see this secret dress you've found for the homecoming dance?" Carly asked as they walked out of the mall.

Rachel rolled her eyes. "We're not in high school anymore, you know."

"Aww, come on. Don't be a spoilsport. With the hundredth anniversary of the school and all, *everyone's* coming back for homecoming."

Rachel grimaced. At the moment, a party sounded about as much fun as a root canal. She replied reluctantly, "My dress is a surprise."

"Fine. Have it your way. Maybe if you're lucky, Finn will stick around long enough to go to the dance."

"Oh, Lord. Can I just slit my wrists now?"

Carly laughed. "You've got it all wrong. This dance is your chance to show the jerk what he's missing. It's all about revenge, girlfriend."

She sighed. "If only I had your killer instinct."

"Stick with me, kid. We'll have you kicking men in the teeth in no time."

There was only one man she wanted to kick in the teeth. And now that Carly mentioned it, the thought of sashaying into that dance and telling him to go to hell made her feel distinctly better.

But by Monday morning, Rachel's bravado had mostly faded. Another set of bills had come in from the nursing home and she'd had to empty her bank account to cover them. Thank God she'd landed this job at Walsh Enterprises. Craig Warner, the chief financial officer, had actually been more interested in her accounting degree than her tarnished reputation and past association with the Coltons. Her next paycheck would arrive this Friday, and then, good Lord willing, she'd be able to start digging out of the mountain of medical bills.

"Good morning, Miss Grant."

She looked up as Craig Warner himself walked through the cubicle farm that housed Walsh Enterprises' accountants and bookkeepers. He paused beside hers. "Good morning, sir."

"How's the new job coming?"

"Just fine. I'm so grateful to be here."

The older man smiled warmly. "We're glad, too, Miss Grant. Let me know if you have any questions. My door's always open."

Enthusiastically, she dived into the financial records of Walsh's oil-drilling venture. Craig had asked her to audit the account with the expectation that she would take over responsibility for it afterward.

She'd been working for an hour or so when she ran into the first snag. Several of the reported numbers didn't add up to the receipts and original billing documents. Who'd been responsible for maintaining this account? She flipped to the back of the file and frowned. Whoever had signed these papers had done so in a completely illegible scrawl. No telling who'd managed the account. She flipped farther back into the earlier records. Still that indecipherable scribble. Until fifteen years ago. Then a signature jumped off the page at her as clear as a bell. Mark Walsh.

Walsh, as in the founder of Walsh Enterprises. The

same Mark Walsh who'd been found murdered only weeks ago. A chill shivered down her spine. How creepy was that, looking at the signature of a dead man? His hand had formed those letters on this very paper.

She went back to the more recent documents and corrected the error. Good thing she'd spotted it before the IRS had. It was the sort of mistake in reporting profits that could've triggered a companywide tax audit. Relieved, she moved on with the review.

By the time she found the third major discrepancy, she was certain she wasn't looking at simple math errors. Something was *wrong* with this account. She double-and triple-checked her numbers against the original documents. There was no doubt about it. Somebody had lied like a big dog about how much money this oil-drilling company had made. Over the years, *millions* of dollars appeared to have been skimmed off the actual income.

What to do? Now that he was tragically dead, was Mark Walsh a sacred cow? Would she be fired if she uncovered evidence that maybe he'd been involved in embezzlement? Who had continued the skimming of monies after he'd supposedly died the first time? Had someone within Walsh Enterprises been in league with Mark Walsh to steal money for him? Had this been where Walsh had gotten funds to continue his secret existence elsewhere for the past fifteen years?

His family had already been through so much. And now to heap criminal accusations on top of his murder? Oh, Lord, she needed this job so bad. The last thing she wanted to do was rock the boat. And it couldn't possibly help that for most of her life her name had been closely associated with the Coltons. There hadn't been any love lost between the Walshes and Coltons since even before Mark Walsh's first murder, the one supposedly at the hands of Damien Colton.

But what choice did she have? She would lose her CPA license if she got caught not reporting her findings. She scooped up all the documents and the printouts of her calculations and put them in her briefcase. Her knees were shaking so bad she could hardly stand. But stand she did. Terrified, she walked to the elevator and rode upstairs to the executive floor. Craig Warner's secretary looked surprised to see her, almost as surprised as Rachel was for being here. The woman passed Rachel into the next office, occupied by Lester Atkins, Mr. Warner's personal assistant. Rachel wasn't exactly sure what a personal assistant did, but the guy looked both busy and annoyed at her interruption.

"Hi, Mr. Atkins. I need to speak with Mr. Warner if he has a minute."

"He has an appointment in about five minutes. You'll have to schedule something for later."

Disappointed, she turned to leave, but she was intercepted by Mr. Warner's secretary standing in the doorway. "If you keep it quick, I'm sure Mr. Warner won't mind if you slip in."

Rachel felt like ducking as the secretary and Lester traded venomous looks. She muttered, "I'll make it fast."

Actually, she loved the idea of not getting into a long, drawn-out discussion with Mr. Warner. She'd just float a teeny trial balloon to see where the winds blew around here and then she'd bail out and decide what her next move should be. In her haste to escape Lester's office, she ended up barging rather unceremoniously into Mr. Warner's.

He looked up, startled. "Rachel. I didn't expect to see you this soon."

She smiled weakly. "Well, I've hit a little snag and I wanted to run it by you."

Craig leaned back in his chair, mopping his brow with a handkerchief before stuffing it in his desk drawer. "What's the snag?"

"I was comparing the original receipts against the financial statements of the oil-drilling company like you asked me to, and I found a few discrepancies. I'm afraid I don't know much about Walsh Enterprises' procedure for handling stuff like this. Do we just want to close the books on it and move on, or do you want me initiate revising the financial statements?"

Craig frowned and she thought she might throw up. "How big a discrepancy are we talking here?"

She squeezed her eyes shut for a miserable second and then answered, "Big enough that the one person whose signature I can read would be in trouble if he weren't already dead."

"Ahh." Comprehension lit Craig's face. She thought she heard him mutter something under his breath to the effect of, "The old bastard," but she couldn't be sure.

The intercom on his desk blared with Lester announcing, "Mr. Warner, your eleven o'clock is here."

Rachel leaped to her feet with alacrity. Her need to escape was almost more than she could contain. She had to get away from Warner before he fired her.

He stood up. "I've got to take this meeting. We'll talk later."

She nodded, thrilled to be getting out of here with her job intact.

"And Miss Grant?"

She gulped. "Yes, sir?"

"Keep digging."

He was going to support her if she found more problems. Abject gratitude flooded her. God bless Craig Warner. Weak with relief, she stepped into Lester's office. And pulled up short in shock. The last person she'd ever expect to see was standing there. And it was *not* a nice surprise. "Finn!" she exclaimed. "What on earth are you doing here?"

He arched one arrogant eyebrow. "Since when is what I do any of your business?"

Good point. But had she not been standing well within earshot of her boss, she might have told him to take his attitude and shove it. As it was, she threw him a withering glare and said sweetly, "Have a nice day." *And go to hell,* she added silently.

"Finn. Thanks so much for coming," Craig Warner said from behind her. "I know it's strange in this day and age to ask a doctor to make a house call—"

Lester pulled the door discreetly closed and Rachel heard no more. Was Craig Warner sick? He looked okay. Maybe he was a little pale and had been perspiring a bit, but the guy had a stressful job. And why call a specialist like Finn? Last she heard, he was an emergency internist—not a family practitioner.

She started back to her desk, her thoughts whirling. *Keep digging.* What exactly did Warner expect her to find? And why *had* Finn agreed to see Craig in his office? Why not tell the guy to call his own doctor? Maybe Finn had come over here to wreck her new job.

After all, he'd successfully wrecked just about every other part of her life. Without a doubt, the worst part of living in a small town was the insanely long memory of the collective populace. You made one mistake and it was never forgotten, never forgiven.

She worked feverishly through the afternoon and found more and more places where money had been skimmed off of the profits of the oil-drilling company and disappeared. She'd have stayed late and continued working if tonight she hadn't volunteered down at the senior citizens' center. It was bingo night, and the retirees didn't take kindly to any delays in their gambling.

Finn rubbed his eyes and pushed back from the computer. He'd been searching various medical databases for symptoms that matched Craig Warner's but so far had come up with nothing. The guy was definitely sick. But with what? His symptoms didn't conform to any common disease or to any uncommon diseases that he could find, either. He'd begged Craig to go to Bozeman and let him run tests there, but Craig had blown off the suggestion. He'd said he just needed some pills to calm his acid stomach and wasn't about to make a mountain out of a molehill.

But in Finn's experience, when a non-hypochondriac patient thinks he's sick enough to seek medical advice, it usually isn't a molehill at all.

He dreaded going home to face more of Maisie's grilling over his latest encounter with his ex-girlfriend. For she'd no doubt heard all about it. She had a network of informants the FBI would envy.

It had been a nasty shock running into Rachel like that today at Walsh Enterprises. The woman was sandpaper on his nerves. As if he fell for a second for that syrupy-sweet act of hers. He knew her too well to miss the sarcasm behind her tone of voice. Once it would've made him laugh. But now it set his teeth on edge. He'd been prepared to act civilized toward her when he'd come back to Honey Creek, but if she was determined to make it a war between them, he could live with that.

Muttering under his breath, he pushed to his feet and headed out of Honey Creek's small hospital.

"What're you doing here, bro?"

Finn pulled up short at the sight of his brother, Wes. It still looked funny to see him in his sheriff's uniform and toting a pistol. Wes had been as big of a hell-raiser as the rest of the Colton boys. Finn supposed there was a certain poetic justice in Wes being the guy now who had to track down wild kids and drag them home to their parents.

Belatedly, Finn replied, "I was just using the hospital's computer to look up some medical information on their database."

"Trying to figure out how to poison certain of the town's females, maybe?"

Finn snorted. "Yeah. Maisie. That woman gets nosier every time I see her."

Wes shook his head. "Sometimes I wonder if they switched her at birth and Mom and Dad brought home the wrong baby. I stopped by to see if you'd want to get a bite to eat?"

"Yeah, sure. Lily working late tonight?"

"Mother-daughter Girl Scout thing. I'm baching it for supper. I saw your truck in the parking lot."

Finn walked out onto the sidewalk with Wes. It was strange enough thinking of his older brother as sheriff. But a family man, too? That was downright weird. It made Finn a little jealous, though. He'd been so sure he and Rachel would have a passel of towheaded ankle-biters by now. Funny how things turned out.

The sun was setting, outlining the mountains in bloodred and throwing a kaleidoscope of pinks and oranges and purples up into the twilight sky. His thoughts circled back to Wes's comment about Maisie not belonging to the family. He commented reflectively, "I dunno. Sometimes I see a bit of Dad in Maisie. The two of them get an idea stuck in their craw and they won't let it go."

Wes laughed. "Right. Like the rest of us Coltons aren't that same way? Stubborn lot, we are."

Finn grinned. "Speak for yourself, Sheriff. I'm the soul of patience and reason."

Guffawing, Wes held the door to his cruiser open for him. "Then you won't mind paying for supper, will you, Mr. Patience and Reason?"

Finn cursed his brother good-naturedly. He didn't mind, though. He made decent money as a physician, and public servants didn't rake in big bucks. He did roll his eyes, though, when Wes drove them to Kelley's Steakhouse, which was without question the most expensive restaurant in town. They ordered steaks with all the trimmings, and then Finn picked up the conversation. "How's the murder investigation coming?"

Wes shrugged. "Frustrating. There are damned few clues, and everywhere I look I find another suspect with a motive for killing Walsh."

"No surprise there," Finn commented. "He wasn't exactly cut out for sainthood."

"No kidding. It just stinks that Damien had to pay for something he didn't do."

They fell silent, both reflecting on the bum deal life had dealt their brother. Finn had visited Damien regularly in jail and tried to be supportive, but a little worm of guilt squirmed in his gut. Damien had always sworn he didn't kill Walsh. Turned out he'd been telling the truth all along. They all should've tried harder to get him exonerated.

Fifteen years was a hell of big chunk of a person's life to throw away. It hardly seemed like that long to him, but he imagined it had felt like twice that long to Damien.

It seemed like only yesterday Finn had been in high school, excited to play in the district football championship, dating the prettiest girl in the whole school, and counting the days until he was going to blow this popsicle stand for good. Of course, Rachel had a couple more years of high school to go before she could join him, but then…then they were going to run away together and see the world.

And it had all changed with a single phone call. He'd never forget his sister Maisie's voice, delivering the news that had shattered his world—

"Earth to Finn, come in."

He blinked and looked up at his brother. "Sorry. Was just remembering stuff."

"Yeah, Honey Creek has that effect on a soul, doesn't it? Want go down to the Timber Bar and get a beer? I'm off duty."

"Sounds great. But you're paying, cheapskate."

Chapter 3

It was nearly midnight when Rachel pulled into her driveway. The bingo had ended at ten, but the usual volunteers who cleaned up hadn't shown up tonight. Folks knew she was single and had no life of her own, so they didn't hesitate to recruit her for the crap jobs that required sticking around late. And of course, she was too much of a softie to say no.

She got out of her car and locked it. The weather had turned cold and it felt like snow. Soon, winter would lock Honey Creek in its grip and not let go until next spring. She made a mental note to get out the chains for her tires and throw them in the trunk of her car.

She headed across the backyard under a starry sky so gorgeous she just had to stop and look at it. But then a movement caught her attention out of the corner of her eye and she lurched, startled. That was something or someone on her back porch!

She fumbled in her purse for the can of mace that swam around in the jumble at the bottom of it. Where was that can, darn it? Whoever it was could rob her and be long gone before she found it at this rate! She ought to keep the thing on her keychain, but it was bulky, and this was Honey Creek. Nothing bad ever happened here. Not until Mark Walsh's murder. Why hadn't it occurred to her before now that she ought to be more careful?

Whoever was on the porch moved again slightly. The intruder appeared to be crouching at the far end of the porch near the back door.

"I see you!" she shouted. "Go away before I call the police!"

But the intruder only slinked back deeper in the shadows. Her eyes were adjusting more to the dark, and she could make out the person's shape now. There. Finally. Her fingers wrapped around the mace can. She pulled it out of her purse and held it gingerly in front of her like a lethal weapon.

"I swear, I'll use this on you. Go on! Get out of here!"

But then she heard something strange. The intruder whimpered. She frowned. What was up with that? Surely she hadn't scared the guy that bad. She heard a faint scrabbling sound…like…claws on wood decking.

Ohmigosh. That wasn't a person at all. It was some kind of animal! She was half-inclined to laugh at herself, except this was Montana and a person had to have a healthy respect for the critters in this neck of the woods.

She peered into the shadows, praying she wasn't toe to toe with a mountain lion. She wasn't. Actually, the creature looked a little like a wolf. Except he was too fuzzy and too broad for a wolf. They were leaner of build than this guy. Nope, she was face-to-face with a dog.

She lowered the can of mace and spoke gently, "What's the matter, fella? Are you lost?"

Another whimper was the animal's only reply.

She squatted down and held out her hand. Okay, so a stray dog wasn't exactly the safest thing in the world to approach cold, either, but she was a sucker for strays. Heck, she'd been collecting them her whole life. *Yeah, and look where that had gotten me,* a cynical voice commented in the back of her head.

The dog took a step forward, or rather hopped. He was holding his right rear leg completely off the ground. "Oh, dear. Are you hurt? Let me go inside and put down my purse and turn on a light and then we'll have a look at you."

She hurried into the kitchen and dumped her purse and mace canister on the table. She turned on the lights and opened the back door. "Come here, Brown Dog. Come."

The dog cringed farther back behind an aluminum lawn chair. She squatted down and held out her hand. The dog leaned like it might take a step toward her and then chickened out and retreated even farther behind the chair. If she knew one thing about frightened animals, it was that no amount of coaxing was going to get them to go where they didn't want to go. Looked like she had to go to the dog.

"Hang on, Brown Dog. Let me get some more light out there and then just have a look at you on the porch. Would that make you feel better?"

She kept up a stream of gentle chatter as she went inside, opened all the blinds and flooded the back porch with light. She stepped back outside. And gasped. The entire far end of her porch was covered with blood. As she watched, the dog staggered like it was nearly too weak to stay on its feet. Even though the dog had a thick, shaggy coat, she could still see hip bones and shoulder blades protruding. The creature was skeletal, his eyes sunken and dull in his skull.

And then she caught sight of his right hind leg. It was a bloody, mangled mess with white bone sticking out of a gaping wound she could put several fingers into. For all the world, it looked like he'd been shot. And the bullet looked to have nearly ripped his leg off.

Oh, God. This was way beyond her paltry skills with antibiotic cream and bandages. The sight of the wound nearly made her faint, it was so gory. She had to call a vet, and *now.* Dr. Smith, Honey Creek's long-time veterinarian, retired a few months back, and the local ranchers had yet to attract another one to town. She'd have to call someone in Bozeman. She raced into the house and pulled out the phone book, punching in the first number she found.

"Hello," a sleepy female voice answered the phone.

She blurted, "Hi. A dog is on my back porch. He's been shot and he's in terrible shape. I need a veterinarian to come down to Honey Creek right away!"

"I'm sorry, dear, but my husband doesn't cover that far away. And besides, he's out on a call. Said he'd be gone most of the night."

Oh God, oh God, oh God. *Breathe, Rachel.* "Is there another vet in the area I can call?"

"I'm sorry. I don't know any small-animal vets who'll go to Honey Creek. You'll have to bring the dog up to

Bozeman. Can I take your number and have my husband call you? He may have a suggestion."

No way could she pick up that big dog by herself and hoist him into her car. And even if she did manage it, she suspected the dog on her porch wasn't going to live another hour, let alone through a long drive over mountain roads. It might be twenty miles as the crow flew to Bozeman, but the drive was considerably longer. Especially at night, and especially when it got cold. Even the slightest hint of moisture on the roads would freeze into sheet ice in the mountains. "Thanks anyway," Rachel mumbled. "I'll figure out something else."

She hung up, thinking frantically. Now what? She needed someone who could handle a gunshot wound. A doctor. Maybe she could take the dog down to the local emergency room—

No way would they let her in with a stray dog carrying who knew what diseases. She swore under her breath. She got a bowl of water for the dog and carried it outside. Tears ran down her face to see how scared and weak he was and how voraciously he drank. He was *dying.* And for who knew what reason, he'd wandered up to *her* porch. She *had* to get him help.

Without stopping to think too much about it, she pulled out her cell phone and dialed the phone number that hadn't changed since she was in high school, and which she'd had memorized for the past decade and more.

"Hello?" a gruff male voice answered.

She couldn't tell which Colton it was, but it definitely wasn't Finn. She spoke fast before her courage deserted her. "I need to speak to Dr. Finn Colton. This is a medical emergency. And please hurry!"

While she waited a lifetime for him to come to the phone, the dog lay down on the porch, apparently too weak to stand anymore. Panic made her light-headed. He was dying right before her eyes!

"This is Dr. Colton."

"Oh, God, Finn. It's Rachel. You have to come. I tried to call a doc in Bozeman but he can't come and there's so much blood from the gunshot and I don't know what to do and I think I'm going to faint and please, there's no one else I can call—"

He cut her off sharply. "Unlock your front door. Lie down. Elevate your feet over your head. And breathe slowly. I'll be right there."

The phone went dead.

Why would she put her feet up? Time was of the essence right now. She ran into the kitchen and grabbed all the dish towels out of the drawer. The dog let her approach him and press a towel over his bloody wound, indicating just how close to gone he was. Pressure to slow the bleeding. That's what they said in her Girl Scout first-aid training about a century ago.

The dog, which she noted vaguely was indeed a boy, whimpered faintly. "Hang on, fella," she murmured. "Help is on the way." She stroked his broad, surprisingly soft head and noticed that his ears were floppy and soft and completely out of keeping with the rest of his tough appearance. His eyes closed and he rested his head in her hand. The trust this desperate creature was showing for her melted her heart.

Oblivious to the pool of blood all over her porch, she sat down cross-legged beside the dog and gathered the front half of his body into her lap. He was shivering. She draped the rest of the towels over him and cradled him close, sharing her body heat with him. "It'll be all right. Just stay with me, big guy. I promise, I'll take care of you."

The dog's jaw was broad and heavily muscled, somewhat like a pit bull. Maybe half pit bull and half something fuzzy and shaped like a herding dog. Underneath the layer of blood he was brindled, brown speckled with black.

"Hang in there, boy. Help is on the way. Finn Colton's the one person in the whole wide world I'd want to have beside me in an emergency. He'll fix you right up. You just wait and see."

Finn tore into his bedroom, yanked on a T-shirt, grabbed his medical bag and sprinted for the kitchen. He snatched keys to one of the farm trucks off the wall and raced out of the house, ignoring a sleepy Damien asking what the hell was going on.

He peeled out of the driveway, his heart racing faster than the truck. And that was saying something, because he floored the truck down the driveway and hit nearly a hundred once he careened onto the main road.

"Hang on, Rachel," he chanted to himself over and over. "Don't die on me. Don't you dare die on me. We've got unfinished business, and you don't get to bail out on me by croaking," he lectured the tarmac winding away in front of his headlights.

He'd followed her home from the hardware store this morning—at a distance of course, where she wouldn't spot him. He'd been worried at how she looked in her car in the parking lot. It was nothing personal, of course, just doctorly concern for her well-being. Good thing he had followed her, because he knew where she lived now. Turned out she was living in her folks' old place. On the phone, she'd sounded on the verge of passing out from blood loss. And a gunshot? Had there been an intruder in her house? An accident cleaning a weapon? What in the hell had happened to her? First Mark Walsh, and now this. Was there a serial killer in Honey Creek?

He'd call Wes, but he'd left his cell phone back on his dresser at home, he'd been in such a rush to get out of there. He'd have to call his brother after he got to Rachel's place. And after he made sure she wasn't going to die on him.

"Hang on, baby. Don't die. Hang on, baby. Don't die—" he repeated over and over.

In less time than Rachel could believe, headlights turned into her driveway and a pickup truck screeched to a halt behind her car. Finn was out of the truck, medical bag in hand before the engine had barely stopped turning.

"Rachel!" he yelled.

"I'm right here," she called back more quietly. "No need to wake the entire neighborhood."

He raced up to her, took one look at the blood soaking her clothes and flipped into full-blown emergency-room-doctor mode. "Where's the blood coming from? How did you get hurt? I need you to lie down and get these towels off of you—"

"Finn."

"Be quiet. I need to get a blood pressure cuff on you. And let me call an ambulance. You're going to need a pint or two of blood—"

"Finn."

"What?"

"I'm not hurt."

"Are you kidding? With all this blood? Shock can mask pain. It's not uncommon for gunshot victims not to be aware that they've been shot for a while. Where did the bullet hit you?"

"I wasn't shot. He was."

She pulled back the largest towel to reveal the dog lying semiconscious in her lap.

"What the—"

"I'm not hurt. The dog was. Please, you've got to help him. He's dying."

Finn pulled back sharply. "I don't do animals."

"But you do bullet wounds, right?"

"On humans."

"Well, he's a mammal. Blood, bone. Hole in leg. Pretty much the same thing, if you ask me."

Finn rose to his feet, his face thunderous. "You scared ten years off my life and had me driving a hundred miles an hour down mountain roads in the middle of the night, sure you were dying, to come here and treat some *mutt?*" His voice rose until he was shouting.

Oh, dear. It hadn't occurred to her that he'd think she was shot. And he'd driven a hundred miles an hour to get to her? Something warm tickled the back side of her stomach.

"Finn, I'm sorry if I scared you. I was pretty freaked out when I saw all the blood. I called a vet in Bozeman. But he's out on a call that's supposed to take all night and his wife said no small-animal vet would make a house call to Honey Creek anyway. And it's not like I could take the dog to the Honey Creek hospital. You're the only person I know of in town who can take care of a serious gunshot wound and make a house call."

"I'm going home." He picked up his bag and turned to go.

"Wait! Finn, please. I—" she took the plunge and bared her soul "—I've got no one else."

He turned around. Stared down at her, his jaw rigid. Heck, his entire body was rigid with fury.

"I'm sorry for whatever I've done in the past to treat you badly. I'm sorry I did whatever I did that broke us up. If it makes you feel better, I'll take full responsibility for all of it. But please, please, don't take out your anger at me on a poor, defenseless animal who's never done anything to you."

Finn stopped. He didn't turn around, though.

"Please, Finn, I'm begging you. If you ever had any feelings for me, do this one thing."

He pivoted on his heel and glared down at her. "If I do this you have to promise me one thing."

"Anything."

"That you'll never call me again. Ever. I don't want to see you or speak to you for the rest of my life."

She reeled back from the venom in his voice. Did he truly hate her so much? "But you'll take care of Brown Dog?"

His gaze softened as he looked down at the injured animal. "I'll do what I can."

She nodded. "Done."

"We've got to get him inside. Although the cold has probably slowed his metabolism enough to keep him alive for now, he'll need to warm up soon."

Working together, they hoisted the big dog and carried him inside, laying him on her kitchen table. It made her heart ache to feel how little the animal weighed given his size and to feel the ribs slabbing his sides. He was skin and bones.

Finn gave the dog a critical once-over. "This dog's so emaciated that treating his gunshot wound is only going to delay the inevitable. I've got a powerful tranquilizer in my bag. It should be enough to put him down."

"Put him down as in kill him?" she squawked.

"Yes. Euthanasia. It's the humane thing to do for him."

"Since when did you turn into such a quitter?" she snapped. "Our deal was that you'd do your best to save him, not kill him."

Finn glared at her across the table. "Fine. But for the record, you're making this dog suffer needlessly. I can't condone it."

"Just shut up and fix his leg."

"Make sure he doesn't move while I wash up," Finn ordered. He moved to the sink and proceeded to meticulously scrub his hands. He hissed as the soap hit his palms and Rachel craned to see a series of raw blisters on his palms. Where had he gotten those?

Finally, he came back and laid out a bunch of stainless steel tools on the table beside Brown Dog. "You'll assist," he ordered.

Great. She never had been all that good with blood. A person might even say she was downright squeamish. And surely he remembered that. A suspicion that he was doing this to torture her took root in her mind. But if it meant he took care of the dog, so be it. "As long as I don't have to look," she retorted.

"Hand me both pairs of big tweezers." He held out one hand expectantly.

She gasped as she got a better look at his bloody blisters. "What happened to your hands?"

"I helped Damien string fence today. Wasn't expecting to have to scrub for surgery tonight. Had to take the skin off the blisters while I scrubbed up so no bacteria would hide underneath."

She stared. He'd torn up his hands like that for the dog? Awe at his dedication to his work flowed through her.

For the next hour, the kitchen was quiet. Finn occasionally asked for something or passed her a bloody gauze pad. His concentration was total. And she had to admit he was giving it his best shot at saving this dog. He murmured soothingly to the animal, even though it was clear the dog was out cold from the injection Finn had given him.

She couldn't help glancing at the surgical site now and then. It appeared Finn was reconstructing the dog's leg. He set the broken femur and then began a lengthy and meticulous job of suturing tendons and muscles and whatever else was in there that she couldn't name and didn't want to.

Finally, when her head was growing light and she thought she might just faint on him in spite of her best efforts not to, Finn started to close up the wound. He stitched it shut in three different layers. Deep tissue, shallow tissue, and then, at long last, the ragged flesh.

Her stove clock read nearly 2:00 a.m. before Finn straightened up and stretched out the kinks in his back. He rubbed the unconscious dog's head absently. "All right. That's got it. Now we just have to worry about blood loss and infection and the patient's generally poor state of health. I'll leave you some antibiotic tablets to get down him by whatever means you can. If he wakes up, you can start feeding him if he's not too far gone to eat."

Although he continued to stroke the dog gently, Finn never once broke his doctor persona with her. He was cold and efficient and entirely impersonal. If she weren't so relieved that he'd helped her, she'd have been bleeding directly from her heart to see him act like this. Again.

She would never forget the last time he'd been this angry and cold and distant. It had been the night of his senior prom. She'd been waiting for him in the beautiful lemon-yellow chiffon dress her mother had slaved over for weeks making. She'd had a garland of daisies in her hair, the flowers from their garden woven with her father's own hands. Finn had been acting strangely when he came to the door but was polite enough to her parents. Then he'd taken her to the dance, waited until they were standing in front of the entire senior class of Honey Creek High and told her in no uncertain terms how she was worthless trash and vowed he never wanted to see her again.

He'd kept that promise until today. Well, and tonight, of course. Strange how he'd renewed his vow never to see her again within twenty-four hours of seeing her for the first time. She'd never known what had caused him to turn on her then, and she darned well didn't know why he was so mad at her now. He was like Jekyll and Hyde. But mostly the monstrous one. Were it not so late, and she so tired and stressed out and blood covered, she might have asked him. But at the end of the day, it didn't matter. They were so over.

He plunked a brown plastic pill bottle on the counter. "Based on his weight, I'd say half a tablet every six hours for the next week or until he dies, whichever comes first."

She frowned at him. "That was uncalled for."

"I said I'd treat the damned dog. Not that I'd be nice about it."

"Well, you got that right. You're being a giant jerk," she snapped.

Finn scooped the rest of his surgical instruments into his bag and swept toward the door. "Goodbye, Rachel. Have a nice life."

All of a sudden everything hit her. The shock and terror of the past few hours, the stress of the surgery and its gory sights, but most of all, the strain of having to be in the same room with Finn Colton. All that tension and unresolved anger hanging thick and suffocating between them. Watching him walk out of her life *again*. She replied tiredly, "Go to hell."

She thought she heard Finn mutter, "I'm already there."

But then he was gone. All his energy and male charisma. His command of the situation and his competence. And she was left with an unconscious dog lying in the corner of her kitchen, a bottle of pills, and a bloody mess to clean up.

So exhausted she could barely stand, she mopped the kitchen and the porch with bleach and water. How Brown Dog had any blood left inside his body, she had no clue. She was pretty sure she'd cleaned up an entire dog's worth of blood.

Just as she was finishing, he whimpered. Now that his surgery was over, Finn had said it was safe for him to eat. Maybe she'd better start him off with something liquid, though. She pulled out a can of beef consommé that had been in the back of her cupboard for who knew how long and poured it into one of her mixing bowls. She thinned it with a little water and warmed it in the microwave before carrying it over to the groggy animal.

"It's just you and me now, Brownie boy."

She sat down on the floor beside him and used her mother's turkey baster to dribble some of the broth into his mouth. At first he swallowed listlessly, but gradually he grew more enthusiastic about licking his chops and swallowing. By the time she finished the soup, he was actually sucking at the tip of the baster.

"We'll show Finn, won't we, boy? We're survivors, you and me."

Chapter 4

Rachel came home at lunch to change the newspapers under Brownie, give him his antibiotics and use the turkey baster to squirt canned dog food puréed with water down his throat. He was still too weak to do much but thump his tail a time or two, but gratitude shone in his eyes as she tenderly cared for him.

"What's your story, boy? Where'd you get so beat up? Life sure can be tough, can't it?"

She settled him more comfortably in the corner of her kitchen in his nest of blankets and headed back to work. The afternoon passed with her finding more and more discrepancies in the Walsh Oil Drilling Corporation records. She'd be worried about it if she weren't so tired from last night and so concerned about the wounded animal in her kitchen. So when Lester Atkins called her and asked her to come to Mr. Warner's office, she merely grabbed her latest evidence of the embezzlement and headed upstairs.

But when she stepped into the office, she pulled up short. Wes Colton, in full sheriff garb, was standing beside Craig Warner's desk. Wes's arms were crossed. And he was glaring at her. Good lord. What had Finn told him when he'd gone back to the ranch last night? Had Finn sicced Wes on her to get her fired?

"Good afternoon, gentlemen," she managed to choke past her panic.

"Have a seat, Miss Grant," Craig started.

Oh, God. This *was* an exit interview. Wes was here to escort her out of the building. The sheriff parked one hip on the corner of Warner's massive desk, but he still loomed over her. The guy was even bigger and broader than Finn.

"How are you feeling today, Miss Grant?" Wes rumbled.

"Tired, actually. I'm sure Finn told you about my rather adventurous evening last night."

"He did. Any idea who shot your dog?"

She shook her head. "I've got no idea. He just wandered up to my porch already shot. I never saw the dog before last night."

"Kind of you to go to all that trouble to help him," Wes murmured.

Was that skepticism in his voice, or was she just being paranoid? She shrugged and waited in resignation for this travesty to proceed.

On cue, Craig spoke quietly. "Miss Grant, I'd like you to tell Sheriff Colton what you told me on Friday."

She blinked, startled. "You mean about the Walsh Oil Drilling accounts?"

He nodded.

Okay. She didn't see what that had to do with her getting fired, but she'd play along. She turned to Wes. "Mr. Warner asked me to do an internal audit of the financial records of Walsh Oil Drilling Corporation for the past several years. Walsh Oil Drilling is a wholly owned subsidiary of Walsh Enterprises so we have legal purview over—"

Wes waved a hand to cut her off. "I'm not interested in the legal ins and outs of corporate structure. I'm confident that Craig is operating within the law to do the audit."

She adjusted her line of thought and continued. "Yes, well, I looked at last year's records first. I compared the original receipts, billing documents and logged work hours against the financial reports. And I found several major discrepancies. Based on that, I started going back further and looking at previous years."

"And what did you find, Miss Grant?" Wes asked.

"More of the same. Somebody's been skimming funds from this company over at least a fifteen-year period. Maybe since the founding of the company itself seventeen years ago."

Wes definitely looked interested now. "How much money are we talking?"

"Millions. As much as two million dollars the year the company made a major oil strike and had a windfall income spike."

Wes whistled low between his teeth. "Any way to tell who was taking the cash and cooking the books?"

She shrugged. "Mark Walsh himself signed off on the earliest financial reports. If he wasn't taking the initial money himself, he was certainly aware of who was and how much he was taking. After his first death…" The phrase was weird enough to say that it hung her up for a moment. But then she pressed on: "…somebody kept taking it. I can't read the handwriting of whoever was signing off on the financial documents, but it appears to have been the same signature for the past fifteen years."

Wes glanced over at Warner. "You weren't kidding when you said I'd want to hear this." To Rachel he said, "Who else knows about this?"

"Nobody. Just me and Mr. Warner."

Wes nodded, thinking. "I'd like to keep it that way for a while. This may be just the break we're looking for."

She frowned. "Huh?"

"In the Walsh murder investigation."

"You think whoever killed Mark was helping him skim money from his companies and killed him over it?" she asked in surprise.

Wes shrugged. "I wouldn't want to speculate. I just know that Mark Walsh was damned secretive, and it's been nearly impossible to learn much about his life over the past fifteen years. If nothing else, you may have just answered how he was able to pay for his ongoing existence without his family knowing anything about it. Can you give me a complete rundown of how much money went missing and when, Rachel?"

He was using her first name now? Was that a good sign? "Uhh, sure. I can have it for you in a day or so. I've got a few more years' worth of records to review and then I'll be able to compile a report."

"That would be great. And, Craig, thanks for calling me."

The two men shook hands and Wes turned and left. Craig sat down quickly, mopped his forehead with a tissue and then tossed the tissue in the trash. He didn't look good. His skin was pale and pasty and he had that uncomfortable look of someone who was contemplating upchucking.

"Can I get you a glass of water, sir?" she asked in concern.

"Yes, thank you."

She went over to the wet bar on the far side of the room and poured him a glass of water. She carried it to his desk. "Are you feeling all right, Mr. Warner?"

"It'll pass. I've been having these spells for a couple of weeks." He smiled wanly at her. "I'm a tough old bird. I'm not about to go anywhere."

She smiled back at him.

"What's this about a shot dog?" he asked.

Likely he was just looking to distract himself from throwing up. She told him briefly about Brownie and his injuries and Finn coming over to perform surgery on him. She left out the part about Finn's bitter anger toward her.

"You've got a good heart, Miss Grant."

She smiled at her boss. It was a rare moment when anyone in this town said something nice to her. She savored it.

"As soon as you're done with those last financial reports, why don't you take the rest of the day off and go look after your four-legged houseguest?"

She nodded, touched by his kindness. "Thank you, sir."

He waved her out of the office. She suspected he was losing the battle with his stomach and wanted a little privacy to get sick into his trash can. Poor man. She hoped he felt better soon.

* * *

Finn helped Damien string barbed wire all day. The hard labor felt good and helped him burn off a little bit of the residual stress from last night. He still wasn't entirely recovered from that panicked call from Rachel Grant. The woman had about given him a heart attack. Good thing she'd agreed to stay the hell away from him forever. He couldn't take much more of that from her.

"Anything on your mind?" Damien finally asked late in the afternoon.

Finn looked up surprised. "Why do you ask?"

"You're working like a man with a chip on his shoulder."

"What? I can't come out here and help string a fence out of the goodness of my heart?"

Damien cracked a rare smile at that. "Not buying it."

"When did you get so perceptive?" Finn grumbled.

Damien shrugged. "Prison's a tough place. Gotta be good at reading people if you want to stay out of trouble."

Finn was startled. To date, Damien hadn't said more than a few words about his time in jail. "Does it feel strange to be out?" he ventured to ask.

Damien shrugged. He pounded in a metal stake and screwed the fasteners onto it before he finally answered. "It's surreal being back home. Didn't think I'd ever see big open spaces like this again. I missed the sky. It goes on forever out here."

Finn looked up at the brilliant blue sky overhead. Yeah, he might go crazy if he never got to see that. "How'd you do it? How did you keep from losing your mind?"

"Who says I didn't lose it?" Damien retorted.

Finn didn't say anything. He just waited. And sure

enough, after two more posts, Damien commented, "About a year in, I beat the shit out of guy who chose the wrong day to cross me. Growing up with all you punks for brothers served me well. I knew how to handle myself in a fight."

Finn grinned and passed Damien another fastener while he started in on the next post.

Damien continued reflectively. "I got thirty days in solitary. A month in a box broke something in me. It was like I lost a piece of myself. The fight went out of me. It became about just surviving from one day to the next. I played a game with myself. How long could I live in there without losing it again? I made it 4,609 days. And that was when I got word that Walsh had been found dead for real this time and I was going to be released."

Finn shuddered. "God, I'm sorry—"

Damien cut him off with a sharp gesture. "What's done is done. If I learned nothing else in the joint, I learned to keep moving forward. Don't look back. I live my life one day at a time. No apologies. No regrets. It's over."

Finn nodded. His brother was a better man than he. No way could he be so philosophical about a miscarriage of justice costing him fifteen of the best years of his life.

They knocked off when the sun started going down. It got cold fast, and by the time they got up to the main house, he was glad for the fleece-lined coat his brother had tossed him across the cab of the truck.

As beautiful as the log mansion their father had built was, Finn was restless tonight. The heavy walls felt confining and the massive, beamed ceilings felt like they were closing in on him. Hell, Honey Creek was closing in on him.

If his old football coach hadn't extracted a promise out of him to stay for the big homecoming dance this coming Saturday night, he'd be on his way back to Bozeman already. But Coach Meyer was losing his battle with cancer, and he'd asked all his players to come back for one last reunion. It was damned hard to say no to a dying man's last request.

He had to get out of the house. He grabbed his coat and a set of keys and stormed out. As he stomped through the mud room intent on escape, Maisie's voice drifted out of the kitchen. "What's his problem?"

Damien's voice floated to him as he opened the back door. "Woman trouble."

Finn slammed the door shut so hard it rattled in the frame. Woman trouble? Ha!

Rachel raced home from the office to check on Brownie. He seemed more alert and had a little more appetite. He even gave several thumps of his thick, long tail whenever she walked into the kitchen. After both of them had eaten, she signed onto the internet to do some research about care of injured animals. She browsed various veterinary advice sites for an hour or so and then, following the recommendation of several of them, went into the kitchen to check the color of Brownie's gums. Supposedly, pink was healthy and dark red or pale white was bad.

Gingerly, she took hold of his lip and raised it to take a peek. He pulled his head away weakly but not before she glimpsed pasty white gums. She laid her hands on his side and he definitely felt hot to the touch. Oh, no.

Finn had warned her that infection and fever were a major risk to Brownie's survival.

She headed for the phone and dialed the same veterinarian from the night before. "Hi, this is Rachel Grant. I called last night."

"Ahh, yes. The injured dog. How's he doing?"

"I think he's developing a fever."

"If you want to bring him up to Bozeman, I'll meet you at my office."

She winced. The dog had to weigh seventy pounds, even in his emaciated state, and even if she could lift him herself, she doubted Brownie would cooperate with getting into her compact car. At least not without doing even more damage to his injured leg. "I don't think I can get him up to Bozemen by myself."

"You can try giving him some acetaminophen for the fever," the vet suggested.

She forced the suggested medication down Brownie's throat and hovered nervously over him for the next hour. He was getting worse quickly. He stopped wagging his tail at her, and then his eyes went dull and finally he couldn't even raise his head anymore. She eyed the heavy bandage wrapping his leg. Should she take it off and check the wound? Or would that introduce even more chance of infection? If only she knew more about caring for a wound like this!

But she knew someone who did. Small problem: She'd promised never to cross his path again.

Over the next hour, Brownie's breath grew raspy and shallow. She was losing him. What the heck. Finn could get over it. She dialed the Colton phone number. The good news was that Duke answered the phone and was reasonably pleasant with her. The bad news was that Finn wasn't home and Duke didn't know where he was. But he did give her his missing brother's cell phone number. Finn was going to have a fit when he found out Duke had done that.

She hung up and dialed Finn's cell phone.

"Yeah?" he shouted. From the noise in the background, it sounded like he was at a party. Or maybe a bar.

"It's me. Brownie's got a bad fever and he's struggling to breathe."

"Tough shit."

Rachel gasped. "Do you torture small children, too, Doctor?" she asked sharply. "This dog has never done anything to hurt you, and you'd turn your back on him?"

"He's just some mutt."

"Oh, and he's not worthy unless he's a purebred? Kind of like being a Colton or a Kelley or a Walsh in this town? The rest of us are lesser life forms to you purebreds? Is that it? You know, I'm glad whatever happened between us happened. You really are a bastard."

She slammed her phone down and took deep satisfaction in doing so. What a *jerk*. She glanced down at the dog suffering in the corner. "I'm sorry, boy. I may have just driven away your best chance at pulling through." There had to be something she could do. This was the kind of stuff her mother had always been able to handle. *Think, Rachel. What would Mom do?*

Her mother probably would have trotted down the street to visit old Harry Redfeather. He was some sort of medicine man among the local Lakota Sioux. As soon as the idea occurred to her, Rachel knew it to be a good one. If nothing else, the man had a lot more life experience than she did. Maybe he knew of some remedy for a fever.

She grabbed her down ski jacket and gave Brownie a last pat. "Hang in there, buddy. We don't need any nasty old Coltons anyway."

She jogged three houses down to Harry's place and banged on the front door. He was known to be a little hard of hearing. After a minute, his front door opened.

"Rachel, come in and be warm by my fire. Old Man Winter's blowing in tonight. Snow before morning."

She frowned. "I don't think any is in the forecast."

He smiled serenely and said nothing.

"Harry, a dog showed up on my back porch last night. He was starving and shot and half dead. Finn Colton operated on his hind leg to remove the bullet, but tonight the dog's got a terrible fever. Do you know of anything I can do to bring his temperature down? He's burning up. I'm worried that he's got an infection."

Harry nodded. "Come. You can help get my herbs."

He led her to a disreputable-looking wooden shed out behind his house. She ducked inside the low door after Harry and was surprised to find it stuffed with dried plants hanging in bundles from the nearly every square inch of the walls and rafters.

"Get me a sprig of that one over there." Harry pointed at a bundle on the wall. She did as he instructed, pulling various branches and bundles of herbs down for him. "And one stalk only of that one with the purple flowers."

"What is it?" she asked as she handed him the stem of dried flowers.

"Wolfsbane," Harry muttered as he ground leaves together.

She frowned. "Isn't that poisonous?"

"Yes. But a little of it will strengthen the spirit of your dog." In a few minutes, Harry handed her a plastic bag full of ground herbs. "Steep a spoonful of this in warm water and pour the tea down his throat every hour until his fever breaks. And burn this smudge stick around him to help cleanse his spirit. Do you know how to do that?"

Rachel nodded. Ever since she'd been a little girl, she'd seen Harry light up the tightly tied bundles of herbs and waft the smoke around with his free hand. She took the medicines and headed back to Brownie. Over the next several hours she dutifully fed the dog the healing tea. He didn't seem to get any better, but he didn't get any worse, either.

As the hour grew late, the wind began to howl outside, sweeping down out of the high Rockies. She set an alarm for herself and laid down on the couch under a quilt to rest until it was time for Brownie's next dose. It certainly did feel like snow in the air.

She'd dozed off and was warm and cozy when a loud pounding noise dragged her unwillingly from her nap. She glanced at her watch. Not time for the next dose. She rolled over to go back to sleep when the pounding started up again. And this time it was accompanied by shouting. What the heck?

She stumbled upright and headed for her front door. She pulled back the lace curtain to peer through the glass. Her jaw dropped. She had to be hallucinating.

A massive eighteen-wheeler was just pulling away from the curb in front of her house, and a man was standing at her door. Stunned, she opened the front door on a gust of frigid air and icy particles that stung her skin, and the storm blew Finn Colton into her living room.

Chapter 5

Finn didn't know what the hell he was doing standing here, freezing his butt off. But he'd been drinking and chewing on Rachel's phone call ever since he'd gotten it. Despite his tough words to the contrary, he really was worried about that damned dog of hers. He always had had a big soft spot for animals. Truth be told, he'd wanted to be a veterinarian and not a human doctor. But when Damien went to jail, his father got all obsessive about redeeming the Colton name and had pushed him mercilessly to become a physician.

Finn was royally pissed when Rachel called him. She'd broken her promise, and after a few more beers that had ticked him off worse than the fact that she'd called him. Not to mention she'd accused him of being cruel to animals and small children. He was a doctor, for God's sake. A healer.

One thing had led to another, and he'd moved on to slamming down shots of whiskey. Somehow a trucker at the Timber Bar had volunteered to drive him over to Rachel's place, and he'd actually taken the guy up on the offer. The last time a woman had driven him to drunkenness at the bottom of a bottle, it had been Rachel, too. At least he was fairly sure he was drunk. Why else was his head swimming and his feet not attached to his body?

"What on Earth?" Rachel exclaimed. "Where's your coat?"

"What? My… I dunno." He'd remembered to grab his medical bag out of his truck but apparently not his coat. Must be drunker than he'd realized.

"Oh, get in here before you freeze to death." She closed the front door behind him.

With the amount of alcohol in his blood, he doubted any part of him would be freezing anytime soon.

"What are you doing here, Finn?"

He squinted at her, trying to make out her facial features in the dark. "The dog. Came to see the dog. I don't torture little kids, you know."

She frowned for a moment. "Are you fit to see a patient?"

He gave her a bleary glare. "I can do a fever in my sleep. I think I have treated 'em in my sleep." He strode past her toward the back of the house. "Where's my hairy patient?"

As toasted as he was, something made him pause in the kitchen door and proceed more quietly. He moved slowly over to the corner and knelt down beside the motionless dog. "Hey, old man," he murmured. "I hear you're feeling a little under the weather." He stroked the dog's thick fur gently and came away with a handful of dry, coarse hair. The dog was burning up. It didn't take a fancy medical degree, human or otherwise, to know that this animal was in big trouble.

"Get me a bunch of towels and fill your sink up with cold water." He dug in his medical bag and came up with a vial and a syringe. Doing the math on a dosage started a faint headache throbbing at the back of his skull. He did the math a second time to be sure and pulled the antibiotic into the syringe. The dog's skin was dry and pinched as he injected the medication into his unprotesting hip.

"Here they are," Rachel panted. She sounded out of breath like she'd sprinted full out for the towels. The girl sure did seem attached to this mongrel for only having known him a day. Almost made a guy a little jealous.

"Soak those in the sink and then lay them over the dog. Keep his bandage dry."

Rachel followed his directions, bending over so close to him he could smell her vanilla perfume. He remembered the scent well and drew in an appreciative sniff of it. Nothing and no one else in the world smelled quite like that intoxicating combination of homey sweetness and Rachel.

In a matter of seconds the towel was warm to the touch. He passed it up to her and took the next one. They worked for close to an hour in silence. The edge of his buzz was wearing off and he moved automatically in fatigue. And then the dog started to feel a little cooler.

"The fever's breaking," Finn murmured.

Rachel sagged, supporting herself against the edge of the sink. He thought he spied tears tracking down her face.

"Without getting another lecture on my lack of concern for animals and children, why are you so attached to this beast?"

Rachel turned, dashing the tears from her cheeks. "He came to me for help, and that makes me responsible for him. Unlike some people in this town, I don't leave my own behind."

He flared up. "We did what we could for Damien. But there wasn't enough evidence to clear him once he was convicted."

Rachel shrugged. An awkward silence developed between them. He spent it checking the dog's bandages. "What are you calling this mutt, anyway?"

"He started out as Brown Dog. Then it became Brownie Boy and now it's just Brownie."

Finn frowned. "He's a big, macho dog. That's too girly a name for him."

"He chose a girl's porch to nearly die on. He's stuck with whatever name I give him."

"Were you always this bitchy?"

She glared at him. "No, it's your special talent to bring out this side of me."

"Figures. You got something to drink?"

"I've got coffee or water for you. Oh, and milk."

He scowled. That wasn't what he had in mind. If he was going to have to deal with this woman, he definitely needed alcohol and lots more of it. Barring that, he had to find some way to shut her up. The sound of her voice was doing weird things to his gut, and he had to make it stop. He didn't want to feel this way. It was too damned much like old times. Like before she ripped his heart out, when things had been so sweet between them that the joy of it had been nearly unbearable.

She took him by the elbow and steered him into her living room. The light from the kitchen was dim in there and the room was wreathed in shadows. Their silhouettes danced upon the walls, ghostlike. Maybe it was the booze, or maybe it was being up half the night last night and working hard all day today, but the years fell away from him and the two of them were sneaking into her parents' house late from a date, he eighteen, she barely sixteen, both of them innocent and crazy in love.

Regret for the loss of those two carefree kids stabbed him.

"What happened to us?" he whispered.

Rachel turned in surprise to stare at him. The line of her cheek was as pure and sweet as ever. He reached up to touch that young girl one more time before she slipped away from him into the mists of time and bitterness.

She made a soft sound. Whether it was distress or relief, he couldn't tell. But he stepped forward and wrapped her protectively in his arms, hushing her in a whisper.

"Don't leave me, Blondie. Stay with me a little longer. I've missed you so damned much."

Her head fell to his chest and all the tension left her body as she gave in to the magic of the moment. He touched her chin with one finger and raised her face to his. He kissed her closed eyelids and then her cheeks, lifting away the tears. He moved on to her jaw and finally her honeyed mouth. And it was like coming home after many long years away. His relief was too profound for words, his only thought to wonder if this was how Damien had felt when he'd walked out of that prison a free man.

And then she kissed him back. Like always, she was shy at first. But he was patient and slowly, gently, drew her out of herself and into the moment. Before long her slender arms came around his neck and her graceful body swayed into his. And then they were really kissing, deeply, druggingly, with heat building between them that would drive back the night outside and chase away all the old hurts.

He ran his fingers through her silky hair, still as golden and blond and full of light as it had always been. Her skin was still smooth, gliding beneath his fingertips like satin. And that little noise she made in the back of her throat—part moan and part laugh—was exactly the same. Everything about her, how he reacted to her, how he felt about her, was exactly the same.

The realization was like the sun rising in his unguarded eyes, blinding him with its undeniable presence. He turned, spinning her with him on invisible currents of air and light and carried her down to the couch, pulling her down on top of him as he sprawled. The sofa creaked and he chuckled as he threw aside a bunched quilt. And then he kissed her until he thought his heart might burst with the joy of it. His whole world spun around him dizzily and he laughed up at her.

"It's not just me, is it?"

She looked at him questioningly.

"How good this feels. As good as it ever did. We were great together. Could be great together again."

She stared at him in undisguised shock. Finally, she announced, "You're drunk."

"Yup. Ain't it grand?"

She smiled, although regret was thick in her sad

gaze. She shook her head. "Mark my words. You're going to regret this in the morning."

"What the hell. You only live once. Damien's a good case in point. You never know what's going to happen tomorrow, so you'd better enjoy today."

"I'll be sure to tell your hangover that," she commented wryly.

"Kiss me some more."

"How about I go get you that cup of coffee so you can make an informed decision here?"

"Stay."

But she nimbly disentangled herself from his clumsy embrace and disappeared. He kicked off his shoes and stretched out, deliciously content. Damn, life was good. He'd have to thank that dog in the morning for getting sick and forcing him to come over here…

Rachel stood over the couch, coffee mug in hand, and looked down at Finn sleeping like a baby on her couch. And now the $64,000 question was, how much would he remember in the morning? How much did she *want* him to remember? Her rational self prayed he had a total blackout. But something tiny and stubborn in the back of her head wished that he would remember it all.

His kisses had brought it all back. Everything. How desperately she'd loved him. How they'd planned their escape from Honey Creek, sure they'd be together forever. How innocently and completely she'd given him her heart.

For a little while there, he'd kissed her like he remembered it all, too. They really had been great together. Right up until the moment he turned on her.

She covered him with a quilt, stunned at the direction his thoughts had gone when his inhibitions were removed by the Johnny Walker Red she'd tasted on his mouth. He'd wanted her. Asked her to remember how good it had been between them. Had even suggested they'd be that good together again. For a moment there, he'd been her old Finn. The one she'd never really gotten over. Who was she kidding? No matter how mad at him she'd been for dumping her and treating her so badly, there was still something about him…something irresistible between them.

And those kisses of his! Her toes had yet to uncurl from them. If he'd acted like a drunken lout and pawed at her and tried to shove his tongue down her throat, it would have been easy to resist him. But, no. He had to go and be all gentle and tender and caring, like she was made of fine porcelain and was the most beautiful and fragile thing he'd ever seen.

She pressed the back of her hand to her mouth to suppress a sob. Nobody had ever made her feel like that since him. And that was a big part of why she was still single and heading fast for a lonely middle age. Damn him! Why did he have to go and ruin her for anyone else? Worse, he had the gall to come back to Honey Creek and remind her why she couldn't settle for anyone less than him.

She turned and ran for her bed. Her lonely, cold bed. But at least it had fluffy down pillows into which she could cry out all her grief and loss and remembered pain. She'd thought that part of her life was over. She hadn't thought there were any more tears left to shed for Finn Colton. But apparently she'd been wrong.

When the alarm clock dragged her from sleep two hours later to check on Brownie, she stepped into the living room gingerly. Had it all been a dream? An exhaustion-induced hallucination, maybe?

Nope. A long, muscular silhouette was stretched out under her grandmother's quilt, one arm thrown over his head. She paused to examine his hand. A surgeon's hand with long, capable fingers. And then there was the fresh row of blisters not quite scabbed over on his palm. She tucked the quilt higher over his shoulder and tiptoed into the kitchen.

Whether it was Harry Redfeather's tonic or Finn's antibiotics or the cold towels, or some combination of the three, she didn't know. But Brownie seemed to be sleeping more comfortably and even thumped his tail a little for her. She changed the newspapers under him and tucked a blanket around him more securely. She even managed to get a little liquefied dog food down him. Miraculously, he seemed to have turned a corner for the better.

She stood up and reached out to close the kitchen blinds. An odd light was streaming through the window, too bright for moonlight. She stared in delighted surprise. Snow was falling. Big, fat, lazy flakes, drifting down in silent beauty. The entire world was blanketed in white, fresh and shining and clean. She loved new snow better than just about anything on earth.

How appropriate for this night. Brownie had been given a new chance at life. And her and Finn? She didn't have a clue what had happened between them, but it was certainly new and different. Tomorrow morning would tell the tale, she supposed.

She closed the blind quietly and reached down to pet Brownie. "Sleep tight, fella. Enjoy being warm and dry and safe, eh?"

It must've been a trick of the moonlight because for a moment she could swear he'd smiled at her. Then he shifted and settled down, deeply asleep once more.

Yes, indeed. The morning would tell the tale.

Finn blinked awake into light so blinding he thought for a moment he was lying on a surgical table. "What the hell?" he mumbled.

His feet were hanging off the end of his bed, which was barely wide enough to hold him. Something heavy and warm lay across him. Where in blue blazes was he? He squinted and sat up, swinging his feet to the floor. A living room. On someone's sofa. Man, he must've really tied one on last night. He couldn't remember the last time he'd done that. He was the respectable Colton. The good son. He didn't go out and get ragingly drunk.

He did vaguely remember being severely pissed off at something. No, some*one*. He'd tossed back a whole lot more whiskey than he usually did. And then…he frowned. He remembered a semitruck. And getting a ride to somewhere. But where?

He looked around and spied lace curtains at the windows. He reached up to rub his face and caught a whiff of something familiar on his shirt sleeves. *Vanilla.* This was Rachel's couch!

It all came back to him, then. The dog. She'd chapped his butt but good for failing to help her dog get over his fever. He'd tried to drink away the memory of the animal's sad brown eyes and failed. Not to mention the dog's new mistress. He'd ended up piling in that truck and hitching a ride over here while some trucker laughed at him the whole time about being in love. He was *not* in love with Rachel Grant!

He remembered her letting him inside and the two of them working on the dog together for a long time until the fever had finally broken. He frowned, glancing down at the couch, and the rest of it came rushing back. He had pulled her down on top of him and kissed Rachel's lights out...or maybe more accurately they'd kissed each others' lights out.

And he'd said he missed her. That they'd been good together. Could be good together again.

He swore long and fluently. That was possibly the dumbest thing he'd ever done in his entire life. And he'd done some pretty stupid things over the years. He vowed then and there never to mix booze and women again as long as he lived. He should probably be grateful he'd only ended up on her couch and not in her bed. Talk about complicating things!

But then insidious images of what she would look like and feel like, naked and silky and willing in his arms, invaded his mind. His body reacted hard and fast, pounding with lust. Damned, traitorous flesh.

"Hi, there. I thought I heard you moving around," Rachel said from the doorway.

He yanked the quilt across his lap to hide his reaction to thinking about being in bed with her. "G'morning," he grumbled. "How's the mutt?"

"The mutt is doing great. He went out in the backyard under his own steam to pee and hopped back inside all by himself."

"Could you dial down the chipper meter a bit?" he groaned.

"Headache, pukey gut, or both?" she asked sympathetically.

"If the guys jackhammering my eyeballs out of my skull are a headache, let's go with that."

"A pile of aspirin coming right up." She brought the pills along with a big pitcher of cool water. He drank several glasses down, and although his head still throbbed, the jackhammers went on break.

She asked sympathetically, "Do you think you could eat? You might feel better if you got some food into your stomach."

"Something starchy, please."

"Pancakes?"

"Perfect."

"If you want to take a shower while I make you a stack, that's okay."

He nodded wearily and hauled himself to his feet. He glanced across the living room at the shadow he cast on the far wall. Memory of a slender, feminine shadow moving sinuously there last night came to mind. He ought to apologize. Tell her it had all been a terrible, alcohol-induced mistake. But his throat closed on the words and his tongue stayed stubbornly silent. He shook his head to clear the memory—and groaned. Big mistake. It felt like he'd just thrown his brain in a blender. Ugh.

He made a beeline for the bathroom and the hottest shower her house could serve up.

Rachel looked up from the table where she was just setting down two glasses of orange juice and was mortified to see Finn holding the mystery piece from her latest attempt at toilet repair.

He said casually, "You didn't need this, so I took it

out and hooked up the handle properly. You're flushing like a champ, now."

Her face heated up. "Surgery on my dog and now surgery on my toilet. How will I ever repay you?"

He grinned, a self-conscious little thing that looked strange on him. Was he actually embarrassed? About what? She was the one who couldn't fix a toilet. He slid into the chair across from hers, and suddenly her kitchen shrank from cozy to itty-bitty.

He bit into the pancakes cautiously. She hoped it was because he was being respectful of his stomach's propensity to revolt and not because he thought her cooking was that bad. In fact, she was a pretty decent cook when she bothered to do it. It was just that she lived alone and most of the time it was easier to toss something into the microwave.

"Mmm. Good," he murmured.

Relieved, she dug into her own breakfast.

"Don't you have to be going to work?" he asked.

"I have an appointment this morning," she replied. With his brother. To turn over the copies of the financial records Wes had asked for. The same records he'd asked her not to talk to anyone about. So of course, Finn asked the obvious question.

"Who's the appointment with?"

"Nobody," she answered evasively.

"Nobody who? Must've moved into town after I left."

"Ha, ha. Very funny."

"Who's it with?" he pressed.

She sighed. "You're not making it easy to tell you tactfully that it's none of your business."

The open expression on his face snapped into something tight and unpleasant in the blink of any eye. Dang it! And they'd been getting along so well.

She frowned. And she was desperate to get along with him well, *why?* She was the ex. The very-ex ex. There was no way he'd ever contemplate getting back together with her. At least not sober. He'd had going on fifteen years to get around to it and never had. Last night had been a whiskey-induced anomaly. Nothing more. She could only pray that the fact he hadn't mentioned their kiss this morning meant he didn't remember it.

He pushed his plate back. "Thanks for breakfast. I seem to have left my cell phone in my coat pocket, and I have no idea where my coat is at the moment. Could I use your phone to call a cab?"

"I've got some time before my appointment. I can drive you wherever you need to go."

"I've put you out too much already."

She rolled her eyes. "You saved my dog's life. I definitely owe you a ride. Is your truck over at the Timber Bar?"

"Not anymore. Damien and Duke picked it up last night so I wouldn't try to drive it drunk."

"So you need a ride to the ranch?" Internally, she gulped. It was bad enough having to face him again. But the whole Colton clan? Yikes!

He sighed. "I can see from your face you're not thrilled at that prospect. Really. I'll call a cab."

"Really. I'll drive you home." He glared, and she glared back. The same fire that had zinged back and forth between them last night flared up again, and her kitchen went from itty-bitty to minuscule. Even Brownie lifted his head in the corner to study them.

"I'm calling—"

She cut him off. "I'm not some impressionable fifteen-year-old sophomore that a big, bad senior can push around anymore. I'm taking you home and that's that. Now hand me your plate."

A grin hovered at the corners of his mouth as he passed her his plate in silence. She rinsed off the syrup quickly and popped the dishes and utensils into the dishwasher. Maybe later she'd take them back out and put her lips where his had been. Goodness knew, she was all but drooling over him already.

Finn surprised her by going over to Brownie and squatting down beside him. He held his hand out and let the dog sniff it, then scratched him gently under the chin.

Whoever said men weren't capable of being as tender as women was dead wrong. And furthermore, it was as sexy as hell when a man was gentle and sweet. Her racing pulse was proof enough of that.

Finn murmured to the dog, "How're you feeling this morning, buddy?"

Brownie whimpered as if in response.

Finn glanced up at her. "Sounds like he's conscious enough to be in pain, now. We've got some tramadol out at the ranch I can give you."

"What's that?"

"A painkiller. Wouldn't want the big guy to be uncomfortable now, would we?"

The whole time he spoke, Finn was petting the dog easily, trailing his fingers through the dog's thick coat. Rachel could hardly tear her eyes away from the magic his hand wove. What would it feel like if he did that across her skin? The idea made her shiver.

Finn glanced up and caught her red-handed staring at him like he was a two-inch-thick, sixteen-ounce prime rib cooked to perfection. She ripped her gaze away hastily. "Uhh, ready to go?" she mumbled.

He stood up leisurely, which put him about a foot from her in her little kitchen. "Yeah," he murmured. "I'm ready if you are." His voice rolled over her, smooth and masculine. And it didn't sound at all like he was talking about leaving. He sounded distinctly like he was talking about *staying.*

Her breath hitched. Then her heart hitched. And then her brain hitched. Was it possible? In a fog of lust and disbelief, she grabbed her keys and her briefcase and led the way out the back door. Last night's snow was mostly gone, but patches of it remained in the grass.

"Winter's coming," Finn commented.

"My favorite time of year," she commented back.

"I remember that about you. You like the holidays and curling up under a blanket with a cup of hot chocolate and watching it snow."

She all but dropped her keys. He remembered that about her? After all these years? What did it mean? In a lame effort to cover her shock, she said, "Yeah, but now that I have to drive in it, the romance of snow has worn off somewhat."

He grimaced at her compact car. "You need to get yourself something bigger and heavier. With four-wheel drive. You live in Montana, after all."

Like she could afford something like that. Maybe in a year or two after she'd dug out from under the bills. Finn looked comical folded into the passenger seat of her little car. The roads in town were wet, and as they headed east into the hills toward the Colton spread, the pavement started to get slippery.

To distract herself from visions of driving off the side of a mountain and killing them both, she asked, "Did you get roped into going to the Honey Creek High anniversary celebration next Saturday?"

"Only reason I'm sticking around town this week. Couldn't let Coach Meyer down."

Rachel swallowed hard. She should've put it together that he'd be at the dance. The daring gown that was being altered for her right now flitted through her mind. *Ohmigosh.* She'd fallen in love with the dress precisely because it was a defiant statement of sensuality. She'd tried for years to be the person everyone in Honey Creek wanted her to be, and the gown was a big, fat announcement that she was done chasing respectability—or paying penance for a crime they'd never bothered to tell her about. If they thought she were a tart, why not be one? Surely tarts had more fun than she'd had for the past fifteen years.

Maybe she could find a burlap sack at the Goodwill store before Saturday.

Or maybe she'd just skip the dance. Although she'd promised Carly she'd go. No way would her cousin let her back out of it without raising a huge stink. Crud.

She fell silent, contemplating ways to duck both the dance and Carly but coming up empty. Finn stared out the window as the mountains rose around them. The high peaks wore their first caps of snow and wouldn't lose them again until next spring. As the roads grew narrower and steeper, she concentrated carefully on her driving. She might not have a fancy truck like Finn, but she knew how to handle winter road conditions.

She took it easy and finally turned into the familiar driveway. The big, wrought-iron arch over the entrance still held up the elaborately scrolled letter *C.* Yup, the Coltons were royalty in this town.

A wash of old memories swept over her: amazement that someone who lived in this palatial place could be interested in her; the excitement of imagining herself a member of the Colton clan someday, dreaming of living in the magnificent log mansion that sprawled forever along a mountaintop; her intimidation at meeting Finn's parents for the first time. She'd so wanted to make a good impression on them. But then Maisie had been nasty to her, and she'd gotten tongue-tied and ended up standing in front of Finn's family red in the face and unable to form complete sentences. It had been the most humiliating experience of her life...until the night of prom, of course, when Finn had dumped her.

"Pull around back by the kitchen entrance," he directed.

She nodded and to make conversation added, "This place is still as beautiful as ever."

He shrugged. "It's a house." She didn't think he was going to say anything more, but then he added, "You know what they say. A house isn't necessarily a home."

"Your home's in Bozeman for good, then?"

Another shrug. "I haven't found a home yet."

Now what did he mean by that? She was fairly certain he wasn't talking about finding a house. Her impression was that he was talking about having found love. Companionship. Family. Roots. Her father might be gone and her mother gone in all but body, but at least they'd been a close family. They'd stuck together through thick and thin and been there for each other. Heck, they'd had fun together.

Finn interrupted her thoughts. "Come in while I get the pills for you."

"No, that's okay. I'll wait in the car."

His head whipped to the left. "You scared, Blondie?"

Her spine stiffened. "No, I'm not!"

"Yes, you are. You're chicken to face my family," he accused. He looked on the verge of laughing at her.

"Wouldn't you be?" she shot back.

That wiped the grin off his face. "Yeah, I suppose I would be."

"All right then. So, I'll come inside and show you I'm braver than you ever were. I'm not scared to face the mighty Coltons."

Except she *was* scared. And for some reason, Finn went grim and silent as he climbed out of the car. Had he caught her veiled barb about being afraid to stand up to his family? She didn't like the practice of taking pot shots at other people, but it was hard not to take a swipe or two at him after all the years of pain and suffering he'd caused her. Vaguely nauseous, she marched toward the back door behind him, praying silently that none of the other Coltons would be around.

Her prayer wasn't answered, of course. Finn held the back door for her and she stepped through a mud room the size of her living room and into a giant rustic kitchen that could grace the pages of a home-decorating magazine. A big man sat on a bar stool with his back to her, hunched over a mug of something steaming. He turned at their entrance and she started. Although he'd changed a great deal, he was still clearly Finn's older brother.

"Hi, Damien. Welcome home," she said.

"Thanks," he muttered.

"It's good to have you back," she added sincerely.

He glanced up again, surprise glinting in his hard gaze for a moment. "It's good to be back."

"I'll go get the drugs, Rachel. Stay here," Finn ordered. He strode out of the kitchen for parts unknown in the mansion.

"You two dealing drugs now?" Damien asked wryly.

"Yup. Thought we'd corner the market on doggie painkillers."

"Come again?"

Rachel grinned. "A stray dog wandered up to my house night before last. He'd been shot and was bleeding and half starved. I couldn't get him to a vet, so Finn came down to town to help him. Did surgery on my kitchen table to remove the bullet and repair his leg."

"Finn did that for you?" Damien asked in surprise. She nodded and he gestured at the bar stool beside her. As she slid onto it he asked, "Coffee?"

"Yes. Thanks."

He poured her a mug and sat back down beside her. Great. Now what were they supposed to talk about? The guy had never been the chatty type, even before he went to jail for half his adult life. She resorted to, "Finn says you've been doing a lot of work around this place."

He shrugged.

"Do you know what you're going to do next?"

He looked at her questioningly.

"I mean, are you planning to stick around Honey Creek long term?"

He raised his mug to her. "You're the first person with the guts to ask me that outright."

"It's not about guts. I'm just interested. I can speak

from experience that it sucks to be an outcast among people you thought were friends."

"Yeah?"

"Yeah," she replied, warming to the role of advice giver about something she was an expert in. "You stick by your guns, Damien, and do exactly what you want to do. Ignore the funny looks and snarky comments. I wish I had done it sooner."

He surprised her by mumbling, "Do they ever stop? The looks and the comments?"

She looked him dead in the eye and answered candidly, "I'll let you know when they do."

He grunted. She wasn't sure what the sound meant. Maybe agreement. Maybe disgust.

She said reflectively, "The thing about small towns is no one ever forgets."

He muttered into his mug, "Don't need 'em to forget. Just need 'em to forgive."

She laid her hand on his arm and it went rock hard under her palm. "You don't need anyone's forgiveness. You did nothing wrong. You hold your head high in this town, Damien Colton."

"Maybe before I take off I'll stick around long enough to see Walsh's real killer caught."

"I sincerely hope Wes catches the killer for you. And soon."

An actual smile lit Damien's eyes. "You're not so bad, you know. Finn was a fool to—"

A female voice cut sharply across his words. "What in blue blazes are *you* doing in my house? We don't cotton to white trash sluts around here."

Rachel looked up, stunned at the attack, and her heart

fell to her feet. *Maisie.* The woman had always hated Rachel's guts for no apparent reason.

Damien surprised her by cutting in. "Don't be a bitch, Maisie. Rachel brought Finn home."

"Are you telling me he was with her all night last night?" Maisie screeched. "Just couldn't wait to get your hooks back into him, could you? After all these years you still don't get it, do you? You'll never be good enough to be a Colton, missy. You leave my brother alone. You broke his heart but good the last time, and I'll not stand for you doing it to him again, you hear me?"

Rachel eyed the back door in panic. If she was quick about it, she could make the mud room and be outside before the other woman could catch her.

Damien spoke up mildy. "Shut up, Maisie. What Finn and Rachel do or don't do is none of your business." There was steel behind his words, though. Rachel blinked. At the moment, he didn't sound like a guy she'd want to cross in a dark alley.

"Here they are—" Finn burst into the kitchen, took in the scene of Rachel eyeing the back door, Maisie glaring at Rachel and Damien glaring at Maisie, and fell silent.

Hands shaking, Rachel took the brown plastic bottle from Finn and slid off the stool. "Thanks for everything, Finn. I don't know what I'd have done without you." How she got the words out with any semblance of composure, she had no idea.

"Any time," he replied. Whether he actually meant that or just said it out of automatic politeness, she had no idea. If only she could get out of here without any more collateral damage from Maisie Colton. Folks in Honey Creek were about equally split over whether she was just a spoiled bitch or a little bit crazy. Either way,

Rachel usually steered well clear of her. And it was time to do that now.

"Nice talking with you, Damien," Rachel said.

"You, too."

She didn't know how to say goodbye to Finn, so she just nodded at him and turned to leave.

"Be careful driving home, Blondie," he murmured quietly enough that she doubted Maisie heard.

For some inexplicable reason, tears welled up in her eyes. She just nodded mutely and fled like the big, fat chicken she was. So much for being braver than Finn Colton.

Chapter 6

The next few days were busy ones for Rachel. She visited her mother at the nursing home and cried in her car afterward at how delighted her mother had been that the nice young woman had brought her a cup of chocolate pudding. Her mother was continuing to lose weight and looked so frail that a strong wind might blow her away.

Rachel did a volunteer shift at the Goodwill store and was dismayed to discover the place was plumb out of burlap sacks. It didn't even have any conservative dresses that would remotely fit her, either. She was stuck with the one Edna was nearly done altering.

At work, she commenced revising the Walsh Oil Drilling financial statements, a job that was going to take her weeks to complete. Craig Warner was out of the office for a couple of days but had stopped by to say hello to her on Thursday morning. She took that as a sign that maybe she wasn't going to lose her job over exposing the company founder's embezzlement, after all. At home, she slept and ate around caring for Brownie, who was gradually recovering. She thought he might be putting on a bit of weight, too.

The weather was strange all week. After the snow, the next day the temperature went up to nearly eighty degrees. Mother Nature was as unsettled as Rachel felt.

She didn't run into Finn around town again, but she was vividly aware of his presence. It was as if she felt him nearby. Every now and then she got a crazy notion that he was within visual range. But whenever she turned to look for him, he wasn't there. It was probably the lack of sleep making her hallucinate. Either that, or she was as big a lovesick fool as she'd ever been. She tended to believe it was the latter.

Her rational mind argued that she was insane to entertain any thoughts of Finn at all. Maisie was right. Hadn't she learned her lesson the first time around? She would never be good enough to be a Colton. But her heart stubbornly refused to listen to reason. She dreamed of him. The kinds of dreams that made her wake up restless and hot and wishing for a man in her bed. Finn Colton, to be exact.

Why, oh why, did he have to come back to Honey Creek?

She rushed home after work on Thursday to take care of Brownie and change clothes. Walsh Enterprises was throwing a barbecue to kick off the centennial homecoming weekend celebration, and as a Walsh employee, she was invited.

She'd never been out to the Walsh spread other than to drive by at a distance. It looked homey and charm-

ing from the main road. The Walsh house turned out
to be deceptive, though. It looked like a fairly normal
country-style home with a broad front porch and dor-
mer windows in the steep-pitched roof. But when she
stepped inside, she was startled at the size of the place.
Nothing but the best for one of the town's other royal
families, she supposed. These people lived in a world
different from hers entirely.

Lucy Walsh, who was only a couple of years older
than Rachel, ushered her out back to where easily a
hundred people milled around the swimming pool bal-
ancing plates of food and drinking tall glasses of beer
from the Walsh brewery.

He was here. She knew it instantly. Finn's presence
was a tingling across her skin, a sharp pull that said he
was over by the bar. She looked up, and there he was.
Staring across the crowd at her like he'd felt her walk
into the party the same way she'd felt him.

He was, of course, the only Colton at this Walsh barbecue. Frankly, she was surprised he had come. The two
families weren't exactly on friendly terms. But then,
Finn always had been the *good* Colton. The diplomat.
The one who smoothed things over.

He wore a pale blue polo shirt and jeans and looked
like a million bucks. It was all she could do to tear her
gaze away from him. But in a gathering like this, she
dared not look like she bore any interest at all in him.
The rumors would fly like snowflakes in January if
she did.

In fact, she assiduously avoided him for the next
hour. Thankfully, Carly arrived and took her in tow.
Her cousin was outgoing and popular and made lively
conversation with dozens of people. It allowed Rachel

to nod and smile and act like she was having fun, when mostly she was concentrating on keeping tabs on Finn and forcing herself not to look at him. When the strain became too much for her, she went inside in search of a restroom and found a long line of people waiting to use one.

Jolene Walsh, Lucy's mom, stopped to speak to Rachel in the hall. "Why don't you go upstairs, dear? There are several bathrooms, and you won't have to wait."

"Thanks, Mrs. Walsh."

"Call me Jolene, dear."

She thought she detected a hint of sadness in the woman's voice. She'd had a rough go of life, too. It was no secret that Mark Walsh had cheated on his wife and been a rotten husband until his first death. By all accounts, Jolene had kept to herself for years afterward and let Craig Warner mostly run Walsh Enterprises. Then Mark had shown up dead for real and plunged Jolene into yet another scandal. Poor woman.

"Thanks, Jolene," Rachel murmured. She headed upstairs and went in search of a bathroom. She ducked into a bedroom and saw a door that looked promising. She headed toward it and started when it opened.

Finn stepped out.

"Oh! Hi," she murmured, flustered.

"Hi. Enjoying the party?" Finn asked. He glanced warily toward the open bedroom door.

"Uhh, yeah. Food's great."

"How's Brownie?"

"Getting better slowly. He's started trying to put weight on his leg, but he cries every time he tries it."

Finn frowned. "Femurs are intensely painful bones

to break in humans. I suspect it's similar in dogs. Let me know if the pain doesn't seem to subside in a few days."

"Okay. Thanks."

He took a step closer and asked quietly, "How are *you* doing, Blondie?"

She looked up at him, startled. "Tired, actually. Taking care of Brownie around the clock is hard work."

He nodded and reached out to trace beneath her eye with the pad of his thumb. She froze, stunned that he would touch her voluntarily. "Get some rest. He's depending on you."

She nodded, her throat too tight to speak. He *was* talking about the dog, right?

Finn took a step forward, his fingers still resting lightly on her cheek. His head bent down toward hers slightly. *Ohmigosh.* He was going to kiss her!

Someone burst into the room in a flurry of noise and movement. "Finn, come quick! We need a doctor—" Lucy Walsh broke off, looking back and forth between them. "Oh!"

Finn jumped back at about the same instant Rachel did, but he was first to speak. "What's wrong?"

"Craig has collapsed. Hurry!"

Finn spared Rachel an apologetic glance, then raced out of the room after Lucy. Rachel sat down on the edge of the bed, breathing hard. Holy cow. Finn Colton had been about to kiss her. And he wasn't drunk this time. At least, she was pretty sure he wasn't.

As worried as she might be about her boss, she couldn't exactly go busting downstairs immediately after Finn with her cheeks on fire. Not if she didn't want to be the stuff of gossip for weeks to come. She stumbled into the bathroom and splashed cold water over her face until her cheeks had returned to a normal pink in the mirror. Her brown eyes were too big, though, too wide, and her hands were shaking. There was no way she was going to hide the fact that something had happened between her and Finn up here.

Crud. She seemed to have a knack for doing practically nothing yet managing to put herself into prime rumor position. She really wished she would stop doing that. Reluctantly, she walked downstairs. An ambulance siren screamed in the distance. Oh, dear. Craig must be seriously ill. She hoped it was nothing like a heart attack.

She stepped out onto the back patio. A crowd of people was clustered around the far end of the pool, and she spotted Finn kneeling next to a prone figure. At least he wasn't doing CPR on Craig. That was good news, right? A pair of paramedics raced around the side of the house, pulling a stretcher. She watched in dismay along with everyone else while they loaded Craig onto it and, with Finn jogging beside them, rushed Craig out to the ambulance.

Lucy Walsh, who happened to be standing next to Rachel, turned blindly to her, her face pale. "I've got to take my mom to the hospital. She's too upset to drive. Could you keep an eye on things around here? Everyone can stay if they like, but we've got to go."

Rachel nodded, stunned. In moments, the Walsh party was nearly devoid of Walshes. Lester Atkins made an announcement that people should feel free to stay and enjoy the barbecue. But the life had gone out of the evening. People trickled out steadily over the next hour until the place was deserted.

Rachel stepped in to supervise the caterers when

Lester got a call from the Walshes and had to race off to the hospital. That couldn't be a good sign. She said a prayer for Craig and turned to the daunting task of cleaning up after two hundred people. After all, she was the town's resident pitch-in-and-volunteer girl. Thankfully, the caterers were efficient, and it only took an hour or so for them to pick up the mess, pack the tents and tables and leave the remaining food in coolers in the kitchen.

Rachel climbed into her car a little after midnight and started the long drive back to town. Finn was a great doctor and he was looking after Craig. Everything would turn out okay. Except an ominous rumbling in her gut said that everything was not okay in Honey Creek.

Finn parked his truck behind his family's mansion and sat there for a while staring at nothing. What on earth was wrong with Craig Warner? He understood why the local chief E.R. doctor had recruited him to consult on this case. But even as a specialist in gastro-intestinal disorders, he was stumped. He'd seen a lot of strange cases in emergency rooms before, but this one was baffling. He'd ordered up a raft of tests, but the nearest lab was in Bozeman and he wouldn't have any results on most of the lab work until morning. He'd considered ordering a helicopter to transport Craig up to Bozeman, but frankly, he didn't think the man would survive the flight.

Damn it, the guy couldn't die on him! Besides the fact that he took pride as a physician in hardly ever losing a patient, how ironic would it be for one of the mainstays of the Walsh family to die on the watch of a Colton?

He climbed out of the truck, shrugging deep into the jacket he'd snagged from the mud room earlier. He didn't feel like going inside. The weather had swung back from summer warm to cold tonight, and the temperature fit his mood. He strolled out toward the back acreage and spied a light on in the main barn. What was going on out there? He headed for the light.

The dew soaked through his docksiders and the night air bit sharply at his nose. The warmth of the barn was tangible as he stepped inside. A rich smell of cattle and disinfectant washed over him. This always had been his favorite place on the whole ranch. Damien leaned against a stall door at the far end of the cavernous space.

He joined his brother and glanced into the stall. A cow lay on her side, straining in the distinctive spasms of delivering a calf. "Everything okay?" Finn asked.

Damien shrugged. "First calf. She's struggling with it. Thought I'd keep an eye on her in case she needs help."

"Late in the year to be calving, isn't it?" Finn murmured.

Damien shrugged. "I wasn't around ten months ago to know how she got in with the bull."

Finn fell silent. They watched the cow stand, pace around a bit, then lay back down and strain again. Finn asked, "You check the calf's position?"

"Yeah. Presentation's normal."

Funny how both of them had been gone from the ranch for over a decade, but the knowledge of ranching and cattle husbandry came back unbidden. The rhythm of life out here got into a man's bones and never left him.

Damien commented, "I figure we give her another push or two, and if she doesn't make any progress, we go in and help."

"Want me to call a vet?"

Damien replied, "I hear Doc Smith retired. There's no vet in town these days, so we're on our own. But you're a doctor. Some of that fancy medical stuff has to apply to cattle, doesn't it?"

Finn nodded. Something in his gut ached with longing to go to veterinary school and take Doc Smith's place as the local vet. But, no. He had to become a "real" doctor. Respectable. Successful. Distinguished.

Damien looked over at him with that disconcertingly direct stare he'd developed in prison. "What brings you out here at this time of night? I thought you were going to the Walsh barbecue."

"I went. Craig Warner collapsed and had to be rushed to the hospital. I spent most of the evening in the emergency room with him."

"He gonna be okay?"

Finn shrugged. "Don't know. We can't figure out what's wrong with him. He's in critical condition."

Damien frowned. "Can't say as I wish anyone associated with the Walshes well, but I don't wish death on the guy."

Finn nodded. Once upon a time, Damien had been crazy in love with Lucy Walsh until her father ran Damien off. That was what the prosecutors used as Damien's motive for supposedly murdering Mark Walsh. *Women. The root of all evil.*

"You think?" Damien murmured in surprise.

Finn glanced over at his brother. Had he said that out loud?

"You got woman trouble, Finn?"

He frowned. Did he have woman trouble? He wasn't sure. He'd been on the verge of kissing Rachel again at the barbecue before Lucy burst in to announce that Craig had collapsed. And that would've been a colossal mistake.

"Only trouble I'm having with women is staying away from them. Or rather getting them to stay away from me."

"Rachel's not stalking you, is she? She didn't strike me as the type."

"Hell, if anything I'm the one stalking her." He jammed a hand through his hair. "But I know better. The woman's poison. She reeled me in the last time and then betrayed me."

"You mean back in high school?" Damien asked. He sounded surprised again.

"Yeah," Finn answered impatiently.

"You still carrying a torch for her after all this time?"

"I'm not carrying a torch for Rachel Grant!"

"Dunno. From where I stand, it sure looks like you are. Helping her with that dog and spending the night at her house. Were you really only on her couch?"

Rage exploded in Finn's chest. It boiled up within him until his face was hot and his fists itching to hit something. What the hell? He checked the reaction, stunned at its violence. Where had that come from? Was he really so defensive of Rachel? Or was it maybe that it just pissed him off to have someone else see the truth before he did?

The cow lay down abruptly and commenced another contraction.

"Crap," Damien exclaimed softly. "The calf has turned. Those aren't front hooves."

Finn followed his brother into the pen. "I'll hold her down. You're stronger than me. You pull the calf."

They went to work quickly. Finn put a knee on the cow's neck, leaning on it just enough to keep her from getting up. As another contraction started, Damien wrapped a towel around the calf's back legs, braced himself with his boots dug deep into the sawdust and commenced pulling for all he was worth.

"Ease up," Finn said as the contraction ended. Damien and the cow had the calf's entire hind legs out. Damien tore back the silver-white amniotic sac to get better purchase on the slippery calf.

"Big calf," Damien commented, breathing hard.

"Here comes the next contraction," Finn replied.

Damien nodded and commenced pulling again. It took maximum effort from cow and human, but a few moments later, the calf popped out in a rush of fluid. Finn and Damien pulled the sac back from the calf's face and cleaned out its nose. The calf shook his head and snorted, breathing normally. The cow lowed to her baby and after passing the afterbirth got to her feet to examine her offspring. While mother administered an energetic bath to her baby, Finn got a barn shovel, took the afterbirth out of the stall and checked it make sure it was intact and whole.

He and Damien leaned on the stall wall and watched as the calf started struggling to get to its feet. Mom's enthusiastic licking wasn't helping, and she knocked the little guy over a few times. There was something miraculous to watching new life unfold like this. It put everything else in the world into perspective.

Damien murmured, "Rachel seems like a decent woman. Why is it you hate her guts, again?"

Finn was startled. Why had Damien circled back to this subject? "You know why. She slept with some other guy. Hell, she ripped my guts out and stomped on them."

Damien shrugged. "Yeah, yeah. I remember. I was there when Maisie told you." He paused. "But it's been fifteen years. That's a long time. People change."

"Yeah, but just because people change, that doesn't mean it's always for the better."

"They don't always change for the worse, bro."

Finn looked over at Damien in surprise. "When did you become such an optimist about the human race?"

"I'm no great optimist. It's just that…" Damien seemed to search for the right words and then settled on "…life's too short. You gotta do what makes you happy. If you want to give things with Rachel another go, then you should do it."

Finn reared back. "I don't want to give things with Rachel another go!"

"Why the hell not? She's a beautiful woman, and she's plumb tuckered in love with you. If I had a woman like that who wanted me like she wants you, I wouldn't think twice about going for it."

"In love? With me? You're nuts. She hates my guts!" His outburst startled the cow into turning defensively and banging into her calf, who stumbled and fell over.

"Shh," Damien hushed him. "You're upsetting momma and interfering with junior's first meal."

Finn subsided, but his brain was in a whirl. Why on earth did Damien think Rachel still had a thing for him? She might have turned to him for help with her injured dog, but she'd made it plenty clear that she wished he'd leave town and stay gone. Except she'd kissed him back last night when she thought he was too drunk to remember the kiss today. And earlier this evening at the barbecue, she'd definitely leaned toward him when he'd leaned toward her—

Cripes. Was he so desperate that he was analyzing *leaning,* now?

The sound of sucking pulled his thoughts back to the moment. He smiled as the calf butted his mother's udder and sucked some more.

"Nice-looking calf," Damien commented. "Maybe I'll ask the old man to give him to me as a starter bull for my new ranch."

"You still planning to move to Nevada and start your own place?" Finn murmured.

"Nothing to hold me around here anymore," Damien retorted. "Just a whole lot of bad memories and bad blood."

It hurt to hear the pain in Damien's voice. The guy'd been through so much and gotten such a raw deal. Finn really wished there was something he could do to put a smile back into his brother's eyes.

"Things sure didn't turn out how either of us planned, did they?" Finn muttered. "I thought I was going to marry Rachel, go to vet school and live happily ever after, and you were going to run the ranch and marry Lucy."

Damien's gaze went glacial. Finn froze as actual violence rolled off his brother's massive shoulders. For the first time since he'd gotten home, Finn was a little afraid of his older brother. By slow degrees, Damien's bunched muscles relaxed and the violence pouring off of him ebbed. Finn released a slow, careful breath.

Damien glanced wryly over at Finn. "It's not too late for you. You can still have it all."

Finn wanted to shout that he didn't want Rachel Grant, but once again, the words wouldn't come out of his throat. They stuck somewhere in his gut and refused to budge.

Damn, that woman messed him up like no other female ever had. Coming back to Honey Creek had been a big mistake. A huge one. To hell with the homecoming dance. He'd pay his respects to Coach Meyer in the morning and get the hell out of town.

Chapter 7

Rachel dragged herself into work the next morning as exhausted as she'd ever been in her life. Brownie had been restless and uncomfortable last night, and what with worrying over Craig Warner and replaying that almost-kiss with Finn Colton over and over in her head, she'd barely slept at all.

After hours and hours of wrestling with the decision, she'd determined that no matter how much attraction still lingered between the two of them, she and Finn were better off going their separate ways and living their own lives. Too much time had passed and they'd both changed too much. Even if they had been wildly attracted to one another as kids, teen lust was no basis for a long-lasting relationship.

Only a few minutes after she'd sat down at her desk, Lester Atkins summoned her to his office. Alarm coursed through her. What could he possibly want with her? As Craig's personal assistant, he had a great deal of unofficial power at Walsh Enterprises. And some of his power was entirely official. She gathered from her coworkers, for example, that he had the power to fire people at her pay grade.

Craig Warner's secretary wasn't at her desk when Rachel got to the woman's office, so she stepped through into Lester's. He wasn't there. Strange. She glanced into Craig's office and was startled to see Lester sitting at Warner's desk. His palms were spread wide on the leather surface, and a look of satisfaction glutted his features.

Rachel stepped back hastily into the doorway to the secretary's office and cleared her throat loudly. Lester came out of Warner's office immediately, the look in his eyes one of suspicion now.

"Ah. There you are, Miss Grant. I have some paperwork I need you to take over to the hospital and get signed."

"Does that mean Mr. Warner's doing better?" she asked hopefully.

"No. He's still in critical condition. I need Mrs. Walsh's signature."

Rachel frowned. From what she gathered, Craig Warner and Jolene Walsh had quietly been an item for the past year or two. She hardly imagined that Jolene would want to deal with business matters when her lover was fighting for his life.

Lester must've caught the frown, because he snapped, "I wouldn't bother her with trivial matters. This paperwork is vitally important and has to be signed right away." He picked up a thick manila folder off his desk.

"I've marked the spots that need signing with sticky notes. Jolene doesn't need to read any of it. You can tell her I've reviewed it all and she just needs to sign it. Bring it back to me when she's done it."

Rachel nodded and took the file he thrust at her. As she drove to the hospital, she couldn't get the sight of that gloating pleasure on Lester's face out of her mind. She glanced down at the folder resting on her passenger seat several times. What was he up to? She pulled into a space in the hospital parking lot and turned off the ignition. It was none of her business. But the Walshes were bound to be distracted. And she neither liked nor trusted Lester. She picked up the file.

There had to be a hundred pages of dense legal papers in the folder. She tried to read the first few pages but got bogged down in the language so fast that she shifted into merely scanning the pages superficially.

And then the words *Walsh Oil Drilling Corporation,* leaped off a page at her. She stopped and went back to it. She appeared to be in the middle of some sort of contract. She backed up a few pages and read more closely. The contract appeared to be fairly innocuous. Walsh Oil Drilling was leasing mineral rights to several large tracts of land on the West Coast for exploration and possible development. The other party in the deal was a corporation she'd never heard of before— Hidden Pines Holding Company. She plowed through a dozen pages of clauses before she reached the end of the agreement and a sticky note marking where Jolene was supposed to sign the contract.

Rachel jolted as she looked down at the signature blocks on the page before her. She recognized one of the signatures of a Hidden Pines official. Or, more accurately, one of the illegible scrawls. It looked an awful lot like the scrawls on the fraudulent Walsh Oil Drilling financial records she'd been poring over for the past week. She studied the scribble. It had a different loop at the beginning and trailed off a little more horizontally than the one on the financial records, but the rest of it—the way it floated above the line, the aggressive slash of it—was nearly identical.

She needed to show this to Wes Colton. Except Lester would get suspicious if she didn't get Jolene's signature and bring it back to the office right away. Not only would Wes not want the guy involved with this, but Lester had the power to fire her, and she really couldn't afford to lose this job. Maybe she could find a copy machine in the hospital and make a copy of the page.

Who was the owner of Hidden Pines Holding Company? And how was he or she involved with skimming Walsh Oil Drilling monies? It seemed awfully fishy that the two companies were doing business together like this.

She closed the folder and headed into the hospital. It wasn't a big place and she had no trouble finding the Walsh clan. They all but filled the main waiting room.

Jolene Walsh greeted her warmly, if wanly. "Rachel, dear. How kind of you to stop by."

"How's Mr. Warner? He's been so kind to me."

"There's no change. Finn says that's good news. He went down fast last night, but he seems to be holding his own now. He's still having trouble breathing, though, and they can't make heads nor tails of his blood work."

Rachel expressed her sympathy and prayers for Mr. Warner's recovery. Then she winced and said, "Actually, Mrs. Walsh. I'm here on business. Lester Atkins sent me over with some documents for you to sign. But I need to make copies of them before you do."

"Oh!" Mrs. Walsh looked surprised.

Rachel added hastily, "If you'd rather wait on signing these, I'll be glad to tell Lester that. Really, this is no time to be thinking about contracts and the like."

Mrs. Walsh blinked and then examined Rachel more closely. For a moment, Rachel got the impression of acute perceptiveness behind the woman's gaze. Like she'd heard the layers of hidden warning behind Rachel's words. "Yes. Yes, you're right. Now's not the time. Who knows what I might end up signing. Tell Lester I'll take a look at the documents in a few days, when Craig's feeling better."

Rachel nodded, deeply relieved, and turned to leave. And she all but ran into Finn Colton's chest. She didn't need to look up to know those broad shoulders, even if they were covered in a white lab coat this morning.

"Sorry," she mumbled. "I was just leaving."

"Hey," he murmured. "Aren't you even going to say hello?"

Her gaze snapped up to his. "In front of all these people?"

"There's no reason for us not to act civil to one another in public," he replied evenly.

It wasn't the civil bit that worried her. It was the incendiary attraction that flared up between them any time they got into close proximity that had her nervous. It was flaring up, now, in fact, if the heat in her cheeks was any indication. She took a step back from him. "Uhh, hi, Finn. I was here on business, but I'm just leaving. Unless you can tell me where to find a copy machine in this hospital."

"Try the nurses' station. They handle massive amounts of paperwork."

"Thanks." She turned and walked away from him even though every fiber in her body wanted to turn around and fling herself into his arms. But when she heard him murmur, "The blood work is coming back from Bozeman, and it's not good," she did turn around.

Mrs. Walsh collapsed into a vinyl-covered chair and Lucy sank down beside her, holding her mother's hand.

Finn continued gently. "His liver is failing. We don't know why. It seems to be accumulating toxins at a rapid rate, and they're poisoning his body. I'm going to start him on a course of chelation using specially engineered cell salts."

"Cell salts?" Jolene Walsh repeated faintly.

Finn explained. "It's an experimental treatment. I'll introduce specially designed salts into Mr. Warner's body. If all goes well, the salt molecules will bind to the toxins in his liver. And because the body readily flushes salt out of itself, the idea is for his body to flush the salts and take the poisons with them. But we don't have time to do lengthy studies and create a salt specifically for the toxins in Mr. Warner's system. We're going to have to make our best guess at which salt complex to use."

Rachel was impressed by Finn's reassuring calm with Jolene. His explanation had also been clear and easy to follow. Who'd have guessed that the fun-loving teenager she'd once known would have developed into a doctor like this? Of course, the wild recklessness wasn't entirely gone. It had been dangerous in the extreme for him to contemplate kissing her at the Walsh barbecue.

Finn was speaking again. "…need your signature on

some releases before we start the treatment, since it's still experimental."

Jolene glanced up at Rachel, and she smiled at the older woman. These were the sorts of things she needed to be signing right now. Not oil-drilling contracts for Lester Atkins. And on that note, Rachel slipped quietly from the waiting room.

When she approached the nurses' station, the place was in chaos, with nurses rushing every which way. Apparently, there'd been a car accident outside of town and several victims were in the midst of being admitted. Rachel decided to go to the library and make her copies there. She started toward the parking lot but stopped in surprise as she spied Wes Colton standing in front of the hospital. Alarm jangled in her belly. Did his presence have something to do with Craig Warner's mystery illness?

She walked up to him and waited while he finished a call on his cell phone.

"Hi, Rachel. What can I do for you?"

"It's what I can do for you. I've found something I think you might want to take a look at."

"Regarding?"

"Those financial records I gave you. I may have found another place where that one mysterious signature was used. Recently."

"How recently?"

"It's dated two days ago."

Wes glanced around the parking lot and then leaned close to murmur, "Meet me in my office in an hour. And don't say anything about it to anyone."

She nodded, feeling very James Bond-like, and headed for her car. She used the hour to run home and check on Brownie. He was still restless, and she gave him another dose of the painkiller Finn had given her.

Wes was waiting when she arrived at his office. She opened the folder and showed him the signature, and he pulled out his copies of the financial records and compared the two.

"Good eye, Rachel. I'll send these off to a handwriting expert and see what he can make of it."

In short order, Wes had copied the contents of the entire file. As he handed the documents back to her, he asked, "Atkins likely to hassle you over not getting these signed?"

She looked up at Wes in alarm. "I hope not."

"If he gives you any trouble, you let me know. Jolene won't stand for an employee being fired for looking out for her best interest. I'll have a word with her if Lester tries to mess with you."

She smiled her gratitude at him. Who'd have guessed a Colton would look out for her like this? And with a Walsh, no less. *Too bad it wasn't Finn showing such concern.*

As she stood up to leave the sheriff's office, the bell on the outer door rang behind her. A large, familiar shadow filled the doorway. Her heart tripped and sped up.

"Finn!" Rachel exclaimed. "Are you following me?"

"Gee. I was just about to accuse you of the same thing," he retorted, grinning.

Wes looked back and forth between them shrewdly. Rachel squirmed. At this rate, everybody in town would know there were sparks flying between the two of them. But nobody seemed to believe her avowal that even though there might be sparks, she had no intention of starting any fires.

Wes gathered up the papers on the desk. "Let me just put these in the safe and then I'll be ready to go."

Rachel picked up her briefcase and headed for the door. Small problem: the only way out of the sheriff's office was right past Finn. And he wasn't moving. She approached him warily. "Any change in Craig Warner's condition?"

Finn shrugged. "We've started the cell salt therapy. It's too early to tell if it's going to do any good."

"And if it doesn't?"

Finn's jaw tightened and he didn't answer. Which was answer enough.

"I'll say another prayer for him."

"Thanks, Rachel."

"How are you doing? Did you get any sleep last night?"

He shrugged. "Medical school teaches you how to go without sleep. I'm okay. I just wish—"

"Wish what?" she asked quietly.

"I just wish I knew what in the hell is wrong with Craig," he burst out.

"You'll figure it out. I know you will." On impulse, she laid a hand on his chest and sucked in her breath at the heat and hardness of him. She'd meant the spontaneous gesture as a sympathetic one, but in the blink of an eye, tension thrummed between them, hot and thick. She glanced fearfully toward Wes's office and very carefully removed her hand from his chest. *Whoa. Note to self: do not touch Finn even under the most innocent of circumstances.* Not unless she had a burning desire to scorch herself silly.

Finn let out a slow breath. He tried to smile, but the expression seemed more of a grimace to her. "I'll do my best not to let the Walsh family down."

If he could manage normal conversation, she could, too. "Take care of yourself, okay?"

She felt anything but, normal, though. Her stomach was by turns heavy and floating, and her entire body tingled. Why did she only feel this alive when she was around him? Should she ride the wave and enjoy it while it lasted, or maybe she'd be wiser to try to wean herself off the addiction now before it got too bad.

She moved to pass him, but he reached out and stopped her with a hand on her arm. "I—"

She froze, waiting to see what came next.

"I'm sorry we didn't get to finish our conversation at the Walsh barbecue."

She stared, shocked. Okay. Not what she'd been expecting. He wanted to finish that kiss they'd almost started but had never gotten around to? Her gaze ducked away from his. "I'm, uh, sorry, too."

"Give me a rain check?"

"Uh, sure." Positively stunned now, she stumbled as she heard Wes coming back out into the main room. Finn steadied her, a smile playing at the corners of his mouth.

"Thanks," she mumbled. And then she all but ran for the door, her cheeks on fire.

"She okay?" Wes asked.

Finn looked up at his brother, doing his damnedest to hide how shaken he was. He couldn't even be in the same room with Rachel without thinking about pulling her into his arms and kissing her senseless. Who was he kidding? He wasn't leaving town on her account anytime soon. And then she had to go and lay her hand on his chest. He'd thought he was going to come out of his skin when she touched him like that.

Belatedly, Finn answered, "She's great. She just doesn't know it yet."

"Huh?"

"Never mind."

"You thinking about getting back together with her?" Wes asked as they headed out the front door and Wes locked up.

Finn opened his mouth. Shut it. His first impulse was to reply that hell yes, he was getting back together with Rachel. But the inevitable reaction he would get from Wes made him pause.

It was a stupid idea. Hooking up with Rachel would bring him nothing but trouble. If he knew what was good for him, he'd leave well enough alone. Hell, if he really knew what was good for him, he'd get out of Honey Creek as soon as possible. Except he couldn't walk out on Craig Warner right now. No, he definitely had to stick around town until the crisis passed for Warner one way or the other. He didn't know whether to curse the man or bless him.

Rather than try to field any more uncomfortable questions from Wes that had no easy answers, Finn guided the talk into safer waters. "Any progress on the Walsh murder?"

"Maybe."

"Can you talk about it?"

"Nope."

Finn eyed his brother speculatively. Did Rachel have anything to do with the possible break in the case? Why else would she be in the sheriff's office? What did she know? He asked abruptly, "Is Rachel in any danger?"

Wes glanced over at him, startled. "Why do you ask that?"

"Umm, well, with that dog showing up on her porch shot and all…" It was a lame response but the best he could do on short notice.

"Nah. The dog's just one very lucky mutt to have found someone as soft-hearted as Rachel."

"What about whoever killed Walsh?"

"I don't think we have a serial killer on our hands, if that's what you're implying. Whoever killed Mark Walsh wanted him dead and him alone."

Finn exhaled heavily. "Maybe not."

Wes looked over sharply. The squad car slowed and Wes guided it over to the side of the road. When it was parked, he said, "You never did tell me why you called me earlier. That's why I swung by the hospital. But you were tied up with Warner. So talk. Now."

Finn frowned. "There's a chance—a small one, but a chance—that Craig Warner is the victim of foul play."

"How's that?"

"It's too early to be sure, but I've ruled out just about everything else. I think it's possible that Craig has ingested poison."

"Have you got any evidence?"

"Not yet. I wouldn't have said anything at all if you weren't my brother, and I know you won't go off half-cocked."

"When will you be able to say for sure?"

Finn shrugged. "I've sent blood and tissue samples to the crime lab upstate to look for various toxins. It may be a few days before all the results come back."

"Let me know what you find. And I'm saying that in my official capacity."

Great. Another reason he was trapped here in town with Rachel. Part of him was secretly thrilled, and part of him hovered between dismay and disgust. Finn nodded unhappily as Wes muttered to himself. "Different M.O. than the Walsh murder...but, the second Walsh father figure...who'd want to see the head of the family dead?"

Finn had a bad feeling in his gut. First Walsh and now Warner. What was going on in Honey Creek?

Chapter 8

Rachel stared at herself critically in the mirror, remembering another night long ago standing in front of this mirror preparing carefully for prom. The butterflies in her stomach were the same, the nervous anticipation, the worry that she had put on too much makeup and then that she hadn't put on enough—all of it the same. Even the man on her mind was the same.

Finn. Just thinking his name made her sigh. Although she couldn't say exactly what the sigh meant. Maybe it was nostalgic, maybe wistful. Surely it didn't have anything to do with being love struck, though. She knew better. Right?

Fifteen years ago, she'd piled her hair on top of her head in a mass of curls and worn a coronet of daisies. Tonight, she pulled it back into a loose French twist that was more sophisticated. More appropriate to her age. After all, she was thirty years old now—a mature woman. She snorted. *More like a desperate one settling unwillingly into spinsterhood.*

Her prom dress had been a frothy yellow affair with ruffles and bows. This gown, although yellow as well, was anything but little-girly. Edna had done a magnificent job on it. The pale yellow silk draped around her in a smooth sheath, melding with her skin and hair tones until it was barely there. Whisper light, it moved like water against her skin. The long skirt was slit practically to her hip, so its narrow, hourglass cut didn't impede her movement at all. She slipped on the gold and crystal strappy high heels that completed the ensemble. She wore no jewelry at all. The dress didn't need it.

The doorbell rang. That would be Carly, but Rachel couldn't help the moment of flashback as she remembered how excited she'd been the night of prom. She'd had a surprise for Finn. She'd decided she was ready to make love to him, and that night was the night. He'd been sweet and patient and never pushed her, but she knew he'd be thrilled to take their relationship to the next level.

Finn had even hinted that he might be asking her to wait for him while he went off to college, and he'd even not so subtly found out what her ring size was. Had he planned on asking her to marry him? Her heart had told her that was exactly what he had in mind. And the thought made her so happy she could barely contain the joy bursting out of her. She would graduate and join him in college, and then the two of them would start a new life far away from this tiny corner of nowhere. Ha. How terribly wrong she'd been.

She picked up the crystal-encrusted clutch that had

come with the shoes and headed for the front door. She flung it open and Carly stepped inside.

"Oh my God!" Carly exclaimed. "You did it! You finally picked out an outfit all by yourself that I approve of!"

Rachel laughed. "You like it?"

"Like it? I love it! You look practically naked! Finn is not going to be able to take his eyes off you."

"That's not the point," she protested. But then her conscience kicked in. *Okay, so that is secretly exactly the point.*

"Regardless. Every man in the room's going to be drooling over you, girlfriend. *Hoo wee!* Honey Creek isn't going to know what hit it!"

"Carly, I'm not trying to look like a slut. Be honest. Do I look cheap?"

Carly answered with uncharacteristic seriousness. "Rachel, you look like a million bucks. Honest. I've never seen you look more beautiful or classy."

She hugged her cousin. "You look pretty terrific yourself."

Carly twirled in the black cocktail dress and the skirt flared out. "Like it?"

"Yeah. Expecially the part where you twirl and flash your panties at everyone."

Carly grinned. "Not wearing any."

They headed out the front door and Rachel looked up. "You're going commando?"

"I'm thonging it. Makes me feel daring and naughty. How 'bout you? Is there any room under that dress for lingerie?"

Rachel laughed across the top of Carly's red Mustang. "I could never go out in public without underwear."

"Chicken."

"Tart," Rachel retorted as she slipped into her seat.

Carly kept glancing over at her as they headed for the high school. Finally, Rachel asked, "What's wrong with me? Do I have lipstick on my teeth?"

Carly laughed. "No. I'm just thinking about walking into that dance with you. This is going to be fun."

Tonight was going to suck rocks. Finn glared into the mirror as he tied his tie. No way to get out of it, though. The whole Colton clan was going to the dance. Even his younger brothers, Brand and Perry, were going to be there. Darius had decreed it. Only Damien had been excused from the edict to go. He didn't need to become a circus sideshow in front of the entire town. Not to mention Darius had always been so hellbent on Colton respectability. The old man surely wouldn't want to parade his ex-con son in front of everyone. The young doctor in the family, though—that was a different matter. Finn had a sneaking suspicion he'd be on display tonight like some kind of damned trophy.

He shrugged into his suit coat and tugged it into place. An image of prom night all those years ago flashed through his mind. He'd had an engagement ring in his pocket and had been positive that Rachel would say yes. Sure, they were young. But true love was true love. From the moment he'd first laid eyes on her in biology lab, he'd known. She was the One.

He supposed she'd be at the homecoming dance tonight. No reason for her not to be there. But he mentally cringed at the idea. Another dance. The high school gym. Him and Rachel. Both there. But thankfully, not together this time.

Yup, tonight was definitely going to suck.

When they got to the high school, Carly declared the parking lot not full enough for their grand entrance and took a lap around town before coming back to the dance. Rachel's nerves, which were stretched thin already, didn't need the delay. As she glanced down at her gown's plunging neckline and the way her push-up bra all but dumped her out of the top of it, she began to think better of this getup. She'd been feeling unappreciated and defiant the day the dress had come in to the Goodwill store and she'd impulsively bought the thing. But maybe that hadn't been such a good idea. She had the black dress she'd worn to her father's funeral at home...

"I can't do it, Carly. Run me home fast, will you? You can drop me off and come back here while I change."

"Change? Whatever for?" Carly squawked.

"I'm chickening out."

"Oh, no you're not, young lady." The Mustang swung into the high school drive and Carly accelerated threateningly. "You're going into that dance just as you are even if I have to drag you in there by the hair."

Rachel grimaced. She knew her cousin well enough to take the threat seriously. "This is a bad idea."

"This is a great idea. It's high time Finn Colton realized what he's missing. And when he begs you to take him back, you take that stiletto heel of yours and stomp on his heart. You hear me?"

Rachel winced. She hadn't been exactly forthcoming with Carly about her recent encounters with Finn.

Carly wasn't known for her ability to keep a secret, and Rachel really hadn't wanted to be the gossip topic of the whole town again. As it was, enough people were throwing her and Finn speculative looks that rumors had to be swirling behind her back.

"Want me to drop you off in front?" Carly asked.

"No!" Rachel blurted. She flashed back to standing under the porch outside the gym, waiting for Finn to park his truck. He'd been so handsome striding toward her in his tux she'd actually cried a little. He'd been wearing a strange expression as he'd joined her that night, but she had put it down to his nerves at proposing to her. She couldn't have been more wrong!

Carly shrugged and pulled into the parking lot. "There's one of the Colton trucks over there. I wonder how many of them showed up tonight."

"Oh, Lord. If you're trying to make me run screaming from this stupid dance, you're doing a great job."

"C'mon, Raych. Let's go show all those fuddy-duddies just how amazing we Grant women are." Carly linked an arm through hers and marched toward the gym in a fashion that gave Rachel no choice but to go along.

This was dumb. Really dumb. She was going to walk in there and cause a scandal she'd spend another fifteen years living down. What *had* she been thinking to choose this dress? The doorway loomed and two ridiculously young-looking teenaged boys reached for the double doors.

"I can't do this," Rachel wailed in a whisper.

The doors swung open before them.

"Too late," Carly announced cheerfully. "Smile."

What the heck. If she were going to go down in

flames, she might as well pretend to enjoy the ride. Rachel pasted on a smile and stepped inside. The wash of memories that came over her was almost unbearable. A mirrored disco ball spun slowly above the dance floor, and she swore the exact same hand-painted banners and crepe paper streamers decorated the walls. Even the bunches of helium balloons were the same.

She glanced around the room and was shocked to realize that it did, indeed, appear that she had stopped the dance. Every face in the room was turning her way, with varying degrees of amazement and appreciation painted upon them all. She spied the cluster of Coltons in the corner but didn't see Finn among the broad-shouldered group.

Her stomach fell. But then relief kicked in.

"C'mon. Let's turn this town on its head," Carly murmured, dragging her forward into the room. They just about reached the mob of people dancing in the middle of the gym floor when Rachel felt a presence behind her.

She paused. Half turned. And stared.

Whoever said men didn't know how to make a grand entrance had obviously never seen Finn Colton walk into a room. In a tuxedo. With one hand carelessly in a pants pocket like an Italian model. Or a movie star.

He stopped just inside the door, much as she had. And likewise, every head in the place turned his way. But then his gaze locked on her, and everything and everyone else in the room faded away. His gaze traveled slowly down her body to her toes and all the way back up to her face. It was hard to see his eyes in the dim half-light, but the expression on his face came darn near to open lust.

Carly cackled beside her. "Take that, Finn Colton! Now go for the kill, cuz."

"Uhh, how exactly do I do that?" Rachel mumbled back. Not only was her entire face on fire, but it felt like her neck, shoulders and arms were blushing, too.

"Easy. Flirt with him like crazy. Then leave with another guy. He'll never live it down."

"Another guy?" Rachel squeaked. "I don't do that sort of thing. My reputation would be ruined—"

"Like it's not already?" Carly shot back.

Her cousin's flippant remark stopped her cold. Sometimes she forgot what everyone else in town thought of her. She supposed they must be right if they all still believed she was a coldhearted heartbreaker after all these years. After all, she had managed to drive Finn away from her even though he'd been crazy about her.

Rachel's gaze slid in his direction whether she willed it to or not. He had just reached his family and turned. And, oh Lordy, he was looking back at her, a tea cup of punch paused halfway to his mouth. She tore her gaze away from him hoping desperately that the move looked casual. Disinterested.

"Wow!" A male voice exclaimed from nearby. "You two look hot!"

Rachel glanced over at a cluster of young men who didn't look to be much older than college age. As a group, they were big and burly. Had to be some of the recent football players back in town for Coach Meyer's last hurrah.

Carly purred and preened as several of them came over to introduce themselves. Rachel nodded and smiled but couldn't have repeated any of their names if her life depended on it. One of them offered to go get her a drink and she nodded numbly.

A disk jockey was on a platform at one end of the gym spinning a combination of old and new music, most of it with a good dance beat. Back in the day, Rachel had loved to dance. The last time she'd danced in this room, Finn had held her in his arms…and called her the worst kind of human being. Loudly. In front of everyone. And then he'd walked out on her and left her standing in the middle of the dance floor with the whole school staring at her. And then, as she'd stumbled off the floor in a flood of tears that nearly blinded her, they'd laughed at her.

"Here's your punch," one of the nameless college students announced cheerfully. "We spiked it for you, seeing as how you're of legal drinking age."

She smiled ruefully. "Do I look that old?"

The young men laughed. "You look fantastic," one of them retorted. It was gratifying when the others nodded vigorously in agreement.

"You guys are good for a girl's ego," she teased.

"Wanna dance?" one of them asked.

"Will you tell me if I look dopey? It has been a while since I've done it."

"I'll teach you all the latest moves," the one who'd brought her the punch promised.

"You wish," a smooth, deep voice muttered from behind her.

Rachel turned fast and nearly killed herself as she pivoted on the tall heels in her narrow skirt and proceeded to lose her balance. Strong hands caught her and steadied her. Hands whose touch thrilled her to the marrow of her bones.

She murmured to Finn, "It's not nice to sneak up on someone from behind and startle them."

"Sorry."

"Hey, buddy. She and I were just going out for a dance," the college student complained.

Finn sent the kid a quelling look that had the student slinking away in a moment.

"Finn! I was going to dance with him and you just chased him away!"

"He's too young for you."

She stood up to her full, heel-enhanced height. It still was only enough to bring her up to approximately his chin. "Are you calling me old?"

"No. I'm calling you a gorgeous woman in her prime, and he's a snot-nosed kid who wouldn't have the slightest idea what to do with a woman like you."

"Oh, and you do?" Rachel couldn't help retorting.

Finn's gaze went dark and lazy and smoky. "Yeah, I do."

She actually took a step back from all that sexual intensity rolling off of him. "It just so happens that that boy promised to teach me some new dance moves. And I plan to take him up on the offer."

Finn stepped closer and murmured, "Over my dead body. I'm not letting anyone else—boy or man—lay a hand on you, with you looking like that."

Rachel glanced down at her gown in surprise. Everything was where it was supposed to be. "What's wrong with my dress?" she asked defensively.

"Nothing. You look sensational. And that's the problem."

She gazed up at him steadily. Despite Carly's advice to stomp on his heart, she spoke gently. "You're not in any position to dictate who I do or don't dance with, Finn. I don't belong to you."

His jaw rippled and frustration glinted in his eyes.

She continued lightly, "In fact, you made that crystal clear to me in this very room. Or don't you remember?"

"I remember it perfectly well," he gritted out from between clenched teeth.

She nodded and smiled politely at him. "If you'll excuse me, then, I'm going to go collect my dance lesson."

It was hard—really, really hard—but she turned away from Finn and strolled across the room to where the college gang had congregated near the hors d'oeuvre table. And that was how she ended up spending the next hour dancing with a series of college students ten years her junior while Finn furiously avoided looking in her direction. Her heart broke a little every time she spied him across the gym with his back stubbornly turned to her.

The whole Colton clan had come to the dance, with one exception. There was no sign of Damien. Too bad. He was her favorite of the lot of them. But she could see how he might not like a gathering like this, where he might very well become a spectacle. Oh, wait. That was her job.

Another hour later, Rachel was running out of steam at keeping up the charade of enjoying herself. Were it not for the fact that Carly was her ride home, she'd have left already.

As if she wasn't miserable enough, the DJ got the bright idea to ask for all the former homecoming kings and queens to come out onto the dance floor for a spotlight dance. Rachel moved to the side of the room along with everyone else, relieved to get a moment to herself to hide in the shadows.

Then the cursed DJ announced, "Okay, kings and queens. Look around the room. If your date from homecoming is here, go get them and bring them out onto the dance floor. Don't worry spouses…you get the next dance."

Amid the laughter, Rachel's gaze snapped to Finn in horror. He'd been the homecoming king his senior year. And *she'd* been his date. She shrank back behind the biggest of the college students and did her best to fade into the wall. But it was no good. Finn, grim faced and tight jawed, was looking around the room for her.

She swore under her breath as he strode purposefully in her direction. He'd spotted her. In seconds he loomed in front of her. Rachel dimly noted silence falling nearby as locals watched with avid interest to see what happened next between the two of them.

"Well?" Finn muttered, looming in front of her. "Are you going to dance with me or not?"

Chapter 9

Finn was appalled by the look of horror on Rachel's face. Did she despise him so much? He'd thought they had something between them. Had felt it. But she looked as if she'd rather face a firing squad than dance with him.

"C'mon," he said. "People are starting to notice your hesitation. Let's just do this and get it over with."

She squared her bare, slender shoulders…which he'd give a year's salary to kiss right now. Damn, she looked incredible in that gown. She'd been wearing yellow the night of prom, too. It had suited her sunny personality. He'd never believed it possible that she would betray him so completely like she had. He'd loved her, for God's sake. Been sure she felt the same way about him. How could she have cheated on him with some other guy? And then, as if that wasn't bad enough—

"All right. Fine. Let's just get this over with." Rachel stepped forward resolutely.

He held out his forearm to her automatically and led her onto the floor.

The flood of memories was overwhelming. High school dances with her. Looking up into the stands at football games and wanting to play his best for her. Meeting her in the hallway between classes to steal a quick kiss and put a fiery blush on her cheeks. God, the laughter. She'd made him so damned happy. They'd been the two halves of a whole. When he was down, she'd cheer him up. When she was upset about something, she came to him to make it right. And he always did. They'd been magic.

The music wailed around them and she swayed in his arms, bringing back another entire flood of memories. Imagined mostly, but vivid nonetheless of what it would be like to finally make love with her, to become one body and one soul for real. He'd thought about it a lot when they'd been dating but had never pushed. After all, they'd had all the time in the world. The rest of their lives together. No matter how bad he'd wanted to be with her, she was worth the wait.

And then that last night had happened. That last dance. Images came rushing back unbidden, a bitter dessert that ruined the rest of the meal of memories and left a terrible taste in his mouth. His hurt. His disbelief. And ultimately his fury. He must have tensed because Rachel murmured, "Never fear. It will be over soon."

"You don't have to make it sound like I'm torturing you," he muttered back.

"You have no idea," she retorted.

He frowned down at her and words sprang from his

lips before he could think better of them. "You could do a whole lot worse than me, you know."

Her gaze snapped up to his. "Is that an offer?"

"I—uhh—" Her question took him completely by surprise. His mind went blank. Was it an offer?

"Please don't hold me so close," she murmured through a patently plastic smile.

He loosened his arms fractionally. "Why? Do I make you uncomfortable? Remind you of how things used to be between us?"

Her light brown eyes went dark. Troubled. "You can't have it both ways, Finn. You can't flirt with me and try to get into my bed while you continue to throw the past in my face."

That made him pull back. Sharply. "I'm not trying to have it both ways. I'm here for a few weeks to welcome my brother home and then I'm leaving again. And in the meantime, I figured we might as well act civilized with each other."

"Is that what the other night in my living room was? Civilized?"

Ah-ha. So their kiss had had as big an effect on her as it had on him! He studied her closely. "I'm not sure that's the word I'd use to describe it, but it wasn't bad, was it?"

"I think I'd better not answer that question."

He glanced up and wasn't surprised to see that they were the center of attention. And then he spied his family. His brothers mostly just looked concerned. Maisie looked about ready to march out here and commit murder. But it was his father's expression that stopped him in his tracks. The man looked nearly apoplectic. Of course, Maisie and his father knew the whole story of what Rachel had done to him. They were the only ones who did. He'd made them swear fifteen years ago never to tell a soul what they'd learned about Rachel. He might have hated her for her betrayal, but he'd still loved her enough not to want to see her reputation publicly dragged through the mud. To his knowledge, neither of them had ever broken their promise.

But they were a stark reminder of just how treacherous a woman Rachel Grant truly was. Her right hand rested on his shoulder, and her left hand rested lightly on his waist. Where a moment ago her touch had felt like heaven, all of a sudden, her arms felt like a spider's web, sucking him in, luring him into her trap. Again. All the old hurt and betrayal flared up anew. She'd ruined all his dreams for the two of them. And damn her, she seemed to have ruined him for any other woman.

In all the years since he'd left Honey Creek, he'd never been able to trust another woman enough to give away his heart. What if someone else hurt him like she had? He didn't think he could stand it a second time.

They had finished another slow revolution and his family was about to come into sight again. His family, who'd stood by him when he'd wanted to turn down his college scholarship and just run away from Rachel, who'd kept him from falling into a bottle to drown his sorrows. The Coltons might have their problems, but at least they'd stuck by him when his life had fallen completely apart. Or, more accurately, when Rachel Grant had blown it completely apart.

He was being torn in two. And it was killing him.

"You're right," he announced abruptly. "I can't have it both ways. And I don't want it both ways." His arms fell away from her. "I'll never forget or forgive what you did to me, Rachel. No pretty dress or demure charm or injured dog is going change that. I can't do this anymore."

He pivoted on his heel and strode off the dance floor. He headed for the door and some cool air outside. He felt like she'd stuck a knife in his chest all over again. He'd known coming to this dance was a bad idea. That it would dredge up too many old memories and open up too many old wounds.

He burst outside into humid night air that clung heavily to his skin. He tore off his tie and shrugged out of his jacket, but he still felt like he was about to suffocate. He had to get away from there. From her. Far, far away. He'd head back to Bozeman this very minute were it not for Craig Warner lying near death in the hospital. Damn him.

But he could get away from Rachel. He fished the keys out of his pocket and marched into the parking lot. He climbed in his truck, hit the gas and peeled out of the parking lot as fast as he could.

Rachel stood in the door of the gym, tears flowing down her face, and watched him go—again. And he never looked back—again.

"Oh my God. I can't believe he did that to you!" Carly exclaimed. "Let's go to his house and trash his truck."

Her cousin's arm went around her waist; but like the last time Finn had humiliated her and abandoned her in this very spot, Rachel dared not accept the comfort. If she did, she would shatter into a million pieces. She had to hold it together until she could get out of there. Go somewhere far away by herself. And hide. And cry.

And if she were lucky, she wouldn't get to the raving and screaming part until she was safely alone.

"Take me home, Carly," she ground out.

"I don't think you should be alone right now. Besides, I think you should go back in there and show them all that he doesn't—"

"No!" She cut off her cousin sharply.

"Rachel. Do you still have a thing for him? After everything he's done to you? Are you nuts?"

"No!" she snapped a second time. "Of course I don't have a thing for him. I know better than to want Finn Colton. He's poison."

But a poison she was addicted to as surely as she was standing here.

"C'mon, Raych. We'll go to your place, open up a bottle of wine, and drink to what bastards men are!"

"No, thanks. Just take me home," she replied tiredly.

"You sure?"

Sympathy was something she couldn't handle right now. Carly's concern was threatening to break down her last remaining ounce of strength. "Let's just go."

It took determined effort on her part; but when they got to her place, Rachel managed to send Carly on her way without the threatened bottle of wine and man-bashing session.

Finally alone, she hung up the disastrous yellow gown carefully in her closet—no sense taking out her grief and anger on a dress, and besides, she could probably sell it for a little money in Bozeman. She checked in on Brownie, who looked alarmed and licked her hand in concern. Intuitive creatures, dogs.

"Don't worry about me, boy. You just get better. At

least you're on the mend. I got one thing right this week at any rate."

The dog whimpered quietly as if mirroring her distress.

She lay down in her bed but felt numb. She paced her bedroom for a while and experienced alternating bouts of grief and humiliation. She kept waiting for the storm of tears, but it wouldn't come. Shockingly, what finally came was not self-pity at all. It was anger. She was even forced to move her pacing to the living room where she could work up a good head of steam.

She could not believe he'd done it to her again. He'd walked out on her in front of the whole town and left her standing all alone in the middle of the dance floor again. She supposed she ought to be grateful that this time he hadn't reamed her out before turning on his heel and marching away from her. But it was hard to work up much gratitude for that. Her current frame of mind hovered closer to homicidal.

She was a grown woman. She lived a decent life. She was a nice person. There was no reason for her to put up with anyone treating her like this. She'd pack up her things and leave this two-bit town tomorrow were it not for her mother. As soon as Mom passed away, she was out of here forever.

But the moment the thought entered her mind, she shoved it away in dismay. She loved her mother. No reason to wish for her mom's death out of her own selfish anger.

How dare Finn act like that? She hadn't asked him to come back to town. To come to her house and kiss her and make her think they might actually have a chance. He had no right to play with her heart like this!

Who was he to judge her anyway? Just because he was a Colton didn't give him the right to treat other people like dirt. And especially when he couldn't even be bothered to tell them what they'd done to deserve it!

Why had he walked out on her tonight? She went over and over what they'd said; and while she'd called him on his mixed messages, that wasn't the sort of thing that made a person storm out of a room like he had.

And speaking of storming out of gyms, she was sick and tired of him accusing her of all sorts of bad things but refusing to tell her exactly what those bad things were. The guy had owed her an explanation for fifteen years and never had bothered to give it to her. After this latest fiasco, she expected it would be at least fifteen more years before he bothered to show his face around this town again. And by God, after waiting that long already, she wasn't about to wait that long again for some answers!

She was going to go out to that cursed ranch and demand some explanations once and for all. She had grabbed her car keys and stepped out onto the back porch before it dawned on her that it was three o'clock in the morning. Okay, fine. She'd go out there and demand answers when daylight broke.

But when daylight came, she was passed out across her bed, sleeping off the exhaustion and emotional rollercoaster of the night before. It was close to noon before she woke up, and were it not for Brownie whimpering to go out, she might have slept longer.

She stumbled into the kitchen and opened the back door for the dog. A wave of muggy warmth hit her in the face. Indian Summer was late this year. The air was turbulent, and ominous clouds were already building in the west. Looked like a storm brewing. Perfect weather to fit her mood.

Grimly, she fed the dog and moved his bed out to the back porch so he could enjoy the day's unseasonable warmth. She dressed in jeans and a T-shirt, stomped into a pair of cowboy boots and threw on a little makeup for confidence. Her eyes snapping and her cheeks unnaturally ruddy, she headed for the Colton ranch and a showdown with Finn. If she'd owned a six-shooter gun, she'd have strapped it onto her hip in her current state of mind.

Her bravado wavered as she turned into the Colton drive and passed under the big arch, but she took a deep breath and wrapped her righteous indignation more closely around herself. She drove around to the back of the main house.

She knocked on the back door.

No one answered. Cursing under her breath, she knocked again. Still nothing. She looked around for any sign of humans and noticed a barn door open up the hill. She headed for it. She was not leaving this place until she found out what in the hell was going on.

What in the hell was going on? Finn stared down at Craig Warner's latest blood work in dismay. The cell salts had been working. The guy was getting better. He'd even kept a little food down last night. And then this morning he had crashed worse than ever. His heart had stopped an hour ago, occasioning the call from the E.R. asking him to come in to the hospital to watch Warner so the on-call doctor could cover the emergency room.

"Get me a list of everything he ingested last night," he told the nurse hovering beside him.

"Already got it," the woman replied grimly.

Obviously, her thoughts were running in the same direction his were. He smiled his appreciation for her efficiency and took the sheet of paper she thrust at him. Four ounces of chicken broth. Five saltines. Two ounces of strawberry gelatin. Seven ounces of apple juice. Nothing there to explain Warner's cardiac arrest and respiratory distress.

"Double the cell salts," he told the nurse quietly.

"You already have him on a pretty high dosage."

"He'll die if we don't do something."

"Yes, sir."

He jammed a hand through his hair in frustration. What was he missing?

Missing? That would be Rachel.

Oh, for God's sake. He was not missing her. He'd done the right thing. Protected himself from another disaster at her hands. If they had gotten together, how long would it be this time before she turned to someone else? Before she broke his heart for good?

Rachel paused in the dim doorway of the barn while her eyes adjusted. Down the broad alley she saw a big, male figure enter a stall. She marched toward him, battle ready.

She got to the stall and looked inside. A man squatted in the corner, holding a bottle for a red-and-white calf who was noisily and messily drinking from it. He glanced up. *Damien.* Disappointment coursed through her.

"Hey, Rachel. What brings you out here? Looking for Finn?"

"Looking for answers," she replied grimly. "And Finn's the one who can give them to me, yes."

"He's not here. He got called to the hospital a while ago. Craig Warner had a setback, apparently."

"Oh. Too bad. He's a nice man."

Damien shrugged.

"Well, I'll be going, then."

"Before you leave, could you pass me that second bottle and the bucket on the floor beside the door?"

She looked down at her feet at a mash that looked like cracked-wheat cereal in a bucket. "Sure." She picked up bottle and bucket and opened the stall door. She eyed the momma cow warily. "She going to be okay with me?"

Damien glanced up at the gigantic creature casually. "Yep, she's pretty mellow for a first-time mom."

Despite his assurances, Rachel still gave the cow wide berth as she moved slowly across the stall to Damien's side. "What's the mash for?"

"Trying to get this little fella to start eating some solid food."

She gave the calf a critical glance. "He looks a little young for that."

Damien shrugged. "His mother's not making enough milk. Probably the weird time of year he was born. Mother Nature is telling her to preserve energy to get through the winter herself, and she can't spare much for junior. I'm bottle-feeding him until I can get him eating solid food, and the sooner I can do that, the better for his health."

She watched as the calf butted at the nearly empty bottle. "He's a cutie. Looks like he's playing you to get you to give him more milk."

"Animals are honest. They don't play games with you."

Rachel snorted and the cow flung her head up in alarm. "Sorry, momma," she murmured.

"Who's playing games with you?" Damien asked quietly.

"Your brother."

"Finn? That's never been his style. 'Course, I've been gone a long time, and maybe he's changed."

Rachel replied bitterly, "He did the same thing to me fifteen years ago. He hasn't changed his stripes at all."

Damien took the bottle away from the calf—much to its displeasure—and substituted his fingers, dipped in the mash, in the calf's mouth instead. The little guy sucked for a moment but then spit out Damien's fingers in disgust.

Rachel smiled. Damien patiently repeated dipping his fingers in the mash and putting them in the calf's mouth. "You're good with animals," she commented.

He shrugged. "Finn's the one with real magic where animals are concerned. Too bad he never followed his dream to become a vet. He'd have been a great one."

"At least animals would've forced him to be honest with them."

Damien glanced over at her. "You need me to beat him up for you?"

Startled, she looked at him full on. Humor glinted in his eyes. "No, but I'd sure as hell like you to tell me what happened fifteen years ago that turned him against me so suddenly and completely."

Damien blinked, startled. She swore that was guilty knowledge flashing in his gaze before he looked away, busying himself with feeding the calf.

"You know, don't you?" she accused.

He offered the calf the bottle once more and the hungry baby latched on, sucking eagerly. At length, he looked up at her grimly. "Yeah, I know what happened."

Chapter 10

Finn turned at the sound of a male voice calling his name. Wes. "Hey, bro. What brings the sheriff to the hospital on a Sunday morning?"

"How's your patient?"

Finn shrugged. "Had a setback between last night and this morning. Crashed on us about two hours ago. It was a near thing to get his ticker going again."

Wes lowered his voice. "Any idea what caused the crisis?"

Finn frowned. "No. He even was able to eat a little last night. We've tested for food allergies, and nothing he ate should've caused him to nearly die on us this morning. His blood stats are as bad as they ever were, too."

Wes lowered his voice even more. "Who was with him last night? Particularly at or near the time he was eating?"

Finn blinked. "You think one of the Walshes is trying to poison him? A business associate?"

Wes shrugged. "I need a nurse to pull the visitor logs and see who visited Craig last night. Can you arrange that?"

"Yeah, sure," Finn replied, startled. Wes wasn't kidding. He seriously seemed to think one of the Walshes might have poisoned Craig. Why on Earth would one of them do that? Craig was practically a member of the family. He and Jolene were obviously deeply in love, and her kids treated him like a father.

Wes murmured, "Are those blood tests we talked about back yet?"

"Yeah." Finn grimaced. The results weren't going to please his brother.

"And?"

"His arsenic levels are through the roof," Finn said quietly. Wes stared, and Finn continued, "I've ordered another round of tests to determine if his body has been storing up too much of it for a very long time for some reason, or if he has recently ingested massive quantities of the chemical—either by accident or foul play." As his brother's frown deepened, Finn reminded Wes, "It's possible he was exposed through some natural source, like a tainted water source at his home."

"But not damned likely," Wes muttered grimly.

"No. Not likely," Finn agreed. "I'll let you know what the tests show. The tox panel should be back in a day or two."

"Ever heard of an outfit called Hidden Pines Holding Company?" Wes asked abruptly.

"No. Should I have?"

"No." Wes shrugged. "I'm working on a subpoena

to get the state of California to release the names of the company's officers to me. In the meantime, if you happen to overhear any of the Walshes mention it while they're hanging around here, let me know, okay?"

Finn frowned. "You want me to spy on a patient's family?"

"I want you to assist me in a murder investigation and a possible attempted murder investigation."

"I don't think there's anything in the Hippocratic oath to prevent me from doing that." Finn sighed heavily. "All right. I'll do it."

Rachel followed Damien out of the stall like a burr stuck to his back. No way was he getting away from her without spilling his guts. He went to a work area and rinsed out the bottles and bucket, and she waited nearby. Finally, he turned to face her.

"Why are you asking me about all this?" he murmured. "You know what happened as well as I do."

"All I know is that the boy I was crazy in love with turned on me for no reason, dumped me, humiliated me, and didn't come back to town for fifteen years. And I never found out why."

Damien blurted, "The abortion, of course."

Rachel stared. "What abortion?"

"Your abortion."

"What?" Her mind was a complete blank. What on Earth was he talking about? "You mean me? An abortion? I've never been pregnant, let alone had an abortion. Who are you talking about?"

Damien frowned. "I was there. I heard it all."

"Heard what? Tell me what happened, Damien." An awful suspicion was taking root in her head.

He exhaled hard. "It was the night of Finn's senior prom. I was just coming into the kitchen when Maisie told Finn about it. She saw you in Bozeman at an abortion clinic. You were terribly upset. She went in and told them she was your friend who'd come up to be with you. They said you were in having the procedure done, but she could wait for you. She didn't stick around."

"And then she told Finn I'd had an abortion?"

"Yeah."

Rachel didn't know whether to laugh or cry. "Good God, Damien. I was still a virgin the night of prom. I couldn't possibly have had an abortion."

Damien frowned. "Maisie took a picture of you there in the clinic with the snazzy digital camera she'd bought that day. She showed it to Finn."

Rachel frowned. How could that be? She thought back to the spring of her sophomore year in high school. That was right about when her mother was first diagnosed with Alzheimer's. Her mom had only been in her mid-forties and the diagnosis had taken the doctors a while to make. They'd told the family that early-onset Alzheimer's had a tendency to be inherited and had offered Rachel genetic testing—

And then it clicked in her mind.

"Of course. That must have been the day we went to the pregnancy counseling center in Bozeman to get me genetically tested for early-onset Alzhemier's. My mother has that, you know. I had a fifty percent chance of having it, too. And I wanted to know...for my own peace of mind and because of Finn...didn't want to saddle him with me if I was going to lose my memory young...but I don't have the gene and everything was okay..." She trailed off.

Damien stared at her. "So there was no abortion?"

"No."

Eventually he murmured, "Accused of something you didn't do. Been there, done that. It sucks."

"Ya think?" she retorted. Panic was starting to build somewhere deep inside her. Finn had believed all these years that she'd had an abortion? And then the other shoe dropped in her mind. She and Finn had never slept together. They'd agreed to wait until she felt ready. But if he thought she'd had an abortion, he also thought she'd slept with some other guy!

"How could he think that of me?" she exclaimed.

Damien shrugged. "If a woman were carrying my baby and got rid of it without even talking to me, I'd be pretty pissed off."

No kidding. "Not to mention he thinks I slept with someone else. I loved him with every bit of my being. I was dead sure he was my soul mate! Heck, I told him so over and over. How could he possibly think I would have betrayed him?"

"You'd have to ask him that."

Her gaze narrowed. "I will. He's at the hospital?"

"Yeah," Damien answered cautiously. "Should I call him and warn him you're coming down to kill him?"

"Nah," she retorted sarcastically. "It'll be more fun if I surprise him when I do the deed." She spun and headed for the exit with long, angry strides.

Finn frowned at his cell phone as he put it away. That had been a rather strange phone call from Damien. His brother had mentioned in a weird enough tone of voice that Rachel was coming over to the hospital to talk to him that it almost sounded like a warning. And then

Damien had dropped that random comment about listening to people with an open mind. What the hell had that been all about?

As if that wasn't enough, Damien had ended the phone call with some cryptic remark about how he felt a storm coming. A big one. Had the guy been talking about the weather or Rachel? Finn couldn't tell.

He glanced out the window. The sunny day had gone an ominous color outside. He stepped closer to the glass to peer out. Thunder clouds roiled on the horizon, black and menacing. They blocked enough sunlight that the day had taken on a premature twilight cast, but not the cast indicating the serene ending of a day sinking into night. Rather, this greenish twilight presaged violence. Chaos. Storms, indeed.

Everything was big in Montana, including the weather. And it did, indeed, appear that they were in for a severe late-season thunderstorm. He went over to the nurses' station. "If we lose power, I'll need you to check Mr. Warner's ventilator immediately to make sure it switched to the backup power source."

The nurse glanced toward the windows across the waiting area and nodded. "Looks like we're in for a bad one."

Rachel was furious and growing more so by the second. She kept having to take her foot off the accelerator as her speed crept up again and again on her way down the mountain. Oh, yes. She was going to kill Finn. Slowly. And painfully.

The sky overhead grew darker and darker until she was forced to turn on her headlights to see the road. Bizarre. It was still late afternoon. She glanced up at the sky and gasped at the ugly mass of clouds overhead. It was a sickly counterclockwise swirl of purple and yellow, like a spinning bruise. Not good. Her gut told her to get down off this mountain fast and seek shelter before the full fury of this storm broke. As the road straightened out close to town, she stepped on the accelerator. Trash blew in front of her as the sky grew even darker and more ominous. Branches whipped and the trees swayed, groaning, as she entered Honey Creek. People scurried here and there, securing awnings and bringing in outdoor furniture. Leave it to Montana to have snow and then turn around a few days later and have a violent springlike thunderstorm in October.

She parked in the hospital parking lot and ran for the building. It wasn't raining, but the wind was lashing her hair against her face so hard it stung. She ducked into the front lobby. The relative calm was a relief after the violence of the coming storm. She headed for the ICU, where she was bound to find Craig…and Finn.

Finn was at Craig's bedside when she arrived, and she spotted him through the glass wall immediately. Glaring daggers at him, she parked herself next to the nurse's station to wait for him. One of the nurse's cell phones rang behind her.

Then the nurse announced, "My husband says they just issued a tornado warning for Honey Creek. Somebody turn on the local news."

The low drone of the television mounted high in the corner of the waiting area was turned up and tuned in to a Bozeman television station. The meteorologist was speaking with contained urgency: "…take cover immediately. Doppler radar indicates rotation in this cloud five miles west of Honey Creek. A weather watcher reports seeing a funnel cloud forming moments ago. Even if a tornado does not fully form, residents of Honey Creek should expect damaging wind gusts of up to seventy miles per hour and tennis ball-sized hail. The storm is moving east at fifty miles per hour and should reach Honey Creek in the next five to seven minutes. Residents are urged to take cover inside a sturdy building and stay away from windows and doors."

Rachel glanced outside in alarm. The daylight had taken on a strange, green-yellow cast she'd never seen before. A phone rang behind her, and a few seconds later a nurse announced, "All nonessential personnel are to take shelter in the basement."

A nurse beside Rachel grunted. "We're all essential personnel."

Finn's voice spoke up from behind her. "Rachel. What are you doing here? You need to get out of here. Head home and take cover."

"I don't think there's time for that, Dr. Colton," the nurse beside her replied. "Look."

Rachel looked where the woman pointed outside and gasped in dismay. A thick column of spinning cloud snaked down toward the ground no more than a mile away. That window faced west. The storm was moving east. Crap. That tornado was coming straight at them.

Finn ordered sharply, "Get Mr. Warner ready to move. Get all the ambulatory patients down to the basement. Get the nonmobile patients away from the windows and into an interior hall. Cover them with blankets so they don't get hit by flying glass. Move!"

Rachel ran after the nearest nurse. "What can I do to help?"

"Take these blankets. Wrap the patients in rooms

two and four in them and pull their beds out into the hall. Hurry!"

Rachel took the pile of blankets the woman thrust at her and scrambled to do as ordered. One of the patients was either sedated or unconscious and wasn't difficult to wrap up and roll out into the hall. But the other patient, an elderly woman, didn't seem to understand what was happening and kept pulling the blanket off herself. Rachel dragged the heavy hospital bed out into the hall.

The lights flickered and went out and the hall plunged into darkness. Only the faintest light came from the window in the waiting area down the hall. An emergency floodlight came on somewhere in the other direction, sending enough light toward them to see, but not much more.

"Rachel, get the hell out of here!" Finn snapped as he helped her drag the bed across the hall.

"Too late. The storm's almost here, and you guys need the extra hands."

She darted off to help a swearing nurse who was having trouble getting a bed through a door. They wrestled the bed into the hallway and tucked blankets over the frightened man's head.

Rachel noticed Jolene Walsh farther down the hallway tucking more blankets around Craig Warner with all the tender concern of a mother for a child—or a woman for her lover. No doubt about it. Those two were in love. *Good for them.*

She took a step toward Jolene to help her, but then she heard it. A roaring, tearing sound. Huh. The twister really did sound like a freight train. Coming down a set of tracks straight at her at high speed. She glanced out a window as she ran past an open door and gasped.

The entire window was filled with a whirling mass of debris, barely on the other side of the hospital parking lot. Shocked into frozen awe, she stared at the monster coming for her.

And then something big and hard and heavy slammed into her.

"Get moving," Finn barked. "Come with me." He dragged her along by the arm until she started to run under her own power. They raced behind the nurse's station and he shoved her down under the tall desk that formed the front of the station.

He wrapped his arms around her as she spread the last blanket she had around them. He grabbed one end of it and tucked it beneath his hip. The other end he wrapped tightly around them both and over their heads. It was hot and stuffy under the blanket. This was surreal. She was not about to face death, not with Finn Colton's arms tight around her and his cheek pressed against her hair.

"Are we going to die?" she asked blankly.

"Not if I can help it!" he shouted over the roaring wind. "Hang on to me with all your strength!"

That was not a hard command to follow. Her terror was beyond anything she'd ever experienced. But then, as glass shattered nearby, a strange thing happened to her. A calm came over her at all odds with the violence erupting around them. If this were it, so be it. Living or dying was out of her control now. It was up to Fate or God or whatever force controlled such things in the universe. And in the meantime, she couldn't think of another person in the whole world she'd rather spend her last few moments on Earth with.

She might be furious with Finn for believing the

worst of her and never giving her a chance to defend herself, but as debris struck her back through the blanket and Finn wrapped his entire body around her protectively, a single stark fact came into crystal-clear focus. She loved Finn Colton. No matter what he'd done in the past. Against all reason, against her better judgment—heck, against her burning desire not to do so— she loved him.

The roaring got louder and the building shook around her. More glass shattered and the wind shrieked its fury, yanking at her with a violence that was stunning. Her eardrums felt like someone was trying to suck them out of her head. She pressed her right ear against Finn's chest and hung on for dear life as the tornado did its damnedest to tear them apart. And wasn't that just the story of their lives? Everyone and everything around them trying to keep them from each other.

Finn squeezed her suffocatingly tight against his chest. All hell broke loose then. Crashes and ripping sounds joined the banshee wail of the tornado as the hospital was literally torn apart around them. The screams of the wind were so fierce she thought the sound alone might kill them. The blanket tore away from them. She clung to Finn with all her strength in the madness, as desks and chairs and computer monitors flew past.

Something hit Finn's shoulder and he grunted in pain. She'd have spoken to ask him if he were okay, but all the air had been sucked out of her lungs. She tried as hard as she could to pull in a breath, but she couldn't manage it. She couldn't breathe! Panic hit her. She started to struggle, but Finn's crushing embrace held her still. Something about him conveyed an assurance that he would take care of her. That she would be all right. That he was in control of this madness and would see her through it safely. Her heart opened even more as the love she'd held at bay all these years flooded through her.

All in all, it wasn't a bad way to die. In the arms of the one man she'd ever loved wholly and without reservation.

The moment passed and she dragged in a lungful of air. The noise was still horrific, but mostly paper, leaves and light debris were flying around now. And then even that settled. The roaring faded as the tornado passed, and a strange stillness settled around them. And then, as quickly as the silence had come, it shattered with nurses yelling for help and doctors yelling back instructions and patients moaning and crying. Someone screamed, but the noise cut off abruptly.

Finn looked down at her like he was as surprised as she was that they were still alive. "You okay?"

"Shockingly, yes. You? Something hit you."

"It was nothing. I've taken worse hits in a football game." He looked around them and then back to her. "Gotta go do the doctor thing now."

"We need to talk—" she started.

Finn jumped to his feet and held a hand down for her. For an instant his gaze met hers, naked and unguarded, and maybe a touch shell-shocked. The tornado had been a profound moment for him, too, apparently. "Later," he bit out. "I think I'm going to be busy for a while."

She took one look down the hallway at the mess and knew that for the understatement of the century that it was. She prayed that the residents of Honey Creek had heeded the tornado warnings and taken cover and that no one had been seriously hurt or killed. But if the destruction here was any indication, the town probably wouldn't be so lucky.

She pulled out her cell phone, but it had no signal. The tornado must've wiped out the cell phone towers. Scouring the corners beneath a blizzard of paper, she spotted a desk phone and plugged its cord into an outlet she found low on a wall where a desk used to stand. Miraculously, the thing still worked. Quickly, she dialed the nursing home. It was on the other side of town. She hoped it had been completely out of the path of the twister.

"Hello?" someone answered in a completely distracted voice.

"Hi, this is Rachel Grant. I'm just calling to check on my mother. Are you folks okay?"

"Yes, we're fine. We hear the hospital got hit, though."

"It did. I'm there now. The building's standing, but there's a lot of damage and debris inside."

"Well, we've got our hands full over here calming down the residents and assessing the damage."

Rachel wished the woman luck and hung up, so relieved she was faintly ill. She stumbled into the hallway and asked the first nurse she saw what she could do to help. For the next hour she moved robotlike through the motions of helping to clean up the worst of the debris and helping see to the most immediate nonmedical needs of the patients. Carrying her telephone from room to room, she made a number of phone calls for patients so they could reassure their families.

All the while, she felt like she was wading through syrup. Maybe was in a little shock. But then, she'd just lived through a tornado, both the physical and emotional kinds.

Eventually, a horde of medics and firemen, volunteers from several nearby towns, descended upon the hospital and her services were no longer needed. Someone suggested she go home and get some rest and make sure her place was okay. And that was when memory of leaving Brownie out on the back porch broke over her in a wash of horror.

She raced outside into the parking lot and stared in dismay at the flattened remains of her car. It was upside down on its roof and stood no more than two feet tall. No time to stand around mourning the remains of her little clunker, though. She had to get home. Make sure Brownie was okay. She took off jogging toward her place, but even that was a slow proposition as she dodged fallen trees and a variety of mangled debris ranging from entire trees to furniture to giant slabs of roof.

The swath of destruction was neither long nor wide, but within it, the mess was breathtaking. She supposed people would say Honey Creek had been lucky, but it was hard to believe as she wended her way home through the main path of the storm.

She turned onto her street and breathed a massive sigh of relief to see that her house was still standing. A tree in the next door neighbor's yard had fallen over and lay mostly in her backyard, and trash littered her front lawn. It looked like she'd lost some roof shingles, and the bathroom window next to where the tree had fallen had taken a stray branch and was broken. But that looked to be the worst of it.

She made her way around the tree, discovering as

she did so that it had wiped out the three-foot-tall hurricane fence along one side of her backyard. Annoying, but not particularly expensive or difficult to repair.

She picked her way through the broken branches to the back porch and looked around. Where was Brownie? The porch didn't look bad. Her lawn furniture and grill were still there. Even Brownie's blanket was still in its original spot. But the dog was definitely missing.

"Brownie!" she called. "Here, boy!"

But he was not forthcoming. She knelt down to see if he was hiding under the porch perchance. No luck. A frisson of panic started to vibrate low in her gut. She stepped out into the backyard and shouted again. Nothing. Where was he?

Had he made a run for it after the fence came down? He couldn't have gone far on his bum leg. He'd been limping around on his cast a little better last night and hadn't been whimpering every time he put weight on the leg, but still. He couldn't exactly have headed for the hills on it.

He was still taking antibiotics and painkillers, and he needed both. She had to find him. She set off down the street, yelling for him as she went. But before long she got sidetracked into helping her neighbors as they called out to her. Harry Redfeather's herb shed had been blown over and he was picking through it, trying to recover what supplies he could. He was too old and frail to be climbing all over the unsteady pile of broken wood, and she shooed him away from the remains of the shed and took over the job. But all the while, she kept an eye out for a flash of brown fur.

To their credit, most of the citizens of Honey Creek who hadn't been hit by the tornado turned out to help those who had been unlucky enough to fall in its path. Chain saws roared and portable generators rumbled all through the several-block-long and -wide area. By nightfall, huge piles of tree branches and debris stood along the affected streets. Blue plastic tarps were tied down across damaged roofs, and lights began to flicker on in areas that had lost power during the storm.

But Rachel couldn't bring herself to go home. She wandered up and down the streets of her neighborhood long after dark, calling for Brownie. It was all to no avail. There was no sign of her injured dog. Finally, exhaustion began to overwhelm her panic. She hadn't eaten since noon and was getting shaky and lightheaded.

Desolate, she turned her dragging footsteps toward home. The prospect of facing her empty little house alone was almost too much to bear. In desperate hope that Brownie might have come home in her absence to the dishes of food and water she'd left out for him, she picked her way around the stacked woodpile in her yard that had been her neighbor's tree and headed wearily for her back porch. She rounded the corner of her house and her heart leaped in anticipation as she spotted movement at her back door.

But in an instant, she realized she was not looking at a canine form. The shadow crouched over her kitchen doorknob was too big, too vertical for a dog. That was a human. And he looked to be breaking into her house.

"Hey!" she shouted.

The form straightened abruptly. A shadowed face turned her way and then the guy bolted, vaulting the rail at the far end of the porch and taking off around the far end of her house. She might have given chase in her initial outrage that someone was trying to break into her place, but her legs were just too damned wobbly and she was too exhausted to run a single step.

She sagged against the woodpile and dug out her cell phone. Thankfully, it was operational now. She dialed the police station.

"Sheriff Colton," a male voice answered at the other end of the line.

"Hi, Wes. It's Rachel Grant. I just startled someone trying to break into my house. I don't think he got in, but I'm not sure."

"Anything of value in your place missing?"

"I didn't go in. But given that I've still got those contracts I showed you in my briefcase inside, I thought you might want to know."

"Where are you?"

"Standing in my driveway."

"Are you alone?"

"Yes."

"Go to a neighbor's house. Now. Get inside and with other people. You hear me? Don't stop and think about it. Just get moving. Stay on the phone with me until you're with someone. Okay?"

Sheesh. Whoever said men didn't overreact in a crisis was dead wrong. It wasn't as if she were about to die. The would-be intruder was already long gone and probably more scared than she was. Nonetheless, she walked around the woodpile and dutifully knocked on the Johnsons' front door. Thankfully, a few lights were on in their house, powered by a generator she heard rumbling out back like a car with no muffler.

Bill Johnson looked mighty surprised to find her

standing there. She spoke into her phone. "Okay. I'm with Bill Johnson. Now what?"

"Stay with the Johnsons until I send someone over to check out your house. I don't want you going into your place alone. Understood?"

Definitely overreacting. "Yes, sir."

"I'll have a deputy out there shortly."

Her neighbors were understanding, and Mary Johnson fed her a ham sandwich at the kitchen table while they waited for Wes's man to arrive. About halfway through the sandwich the delayed reaction hit her and her knees began to shake. That had been really stupid to charge, shouting, at the intruder like that. The guy could've been armed and shot her dead for all she knew. Why on earth would anyone want to break into her house? She didn't have anything of any great value to steal. Her first impulse had to be the correct one: the guy had been after those damning papers from Walsh Oil Drilling. Had Lester Atkins sent someone to get the contracts from her before she had a chance to read and study them? She chided herself for her suspicions. Just because she didn't like the guy didn't mean she had to assume he was a criminal.

And then the rest of her horrendous day hit. The shocking discovery of why Finn had dumped her all those years ago. The terror of nearly dying. The stunning realization that her feelings for Finn were still there. The worry for her mother. The loss of her dog.

She didn't know whether to cry or scream or just go completely numb. She was saved from having to choose, however, by the Johnsons' front doorbell ringing. She flinched, her nerves completely frazzled. Bill waved her to stay where she was and went to answer the door. She heard a murmur of male voices and then Bill stuck his head into the kitchen.

"Deputy's here."

Rachel murmured her thanks to the Johnsons and stepped out into the front hall. And froze. "You? Since when are you a sheriff's deputy?"

Finn shrugged. "Since a tornado came through town and Wes had to draft every able-bodied man he trusts to help keep order. C'mon. I'll take you home."

Chapter 11

Finn's knees were shockingly wobbly. Thank God Rachel was safe. When Wes had called and told him to get over to the Grant place, he'd felt like someone had knocked his feet out from under him with a two-by-four. He hadn't had a moment to slow down since the tornado and to process what it had been like to nearly die with Rachel in his arms. But he needed to at some point. And in the meantime, the idea that something else might have happened to her, when he wasn't around to protect her—it was nearly as bad as that frantic phone call she'd made that had led him to believe she'd been shot.

"You gotta quit making me think you're dying, Rachel," he muttered as he ushered her out of the Johnson house.

She frowned up at him. "Wes knew I was fine. He made me stay on the phone with him until I was with the Johnsons."

"Yeah, well, he didn't share that with me when he told me to get over here as fast as I could because someone had been seen breaking into your house."

Rachel blinked up at him, looking surprised. "Sounds like your brother was pulling your chain."

Now why would Wes do something like that? Finn scowled. Either Wes was trying to give his little brother heart failure or make the point that Finn's old feelings for Rachel were still alive and well. Wes had laughed his head off when he heard the story of Rachel's phone call about Brownie that'd had Finn tearing down the mountain thinking she'd been shot. *Bastard.*

Without any real heat, Finn murmured, "Remind me to kill Wes next time I see him." He took Rachel's elbow to steady her as they picked their way around the pile of smaller tree limbs left over from a tree that had been blown over by the tornado. The big branches and the trunk had already been cut up into neatly stacked cord wood. Nobody in Honey Creek was going to run out of firewood this winter.

"I checked out your house," he told her. "It's all clear."

"How did you get in?" she blurted.

"The back door was unlocked."

That made her frown. "I wonder if the intruder was breaking in or letting himself out, then."

"Your place isn't messed up like someone tossed it, looking for valuables. At a glance, it didn't look like anything obvious was missing, like your computer or your television. Did you have cash or jewelry in the house? Something small that someone might have known about and gone in specifically to steal?"

Rachel rolled her eyes at him. "Are you kidding? I'm

broke. My mom's medical bills are taking everything I've got and then some."

A stab of desire to make it all better pierced him. He could afford her mom's bills, no problem. If they were married, she wouldn't have to worry about—whoa. Married? Not a chance. He could never trust her not to betray him, and he wouldn't survive losing her a second time. He could never go down that road with her.

"You're sure it's safe to go inside?" Rachel asked in a small voice as they stepped up onto her porch.

"Want me to go first?" he offered.

"If you don't mind." Damned if that grateful look she threw him didn't make him feel like some kind of hero. No wonder Wes liked being sheriff so much. He got to rescue people and get looks like this every day.

Finn stepped into the kitchen and flipped the light switch. Nothing happened. "Looks like you don't have electricity back, yet. Electric company's working on the downed power lines now. Wes expects everyone to get power back by morning."

He felt Rachel's shiver behind him. Since the evening was still unseasonably warm and muggy, he gathered the shiver was less about temperature and more about not being thrilled to spend a night involuntarily in the dark. "Come with me. I'll show you there's no one here."

She tagged along behind him reluctantly as he pointed his flashlight into every room again, looked behind every door and under her bed again and checked in all the closets. She made a little sound of relief when he shined his light on her briefcase standing unopened beside her nightstand. Finally, as they stood back in her living room at the end of his second search, she let out a long, slow breath.

"You gonna be okay now?" he asked.

"Not hardly. But I'll survive."

His eyes were pretty well adjusted to the dark and Rachel looked just about done in. He frowned. Whether it was his usual physician's compassion kicking in or specific concern for Rachel, he didn't know and couldn't care less. Either way, that haunted look in her eyes goaded him to action. He asked, "How can I make it better?"

A frown gathered on her brow. "Now's probably not the time…"

"For what?" he prompted.

"You're a deputy. You probably have other people to go save from the boogey man."

"Actually, I was on my way back to the ranch when Wes called me. Things have pretty much settled down around town for the night." Which was to say, he didn't have anywhere he needed to be right now, and frankly, he'd be glad for some excuse to spend a few more minutes with her. He didn't know what in the hell had happened to him during that tornado, but he did know his compulsion to be with her was stronger than ever.

She shook her head. "We're both wiped out, and I'll say something I'll regret."

Alarm lurched through him. Regret? Was she going to break things off between them for good? Had nearly dying put her life into some new perspective that didn't include him at all? The thought made him faintly nauseous. Why did he care if she didn't want him in her life? After all, he knew better than to make her part of his life. *Although,* a tiny voice whispered in the back of his head, *a little fling wouldn't be such a bad thing, would it?* Maybe he ought to scratch the itch she'd been to him for most of his adult life. Maybe it would get her out of his system once and for all.

But then his better self kicked in. He didn't go to bed with women just to get them out of his system. Regardless of what she'd done to him, it was beneath him to sleep with any woman for purely selfish reasons. Better for her to end it now between them once and for all. He sighed. "Go ahead and say it, Rachel."

Except she didn't say anything at all. She took a deep breath. And another. And then her shoulders started to shake. And then…oh, for crying out loud…those were tears on her face. With deep alarm, he spotted their glistening tracks streaking her cheeks in the dim night.

He didn't stop to think. He merely stepped forward and swept her into his arms. "Hey, Blondie," he murmured. "What's wrong?"

"Everything's wrong," she mumbled, sniffing.

"You lived through the tornado. Your house wasn't blown over. It doesn't look like anybody got into your place, after all. There's nothing to be scared of."

But in spite of his comforting words, she cried all the harder. He tightened his arms around her. He shouldn't be enjoying the woman's distress, but darned if she didn't feel like a slice of heaven in his arms. "Hey, honey. It'll be all right."

Another burst of tears. Maybe he shouldn't try to say anything soothing to her. Flummoxed, he tucked her more closely against him, pressing her head gently down to his shoulder. Their bodies fit together as perfectly now as they had fifteen years ago. More so. Her teenaged skinniness had filled out to slender curves any man would drool over.

He'd buried his nose in her hair and was already

kissing it lightly before he realized what he was doing. It might be madness, but what else could he do? It wouldn't be gentlemanly to turn away a damsel in distress.

Her arms crept around his waist as she cried out what was undoubtedly the stress and terror of an awful day. And something moved within him. Deep and fundamental. Profound. Who was he kidding? This was his Rachel. He'd always looked after her. Taken care of her. Comforted her when she needed it. He could no more walk away from her when she needed him than he could order himself to quit breathing. Like it or not, she was a part of him. Weird how his head could be so opposed to being with her, but his heart could be so completely uninterested in what his head thought.

"I'm sorry," she murmured. "I'm getting your shirt all wet."

"No worries. It's better than some of the stuff that gets on my shirts at the hospital."

That got a little chuckle out of her.

"What's on your mind, Rachel?" Crap. The question provoked another flood of tears. Must not have cried out all the stress yet. He guided her over to the sofa and pulled her down into his lap. He maybe should've thought better of that idea before he did it, but it was what he'd always done with her and it had just come naturally to do it. Just like when they were kids, she curled into his lap like a kitten finding its perfect nest, her cheek resting in the hollow of his shoulder. And it felt like…home.

How long she cried into his collar, he couldn't say. But he did know that every minute of it was sheer bliss. And sheer torture. He wanted this woman so badly he could hardly breathe. And yet with every breath he took, he knew it to be a colossal mistake to even consider making her his.

"I'm so sorry, Finn—" she started.

"I think we already covered the 'no apologies needed' bit," he replied gently. "I'm still waiting for the part where you tell me what's wrong so I can fix it."

He felt her lips curve against his neck into a tiny smile. The feel of it instantly had him thinking thoughts that had nothing whatsoever to do with comfort and everything to do with hot, sweaty sex.

Finally, she mumbled, "Brownie's missing."

"I thought you'd taken him to a neighbor's or something."

"I left him out on the back porch this morning. He—" her voice hitched, but she pressed on "—he loves to lie in the sun. The Johnsons' tree knocked over my back fence, and when I got home he was gone. Oh, Finn, he must be scared. And he needs his antibiotics. And he doesn't have his painkillers. He must be hurting so bad after walking around on his leg this long…"

Finn's gut twisted, too, at the idea of her having lost the mutt. Brownie kind of grew on a person. More important, Rachel loved him, and if he was being honest with himself, he'd grown a little attached to the critter, too. "He's a smart old dog. He'll have found somewhere safe and dry to hunker down for the night. He'll show up tomorrow morning bright and early wanting to know where his breakfast is."

"I left his supper out for him, but he didn't come home to eat it."

Finn shrugged. "He might still have been too scared after the storm. Give him overnight to come to his senses. Trust me. When he gets hungry enough, he'll come back to you."

"If he can. Oh, I hope he wasn't hurt or killed in the storm. Something could've fallen on him. Or he could've reinjured his leg and not be able to walk. Or coyotes—"

Finn kissed her. He didn't know what else to do. But he knew Rachel would work herself up into a state of hysteria if he let her. She was exhausted and distraught and in no mood to listen to reason. Not that he blamed her. She'd had a hell of a day. They all had.

At first, his goal was simply to silence her and distract her. And those were accomplished in the first moment of their kiss. Why he kept on kissing her after his initial missions were accomplished...well, he'd rather not examine that too closely. He really ought to stop this insanity—

And then, oh Lord, she kissed him back. So much for logic and reason. His hand went to the back of her head lest she consider escaping this kiss any time in the next century, and then he let go of everything else. All of it. The restraint and control and sensible arguments against having anything to do with her. The long years of wanting and wondering what it would have been like between them. His ethics and values and codes of personal conduct. His obligations to his family, of his sense of responsibility, of always being the Colton to do the right thing.

He was Finn. She was Rachel. He wanted her. And apparently, she wanted him. It was a miracle. And he wasn't about to walk away from it. To hell with his head and every cursed reason why he shouldn't do this. He'd missed her like a desert missed the rain, like a new shoot missed the sun. She was his life. And for now, that was enough.

He slanted his head to kiss her more deeply, and she met him halfway, her mouth opening and her tongue swirling against and around his as if she were starving as badly for him as he was for her. She moaned deep in her throat and the sound resonated through him more forcefully than the tornado.

"Rachel." He sighed. "My Rachel. Always mine." He kissed her eyelids, her brows, her jaw, every part of her lovely face. Her hands splayed through his hair as he shifted, lowering his mouth to her neck. He lapped at the hollow of her collarbone, then kissed his way up to her earlobe, which he sucked into his mouth and scraped with his teeth lightly, but with enough emphasis for her to know he was marking her as his. She threw her head back, and her thick, honey hair spilled over his hand, cool and silky. He reached for the first button of her shirt and popped it open, baring more of her shoulder to him. His lips encountered the satin of a bra strap, and the sudden need to have it off of her, to have no more obstacles between him and all of her, surged through him. He worked his way down the row of remaining buttons quickly, all but tearing the cotton off her body.

White lace. As demure and sexy as she was. He smiled and lowered his mouth to the valley between her breasts. "My God, you're perfect," he muttered.

She replied breathlessly, "Lucky for me the power's out and there's no way you can see how wrong you are."

"You've always been perfect, Rachel. At least to me."

Her answering laugh was breathless and maybe a little sad.

"I'm not kidding," he insisted. "I've never met another woman like you. You're absolutely perfect."

"And that's why I snap at you and lose my temper and—"

"That's my fault. I can be an insufferable jerk sometimes."

"Can I quote you on that?" she replied humorously.

"Sure, if you'll keep on kissing me."

Her hands closed on either side of his head and raised his mouth to hers. "Oh, Finn." She sighed. "This is crazy."

"I know."

Thankfully, she kissed him then and said no more. Her mouth was sweetness itself against his. The shy little girl had grown up into a confident woman, but her essential femininity was still the same, still intoxicating, still entirely irresistible. Her tongue explored his mouth, and she sipped at him like he was nectar from the gods, but he knew the truth. She was the true gift from heaven.

She threw a leg over his hip and straddled his lap in her impatience to kiss him more deeply, and he shifted beneath her until her core was nestled against his groin so tight and hot that white lights exploded in his brain and stringing words together into thought became nearly impossible.

"Clothes. Off…" he gasped out.

She laughed, a throaty purr that all but had him coming undone. "I thought you'd never ask." Her hands worked at the buttons of his polo shirt, and then her fingers were hooking under the garment's hem. She tugged at it and he raised his arms for her. Her hands ran up his ribs, across the ticklishness that was his underarms, then up the length of his arms, which were corded with muscle from the strain of not grabbing her, pulling her beneath him and ravishing her on the spot.

"You've gotten bigger since high school," she murmured.

He groaned. She had no idea what all had gotten bigger, but it was straining with eagerness to feel her flesh.

"Do you still work out?" she asked.

He struggled to focus. Work. Out. "Uhh, yeah. Weights. Run. Swim some."

"Mmm," she murmured as if he were a tasty treat. He about leaped out of his skin as she leaned forward and—merciful heaven—licked his chest. And then her hands were fumbling at his belt and he was pretty darned sure he was going to explode.

"Let me get that," he rasped.

But she pushed his hands away and insisted on doing it herself. His belt slithered slowly from around his waist. He'd swear she was teasing him, drawing it out until he couldn't take a proper breath. And then his zipper started down, one tantalizing tooth at a time. Oh, yeah. She was messing with him.

"Payback is a bitch," he managed to grit out from between his clenched teeth.

Damned if the little tease didn't grin back at him. "I'm counting on it," she murmured.

He lifted his hips so she could push his pants down, and she hooked his boxers on the way. He kicked the tangle of fabric off his ankles. "What's wrong with this picture?" he asked up at her, his fingers hooked in the top of her jeans.

She sighed. "You always were a little slow on the uptake. You have to keep up here, Finn."

He laughed darkly and hooked a finger under the front of her bra, popping the sassy little catch there. And all of a sudden, her breasts were spilling forth in all their glory, pale and shapely. He inhaled sharply. They fit perfectly in his hands, smooth and firm, and one hundred percent Rachel. He closed his eyes. Opened them again. Nope. Not a dream.

He leaned forward slowly, giving her time to reconsider. But she didn't stop him, and his mouth closed upon her breast. She arched sharply into him, and he took more of her into his mouth. His tongue laved her nipple and she cried out. The sound made him freeze in pure wonder. He licked again, and again she gifted him with a cry of pleasure so intense that it sounded like it almost bordered on pain.

He turned his attention to her other breast and was rewarded with gasps that quickly turned into pants of desire. He surged to his feet, pulling her with him, and stripped her jeans off of her in a single powerful yank. She got tangled up in the legs of the jeans and stumbled into him laughing. He bent down and lifted first one slender foot, then the other, and pulled the slim pants off of her. He kissed her hip and then worked his way over to her soft, flat belly. How he got to his knees in front of her, he wasn't quite sure. But he kissed his way down her abdomen while his hands slid up the back of her thighs. His fingers tested the warm crevice of her buttocks, holding her still while his kisses became more intimate.

He felt the moment when her legs went weak and caught her easily. He shifted back to the couch and pulled her down on top of him, savoring the silky glide of her naked body against his.

"Do you know how many times I imagined getting you naked on this couch?" he murmured.

She lifted enough to gaze down at him. "How many?"

He grinned up at her. "At least twenty times a day. And getting you naked in the my truck. And in the hayloft. And under the stars. And in the boys' locker room—"

"The boys' locker room?" she exclaimed.

"Well, not when anyone else was there. But yeah. In the showers. I had some pretty creative ideas about what I could do in the weight room with you, too. Oh, and the biology lab…"

She laughed, and he could swear she was blushing. "Okay, I confess. I had some rather…steamy…thoughts that involved those big lab tables, myself."

"Ha!" He rose up beneath her to capture her mouth with his. To capture all that joy and laughter and draw it into his soul. "Maybe I'll get the key to the high school from Wes and you can show me your ideas."

"Don't you dare, Finn Colton!"

He pulled her down to him an inch at a time, abruptly serious. "I'd dare just about anything with you, it seems."

"Oh, Finn—"

Alarmed at what she might say next, he closed the remaining distance between them. "Kiss me," he commanded.

Her arms looped around his neck and he held her tightly around the waist as he rolled off the couch in a controlled move, lowering her to the floor beneath him. He propped an elbow on either side of her head. Her eyes opened and she gazed up at him, her eyes wide and serious. He gazed into their depths, letting everything he felt for her show in his eyes. For once, he held nothing back from her.

And then he nudged her thighs apart with his knees, positioning himself so she was wide open beneath him. It was all he could do not to plunge into her and take her like a mindless animal.

"You're sure about this?" he asked tightly.

Her answer was no more than a sigh. But it fell on his ears like a blessing. A benediction. And then he did plunge into her in a single strong, steady stroke that left her no room whatsoever to change her mind.

His eyelids wanted to drift closed, to lose himself in the pure wonder of the moment, in the excess of sensation flooding through him. Rachel. Tight. And hot. And wet. And clenching him so tightly he was about to go over the edge this very second. But he forced his eyes to stay open. To continue gazing into her eyes. To see the matching wonder exploding in her gaze. The limpid delight, the spreading, languishing pleasure rolling over her.

The building wonder in her eyes was astonishing to watch. In a matter of seconds her breathing had shifted, becoming shallow and rapid, little gasps of pleasure that ravaged his soul. Her internal muscles pulsed spasmodically, and before his very eyes, she climaxed. Her gaze went unfocused and stunned but never left his.

It was the most incredible, vulnerable, intimate thing he'd ever experienced. And she'd shared it with him. *Him.* He was profoundly humbled by it. Something moved deep in his heart that he couldn't name. But he knew without a shadow of a doubt that he would never forget that moment for as long as he lived. Hell, he suspected that when he died, it would be the last thing he ever thought of.

The joy in his chest expanded and built until he couldn't contain it any longer. He began to move within her, slowly at first, his strokes lengthening and growing in power like a force of nature, wild and uncontrollable. Rachel found the rhythm with him, her breath quickening once more. She arched up suddenly, crying out and then shuddering beneath him in abandon. He drank in her cries but never stopped driving into her. Something within him wanted to make her go completely out of her mind with pleasure.

Her eyes went dark and wide and a smile curved her lips. And still, their gazes remained locked together. They stared deep into each other's souls as their bodies became one and galloped away with both of them.

He felt his own climax start to build within him, his entire body beginning a slow and exquisite implosion that grew and grew and grew. Amazement widened his eyes, and triumph glittered in hers. And then his entire being clenched. For an instant, everything stopped and even time was suspended. He might have been afraid of the power of it, but Rachel was there with him, her arms and legs clinging desperately to him, her soul completely naked before him.

And then the entire universe exploded. He shouted his release and surrendered every last bit of himself to her as he emptied body and soul into her in an orgasm of such power it drained his being. Disbelief shone in Rachel's eyes, and he mirrored the feeling in his own stunned mind. Never, ever, had he given himself to a woman in even remotely that way. But, Rachel... Rachel took it all. And in return, she'd given everything to him of herself down to the very last dregs.

There were no words. He panted as he tried to catch his breath and pushed the damp hair off her forehead. And still they stared at one another. A world of silent communication passed between them. So much that he didn't know how to catalog it all.

He was quite simply…amazed. He'd always known it would be good between them, but he'd never dreamed it could be like this with anyone, let alone her. What was it about her that drew so much out of him? Was this the difference between sex and making love? Or was it a simple matter of them being soul mates, like it or not? Why on earth had they waited this long to find this?

Rachel was the one to finally break the silence. "Wow," she said on a breath.

He laughed, still a little out of breath. "Yeah. Wow."

"Thanks."

"You're welcome. And thank *you*."

She smiled up at him. Silence fell between them again.

"Are you uncomfortable? The floor must be hard."

"I hadn't noticed," she murmured.

Laughter bubbled up in his chest again. Or maybe it was just that he couldn't ever remember being this happy. "How about we adjourn this to your bed so you're not too bruised in the morning?"

"The damage is already done," she replied, smiling.

"Yes, but the next time I may not be so gentle."

Her eyes widened at that, and her body went languid beneath his. Yup, the lady liked that idea. He pushed up and away from her and reached down to scoop her in his arms.

"Who knows?" she murmured, looping her arms around his neck. "Maybe I'm the one who won't be gentle with you."

Chapter 12

When Rachel opened her eyes in the morning to bright sunshine, she was pretty sure she was hallucinating. Finn Colton was actually asleep in her bed beside her. It hadn't been a spectacular dream after all. Sleepy and content, she lay there, remembering the magic of it. At some level, she'd always known it would be like that between them. They were the two halves of a whole and knew each other better than anyone else in the world. No surprise, then, that they were such a perfect match in bed. They could anticipate the other's desires and pleasures at some instinctive level that transcended conscious thought.

At least, that was what it felt like Finn had done with her. At one point, she'd asked him if they taught students how to be fantastic lovers in medical school, and he laughed heartily at that. Finally, he'd murmured that what they had between them had nothing to do with medical school and everything to do with fate.

Whoever said making love with a man couldn't be absolutely, magically, fairy-tale perfect was dead wrong. Obviously, they'd just never found their true soul mate. Or, let fifteen years pass to build the anticipation to epic proportions. The thought made her smile.

A hand passed lightly over her tangled hair. "Good morning, Blondie."

She turned her smile lazily to Finn. "Good morning. Sleep well?"

His smile widened. "I didn't sleep much, but it was the best rest I've had in years. Maybe ever."

"Feeling rested, are you? Maybe I'll have to do something to change that," she teased.

He rolled onto his side and gathered her close. "Don't change a thing, Rachel. You're perfect just the way you are."

She inhaled the spicy smell of him and couldn't resist dropping a kiss on his chest.

He shifted and his mouth was there all of a sudden, capturing hers and drawing her up higher against him. Their bodies fit together like two pieces of a puzzle, and she sighed as their legs tangled together familiarly.

"Sore?" he murmured.

She was a little, but she wasn't about to admit it. She wouldn't trade this morning's soreness from last night's magic for anything in the world. She merely smiled invitingly. "Why? You all tuckered out?"

He grinned. "Not hardly. I've waited fifteen years for you."

A shadow passed over her heart and she frowned. But then Finn was there kissing her so she couldn't talk and then until she couldn't think at all. Their lovemaking this morning was slow and lazy and exquisitely intimate. Finn looked deep into her eyes again as they made love, and it went beyond personal, forced her to completely open her soul to him, and he to open his to her. If she thought she'd known him well before, it was nothing compared to now that they'd given each other these intensely private pieces of themselves.

She reveled in the slow, powerful glide of his body upon and within hers. He knew just how to draw her out, to steal her breath away, to take her to heights of pleasure she'd never dreamed existed. She clung to his muscular shoulders and shuddered her release to the sight of a smile unfolding on his handsome face.

"You're magnificent," he murmured. And then he shuddered with pleasure into her arms.

When they'd both caught their breath, they lay side by side, gazing at one another. And that was how she saw the moment when the first frown crossed his brow.

"What?" she asked, trying to mask the frisson of alarm streaking down her spine.

He swore under his breath. "We didn't use any protection. I didn't even think about it. I don't do this sort of thing often, and I didn't expect to end up in bed with you last night…" He swore again. "I'm a doctor, for God's sake. I'm supposed to think about these things. I'm sorry, Rach—"

She pressed her fingers to his lips. "I didn't think about it, either. And we're both adults, here. I'm as much to blame as you are. But for what it's worth, I haven't slept with anyone in a few years, so I highly doubt I have any contagious diseases."

His frown deepened. "I was more worried about pregnancy—" He broke off abruptly.

Oh. *Pregnancy.* The word thudded between them heavily. It was like someone had punched her in the stomach. Hard. Everything from yesterday came crashing back in on her. For a brief, shining moment, she'd managed to hold all the rest of it at bay. But no more. A new day had dawned. The magic of the previous night was over.

She closed her eyes and released a long, slow breath.

"Please look at me," Finn murmured.

She opened her eyes, but the link between them was broken. They were strangers once more with all their ugly history hanging between them. Amazing that a single word had the power to do that. Pregnancy.

"About that," she started. She took another deep breath for courage and then plunged ahead. "You and I need to talk."

"So talk," he muttered grimly.

"Not like this."

"Why not like this?" he retorted. "It's not like either one of us can deny that last night happened."

But it was just so darned...vulnerable...lying here naked beside him. She had nowhere to hide. Maybe he was right, though. Maybe it was time to quit hiding from him. From their past. "All right, then," she answered. "Here goes. Would you mind telling me why you walked out on me night before last at the homecoming dance? Again?"

He blinked and looked startled, but she waited resolutely.

"Seriously?" he muttered.

"Yes. Seriously. I've spent the last fifteen years wondering what in the hell happened on prom night, and I'm not about to spend another fifteen wondering what the hell happened Saturday night."

His brow knitted into an ominous expression that hinted at surfacing anger. But he answered evenly enough. "I left the homecoming dance because I couldn't stand to be with you any longer."

Stunned, she exclaimed, "And yet you spent most of last night making love to me?"

"My family was at the homecoming dance."

She frowned. "What the heck do they have to do with anything?"

Finn struggled for words, but then he blurted, "They haven't exactly been your biggest fans over the years. And they were all standing there glaring daggers at me for being dumb enough to have anything to do with you. They reminded me of why I can't ever be with you. Of how you betrayed me and broke my heart. I don't think I could survive it if you did that to me again. You all but killed me the last time."

Rachel stared at him. After everything they'd shared last night, after all the intimacy and honesty and heart-felt sharing, he could still say that? Tearing pain bubbled up from somewhere deep inside her. But along with it came a generous measure of anger.

"Speaking of this supposed betrayal, I had a rather enlightening conversation with your brother yesterday before the tornado."

"With Damien?" Finn asked.

She nodded, her fury gathering a head of steam. "I went out to the ranch to confront you. But you weren't there. I cornered your brother in the barn and forced him to tell me why you dumped me the night of prom."

Finn's eyes went dark. Closed. Angry. "Surely you knew I'd react like that when I found out. You knew how much I cared about you. Hell, I was planning to ask you to marry me."

Something sick rolled through her. Oh, God. He *had* been planning to propose. They could've had it all. All those years of blissful happiness and sharing life's joys and sorrows...

"Here's a news flash for you, big guy. *Maisie was wrong.*"

He stared at her blankly. Finally he said in a stran-gled voice, "I beg your pardon?"

She couldn't stay in bed with him any longer. She had to get away from him. To get dressed. Cover her-self and her pain from him. It was too raw like this. She rolled away from him and, horribly self-conscious all of a sudden, reached into her closet for a robe. She flung it about herself and knotted the belt jerkily. When she turned around, Finn was sitting on the side of the bed, a quilt thankfully pulled across his lap.

"Would you care to explain exactly how Maisie was wrong?" he repeated tightly.

Rachel jammed her hands into the robe's pockets, her hands tightly fisted. "I was at a pregnancy coun-seling center in Bozeman the morning of prom. But not to have an abortion. My mom had just been diag-nosed with early-onset Alzheimer's, and I was there to have genetic testing done to see if I had inherited the gene or not."

Finn was staring at her as if he didn't comprehend a word she'd said.

She continued doggedly. "I was not pregnant. Heck, I'd never had sex." She turned and paced the length of her bedroom and back. "You know what's really ironic? I had decided that I was ready to make love with you. That I wanted you to be my first and only."

Finn sat completely still. He might as well have been a marble statue for all the reaction he was showing to her revelations.

She flung a hand at the bed. "I knew it would be like that between us. And I wasn't wrong, was I? We were made for each other. But you had to go and believe a lie. Why didn't you at least give me a chance to defend myself? If you had bothered to ask me about it, I would've told you. The only reason I was in Bozeman having that stupid test done was because I wanted to marry you and spend the rest of my life with you, but I was afraid that I might get Alzheimer's at age forty like my mom did." She paced another lap of the room before adding, "And I loved you too much to saddle you with a burden like that."

Still, Finn said nothing. She paused to glance at him on the next lap, and he looked pale, maybe a little ill, even.

He mumbled, "She'd bought a digital camera that day. She used it to take a picture of you in the clinic. She showed it to me," he finally said. He sounded almost…confused.

"Maisie? I'm sure she did. She's quite the interfering bitch, you know. And I was, indeed, at that clinic. For blood testing. Finn, I was a virgin. I never slept with any other guy, and I bloody well wasn't pregnant. Besides, I would never have had an abortion—and certainly not without talking to you about it, your child or not. I love kids. How could you have thought any of that of me? I *loved* you."

He opened his mouth to speak twice but closed it both times.

She couldn't take it anymore. She was going to shatter into a million pieces, and she darned well wasn't going to do that in front of him. Not after what they'd shared last night. Not after finally knowing the true measure of just what they could've had. Sleeping with Finn Colton had been the dumbest thing she'd ever done in her entire life. Now she would have to live out her remaining years *knowing* what he'd cost them. It had been so much better merely wondering what it could've been like between them. At least then she'd had the comfort of the possibility that they wouldn't have suited one another at all.

She turned on the shower and was thrilled to feel hot water coming out of the tap. The power had come back on sometime in the night, apparently. She stepped under the pounding stream of water. And as she scrubbed the feel and taste and smell of Finn off her skin, she cried her heart out.

The water was starting to go tepid when she finally turned off the shower and stepped out onto the cold tile floor. Shivering, she dried quickly and jumped into the clothes she'd had the foresight to grab before she'd retreated in there.

She opened the bathroom door. Her bedroom was empty. Finn was gone. Her bedroom, her house, her life was the back the way it had been before last night's crazy magic. Some of the light went out of the bright morning, and the colors of her grandmother's quilt seemed a little duller.

The sense of loss within her was every bit as heavy

and suffocating as the day her father had died. Something inside her shut down. Grief. She knew how to do that. One foot in front of the next. Make lists. Force herself to do each thing on the list. Sleep. Eat now and then. And eventually, after a very long time, the pain would begin to ease. A little. But maybe not in this case.

First, she had to take a step. Kitchen. She'd go in there. Make herself something tasteless to choke down. Feed Brown—

A new wave of grief and loss slammed into her. Her dog was gone, too. Her desire to do something nice for Brownie had backfired, and his pleasant afternoon on a sunny porch had turned into a disaster. She seemed to have a knack for doing that with the men in her life, apparently.

She turned the corner into the kitchen and stopped, startled. Finn was there. Cooking something on her stove.

"Scrambled eggs okay?" he asked.

"What are you doing here?" she asked blankly.

"We're not done talking."

She frowned. "Yes. We are."

"I haven't apologized yet. I'm not sure how I'm going to be able to apologize adequately for being such a colossal idiot, but I'd like to give it a try."

She sat down at the kitchen table. "It's not as simple as an apology, Finn."

"Okay, so I'll have to find a way to make it up to you."

Pain rippled through her almost too intense to stand. As it was, she had trouble breathing around it. He took the eggs off the stove and shoveled them onto plates beside slices of toast. He set them down and slid into the chair across from her.

"I've just found you, Rachel. I don't plan to lose you again."

She closed her eyes in agony. She couldn't believe she was going to say what she was about to. But for the first time in her life, she knew what she had to do about Finn Colton. "Finn, you never had me to lose. Last night was an anomaly. You and I both know it. It doesn't change anything."

Something dark flickered through his gaze, but he answered steadily, "I disagree. I was wrong to break up with you at prom. You never betrayed me. If I got into a relationship with you now, I could trust you. Don't you see? That changes everything."

It was a struggle to keep her voice even, but she did her best. "Maybe that changes things for you. But not for me. The fact remains that you were all too willing to believe the worst of me. You never gave me a chance to explain myself. You judged me without ever hearing me out. And I have a problem with that. You didn't trust me or our love. And I have a bigger problem with that."

Finn stared at her incredulously. "So what was last night, then? Revenge sex? You knew you were going to rip my heart out and shred it this morning, so you jumped into the sack with me to make sure the destruction was complete?"

"There you go again," she said miserably. "Making assumptions about me. If you really think I'm capable of such cruelty, then clearly we have no business being together."

He closed his eyes and pinched the bridge of his nose with his fingers. Then he said more calmly, "You're right. I apologize. But please understand, this has been an incredibly stressful morning for me. I tend to lash out when I'm this confused and upset and angry at myself. It's one of my worst flaws."

She almost wished he would shout and rant and lose his temper. This tightly controlled, polite version of Finn was painful to see. It was all so civilized, and yet her world was crumbling all around her.

She took a wobbly breath. "I'm sorry, too, Finn. But I just don't see how it could work between us. I've spent most of the last fifteen years hating myself for driving you away from me, even though I didn't have the faintest idea what I'd done wrong. And then I found out yesterday that I hadn't done anything wrong at all. And I realized that I had been far too willing to believe the worst of myself. How can I expect anyone else to love me, or for me to love anyone else in a healthy way, if I can't love myself?"

"So that's it?" he murmured. "It's over?"

She couldn't bring herself to say the words. She looked down at her hands, clenched tightly in her lap, and nodded. His chair scraped. She felt him stand up, towering over her, but she couldn't look up at him. Her eyes were filling up fast with tears, and they'd spill over if she moved a millimeter.

"I'm sorry, Rachel. For last night. For everything. Goodbye."

And then he was gone.

Chapter 13

Rachel stepped out onto her back porch to see if Brownie had come back for his breakfast like Finn had predicted. But the food in the bowl was untouched and his bed of blankets wasn't disturbed. And that was when the last spark of light in her world went out.

She visited her mother after breakfast because it was on the list of things to force herself to do today. Her mom was agitated and upset after the tornado, and for a little while, Rachel was glad of the wet blanket of grief smothering her emotions. Otherwise, the visit would have been deeply upsetting.

She got to Walsh Enterprises a little before lunch to find the place in an uproar. Although the tornado hadn't hit the Walsh building, the hail and flying debris had knocked out a row of windows on the third floor. The accompanying rain had caused a fair bit of water damage on the second floor where she worked. As she picked her way past the mess and the cleanup effort, she was vaguely relieved that her cubicle was on the other side of the floor.

Until she reached her desk. Or rather the remains of her desk. A massive steel pipe lay diagonally across a pile of kindling and plastic that had once been her desk and chair.

"What happened here?" Rachel gasped at the man examining the wreckage. "Who are you?"

"Roger Thornton. Building inspector in Bozeman. Got sent here by the county to help check out structures in town. Make sure they're safe."

"Well, that doesn't look very safe to me," she said in dismay as she edged into her office and peered up into the dark cavern of the ceiling space overhead.

"I've never seen a plumbing main come down like this. Should've been bolted to the ceiling with steel bands. But it looks like they were never installed or were removed for some reason."

"You mean the tornado didn't do this?" she asked, aghast.

He shrugged. "Seems like it's gotta be the twister. But I just don't see how. Good thing you weren't sitting at your desk when it came down. Thing would've killed ya if it landed on yer head."

She stared at the pipe, horrified. "When did it fall?"

"Folks say it came down about an hour ago. I got here a few minutes ago."

An hour ago? Had she not swung by to visit her mother first, she'd have been sitting at her desk when that pipe fell. She stared in renewed horror at her mangled chair. "Have you called the police?" she demanded.

"Why? It's a structural failure caused by the tornado. It's Walsh's insurance company somebody oughta call."

Rachel nodded warily. She might have argued with him that he shouldn't rule out foul play so quickly, but Lester Atkins spoke from behind her, startling her. "Rachel. Why don't you take the rest of the day off? It's going to take the cleanup crew a while to clear this out. You do have most of your work stored in a backup file or hard drive of some kind, don't you?"

"Uhh, yes. I've got it all in my briefcase."

He glanced at the case she clutched in her hand. "Perfect. Go home. We'll see you tomorrow when we've got you a new desk and computer set up."

She wasn't about to argue with the uncharacteristic kindness from the man. But the idea of going to her lonely home and its painful memories was too much for her. She went over to the senior citizens' center and spent the afternoon helping with the cleanup there. After eating a tasteless dinner, she went out and wandered the streets of her neighborhood, looking fruitlessly for a brindled brown dog with a limp.

Over the next few days, life went nominally back to normal. She got her new desk and computer and started working on the payroll audits Lester had assigned her to. She had to finish the Walsh Oil Drilling audit in her evenings at home. But that was just as well. It gave her something to do besides stare at her walls and slowly go crazy. The final tally for all the embezzled funds over fifteen years ran to in excess of ten million dollars. Mark Walsh must have lived nicely off of all that money.

She printed off a final copy of her report and put it in her briefcase. At lunchtime, she left the building and headed for the sheriff's office. She parked down the street and took a careful look in the parking lot beside the building to make sure Finn's truck wasn't there before she got out of the rental car her insurance company had provided her until she could buy a new car. When she was going to find the time or energy to head up to Bozeman and take care of that, she had no idea. She'd put it on her list of things to make herself do soon.

She stepped into the sheriff's office to the tinkle of the bell over the door.

"Hi, Rachel. How are you doing?" Wes asked warmly as he came out of his office.

She shrugged, dodging his question. It was easier than trying to lie about being just fine, thank you. "I've got the complete, revised Walsh Oil Drilling financial report. I thought you might want a copy." She held the thick file out to him.

He took it and laid it on the counter. "Thanks." He studied her closely enough that she had to restrain an urge to squirm.

"Any word on who might belong to that signature?" she asked in a blatant effort to distract him.

"The State of California claims it can't find the Hidden Pines incorporation documents. I'm going to hire a private investigator to look into it. He might contact you, and I'd appreciate it if you could give him any help you can."

"Of course," she replied. She probably ought to say something chatty along the lines of how strange the weather had been, but she just didn't have the energy for it.

She started to turn to leave, but Wes reached out and touched her arm. "Rachel. How are you really doing?"

She frowned.

Wes continued, "I wouldn't have sent Finn over to your place if I'd known how much it would upset you."

Oh, Lord. What had Finn told his brother about their torrid night together or their disastrous argument the next morning?

"For what it's worth, he's a wreck," Wes commented.

Vague sorrow registered in her heart that Finn was hurting. She couldn't find it in herself to wish this sort of misery on anyone.

"Is there anything I can tell him for you?" Wes pressed.

She blinked, momentarily startled out of the fog that enveloped her life. "Uhh, no. No message."

"Don't be a stranger, Rachel. If you ever need anything, or you need to talk…"

She glanced up at him, surprised.

He shrugged, looking a little embarrassed. "Just take care of yourself, okay?"

"I will." She left the office, bemused. What was that all about? Was Wes feeling that guilty about throwing her and Finn together, or was there more to it than that? What was going on with Finn?

She knew from the grapevine at Walsh Enterprises that Finn was still in town caring for Craig Warner, who was improving slowly. Apparently, no one but Jolene Walsh was allowed in to see Craig yet, though. Rachel certainly wanted the best care for her boss, but she couldn't help counting the days until Craig left the hospital and Finn left Honey Creek.

She'd done the right thing, darn it. She had to learn to like herself. To come to terms with the fact that she hadn't done anything wrong all those years ago. It was a lot to absorb. She was going to be mature, darn it.

A few days more after her disastrous night with Finn, the fog enveloping her was interrupted once more by Lester Atkins calling her into his office, which was actually Craig's office, which Lester had appropriated while his boss was out sick.

"Rachel, you didn't get Jolene's signature on those documents, like I asked. You've interfered with a very important business deal."

Fear blossomed in her gut and the usual litany started in the back of her head. She couldn't lose this job. She couldn't lose this job....

"I'm sorry, Mr. Atkins. Jolene was too busy signing medical release forms for treatments for Mr. Warner to look at the papers. She said she'd take a look at them later, when Mr. Warner was out of danger."

She thought Atkins might have sworn under his breath, but she didn't quite hear what he mumbled to himself. Then he said abruptly, "I want those documents back. I'll get her to sign them myself."

"Of course, sir. They're at my desk. I'll go get them now."

When she brought the thick file back to Lester, he snatched it out of her hands and immediately thumbed through the stack of documents. She thought he might have slowed down in the middle of the pile, right about where the Hidden Pines drilling contracts were, but she couldn't be sure.

"Did you look at these?" he demanded abruptly.

Startled, she stammered, "Uhh, no, sir."

He glared at her suspiciously. She was such a lousy liar. She felt the heat creeping up her neck against her will. Cursing her fair skin and telltale blush, she mumbled, "I'd better be getting back to work. I have a lot to do."

Still giving her a damning look, he waved her out of

his office. She wasted no time leaving and went back to her desk and resumed plowing through the tall pile of tedious payroll records for Walsh Enterprises. Interesting how Atkins had pulled her off the Walsh Oil Drilling records practically the moment Craig Warner had gone into the hospital.

It was dark when Rachel left the Walsh building that evening. She'd stayed late to catch up on the mounds of work Atkins had heaped upon her in what she suspected was an attempt to keep her so busy she wouldn't go anywhere near the Walsh Oil Drilling records again anytime soon. She probably ought to mention it to Wes. But in her dazed state, she was having trouble working up the energy to get around to it.

The warm spell that had spawned the tornado had passed, leaving the night air bone-chillingly cold. It always took her a few weeks to acclimate to the winter's cold each fall, and she wasn't there yet.

As had become her habit, she didn't drive directly home. Rather, she drove slowly down streets along the edge of town, peering into the night for a glimpse of a brindled brown dog with a limp. She figured by now he'd chewed the cast off his leg.

She approached a dark corner behind a row of warehouses, and maybe because her attention was focused on the tall weeds of an empty lot to her right, she didn't see the other car coming from her left. She started out into the intersection, and before she knew it, something had crashed into her car, sending it careening into a spin that threw her forward into the exploding airbag, which slammed her back in her seat, pinning her in place and blinding her to the other car.

Shockingly, the vehicle sped away into the night.

By the time the airbag deflated enough for her to see around it, she caught only a glimpse of red taillights disappearing in the distance. Fast.

Stunned, she sat in the car, replaying the last few moments. And something odd occurred to her. The other car hadn't had its headlights on when it barged out into the intersection. Given that it was pitch black out here, that was really strange.

Her brain finally kicked in and she fished her purse off the floor where it had fallen in the collision. She pulled out her cell phone and called the sheriff's office.

"Sheriff Colton."

"Hi, Wes. It's Rachel Grant. I'm sorry to bother you, but I was just in a car accident."

"Are you hurt?" he asked in quick alarm.

"No. Just shook up. The airbag deployed."

"Where are you?"

She gave him a rough description and he said he'd be there in five minutes. She was to lock her door and not move a muscle in the meantime. Sighing, she leaned her head back against the headrest to wait. Wasn't it odd for him to tell her to lock her door? Shouldn't she unlock it in case she passed out or something? That way he or a paramedic could get into the car easily to treat her. Did he think she was in some kind of danger? The guy who'd hit her had taken off. She wasn't in any danger if he'd fled the scene, was she?

Wes was the sheriff. Probably just erring on the side of caution. It was his job to be paranoid and protect everyone, after all.

Someone knocked on her window and her eyes flew open in fright. Wes. She unlocked the door and started to open it, but he stopped her.

"Stay right there. I want a doc to look at you before you move. He's right behind me. While he's checking you, I'm going to take a few pictures of your car."

On cue, another vehicle pulled up to the scene, a heavy-duty pickup truck. A silhouetted figure climbed out and strode over to join Wes, who was just finishing up. Her heart sank. Finn.

Darn that Wes. Why couldn't he leave well enough alone? Whoever said men weren't nosy matchmakers would be dead wrong. They were as bad as any interfering auntie or momma impatient to be a grandma. Men were just clumsier about it than their female counterparts. The two men strode over to the car.

It was as if someone had thrown a bucket of ice water over her, shocking her system fully awake for the first time in days. She shivered, stunned at the intensity of the emotions coming back to life within her. Who was she kidding? She was as in love with Finn Colton as she'd ever been. *But loving someone doesn't necessarily mean he's good for me.*

Finn had believed the worst of her, and she'd let him. That last part wasn't his fault. It was hers. And until she knew she would never lose her sense of self-worth again, she dared not engage in any romantic relationships.

Her door opened and Finn's achingly familiar voice said, "Don't move. Let me have a look at your neck first."

Oh, for crying out loud. She glared at Wes as Finn reached into the car to slide a big, warm hand carefully behind her neck. "My neck is fine. I'm fine," she groused.

"Why don't you let me be the one who decides that," Finn murmured back, his concentration clearly on examining her vertebrae. "Does this hurt?" He pressed two fingers gently on either side of her spine.

"A little."

"Describe the pain."

"Like a sore muscle getting poked."

"Any nausea? Headache? Blurred vision? Tingling in your hands or feet? Numbness anywhere?"

"No to all of the above."

"Slowly tilt your chin down and tell me if it hurts."

She did as he directed. "It hurts a little. Like I've strained my neck and it doesn't want me to move it."

"I'd say that's a pretty fair description of your injury. You can get out now." Finn held a hand out to her. She would have to shove past it to get out of the car without accepting the offered help anyway, so reluctantly she took his hand and let him half lift her out of the vehicle.

She turned around to survey the damage. The rental car's entire left side was caved in and had a huge, black scrape down its white side. "I guess the car that hit me was black, then?" she said drily.

Wes nodded. "Yup. Nailed you pretty good."

Finn commented grimly, "If he'd hit her much harder, he'd have rammed her car right over that embankment."

Rachel glanced behind her car and gulped. Only a few feet beyond its rear tires was a steep drop-off, at least twenty feet. At the bottom lay a double set of train tracks. If she'd gone over the edge of that, she could've been seriously hurt, or worse.

"What can you tell me about the car that hit you?" Wes asked grimly.

"Not much. I was looking off to my right. Although I did notice its headlights weren't on." An awful thought occurred to her. "*Ohmigosh.* Did I run a stop sign?" She looked back over her shoulder in alarm.

"No. In fact, the other guy was the one with the stop sign."

Rachel frowned. "He must have run it then, because he came at me way too fast to have been stopped a moment before."

Wes nodded. "Given how far your car was pushed beyond the point of impact, I'd estimate he was going fifty miles per hour or so. So there's nothing you remember about the car, Rachel?"

"Nothing. I never really saw it. I was driving along here slowly, looking into the weeds, and then all of a sudden he was coming at me and there was nothing I could do. Then the airbag inflated and I couldn't see a thing."

"Thank goodness for the airbag," Finn muttered fervently enough to make her turn her head and look at him. Come to think of it, he didn't look all that great. "Are you feeling okay?" she asked.

He scowled at her. "I swear you're going to give me heart failure if you keep having these near-death experiences."

She rolled her eyes. "I was in a little car accident. It was hardly a near-death experience. Now, that pipe falling on my desk at work—that could have been a near-death experience."

Wes asked sharply, "What pipe?"

"The one that fell out of the ceiling at Walsh Enterprises and smashed my desk to smithereens. The building inspector said it was a good thing I wasn't sitting at my desk or I'd have been crushed."

The two men traded glances. Wes looked grim and

Finn looked furious. "All right, all right," Wes muttered. "So someone is trying to hurt her."

Rachel spun to face him. "I beg your pardon?"

Finn answered for his brother. "Wes let you get mixed up in the Walsh murder investigation by having you give him all those financial records. I *told* him he was going to draw the killer's attention to you." Finn made a sound of disgust.

Wes asked, "Have there been any more accidents or incidents in the past few days like the pipe or this hit-and-run?"

"You don't think the driver hit me intentionally, do you?" she asked, aghast.

Wes frowned. "I can't be certain until I analyze the crash scene fully, but yes. Basically, I do think someone crashed into you and hoped to shove your car over the embankment."

Rachel stared. He had to be kidding. This was Honey Creek. The world capital of "nothing ever happens around here." Oh, wait. Until Mark Walsh was murdered.

Finn shook his head. "First Walsh. Then Warner. And now this. Someone's trying to hide something over at Walsh Enterprises. And it's too damned dangerous for Rachel to be involved anymore. I'm calling an end right now to her snooping around there for you."

Wes sighed. "You may be right. I may have to go ahead and talk to Peter Walsh. See if he might be willing to poke around the company. He is a private investigator, and he's also a Walsh. He ought to be able to have a look around without arousing too much suspicion."

Rachel interrupted. "Wouldn't it be some sort of conflict of interest to let him help investigate his own father's murder?"

Wes exhaled hard. "Yeah, that's a big problem. It's why I haven't hired him already. And the district attorney would probably have my badge if I did. But I don't know how else I'm going to get inside that place and figure out exactly who's hiding what."

Finn stepped closer to Rachel. And if she wasn't mistaken, he'd gone all protective and he-man on her. It was kind of cute, actually. Well, actually, it was totally hot. "And in the meantime, she's not staying alone. Until you catch the bastard who's pulling this stuff on her, I'm not leaving her side."

Rachel gaped. *Not leaving*— "Oh, no you're not!" she exclaimed. An unreasonable terror of being alone with Finn swept over her. It was hard enough to resist the pull of him when she didn't have to see him at all. But if she was with him 24/7, no way would she be able to control her urges. And she positively *knew* that that would be a disaster.

Finn gave her a stubborn look she knew all too well and announced, "I'm not arguing with you about this. End of discussion."

Her gaze narrowed. "I'll remind you one more time, Finn. I am not fifteen and willing to be bullied by you. I'm an adult, and no way will I stand for you hovering over me day and night."

"Then act like an adult and make a sensible decision," he snapped.

Wes murmured, "Let me handle this, Finn."

Rachel turned to Wes for support. "They were accidents. Who in their right mind would remove the supports holding up a giant pipe exactly over my desk? And as for the guy tonight, he probably just didn't expect there to be any cars out in this part of town at this time of night."

"What were you doing in this area, anyway?" Wes asked.

"Looking for Brownie," she answered miserably.

"Who?" Wes echoed.

"Her mutt," Finn replied. "No luck finding him?" he asked her sympathetically.

"No."

"I'm sorry."

Tears threatened to fill up her eyes. Since when had she turned into such a baby? She sniffed angrily. She was *not* going to cry in front of Finn. But at least it looked like she'd distracted him from his harebrained scheme to become her personal bodyguard.

But then Wes had to go and say, "I have to agree with you, Finn. I'd feel better if Rachel wasn't alone until we figure out who's behind these accidents of hers."

"Wes Colton, you can stop trying to play match-maker right this—"

He held up a hand. "I'm speaking as the sheriff. And Finn's right. This is not open to discussion. I'm worried about your safety. Either you let Finn stay with you or I'm taking you out to my family's ranch to stay until I catch your assailant."

"The Colton ranch?" she squeaked.

"Yes," Wes answered, crossing his arms over his chest resolutely.

She glanced over at Finn, who was gaping at his brother. Crap. He thought Wes was serious, too. She glared at both of them. "Wild horses couldn't drag me out to that ranch. And no power on Earth is making me stay there."

Wes's eyebrows went up and he looked prepared to

demand to know why. But Finn intervened hastily. "And that's why I'm going to stay with you until this guy's caught."

Rachel glared. "I don't like it."

"Do you have a better idea?" Finn demanded.

"Sure. Hire Peter Walsh to keep an eye on me. He's a trained private investigator. They do that sort of thing, right?"

Thunder gathered on Finn's brow. "Rachel, we need to talk."

She scowled back at him. "No, we don't. We said everything we had to say to each other the last time we talked."

"No, *you* said everything *you* had to say. I didn't say everything I wanted to by a long shot."

Alarm skittered through her. The man did not sound happy.

"Uhh, okay then," Wes said uncomfortably. "It sounds like you two have some stuff to work out. Finn, you take Rachel back to her place and don't let her out of your sight until we talk again."

Finn nodded briskly and took Rachel by the arm.

"I am *not* a sack of potatoes to be hauled around wherever you want," she barked.

"Fine. Then walk over to my truck and get into it of your own volition like the adult you claim to be. Otherwise, I'm going to throw you over my shoulder exactly like a sack of potatoes and haul you over there."

Oooh, that man could be so infuriating! And it didn't help one bit that a creeping sense of relief was pouring over her like warm water.

Chapter 14

Finn's big pickup wouldn't fit in Rachel's driveway with the giant pile of fire wood taking up most of it. Nor could he park in front of her house, given the pile of stacked debris awaiting removal. Honey Creek was mostly cleaned up from the tornado, but pockets of town, like this street, weren't quite back to normal. The guys at the landfill had been working around the clock all week to get caught up.

He ended up parking a few houses down on the street and walking Rachel back to her place. For her part, she'd been silent and sullen on the ride back to her house. And frankly, he didn't give a damn. No way was he leaving her alone to face whoever was out to hurt her. An itch to get his hands around the guy's neck and snap it came over him. He took her elbow as she climbed the steps onto her front porch.

"I can go up a few steps by myself, thank you," Rachel muttered.

"Get used to it. I'm not leaving your side." Not *ever*, if he had his way. But one step at a time. First he had to make her safe. Then he'd move on to the subject of their future.

"Really, Finn. Did you *have* to go all caveman on me? I'll be fine. I've been…distracted…since the tornado, and it's made me accident-prone."

Since the tornado, or since their mind-blowing night together? He didn't voice the question aloud, however. No sense provoking open warfare with her if they had to be together for a while. He followed her into her living room and sighed with pleasure as its homeyness wrapped around him like a blanket. He'd always preferred her family's cozy home to his family's cold mansion. They'd been happy together, the Grants.

"I always envied you for having the parents you did," he commented.

"Really?" she asked, surprised, as she set her briefcase down and shrugged out of her coat.

"You were a real family. We Coltons never were."

"I don't know about that," she disagreed. "You guys seem to stick together pretty close."

"My old man is a big believer in survival of the fittest. He saw it as his mission in life to toughen us all up. To make 'men' out of us."

"While his methods might leave something to be desired, I'd say he didn't do too bad a job all around. I don't know your younger brothers all that well, but Duke and Damien and Wes all turned out pretty good."

He shrugged. Maybe. But he was inclined to believe it was in spite of his father and not because of him. "Stay here. Let me have a look around the place and check for bad guys under your bed and in your closet, okay?"

He hated the fear that flickered across her face. Thank God he was here to look out for her. The house checked out fine and he returned to her in the living room. She'd turned on a lamp, and in its warm light he got a good look at how pale and drawn she looked. Her skin had gone almost transparent, and violet smudges rested under her eyes.

His doctor side kicked in. "When's the last time you ate?"

She frowned, thinking, and that was answer enough for him. He headed for the kitchen. "And when was the last time you got a decent night's sleep?" he called over his shoulder.

Her sharply indrawn breath was answer enough to that question, too. It was the last decent night's sleep he'd gotten, too. He considered the odds of them spending tonight in each other's arms again and decided regretfully that it would be too much too soon. He had a lifetime with her to consider. He could behave himself for a few more nights.

Her kitchen was shamefully bare of food, but he found eggs, some cheese and the remnants of a few vegetables in the refrigerator and whipped up omelettes for them. Over the meal, she kept sneaking looks his way that looked like a mixture of disbelief and relief. He'd take that as a good sign.

After supper, he ordered her into the bathroom for a long soak in the hottest bath she could stand. In particular, he wanted her to soak her neck and try to keep the muscles from stiffening up too badly after her car accident. As it was, he suspected she'd be pretty sore for a few days.

She emerged a while later, rosy pink, wisps of her hair curling around her face, wearing a pair of fuzzy pink pajamas that made her look about eight years old. He was ready and waiting with the next salvo.

"Here." He held out two pills in his hand with a glass of water.

"What are those?" she asked.

"Muscle relaxants. Consider them a preemptive strike against the discomfort to come from your wrenched neck."

She took the pills without argument. Must already be starting to feel a little creaky. He held out the mug of hot chocolate he'd made for her next.

That, she was suspicious of. "What's going on here, Finn?"

"I'm trying to make you as comfortable and relaxed as possible before we talk."

"Oh." Caution blossomed in her eyes as she studied him over the rim of her mug.

"Sit down," he ordered gently. He noted wryly that she chose her father's old armchair across the room from the sofa, which was left for him to occupy.

"Finn—"

He raised a hand. "Please, Rachel. Hear me out. I think you owe me that much. I heard you out the other day."

She subsided.

He took a deep breath. He'd been rehearsing this speech for the past several days. But now that the moment was here to deliver it, fear twisted in his gut. So damned much rode on him getting it right.

"Rachel, I love you."

She lurched at that and he thought she made a tiny sound of distress, but he pressed on. "I always have loved you. And I expect I always will love you. You've been part of the fabric of my life forever. You're a part of me."

She shifted restlessly and he waited for her to settle once more before continuing. "I fought that fact for a long time. But it was no use. I love you and nothing's going to change that."

"But, Finn, I already explained that love isn't always enough."

His jaw clenched, but he forced it to relax. "Yes, you did. You also said you had to learn to love yourself before you could love anyone else or let anyone else love you. And I can see where you might feel that way. I happen to agree with you, in fact."

That sent her eyebrows up behind her hot chocolate.

"And I'm willing to wait for you to work through that."

"But I have no idea how long it might take."

He shrugged. "Take as long as you need."

"But you can't know that you won't meet someone else in the meantime. Or maybe you'll lose patience or just…get over me."

He laughed, but there was no humor behind it. "I can assure you, I've tried everything to get over you already. That's not happening."

"So even you agree that we're not good for each other, then?" she challenged.

"When I thought you'd betrayed us, I might have agreed with that. But now that I know what really happened, I'm convinced we're perfect for each other. Admit it. You know I'm right."

She stared into her cup for a long time. Then she raised sad eyes and said, "Love isn't the only requirement for a relationship to work. The timing has to be right. The right place, the right time in life. And then, of course, the love itself has to be healthy and good for both people involved."

"How can love not be good for a person?" he exclaimed.

"Trust me. Loving you over the past fifteen years all but destroyed me."

Pain sliced through him. "Rachel, there was a terrible misunderstanding. That's resolved now. Our love doesn't have to hurt anymore."

She sighed. "Along with love's power to make people feel good comes great power to harm another person. Can you honestly say you've felt great this past week? Wes said you were a wreck. Love did that to you."

"I'll admit, love is a risk. Maybe the biggest risk any person ever takes. But that doesn't mean we should run away from it."

He barely heard her whisper, "But I'm not that brave."

That pulled him up off the couch and across the room to kneel in front of her. "You're one of the bravest people I know. You've faced the loss of your dad, taking care of your mom, being alone, financial burdens, taking care of this place by yourself—heck, you've faced the whole damned town of Honey Creek and not flinched."

"Oh, I flinched, all right. I just didn't let anyone see it."

He smiled gently at her. "Let me help you. Let me shoulder some of the burden for you. No, *with* you. I want to be there for you, Blondie."

"But you don't even live in Honey Creek. You're a busy doctor. Your patients need you. Let's be real, Finn. You can't commute between me and your real life in Bozeman. Besides, you hate this town. You and I both were desperate to get out of Honey Creek. I couldn't ask you to come back. And I can't leave. Not until my mom—" Her voice broke.

"We'll work it out. Just tell me you're willing to give it a try."

"I—" She fell silent. Eventually, she murmured, "I can't make you any promises."

It was better than the outright rejection he'd expected. He took the mug out of her grasp and set it aside. He took both her hands in his and captured her gaze, gently forcing her not to look away.

"Know this, Rachel Grant. I'm not going anywhere. I'm here to stay in your life. I'll wait for you as long as it takes for you to be ready to love me. I love you, and we *are* going to be together."

"Are you planning on stalking me?" she asked with patently false flippancy.

"Nope. I'm not getting far enough away from you to follow you. I'm going to be right here."

She frowned skeptically.

That, he'd expected from her. He'd laid down the gauntlet. Now it was up to him to follow through on his big words and show her just how much he loved her.

"You probably ought to crawl into bed, sweetheart. You look like you could use the rest. I'll be on the couch tonight, and I'm a light sleeper. No one's getting past me to bother you. Okay?"

She nodded thoughtfully and retreated to her bedroom.

Rachel slept deeply that night, although she figured it had as much to do with the pills Finn had given her as it did feeling safe for once. When she woke up in the morning, delicious smells were coming from her kitchen. That man was going to fatten her up but good at this rate. She realized she was smiling for the first time in a long time.

So. Finn was planning to wait for her, was he?

One part of her was deeply skeptical. That would be the part that remembered him abandoning her without so much as giving her a chance to explain herself. But another part of her, a tiny kernel deep inside her heart, was…hopeful. If only he were telling the truth. She'd give anything for that to be the case.

When she strolled into the kitchen a few minutes later, Finn was dishing up biscuits and sausage gravy and a fresh fruit compote that looked scrumptious. "Where did all this food come from?" she exclaimed.

"I made a quick run to the grocery store before you woke up. I had Wes come over and sit in front of your house while I was gone."

Horrified that he'd put the sheriff out like that so she could have a nice breakfast, she opened her mouth to protest, but he waved her to silence. Frustrated, she sat down and dug into the delicious fare. She insisted on doing the dishes after breakfast and shooed him out of the kitchen to go take a shower. She opened her refrigerator to put away the leftovers and was stunned to see the thing jammed with food. Suspicious, she opened the pantry. It was fully—fully—stocked. Finn must have bought her three months' worth of food.

Bemused, she let him drive her over to the nursing home to visit her mother, as was her daily habit before work. He let her go in alone to see her mother, which was probably best. Strangers seemed to bother her mother, who worried that she was supposed to recognize them and didn't.

When Rachel came out to the front desk to rejoin Finn, the nurses were all smiling broadly. Clearly, he'd been working his considerable charms on them.

The floor supervisor handed her a sealed envelope, and Rachel winced. This month's bill for her mother's care. At least she would get her second paycheck from Walsh Enterprises today, and it should cover this bill plus a little.

She tucked the envelope in her purse and let Finn escort her out to his truck and drive her to work. He'd tried to talk her out of going to Walsh Enterprises, but she wasn't hearing of it. She needed the paycheck too much.

"Don't be alone and don't leave the building unless I'm with you, okay?" he asked.

"Really. You don't have to—"

He waved a hand. "No arguments. Not until the bastard's caught."

She sighed. Okay, so it felt nice knowing that someone big and strong was looking out for her.

"Are you busy for lunch? I have an errand I need to run and I thought you could come along if you like," he suggested casually.

"Uhh, okay."

"I'll be here at noon," he said. Something thawed a

little in her heart. He did, indeed, seem committed to being around for her as long as it took to prove that she could count on him not to leave again.

When she got to her cubicle and bent down to put her purse under her desk, the nursing home bill fell out. She picked up the envelope and opened it idly. And stared. There must be a mistake. The outstanding balance on the account was zero. *Zero.* It should be close to fifty thousand dollars. She picked up her desk phone.

"Hi, Jason. It's Rachel Grant. I think there's been a mistake on my mother's bill."

The floor supervisor at the nursing home laughed heartily. "I was wondering when you were going to open that envelope. It's no mistake."

"I don't understand."

"While you were in visiting your mom this morning, Finn Colton paid off your mom's account."

Rachel gasped. "But it was *thousands* of dollars!"

"He stood right here and wrote a check for the whole amount. Must be nice to have that kind of money, huh?"

Rachel mumbled something and hung up the phone, stunned. It was too much. She dialed Finn's cell phone.

"Hi, Blondie," he answered cheerfully.

"You shouldn't have, Finn. I'll pay you back. I insist."

"Ahh. The nursing home bill. Marry me and we'll call it good."

"Finn!" she said on a gasp. "You can't buy me like that!"

"I know I can't. But I told you I was going to help shoulder your burdens. Get used to it."

"We're going to talk about this when we get home tonight." she said darkly.

"I like the sound of that. When *we* get *home*. Let's do that every night."

"Finn Colton, you are the most exasperating man on the planet."

"Yup, and you love every bit of me."

"I—" She opened her mouth to deny it, but the words wouldn't come out.

"You're welcome," he said gently. "It was my pleasure to pay your mom's bill. She was more of a mother to me over the years than my own mother. It was the least I could do to repay her for her kindness."

Rachel stared at the wall of her cubicle. What was she supposed to say to that?

"Have a nice morning, and I'll see you at noon. Lunch. Don't forget. I love you," Finn said.

She hung up, stunned. Her mountain of debt. Gone. Just like that. The load off her shoulders was unbelievable. She'd had no idea how much it was weighing her down until Finn had lifted it away from her. She was going to find a way to pay him back, though. She hated the idea of being beholden to anyone like that, even if it was Finn, and even if he did have a great explanation for his act of generosity.

Craig Warner's secretary delivered a mountain of payroll records to her from Lester Atkins with instructions to report to him by the end of the day with an audit report. She spent the morning digging through the dust-dry records, sure that the assignment was petty revenge from him for her not getting his precious contracts signed.

The clock registered five minutes till twelve and her stomach started to flutter. She left her desk a few minutes early and headed downstairs to the front door. Sure enough, Finn's pickup truck was there and he was leaning against its side, tall and rugged. Lord, he was handsome. Smiling, she stepped out into the brisk sunshine.

He leaned down to kiss her cheek and her pulse leaped as he held the passenger door open for her. He pointed his truck toward the highway and she frowned. "Where are we going?"

"Bozeman."

"What for?" she asked.

"I have to check in briefly at my hospital. It won't take more than five minutes. But I have to let them know I'm extending my leave of absence for a while. And then I have another errand."

The drive to Bozeman was pleasant. The easy camaraderie they'd shared all those years ago when they'd been young and in love came back to them, and they fell into their usual pattern of fun banter and wide-ranging discussions. She enjoyed his quick mind and his knowledge of seemingly everything under the sun.

The staff of the Bozeman emergency room eyed her speculatively enough that she grew uncomfortable, and Finn didn't help matters when he looped an arm around her shoulders and dropped an absent kiss on top of her head while they waited for his boss to leave a patient to speak with Finn.

As advertised, the stop didn't take long. Finn's boss commented that he was glad Finn was finally taking some of his accumulated vacation time and to go with his blessing.

They got back into Finn's truck, and Rachel frowned at his palpable excitement. "Where are we going?"

"To pick up something I ordered this morning," he answered mysteriously.

"What have you done now?"

He merely grinned...and turned into a car dealership.

"Finn..."

"Shared burdens, kid. Deal with it."

And before she knew it, the keys to a brand-new loaded-to-the-hilt, four-wheel-drive SUV were handed to her. And, no surprise, the title was handed to her as well. The vehicle was paid in full, of course.

"I'm going to kill you, Finn," she muttered direly.

"I look forward to you trying," he grinned back unrepentantly. "I'll follow you back to Honey Creek. And I'm still meeting you when you get out of work to follow you home."

"After this long lunch and given the amount of work on my desk, I'll be late tonight."

"What time should I be there?" he asked.

"Say, six-thirty?"

"Done."

Shell-shocked, she got into her brand-spanking-new SUV and headed back to Honey Creek. The vehicle drove like a dream. It was smooth and powerful and wrapped around her as comfortably as the man who'd bought it for her. She was *not* letting him buy her affections, darn it. She'd find a way to pay him back for this, too, she vowed grimly.

True to his word, Finn watched her walk into the Walsh building and blew her a kiss when she turned around to wave goodbye. As campaigns went to blow her away, his was proceeding very nicely. And that alarmed her. Things were moving too fast for her to process. He was intentionally sweeping her off her feet, not giving her any time to think. The man was a bulldozer. A really, really sexy, thoughtful bulldozer. But still.

She dived into her work with a vengeance but it was still nearly six o'clock before she finished the report Lester had requested. She printed it off on her computer and grabbed the papers. If she were lucky, he'd already left for the day. She'd just put the thing in his in-basket and pack up to meet Finn. Darned if her tummy didn't go all aflutter at the thought of seeing him again. After she kicked his butt for all the things he'd done for her today, she was imagining all kinds of ways to demonstrate her gratitude.

A smile on her face, she passed the empty desk of Craig Warner's secretary. Drat. A light was on in Warner's office. She sighed and knocked on the door.

"Who is it?" Atkins's voiced called out.

"Rachel Grant, sir. I've got your payroll report."

"Come in."

She stepped into the office. Lester wasn't sitting at the desk like she'd expected. He was standing over by the wet bar. One hand was awkwardly behind his back and he had a strange look on his face.

"Lay it on my desk," he directed.

She crossed the room while he watched and did as he'd ordered.

"Turn around," he barked, startling her.

She whirled to face him. What was wrong with him? And then she saw it. The gun pointed at her. Terror erupted in her gut and her knees all but collapsed out from under her. Belatedly, Finn's warning never to be alone came to mind. Of course, she wasn't alone now. Apparently, she was in the company of a certified lunatic.

Atkins ranted, "You think you're so smart, don't you? Finding those discrepancies in the Walsh Oil Drilling documents. And then you had to go and tell the damned sheriff about them. Ruining all my plans, are you? Well, I won't have it. I won't stand for that. I've worked too hard for too long to let some filthy little slut like you wreck it for me now."

She stared. What on earth was he talking about? Was he the insider behind the embezzlement after all?

"What's going on with the Hidden Pines deal?" she blurted. "Are you involved with that in some way?"

He jolted and the gun wavered dangerously. Yikes. Maybe bringing up Hidden Pines hadn't been such a great idea. But if she could get him talking…keep him talking…she glanced at the clock on the wall—6:02. Lord. Almost a half hour before Finn was supposed to pick her up. Could she keep Lester occupied for that long?

"Tell me about Hidden Pines," she demanded.

"I have a better idea. Come over here, bitch," Lester snarled.

She walked as slowly as she could toward him. He sidled away from the bar toward the window, staying well out of her reach. Although it wasn't like she was about to jump an armed and clearly crazy man.

"Drink that," he ordered.

She looked down at the bar and noticed a glass with a few ounces of clear liquid in the bottom of it. "What's that?" she asked.

"Drink it, or I'll kill you here and now. Everyone's left the building. I've made sure of it. It's just you and me."

She recalled the rows of empty and half-dark cubicles she'd walked past on her way to his office. He was right. Panic skittered down her spine.

"Drink it!" he repeated more forcefully. The barrel of the gun wavered and then steadied upon her, deadly and threatening.

She reached out to pick up the glass and noticed her hand was shaking. She sniffed at the glass. It didn't smell like anything.

"Drink!" he shouted.

She tipped the glass and took a sip. Oh, God. It was bitter.

"Drink it all or I'll shoot!" he screamed.

Terrified, she tossed down the entire contents of the glass. At least she didn't immediately start choking or convulsing or anything. She turned to face Lester. "Okay, I've drunk whatever that was. Now you can tell me. What was in that? Did you just poison me?" Visions of her future with Finn danced through her mind's eye. They'd been so close to having it all. Had this madman just taken it all away from them? Panic and grief and rage swirled within her at the thought.

"Craig's the only one I poisoned," Lester answered slyly. "Slipped it into his drinks a little at a time. Idiot never had a clue. Just got sicker and sicker. And then that damned doctor had to come along and figure it out."

Finn. He was talking about Finn. Her head was beginning to swim a little. The lights overhead were swaying slightly. Or maybe that was her doing the swaying. "What did you give me?" she asked thickly.

His gaze narrowed. "You'll feel it soon enough. Stupid bitch. Had to go and try to ruin everything my associate and I have worked so long and hard for."

She tried hard to concentrate. He'd said something important. An associate. He wasn't working alone.

"Who's your associate?" The word came out closer to "ashoshiate," but it made him scowl either way.

"Do I look dumb? Do I look like I'd tell you something like that?"

"Uhh, I guesh no'..." She'd passed through woozy to stoned in about two seconds flat. She was having trouble following anything the guy said.

Only snatches of his next words registered with her: "...get yôu out of here...can't kill you here...too messy... find somewhere to stash you first...then kill you..."

The lights spun crazily overhead, and then everything went dark.

Chapter 15

Finn looked at his watch—six forty-five. It wasn't like Rachel to be late. But she had said she had a lot of work to do, and he'd kept her out of the office for nearly two hours at lunch. The look on her face when the salesman had handed her the car keys had been priceless. He'd never forget the wonder and delight in her eyes. He wanted to put that expression there every day for the rest of their lives.

He shouldn't bug her. But worry niggled at the back of his mind. He pulled out his cell phone and dialed hers. It went straight to voice mail. That was strange. He dialed it again and got the same result. Somebody had just turned off her phone.

He leaped out of his truck and hit the ground running. Something was wrong. Very wrong. He reached the Walsh building and yanked on the front doors. Locked. He swore violently. He punched another number into his cell.

"Wes, it's Finn. Get over to the Walsh Enterprises building right away."

"I'm on my way, bro. Talk to me."

Finn heard a siren go on in the background and an engine gun. "I was supposed to pick Rachel up at six-thirty. When she didn't come out I called her cell phone and somebody turned it off. The Walsh building's locked up tight. Do you have a key or can I break in now?"

"Bust the door. I'll be there in five minutes," Wes replied sharply.

Finn had already checked her cubicle and found her purse under the desk by the time Wes came storming inside. They searched the building by floor and found nothing until they reached Craig Warner's office. Over by the wet bar, Finn found several printed papers scattered on the floor and—oh, crap—one of them had Rachel's signature on it. The document was dated today.

"She's been in here," Finn bit out.

Wes glanced at the document and then at the bar. "That glass still has a little fluid at the bottom of it. Someone's been here recently."

"Then where is she?" Finn demanded.

"Hang on. We'll find her. We've been watching this place." Wes had his phone out and was dialing a number. Finn listened as the panic mounted in his gut.

"This is Sheriff Colton. I need you to run back the surveillance tapes of Walsh Enterprises for the past hour. And pull up the entry and exit logs for the security system. Who's gone in and out of the building since, say, six o'clock?"

Finn waited in an agony of impatience for Wes to get off the phone. "Well?" he demanded when his brother ended the call.

"Lester Atkins is the only person to leave the building since six o'clock. And the security cameras at the rear of the building show him carrying a large cloth-wrapped object outside."

"The bastard's got her," Finn rasped.

Wes was already on the phone again, ordering police units to Lester's home.

Finn paced. Nothing could happen to her. He'd promised her he'd keep her safe! They were going to live happily ever after with each other. Have a home together. Kids. Grandkids. This couldn't be happening.

"He won't be at his house," Finn announced, certain deep in his gut that he was right. "Atkins is too smart to go there. He knows that's the first place we'll look for him."

Wes nodded, thankfully not arguing. "Lester must have figured out that she stumbled onto the embezzlement and the Hidden Pines deal. He needs to get her out of the picture. Silence her."

"My God. He's going to kill her!" Finn gasped.

Wes frowned, working through the logic. "Looks like your suspicions that he was the one to poison Warner were right." Finn looked over at the empty glass standing on the bar. Atkins had access to Warner's office. It would have been an easy matter to slip a little arsenic into all of the man's drinks.

Wes continued, "Good news is he didn't try to kill Warner outright. He used indirect means. Assuming he's behind the attacks on Rachel, he didn't use direct means on her, either. He sabotaged the pipe over her desk and then hit her with a car."

"And that's important why?" Finn asked impatiently.

"He's not a naturally violent criminal. He's probably

going to have to work himself up to the idea of killing Rachel outright. I think we've got a window of time before he actually kills her. He's careful. A planner. He'll want to know where he's going to stash her body. How and where he's going to kill her. I think maybe he grabbed her today on impulse."

"Rachel told me he'd given her a pile of work to do today and wanted a report on it by close of business."

Wes frowned. "Then snatching her today might have been a premeditated act after all. C'mon. Let's head out to his place and see what the boys find."

But even as Finn rode out to Lester's home on the outskirts of Honey Creek, he knew the visit would be fruitless. He racked his brain for where he'd take someone if he wanted to kill a person neatly and quietly. But his panic for Rachel was too much. He couldn't think past it.

A half hour later, Wes stood beside Finn in Lester's living room, swearing under his breath. "Nothing."

"What now?" Finn asked, barely containing himself from tearing the room apart.

"Helicopters are searching the surrounding area and the state troopers have set up road blocks for sixty miles around town. We'll find her."

Yeah, but would they find her in time? Or would they find a corpse? Unfortunately, because of his medical training, he knew all too well what a corpse looked like. And the idea of his Rachel blue and still and lifeless made him want to throw up.

"Let's head back to Walsh Enterprises," Wes said. "It's where the trail starts. There has to be a way to track her, damn it."

"Has anyone local got a tracking dog?" Finn asked hopefully.

"A pair of police bloodhounds are on their way down from Butte, but it'll be midnight before they get here," Wes replied.

Finn's gut told him they didn't have that much time.

"Go home, Finn. You can't do any good here. Let us do our job. I'll call you if there are any developments."

Because he couldn't stand here any longer without exploding, he did as he brother suggested. He blinked when his truck stopped in front of Rachel's house, though. Her place was already "home" to him, and in his distraction and terror, he'd driven here. He got out of the truck and went inside.

His knees all but buckled when he stepped into the living room and smelled the vanilla scent that always pervaded the place and reminded him so much of her. He couldn't fall apart. He had to hold it together for her. He tried to sit. To turn on the television and watch the news segments the Bozeman channels were breaking in with to cover the search for a missing woman in the Honey Creek area.

But his agitation was too great for stillness. He straightened up the already neat living room and moved into the kitchen with the intent to eat or maybe clean the sink. Something, anything, to keep his hands busy so he wouldn't tear his hair out.

Where are you, baby? Talk to me!

Rachel regained consciousness slowly, registering small things first. She was cold. And she was lying on dirt. The air was perfectly still around her. And it stank. Something rustled nearby. She wasn't alone, then. She kept her eyes closed as her mind slowly started to work again. Her wrists were tied behind her back. And her ankles were tied together. Her left arm was asleep. She would roll off of it except the movement might alert her captor that she was awake. Gritting her teeth against the pain, she slitted her eyes open. A dark figure moved in the near total darkness, maybe a dozen feet away from her.

It looked like she was in some sort of cave. Slowly, she turned her head a little to look out of the opening. A mountain loomed in front of her at close range. It was oddly colored, a speckled white in the darkness. And strangely symmetrical. Its sides were smooth and its slope consistent. No trees or gullies marred its side. Odd. Too bad the night was cloudy and no moon shone to illuminate it more clearly.

And why would a cave opening be facing a mountainside like that? Wouldn't a cave open up out of the side of a mountain so she was looking down into a valley. In this area, caves didn't form at the bottom of valleys. She was too groggy to make sense of it, though. Dang, her arm was killing her.

Killing. Was that what Lester had in mind for her? She vaguely remembered hearing him say something to that effect before she passed out. Terror, sharp and bright and sudden, pierced her, doing more to wake her up than a bucket of cold water in the face.

She was not going to go down without a fight, damn it. She and Finn were just finding each other again, and she wasn't about to lose him now.

Lester, silhouetted in the cave opening, tipped a bottle up to his mouth and took a long drink. He shuddered as if the liquid burned. Oh, God. He was getting drunk to work up the courage to kill her.

Finn, where are you? Find me, please. And hurry.

* * *

Urgency rolled through Finn. Rachel didn't have until midnight for the tracking dogs to arrive. He knew it as surely as he was standing there breathing and sweating bullets. There had to be something he could do. But what? He finished emptying the dishwasher and turned to stare out the back window into the blackness of the night. The woman he loved was out there somewhere. *But where?*

He took a step forward and kicked something metallic with a clang that startled him. Brownie's food dish. Too bad the mutt wasn't here. Maybe he could track down Rachel. Lord knew, the dog adored her.

It was a thought. If he could find Brownie, maybe the dog *could* track her. But Rachel had been looking for Brownie for a week to no avail. And Finn had only a matter of hours at most to find the dog *and* find her.

Think. Brownie had left during or immediately after the tornado. No one had seen hide nor hair of the mutt since, which meant he'd either died or gone somewhere with few or no people. And given the animal's general terror and state of abuse when he'd come to Rachel's porch, it was a good bet the beast had headed away from humanity.

He refused to believe Brownie had died from exposure or coyotes or the like. The animal'd had enough common sense and survival instinct to drag himself to Rachel's porch for help. He was still alive, damn it.

Okay. People-hating dog. Bum leg. No way could he have gone far on that broken femur. He would need food and shelter. Finn racked his brains on where the dog could find both within a few miles of Rachel's house.

And he hit on an idea. The landfill. It was about a

mile from here. Outside of town. Good pickings for a scavenger like a dog. It was a long shot, but chasing it down was better than sitting around here staring at the walls and losing his mind.

He drove to the landfill and got out to examine the chained gates. He was startled to see the chain was merely looped around the gates and wasn't locked. He opened the gates and drove through. The stench was thick enough to stand up on its own and slug him in the gut. He climbed toward the symmetrical mountain of trash and trudged up the rough road carved into its side by the garbage trucks coming up here to dump their loads. A pair of bulldozers were parked on top of the acres-wide mound, quiet and dark in the cloudless night.

"Brownie," Finn called. "Here, boy." He strode across the landfill, calling as he went. He had no way of knowing if the dog would come to him or run for cover from the human who'd caused him pain. He would like to think the dog knew he'd been helping to heal his broken leg.

A cloud of seagulls flushed up in front of Finn, startling him badly. Their cries grated on his already raw nerves.

"Brownie!" he called again. "Come here, boy. Rachel needs you."

He'd reached the far edge of the mountain and had turned around to hike back when he thought he heard something. A whimper. He turned sharply. "Brownie?"

A shape, low and broad, moved in the darkness.

"Is that you, boy?" he asked gently.

Another whimper. The dog always had been talkative with Rachel.

Urgency rode Finn hard. He squatted down patiently,

though, and held out one of the dog treats he'd grabbed from the kitchen before he left the house. "Are you hungry? I brought your favorite snack."

A furry shape sidled forward. The fur resolved itself into speckled brown, and the familiar gray muzzle took shape. "Hey, buddy. How are you? Miss Rachel and I have been plenty worried about you."

The dog inched forward, sniffing at the snack. Finn didn't rush the dog but let him come in his own time. Brownie finally took the bone and Finn reached out slowly to scratch the special spot on the back of the his neck. Brownie still had his collar on. Finn held it lightly while he pulled a leash out of his pocket and snapped it onto the collar.

He gave the leash a gentle tug and the dog went stiff. Finn swore under his breath. Lester Atkins could kill Rachel any second. Improvising, Finn pulled out Rachel's nightshirt that he'd stuffed inside his jacket and held it out to the reluctant dog. Lord knew if Brownie could smell anything but trash out here, but it was worth a try.

"We're going to find her, buddy. You're going to help me. Let's go get in my truck and head over to Walsh Enterprises. And if the gods are smiling on me and Rachel, you'll pick up her scent and lead us to her in time to save her."

His voice broke. No way was this harebrained scheme going to work. But he had nothing else. And he couldn't just give up hope. He loved her too damned much for that.

Brownie sniffed the nightshirt deeply and wagged his tail.

"That's right, buddy. We're going to find her, you and me."

Brownie whimpered and danced a little with his front feet as if he were excited at the prospect.

"C'mon. Let's go."

But the big dog balked. Finn swore aloud this time. He didn't have time for this. Rachel didn't have time for this. He pulled harder on the leash. "I'm sorry, but you've got to go with me. Rachel's life depends on this. I swear, I'll make it up to you later. Just help me now, dog."

But Brownie set his feet and yanked back. Finn watched in horror as the collar slipped over the animal's broad head. Crap! The dog turned and took off running, a limping half skip that was faster than Finn would have thought possible. He took off after the dog, frantic to get him back. Everything depended on catching him!

The dog scampered across the landfill, moving rapidly back toward the rear of the massive hill. Finn stumbled in the uneven landscape of garbage bags and dirt, cursing grimly. He couldn't lose Brownie!

The dog started down the steep slope at the back of the fill, which was blessedly covered with dirt and weeds. White plastic bags and bits of trash speckled the hillside, but it was smoother going for Finn. The incline gave the injured dog some trouble, though, and Finn closed the gap quite a bit. Brownie reached the bottom of the hill and paused to sniff the air. The act struck Finn as strange. But at the same time he was grateful for the extra yards the dog's pause had given him.

"Brownie!" he called with frantic, fake cheer. "Do you want another snack?'

The dog looked over his shoulder once, almost as if to check that Finn was still following him, and then took off running again.

Damn, damn, damn.

Brownie ran along the gully at the back of the land-fill for a few moments and then veered away from the trash heap and up an uneven dirt slope. It was dark, and boulders littered this side of the narrow valley. Finn lost sight of the dog and darted forward urgently. He had to get that dog back!

There. He caught sight of a dog shape disappearing into an inky black shadow. What the hell? Was that a cave? Maybe Brownie's hideout since he'd run away? Huffing, Finn followed. If he was lucky, the dog had just cornered himself.

Rachel started as a dark shape hurtled forward into the cave low past Lester's legs. *What the heck?*

Lester swore and dropped his whiskey bottle, grab-bing for the pistol jammed in the back of his waistband.

And then the shape was headed for her. Rachel re-coiled in terror. Had they invaded the cave of a coyote or a pack of wolves who'd come back to reclaim their home? Was she about to be torn apart? She'd almost prefer being shot to that.

"Hold still, you damned wolf!" Lester shouted.

Her wish to get shot looked like it might just come true as the beast closed in on her rapidly and Lester pointed his gun at both her and the beast. And then she heard a familiar whimper.

Oh my God. Brownie. How he'd found her or what he was doing here, she had no idea. But Lester was about to shoot the dog!

"Hey!" she shouted sharply at Lester. "Stop that!"

The gun wavered as she startled him. He was just

drunk enough to be a little confused by an outburst from the supposedly unconscious prisoner.

"Put that gun down!" she ordered.

But unfortunately Lester wasn't that drunk. He snarled. "You wish, bitch. That your dog?"

It was kind of hard to deny belonging to Brownie when the dog had closed in on her and commenced licking her face.

"I love you, too, buddy," she whispered, "but you have to get of here. Go away, boy." When he merely wagged his tail enthusiastically, she said more sternly, "Go on. Shoo!"

Lester laughed. "I was going to kill just you, but now I'm going to shoot your dog and let you watch him bleed first. And then, after you've suffered for a while, *then* I'll kill you."

She didn't waste her time trying to argue with him. He was obviously crazy as a loon. She'd never done a darned thing to hurt him. There was no reason for the man to want to make her suffer. But every minute she could delay him killing her was another minute for Finn to find her. She had faith that their love had to count for something. It had to be of some help in locating her.

"Go on, Brownie," she murmured. "Run, boy!"

Lester was no more than five feet away now, squinting down at her and the dog.

"Lester, who are you trying to kid? You're not going to get away with this. You're not a killer," she said with desperate calm. Anything to distract him. To give her an extra few seconds to convince the dog to leave. The idea of watching poor old Brownie suffer again broke her heart almost worse than the idea of dying.

He laughed wildly, and his words were vaguely

slurred when he retorted, "I got away with poisoning that bastard, Warner. Almost killed him, too. One more good dose of arsenic would've had him. And I got away with setting up fake contracts at Walsh that will net me millions. No one's ever going to find your body way out here. In another year or so, this hillside will be covered up with trash and you'll rot beneath it for all eternity."

"Just put the gun down, Lester," she said patiently.

"Not only no, but *hell no!*" he exclaimed.

And then a new voice came out of the darkness by the cave opening. "I'd do what the lady says, Lester."

Rachel's heart leaped first in jubilation at the sound of Finn's voice, and then in terror as Lester spun, gun and all, to face the man she loved.

"He's got a gun!" she shouted.

Finn's silhouette charged forward and went airborne, flying toward Lester. From beside her, Brownie growled and charged as well, going low.

Bang!

The sound of the gunshot inside the stone walls of the cave was deafening. She screamed, but her ears were too full of the report of the gun to hear herself.

All three shadowed shapes fell to the ground. They rolled around for a few moments, and then became still.

"Finn! Oh, God. Finn!" she cried.

"I'm fine, Blondie," he grunted. "You okay? Are you hurt?"

"I'm fine," she answered breathlessly. *Please, God. Let it be true. Let Finn be unharmed.* She loved him more than life itself.

"Just lemme tie up Lester here, and make a quick phone call to Wes," Finn said. "Then I'll come over and untie you."

"Is Brownie okay?"

Finn laughed. "Yeah. I owe the mutt one. He bit Lester's leg and made the guy jerk just as he pulled the trigger. At this close range, I expect the mutt saved my life."

"Good boy, Brownie," Rachel called out. The dog whimpered happily and came over to her to lick her face. Laughing, she tried to dodge the persistent tongue but failed.

It took a few minutes, but then Finn was there, his hands deft and gentle on the knots holding her wrists. Her bonds fell away. She started to move her shoulders and then cried out in pain.

"Easy. Don't try to move all at once," Finn directed. He probed her shoulder joints gently, no doubt checking for injuries, and then apparently finding nothing, rubbed her shoulders lightly. Pins and needles exploded from her neck to her fingertips as her circulation gradually returned to normal.

She wasn't thrilled when Finn passed her the gun and left to guide Wes to the isolated cave. Thankfully, Lester chose to sulk in silence.

But as Wes slapped handcuffs on Atkins and hauled the man to his feet, Lester screamed, "I'll kill you!"

Finn wrapped her in a protective embrace. "Don't worry. He's hog-tied and not going anywhere anytime soon. And I'll take his gun back."

Rachel sagged in relief, and Finn murmured, "It's over, baby. You're safe. Brownie led me right to you."

"I guess we both owe him our lives, then," she mumbled against Finn's chest.

"Yup. That dog's earned being spoiled rotten for the rest of his life. He can even sleep on our couch if he wants. But you and I get the bed all to ourselves."

Wes dragged Lester out of the cave and it wasn't until Atkins's complaints and threats died away that the significance of Finn's words sank in. "Our couch?" she echoed.

"Well, unless you just want chairs in our living room, I suppose," Finn replied. "I'll leave the decorating of our home up to you if you don't mind. I'm no good at that design stuff."

"Our home?" she repeated.

Whoever said men weren't dense at times would be dead wrong. But then, sometimes women were dense, too. And she was feeling decidedly dense at the moment. "Did I miss something here?" she asked.

Finn held her far enough away from him to grin down at her. "We are getting married, right? I almost lost you tonight, and I'm not taking any more chances with losing you again. I'll still wait for you to work out whatever issues you want to work out. But sooner rather than later, I plan to make you my wife and spend the rest of my life adoring you."

Rachel blinked, shocked into a stillness that went all the way to her soul. "Well, then. I guess you've got it all planned out, don't you?"

He laughed and gathered her close. "Not hardly. Life with you is going to be one surprise after another, if I don't miss my guess. But I can't wait to see what happens. How about it? Will you make me the happiest man in the world and marry me?"

"Oh, Finn." She couldn't help it. She burst into tears and promptly soaked his shirt through.

He stiffened, alarmed. "What does this mean? Are you crying because you're saying yes and you're overcome with joy, or are you saying no and crying because I've made you so unhappy?"

"Of course I'll marry you," she answered through her tears.

Brownie whimpered and pushed between them, and they both bent down to pet him. The dog wasted no time licking the salty tracks off her cheeks. Finn and Rachel laughed. "Guess I'll have to get used to sharing you with the mutt," Finn commented.

"Do you mind?" she asked.

Finn laughed. "Hell, no. Brownie brought us together in the first place and then saved us both tonight. He can be the best dog at our wedding if he wants."

"That sounds perfect." Rachel sighed.

"It will be," Finn replied softly. "No matter what happens in our lives from now on, we'll have each other. And I can't think of anything in the world more perfect than that."

Whoever said men weren't capable of being as tender and romantic as women would be dead wrong. Obviously that person had never met Finn Colton. But for her part, Rachel counted herself the luckiest woman alive to not only have met Finn Colton but also to have won his heart.

She opened one arm and Brownie stepped eagerly into her embrace, warm and fuzzy and wiggly. Finn laughed and kissed Rachel over the dog's head. "Find your own girl to kiss, mutt," he muttered.

Rachel smiled against Finn's mouth. Yup, life was just about perfect.

* * * * *